W9-CII-607

SCOOBY-DOO SPACE FRIGHT!

Written by:
Chris Duffy
Joe Edkin
Terrance Griep
Chuck Kim
John Rozum
Rurik Tyler

Colored by:
Paul Becton

Illustrated by:
John Delaney
Vincent DePorter
Stephen DeStefano
Dave Hunt
Andrew Pepoy
Don Perlin
Joe Staton

Lettered by:
John Costanza

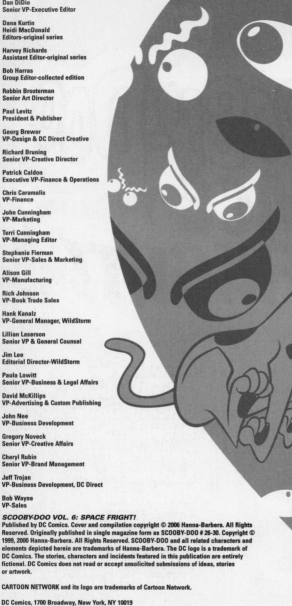

Dan DiDio
Senior VP-Executive Editor

Dana Kurtin
Heidi MacDonald
Editors-original series

Harvey Richards
Assistant Editor-original series

Bob Harras
Group Editor-collected edition

Robbin Brosterman
Senior Art Director

Paul Levitz
President & Publisher

Georg Brewer
VP-Design & DC Direct Creative

Richard Bruning
Senior VP-Creative Director

Patrick Caldon
Executive VP-Finance & Operations

Chris Caramalis
VP-Finance

John Cunningham
VP-Marketing

Terri Cunningham
VP-Managing Editor

Stephanie Fierman
Senior VP-Sales & Marketing

Alison Gill
VP-Manufacturing

Rich Johnson
VP-Book Trade Sales

Hank Kanalz
VP-General Manager, WildStorm

Lillian Laserson
Senior VP & General Counsel

Jim Lee
Editorial Director-WildStorm

Paula Lowitt
Senior VP-Business & Legal Affairs

David McKillips
VP-Advertising & Custom Publishing

John Nee
VP-Business Development

Gregory Noveck
Senior VP-Creative Affairs

Cheryl Rubin
Senior VP-Brand Management

Jeff Trojan
VP-Business Development, DC Direct

Bob Wayne
VP-Sales

SCOOBY-DOO VOL. 6: SPACE FRIGHT!

DC Comics, 1700 Broadway, New York, NY 10019
A Warner Bros. Entertainment Company.
Printed in Canada. First Printing.
ISBN: 1-4012-0937-8   ISBN 13: 978-1-4012-0937-7
Cover illustration by Joe Staton and Andrew Pepoy.
Publication design by John J. Hill.

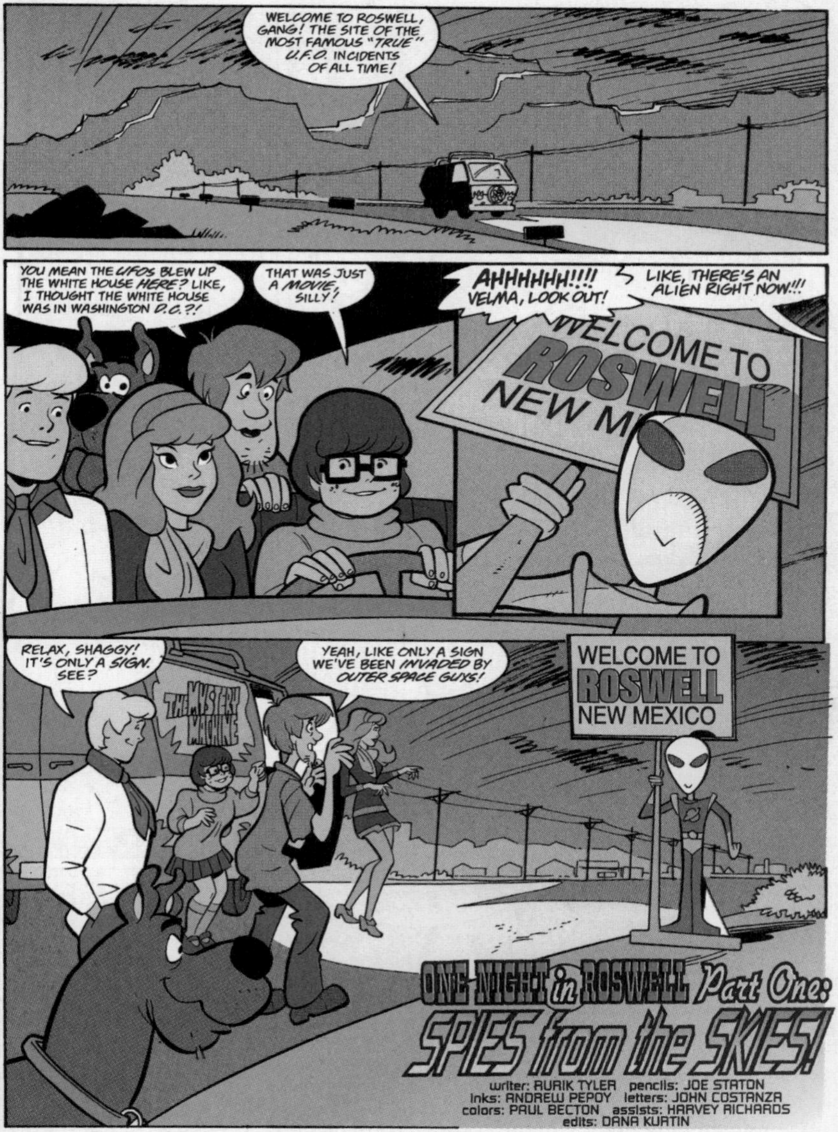
WELCOME TO ROSWELL, GANG! THE SITE OF THE MOST FAMOUS "TRUE" U.F.O. INCIDENTS OF ALL TIME!
YOU MEAN THE UFOS BLEW UP THE WHITE HOUSE HERE? LIKE, I THOUGHT THE WHITE HOUSE WAS IN WASHINGTON D.C.?!
THAT WAS JUST A MOVIE, SILLY!
AHHHHHH!!!! VELMA, LOOK OUT!
LIKE, THERE'S AN ALIEN RIGHT NOW!!!
WELCOME TO ROSWELL NEW M
RELAX, SHAGGY! IT'S ONLY A SIGN. SEE?
YEAH, LIKE ONLY A SIGN WE'VE BEEN INVADED BY OUTER SPACE GUYS!
THE MYSTERY MACHINE
WELCOME TO ROSWELL NEW MEXICO
ONE NIGHT in ROSWELL Part One:
SPIES from the SKIES!
writer: AURIK TYLER pencils: JOE STATON
inks: ANDREW PEPOY letters: JOHN COSTANZA
colors: PAUL BECTON assists: HARVEY RICHARDS
edits: DANA KURTIN

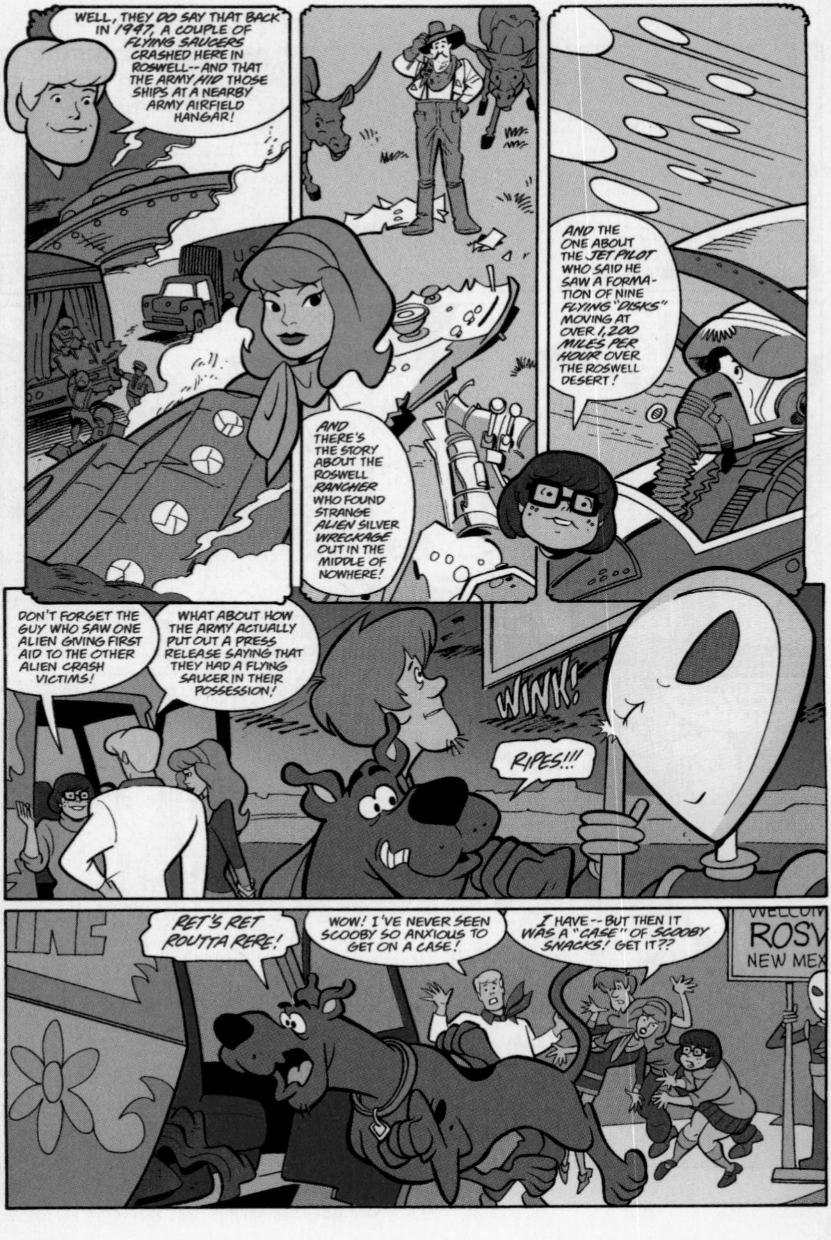

WELL, THEY DO SAY THAT BACK IN 1947, A COUPLE OF FLYING SAUCERS CRASHED HERE IN ROSWELL--AND THAT THE ARMY HID THOSE SHIPS AT A NEARBY ARMY AIRFIELD HANGAR!
AND THERE'S THE STORY ABOUT THE ROSWELL RANCHER WHO FOUND STRANGE ALIEN SILVER WRECKAGE OUT IN THE MIDDLE OF NOWHERE!
AND THE ONE ABOUT THE JET PILOT WHO SAID HE SAW A FORMATION OF NINE FLYING "DISKS" MOVING AT OVER 1,200 MILES PER HOUR OVER THE ROSWELL DESERT!
DON'T FORGET THE GUY WHO SAW ONE ALIEN GIVING FIRST AID TO THE OTHER ALIEN CRASH VICTIMS!
WHAT ABOUT HOW THE ARMY ACTUALLY PUT OUT A PRESS RELEASE SAYING THAT THEY HAD A FLYING SAUCER IN THEIR POSSESSION!
WINK!
RIPES!!!
RET'S RET ROUTTA RERE!
WOW! I'VE NEVER SEEN SCOOBY SO ANXIOUS TO GET ON A CASE!
I HAVE--BUT THEN IT WAS A "CASE" OF SCOOBY SNACKS! GET IT??
ROSW
NEW MEX

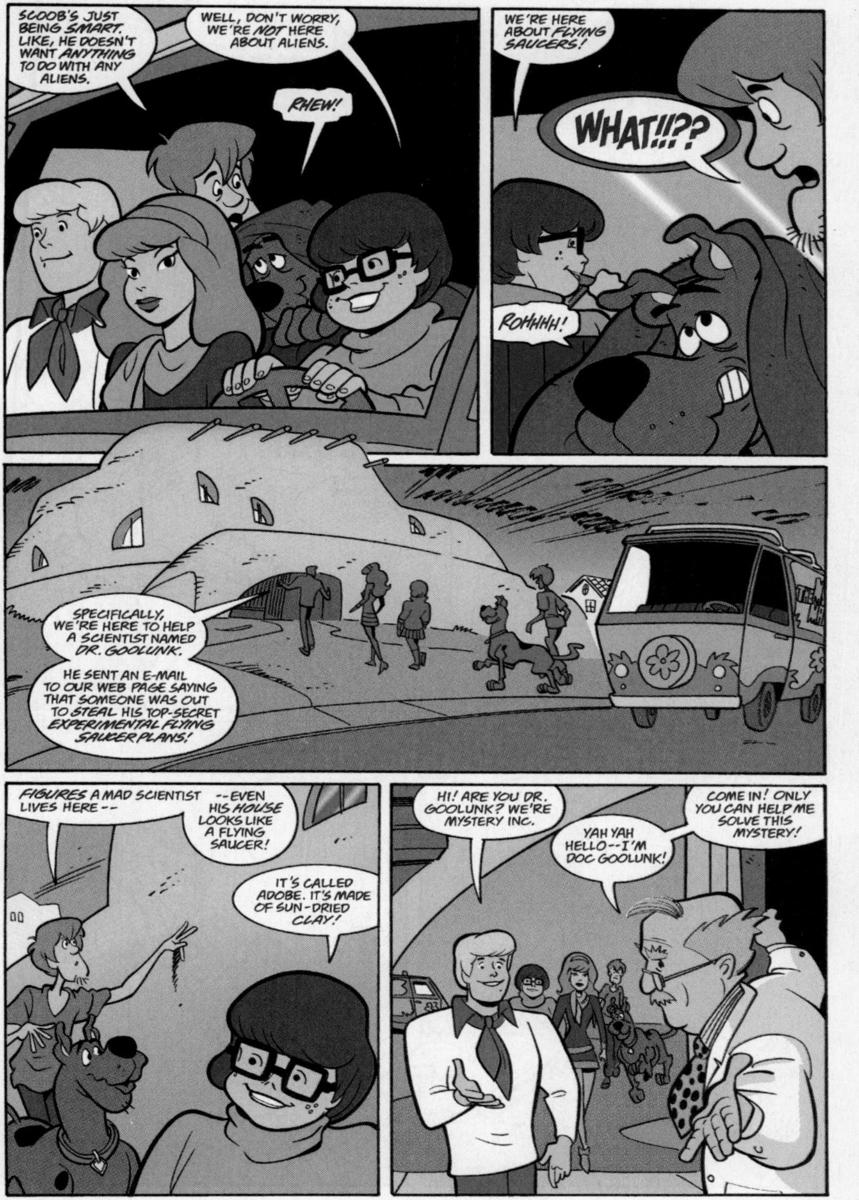
SCOOB'S JUST BEING SMART. LIKE, HE DOESN'T WANT ANYTHING TO DO WITH ANY ALIENS.
WELL, DON'T WORRY, WE'RE NOT HERE ABOUT ALIENS.
RHEW!
WE'RE HERE ABOUT FLYING SAUCERS!
WHAT!!??
ROHHHH!
SPECIFICALLY, WE'RE HERE TO HELP A SCIENTIST NAMED DR. GOOLUNK.
HE SENT AN E-MAIL TO OUR WEB PAGE SAYING THAT SOMEONE WAS OUT TO STEAL HIS TOP-SECRET EXPERIMENTAL FLYING SAUCER PLANS!
FIGURES A MAD SCIENTIST LIVES HERE --
--EVEN HIS HOUSE LOOKS LIKE A FLYING SAUCER!
IT'S CALLED ADOBE. IT'S MADE OF SUN-DRIED CLAY!
HI! ARE YOU DR. GOOLUNK? WE'RE MYSTERY INC.
YAH YAH HELLO--I'M DOC GOOLUNK!
COME IN! ONLY YOU CAN HELP ME SOLVE THIS MYSTERY!

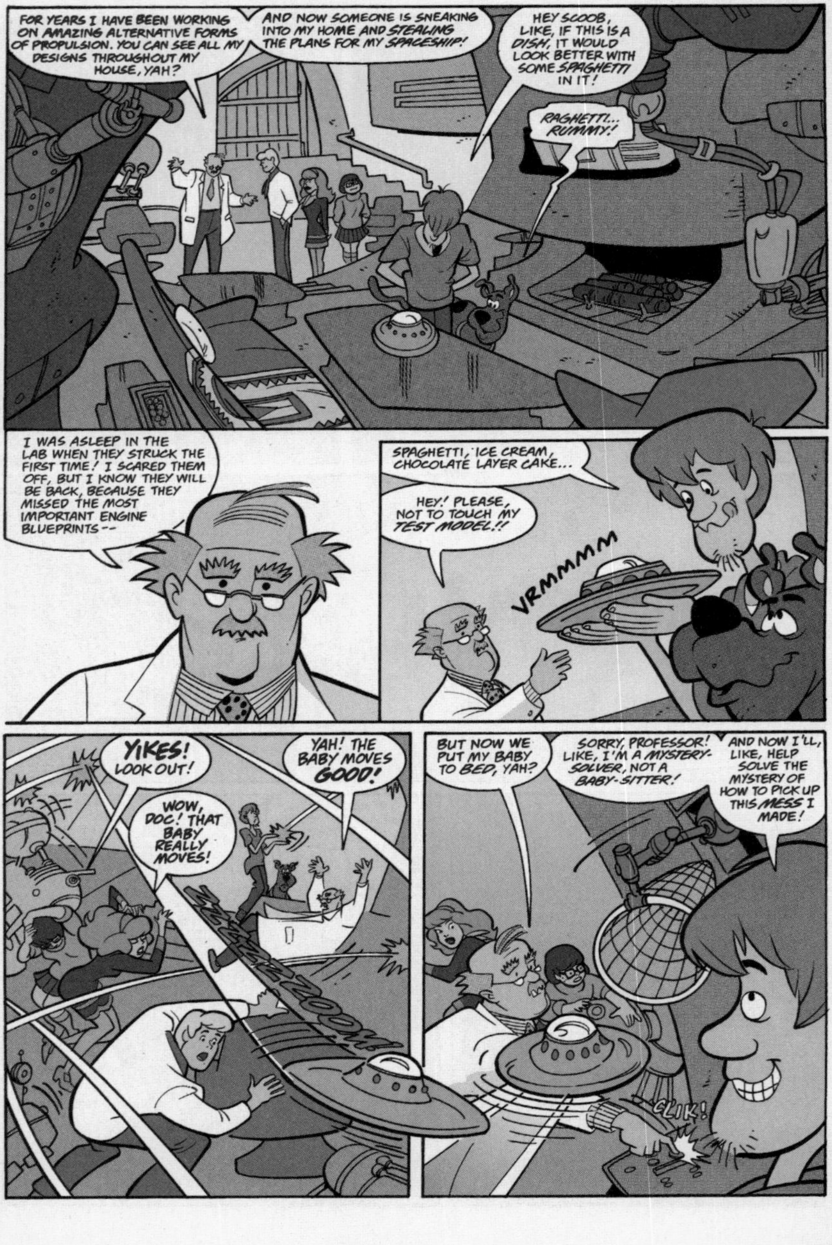
FOR YEARS I HAVE BEEN WORKING ON AMAZING ALTERNATIVE FORMS OF PROPULSION. YOU CAN SEE ALL MY DESIGNS THROUGHOUT MY HOUSE, YAH?
AND NOW SOMEONE IS SNEAKING INTO MY HOME AND STEALING THE PLANS FOR MY SPACESHIP!
HEY SCOOB, LIKE, IF THIS IS A DISH, IT WOULD LOOK BETTER WITH SOME SPAGHETTI IN IT!
RAGHETTI... RUMMY!
I WAS ASLEEP IN THE LAB WHEN THEY STRUCK THE FIRST TIME! I SCARED THEM OFF, BUT I KNOW THEY WILL BE BACK, BECAUSE THEY MISSED THE MOST IMPORTANT ENGINE BLUEPRINTS--
SPAGHETTI, ICE CREAM, CHOCOLATE LAYER CAKE...
HEY! PLEASE, NOT TO TOUCH MY TEST MODEL!!
VRMMMMM
YIKES! LOOK OUT!
YAH! THE BABY MOVES GOOD!
WOW, DOC! THAT BABY REALLY MOVES!
ZZZZZZZOOOM!
BUT NOW WE PUT MY BABY TO BED, YAH?
SORRY, PROFESSOR! LIKE, I'M A MYSTERY-SOLVER, NOT A BABY-SITTER!
AND NOW I'LL, LIKE, HELP SOLVE THE MYSTERY OF HOW TO PICK UP THIS MESS I MADE!
CLIK!

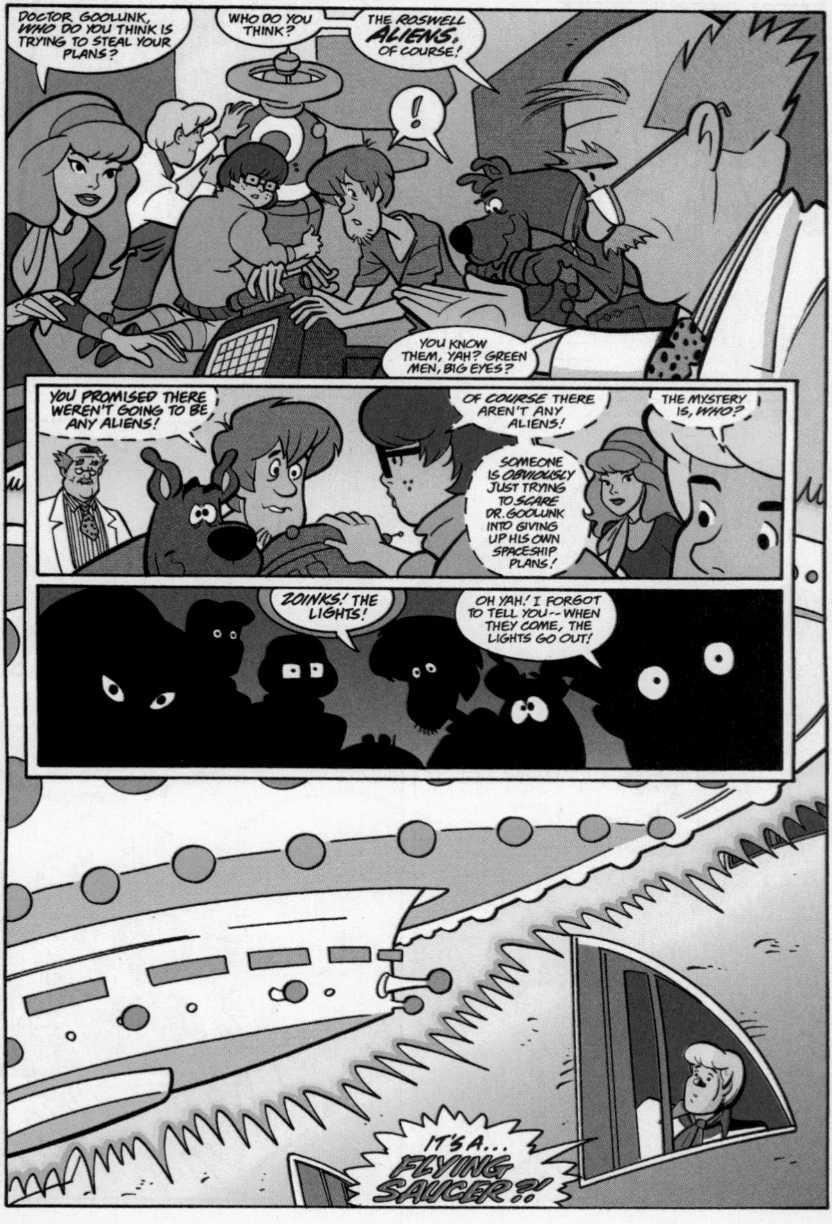
DOCTOR GOOLUNK, WHO DO YOU THINK IS TRYING TO STEAL YOUR PLANS?
WHO DO YOU THINK?
THE ROSWELL ALIENS, OF COURSE!
!
YOU KNOW THEM, YAH? GREEN MEN, BIG EYES?
YOU PROMISED THERE WEREN'T GOING TO BE ANY ALIENS!
OF COURSE THERE AREN'T ANY ALIENS!
SOMEONE IS OBVIOUSLY JUST TRYING TO SCARE DR. GOOLUNK INTO GIVING UP HIS OWN SPACESHIP PLANS!
THE MYSTERY IS, WHO?
ZOINKS! THE LIGHTS!
OH YAH! I FORGOT TO TELL YOU-- WHEN THEY COME, THE LIGHTS GO OUT!
IT'S A... FLYING SAUCER?!

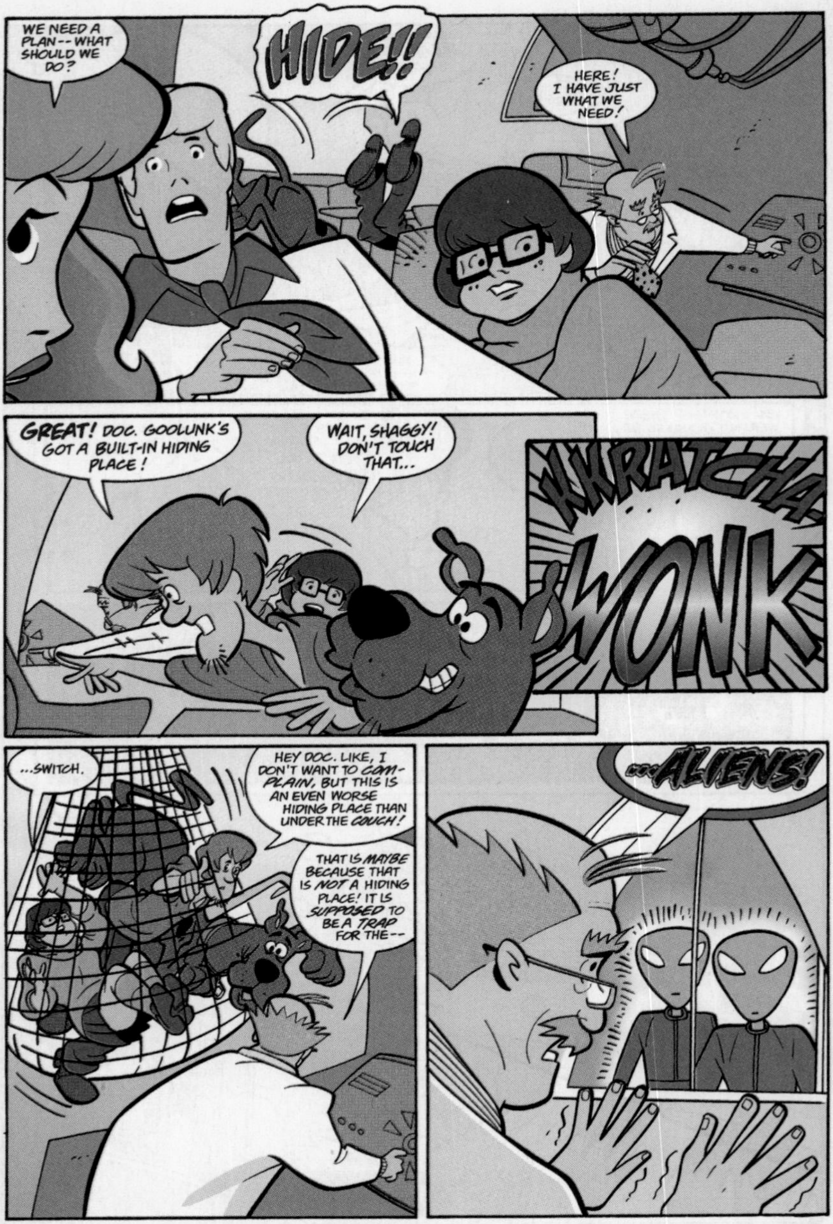

WE NEED A PLAN-- WHAT SHOULD WE DO?
HIDE!!
HERE! I HAVE JUST WHAT WE NEED!
GREAT! DOC. GOOLUNK'S GOT A BUILT-IN HIDING PLACE!
WAIT, SHAGGY! DON'T TOUCH THAT...
KKRATCHA-WONK
...SWITCH.
HEY DOC. LIKE, I DON'T WANT TO COMPLAIN, BUT THIS IS AN EVEN WORSE HIDING PLACE THAN UNDER THE COUCH!
THAT IS MAYBE BECAUSE THAT IS NOT A HIDING PLACE! IT IS SUPPOSED TO BE A TRAP FOR THE--
...ALIENS!

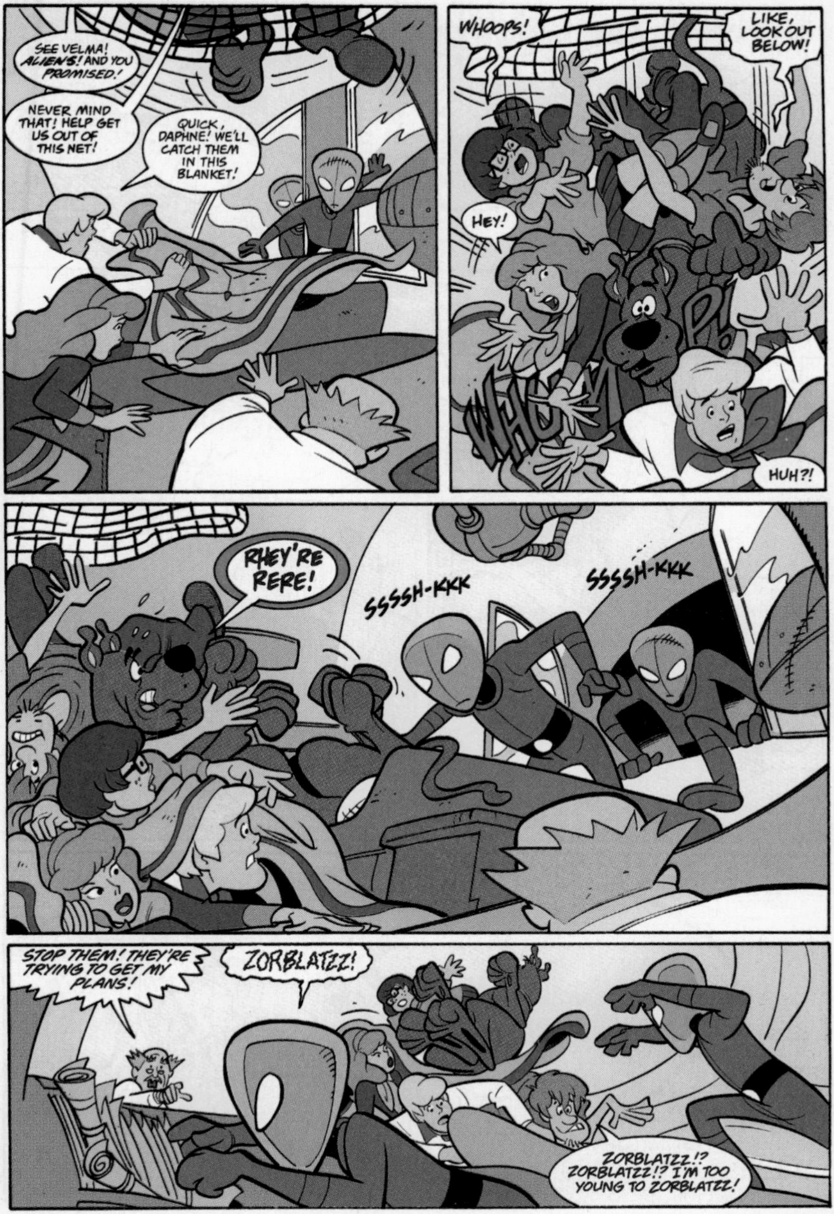
SEE VELMA! ALIENS! AND YOU PROMISED!
NEVER MIND THAT! HELP GET US OUT OF THIS NET!
QUICK, DAPHNE! WE'LL CATCH THEM IN THIS BLANKET!
WHOOPS!
LIKE, LOOK OUT BELOW!
HEY!
WHUMP!
HUH?!
RHEY'RE RERE!
SSSSH-KKK
SSSSH-KKK
STOP THEM! THEY'RE TRYING TO GET MY PLANS!
ZORBLATZZ!
ZORBLATZZ!? ZORBLATZZ!? I'M TOO YOUNG TO ZORBLATZZ!

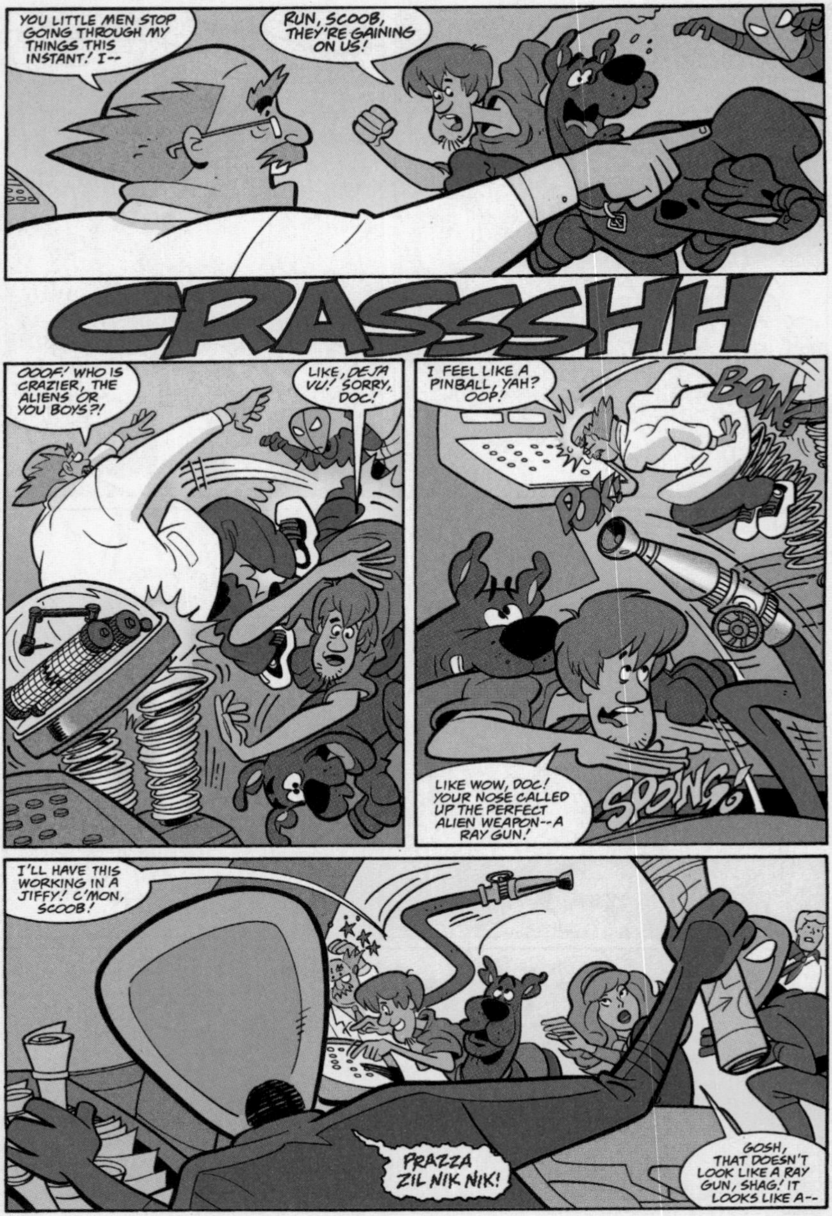

YOU LITTLE MEN STOP GOING THROUGH MY THINGS THIS INSTANT! I--
RUN, SCOOB, THEY'RE GAINING ON US!
CRASSSHH
OOOF! WHO IS CRAZIER, THE ALIENS OR YOU BOYS?!
LIKE, DEJA VU! SORRY, DOC!
I FEEL LIKE A PINBALL, YAH? OOP!
BONG
POK
LIKE WOW, DOC! YOUR NOSE CALLED UP THE PERFECT ALIEN WEAPON--A RAY GUN!
SPOING!
I'LL HAVE THIS WORKING IN A JIFFY! C'MON, SCOOB!
PRAZZA ZIL NIK NIK!
GOSH, THAT DOESN'T LOOK LIKE A RAY GUN, SHAG! IT LOOKS LIKE A--

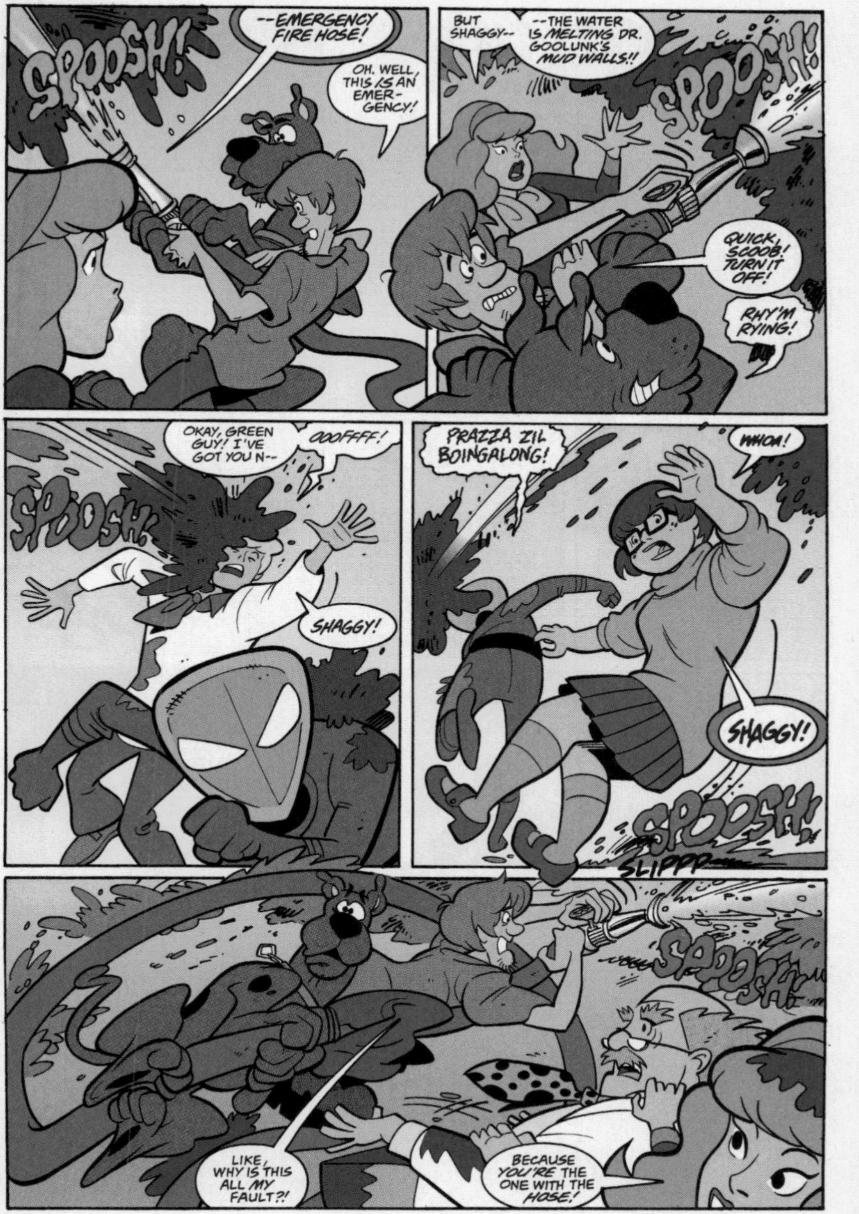
SPOOSH!
--EMERGENCY FIRE HOSE!
OH. WELL, THIS IS AN EMER-GENCY!
BUT SHAGGY--
--THE WATER IS MELTING DR. GOOLUNK'S MUD WALLS!!
SPOOSH!
QUICK, SCOOB! TURN IT OFF!
RHY'M RYING!
OKAY, GREEN GUY! I'VE GOT YOU N--
OOOFFFF!
SPOOSH!
SHAGGY!
PRAZZA ZIL BOINGALONG!
WHOA!
SHAGGY!
SPOOSH!
SLIPPP
SPOOSH!
LIKE, WHY IS THIS ALL MY FAULT?!
BECAUSE YOU'RE THE ONE WITH THE HOSE!

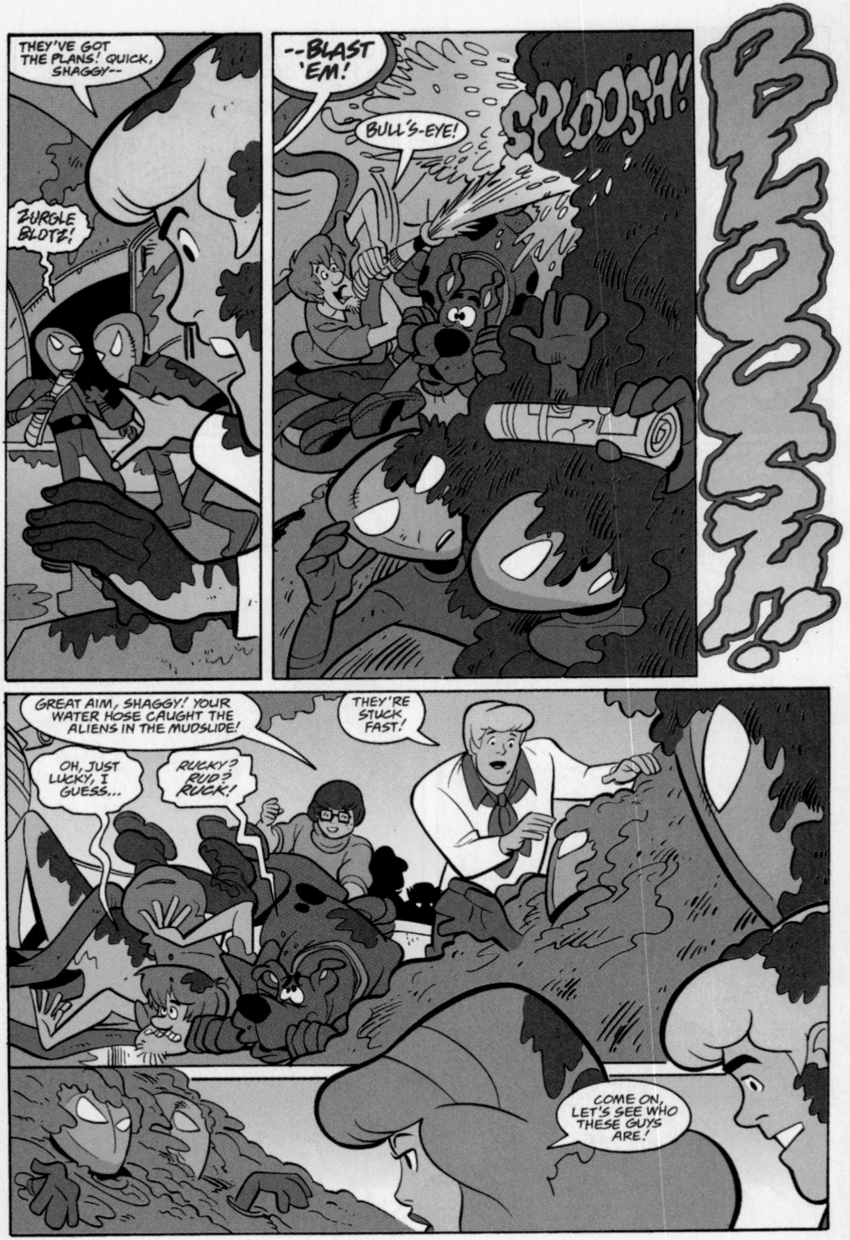
THEY'VE GOT THE PLANS! QUICK, SHAGGY--
ZURGLE BLOTZ!
--BLAST 'EM!
BULL'S-EYE!
SPLOOSH!
BLOOMSH!!
GREAT AIM, SHAGGY! YOUR WATER HOSE CAUGHT THE ALIENS IN THE MUDSLIDE!
THEY'RE STUCK FAST!
OH, JUST LUCKY, I GUESS...
RUCKY? RUD? RUCK!
COME ON, LET'S SEE WHO THESE GUYS ARE!

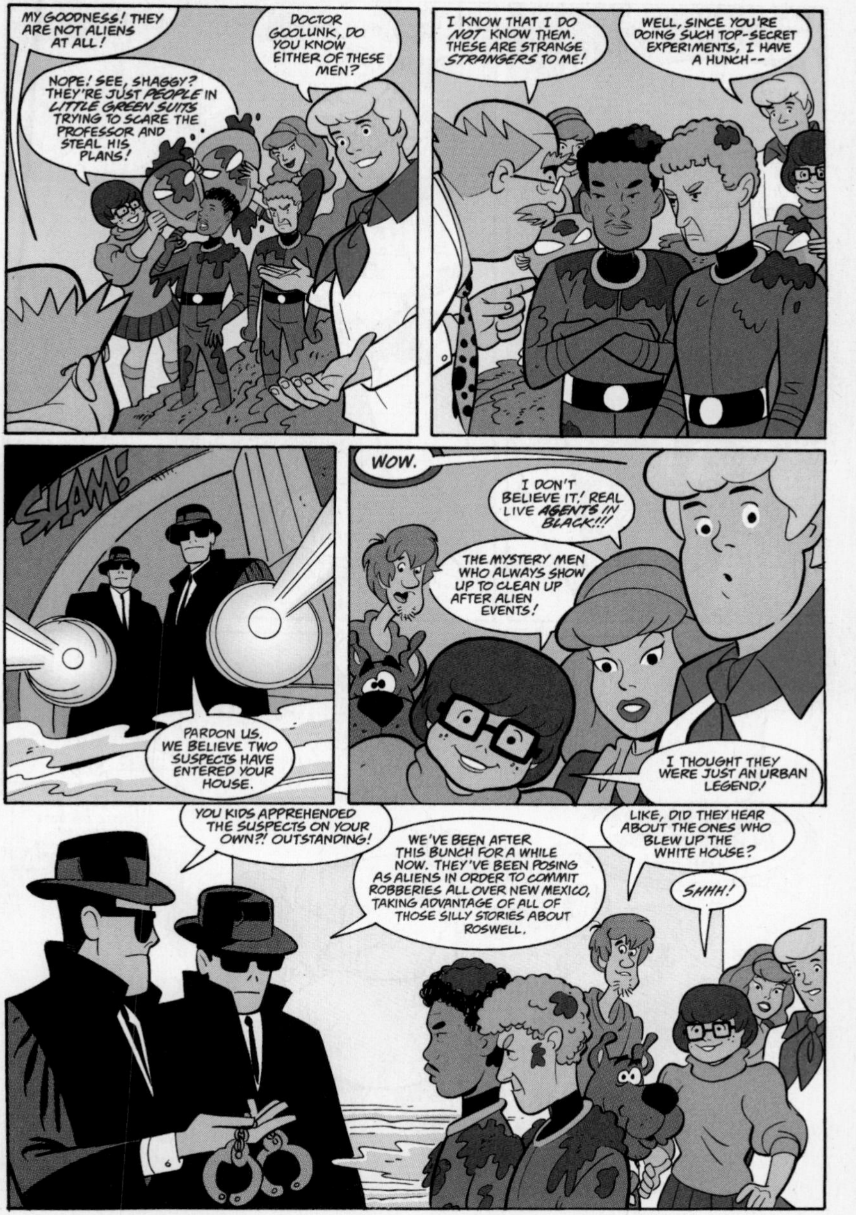

MY GOODNESS! THEY ARE NOT ALIENS AT ALL!
DOCTOR GOOLUNK, DO YOU KNOW EITHER OF THESE MEN?
NOPE! SEE, SHAGGY? THEY'RE JUST PEOPLE IN LITTLE GREEN SUITS TRYING TO SCARE THE PROFESSOR AND STEAL HIS PLANS!
I KNOW THAT I DO NOT KNOW THEM. THESE ARE STRANGE STRANGERS TO ME!
WELL, SINCE YOU'RE DOING SUCH TOP-SECRET EXPERIMENTS, I HAVE A HUNCH--
SLAM!
PARDON US. WE BELIEVE TWO SUSPECTS HAVE ENTERED YOUR HOUSE.
WOW.
I DON'T BELIEVE IT! REAL LIVE AGENTS IN BLACK!!!
THE MYSTERY MEN WHO ALWAYS SHOW UP TO CLEAN UP AFTER ALIEN EVENTS!
I THOUGHT THEY WERE JUST AN URBAN LEGEND!
YOU KIDS APPREHENDED THE SUSPECTS ON YOUR OWN?! OUTSTANDING!
WE'VE BEEN AFTER THIS BUNCH FOR A WHILE NOW. THEY'VE BEEN POSING AS ALIENS IN ORDER TO COMMIT ROBBERIES ALL OVER NEW MEXICO, TAKING ADVANTAGE OF ALL OF THOSE SILLY STORIES ABOUT ROSWELL.
LIKE, DID THEY HEAR ABOUT THE ONES WHO BLEW UP THE WHITE HOUSE?
SHHH!

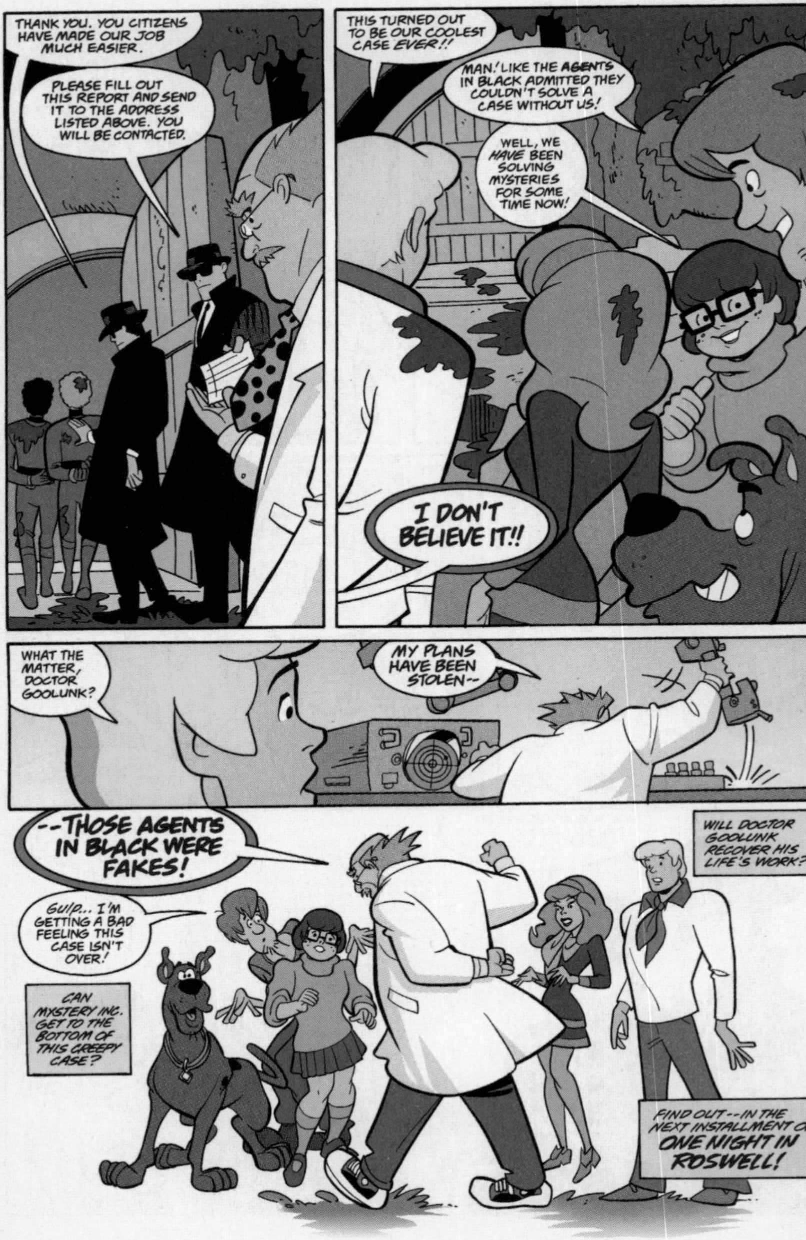

THANK YOU. YOU CITIZENS HAVE MADE OUR JOB MUCH EASIER.
PLEASE FILL OUT THIS REPORT AND SEND IT TO THE ADDRESS LISTED ABOVE. YOU WILL BE CONTACTED.
THIS TURNED OUT TO BE OUR COOLEST CASE *EVER!!*
MAN! LIKE THE AGENTS IN BLACK ADMITTED THEY COULDN'T SOLVE A CASE WITHOUT US!
WELL, WE *HAVE* BEEN SOLVING MYSTERIES FOR SOME TIME NOW!
I DON'T BELIEVE IT!!
WHAT THE MATTER, DOCTOR GOOLUNK?
MY PLANS HAVE BEEN STOLEN--
--THOSE AGENTS IN BLACK WERE FAKES!
WILL DOCTOR GOOLUNK RECOVER HIS LIFE'S WORK?
GULP... I'M GETTING A BAD FEELING THIS CASE ISN'T OVER!
CAN MYSTERY INC. GET TO THE BOTTOM OF THIS CREEPY CASE?
FIND OUT--IN THE NEXT INSTALLMENT OF ONE NIGHT IN ROSWELL!

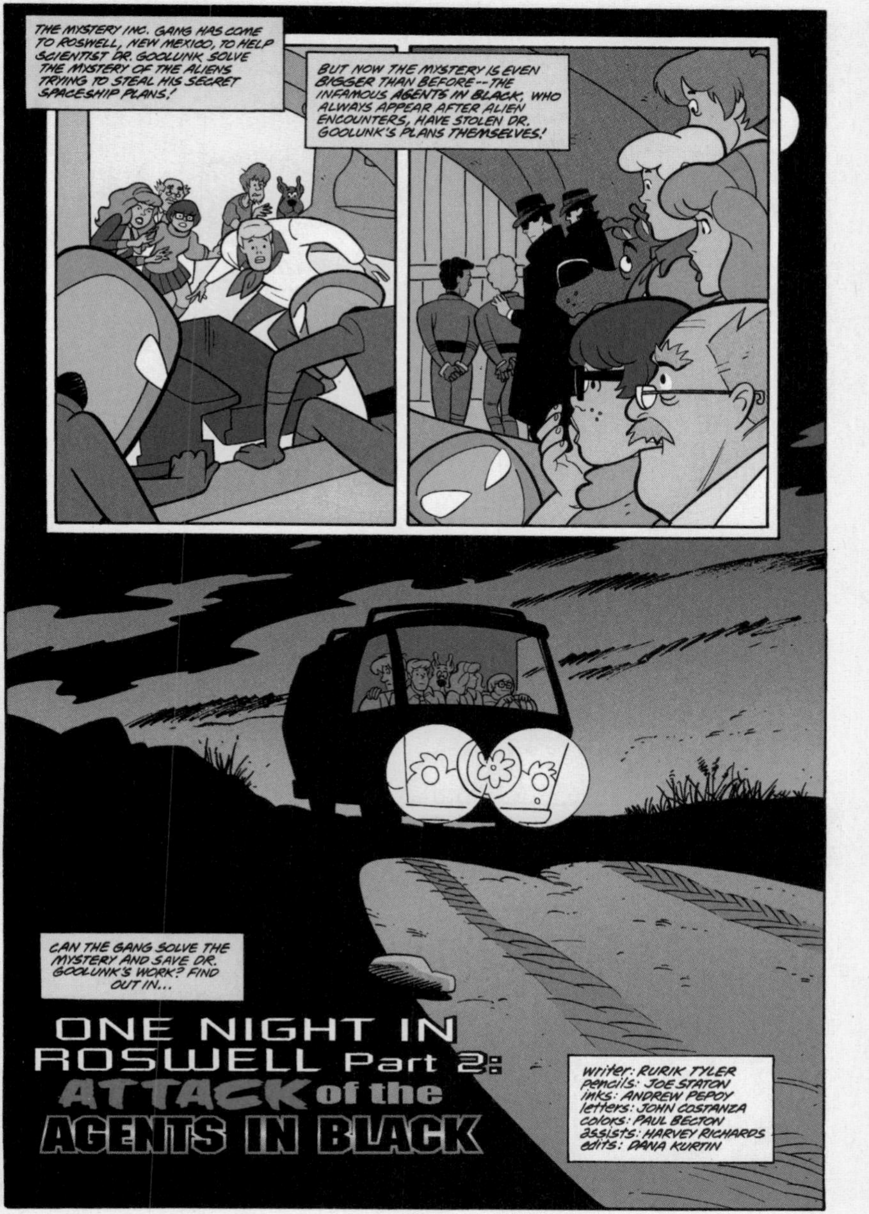
THE MYSTERY INC. GANG HAS COME TO ROSWELL, NEW MEXICO, TO HELP SCIENTIST DR. GOOLUNK SOLVE THE MYSTERY OF THE ALIENS TRYING TO STEAL HIS SECRET SPACESHIP PLANS!
BUT NOW THE MYSTERY IS EVEN BIGGER THAN BEFORE--THE INFAMOUS AGENTS IN BLACK, WHO ALWAYS APPEAR AFTER ALIEN ENCOUNTERS, HAVE STOLEN DR. GOOLUNK'S PLANS THEMSELVES!
CAN THE GANG SOLVE THE MYSTERY AND SAVE DR. GOOLUNK'S WORK? FIND OUT IN...
ONE NIGHT IN ROSWELL Part 2:
ATTACK of the AGENTS IN BLACK
writer: RURIK TYLER
pencils: JOE STATON
inks: ANDREW PEPOY
letters: JOHN COSTANZA
colors: PAUL BECTON
assists: HARVEY RICHARDS
edits: DANA KURTIN

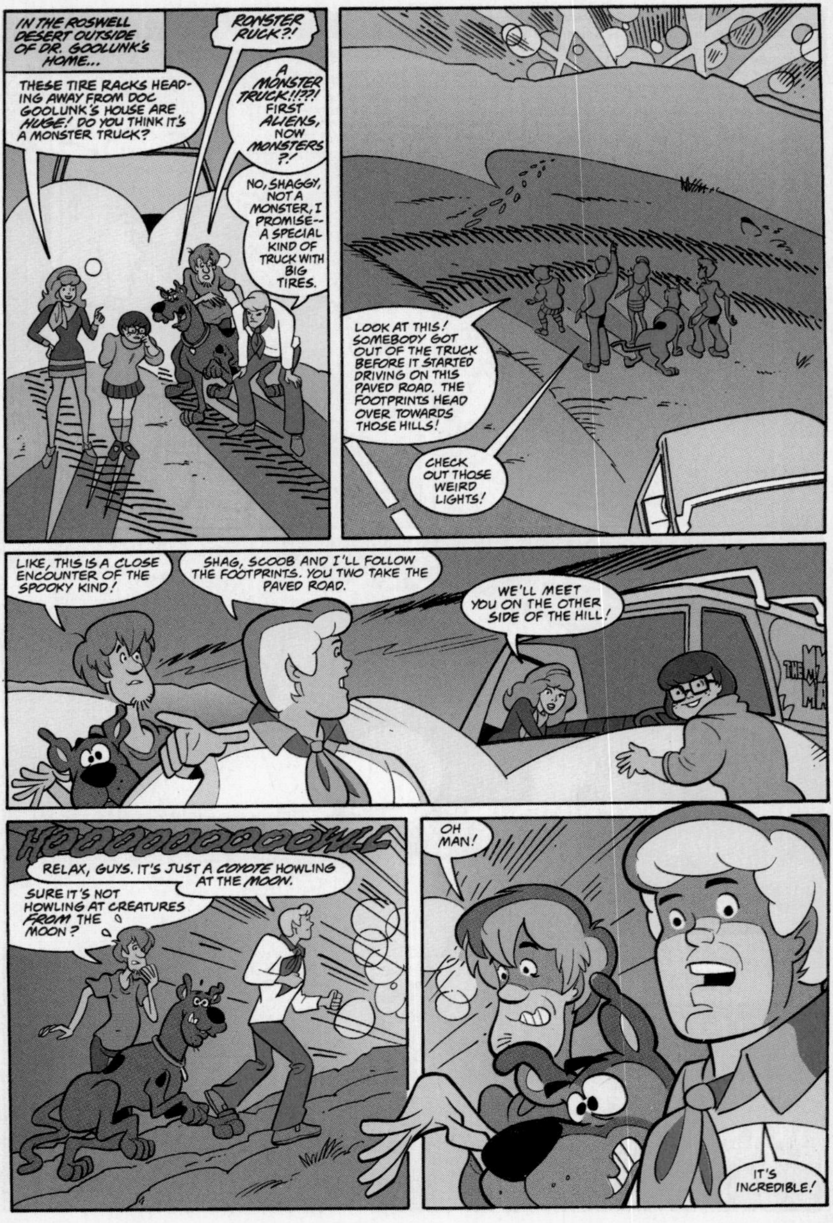
IN THE ROSWELL DESERT OUTSIDE OF DR. GOOLUNK'S HOME...
THESE TIRE RACKS HEADING AWAY FROM DOC GOOLUNK'S HOUSE ARE HUGE! DO YOU THINK IT'S A MONSTER TRUCK?
RONSTER RUCK?!
A MONSTER TRUCK!!??! FIRST ALIENS, NOW MONSTERS?!
NO, SHAGGY, NOT A MONSTER, I PROMISE-- A SPECIAL KIND OF TRUCK WITH BIG TIRES.
LOOK AT THIS! SOMEBODY GOT OUT OF THE TRUCK BEFORE IT STARTED DRIVING ON THIS PAVED ROAD. THE FOOTPRINTS HEAD OVER TOWARDS THOSE HILLS!
CHECK OUT THOSE WEIRD LIGHTS!
LIKE, THIS IS A CLOSE ENCOUNTER OF THE SPOOKY KIND!
SHAG, SCOOB AND I'LL FOLLOW THE FOOTPRINTS. YOU TWO TAKE THE PAVED ROAD.
WE'LL MEET YOU ON THE OTHER SIDE OF THE HILL!
HOOOOOOOOOOWLL
RELAX, GUYS. IT'S JUST A COYOTE HOWLING AT THE MOON.
SURE IT'S NOT HOWLING AT CREATURES FROM THE MOON?
OH MAN!
IT'S INCREDIBLE!

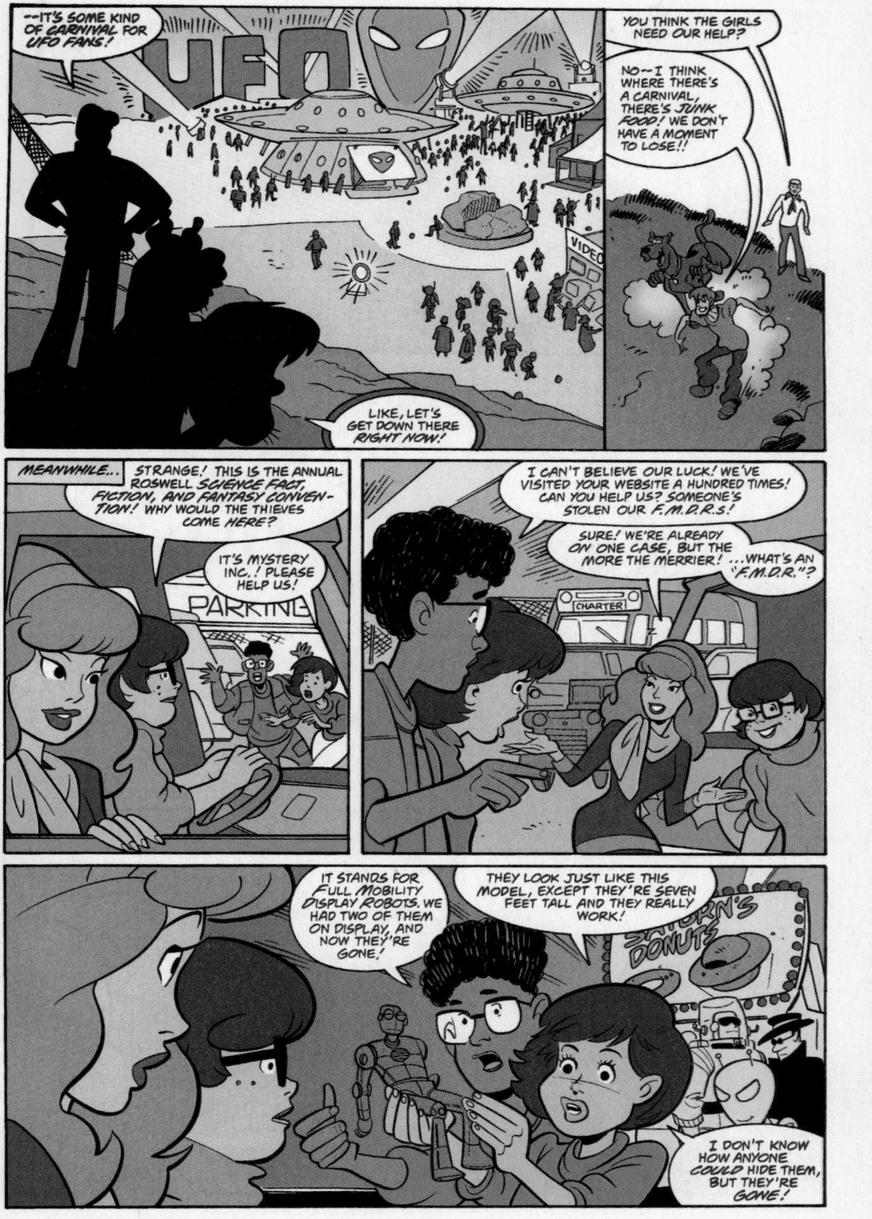
--IT'S SOME KIND OF CARNIVAL FOR UFO FANS!
UFO
LIKE, LET'S GET DOWN THERE RIGHT NOW!
YOU THINK THE GIRLS NEED OUR HELP?
NO--I THINK WHERE THERE'S A CARNIVAL, THERE'S JUNK FOOD! WE DON'T HAVE A MOMENT TO LOSE!!
MEANWHILE...
STRANGE! THIS IS THE ANNUAL ROSWELL SCIENCE FACT, FICTION, AND FANTASY CONVENTION! WHY WOULD THE THIEVES COME HERE?
IT'S MYSTERY INC.! PLEASE HELP US!
PARKING
I CAN'T BELIEVE OUR LUCK! WE'VE VISITED YOUR WEBSITE A HUNDRED TIMES! CAN YOU HELP US? SOMEONE'S STOLEN OUR F.M.D.R.s!
SURE! WE'RE ALREADY ON ONE CASE, BUT THE MORE THE MERRIER! ...WHAT'S AN "F.M.D.R."?
CHARTER
IT STANDS FOR FULL MOBILITY DISPLAY ROBOTS. WE HAD TWO OF THEM ON DISPLAY, AND NOW THEY'RE GONE!
THEY LOOK JUST LIKE THIS MODEL, EXCEPT THEY'RE SEVEN FEET TALL AND THEY REALLY WORK!
DONUTS
I DON'T KNOW HOW ANYONE COULD HIDE THEM, BUT THEY'RE GONE!

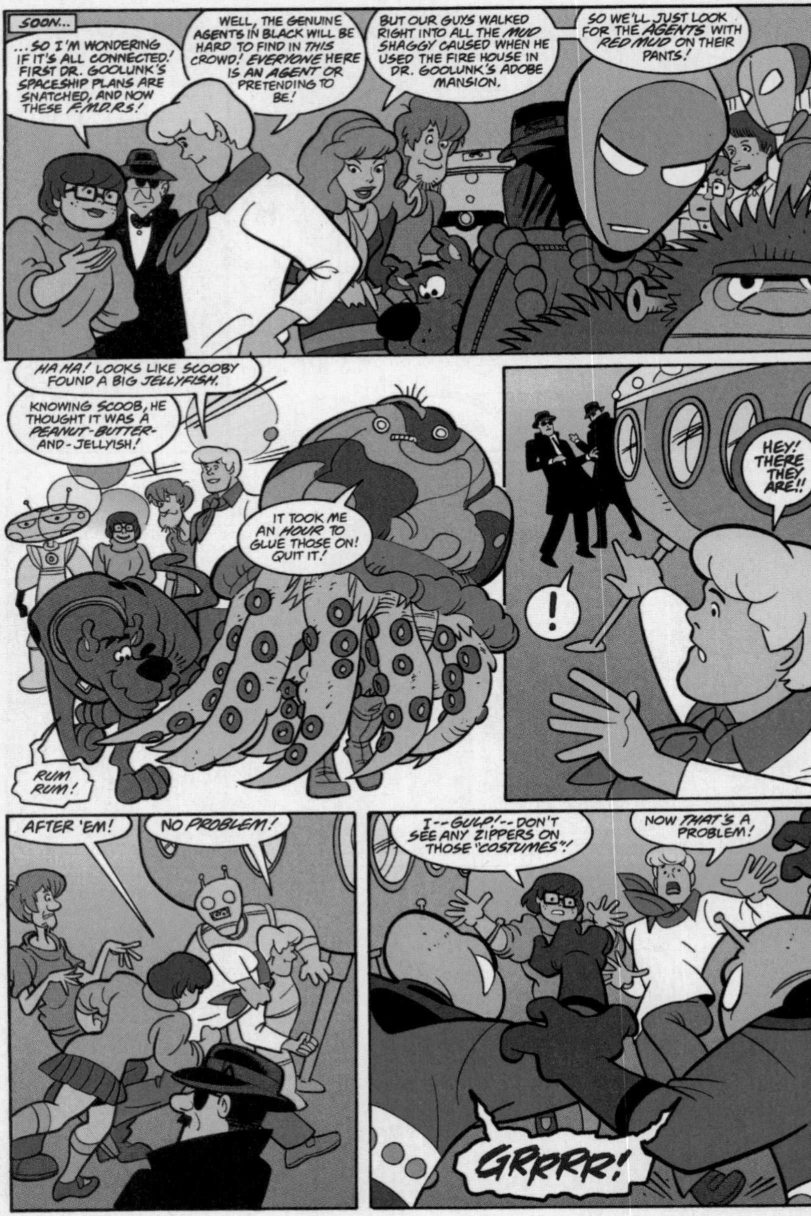
SOON...
...SO I'M WONDERING IF IT'S ALL CONNECTED! FIRST DR. GOOLUNK'S SPACESHIP PLANS ARE SNATCHED, AND NOW THESE F.M.D.R.S.!
WELL, THE GENUINE AGENTS IN BLACK WILL BE HARD TO FIND IN THIS CROWD! EVERYONE HERE IS AN AGENT OR PRETENDING TO BE!
BUT OUR GUYS WALKED RIGHT INTO ALL THE MUD SHAGGY CAUSED WHEN HE USED THE FIRE HOUSE IN DR. GOOLUNK'S ADOBE MANSION.
SO WE'LL JUST LOOK FOR THE AGENTS WITH RED MUD ON THEIR PANTS!
HA HA! LOOKS LIKE SCOOBY FOUND A BIG JELLYFISH.
KNOWING SCOOB, HE THOUGHT IT WAS A PEANUT-BUTTER-AND-JELLYISH!
IT TOOK ME AN HOUR TO GLUE THOSE ON! QUIT IT!
RUM RUM!
HEY! THERE THEY ARE!!
!
AFTER 'EM!
NO PROBLEM!
I--GULP!--DON'T SEE ANY ZIPPERS ON THOSE "COSTUMES"!
NOW THAT'S A PROBLEM!
GRRRR!

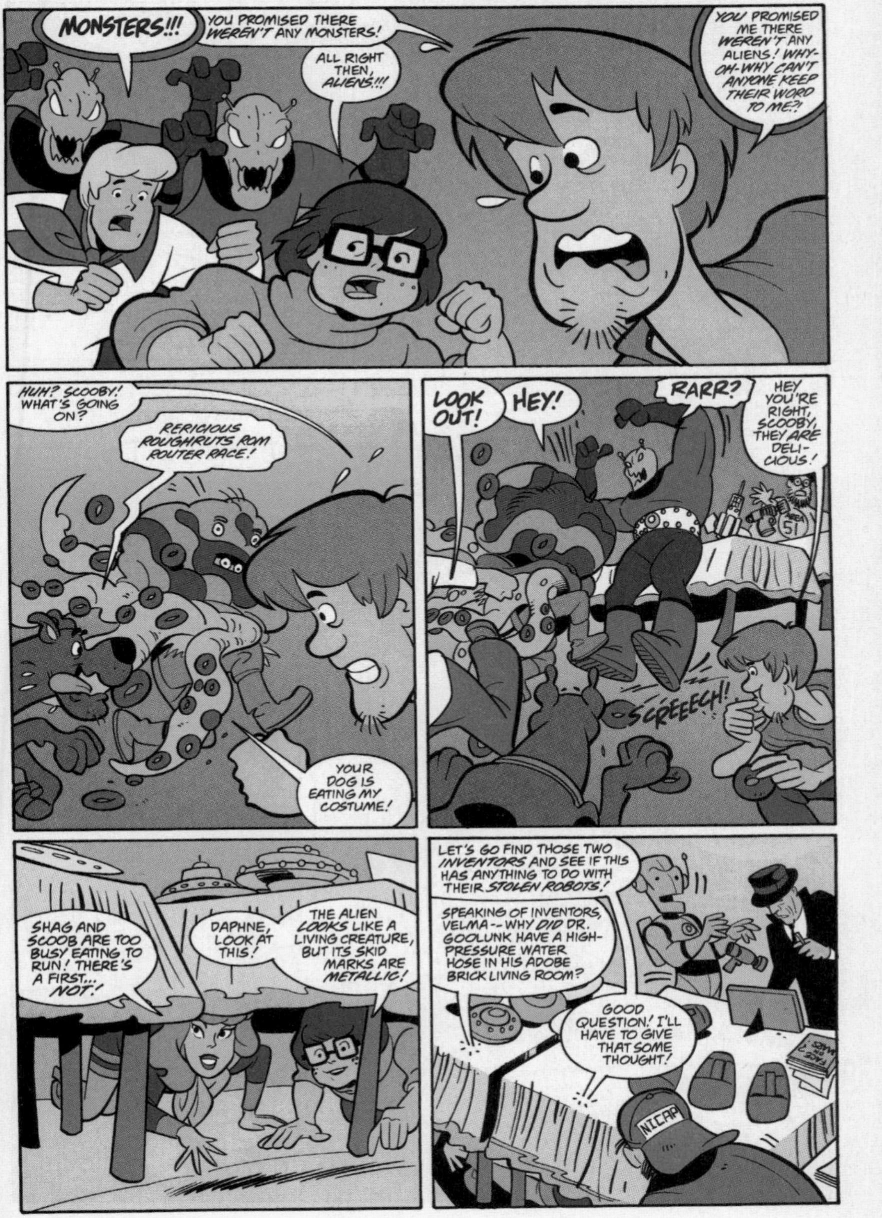
MONSTERS!!!
YOU PROMISED THERE WEREN'T ANY MONSTERS!
ALL RIGHT THEN, ALIENS!!!
YOU PROMISED ME THERE WEREN'T ANY ALIENS! WHY-OH-WHY CAN'T ANYONE KEEP THEIR WORD TO ME?!
HUH? SCOOBY! WHAT'S GOING ON?
RERICIOUS ROUGHRUTS ROM ROUTER RACE!
YOUR DOG IS EATING MY COSTUME!
LOOK OUT!
HEY!
RARR?
HEY YOU'RE RIGHT, SCOOBY, THEY ARE DELI-CIOUS!
SCREEECH!
SHAG AND SCOOB ARE TOO BUSY EATING TO RUN! THERE'S A FIRST... NOT!
DAPHNE, LOOK AT THIS!
THE ALIEN LOOKS LIKE A LIVING CREATURE, BUT ITS SKID MARKS ARE METALLIC!
LET'S GO FIND THOSE TWO INVENTORS AND SEE IF THIS HAS ANYTHING TO DO WITH THEIR STOLEN ROBOTS!
SPEAKING OF INVENTORS, VELMA -- WHY DID DR. GOOLUNK HAVE A HIGH-PRESSURE WATER HOSE IN HIS ADOBE BRICK LIVING ROOM?
GOOD QUESTION! I'LL HAVE TO GIVE THAT SOME THOUGHT!
NICAP

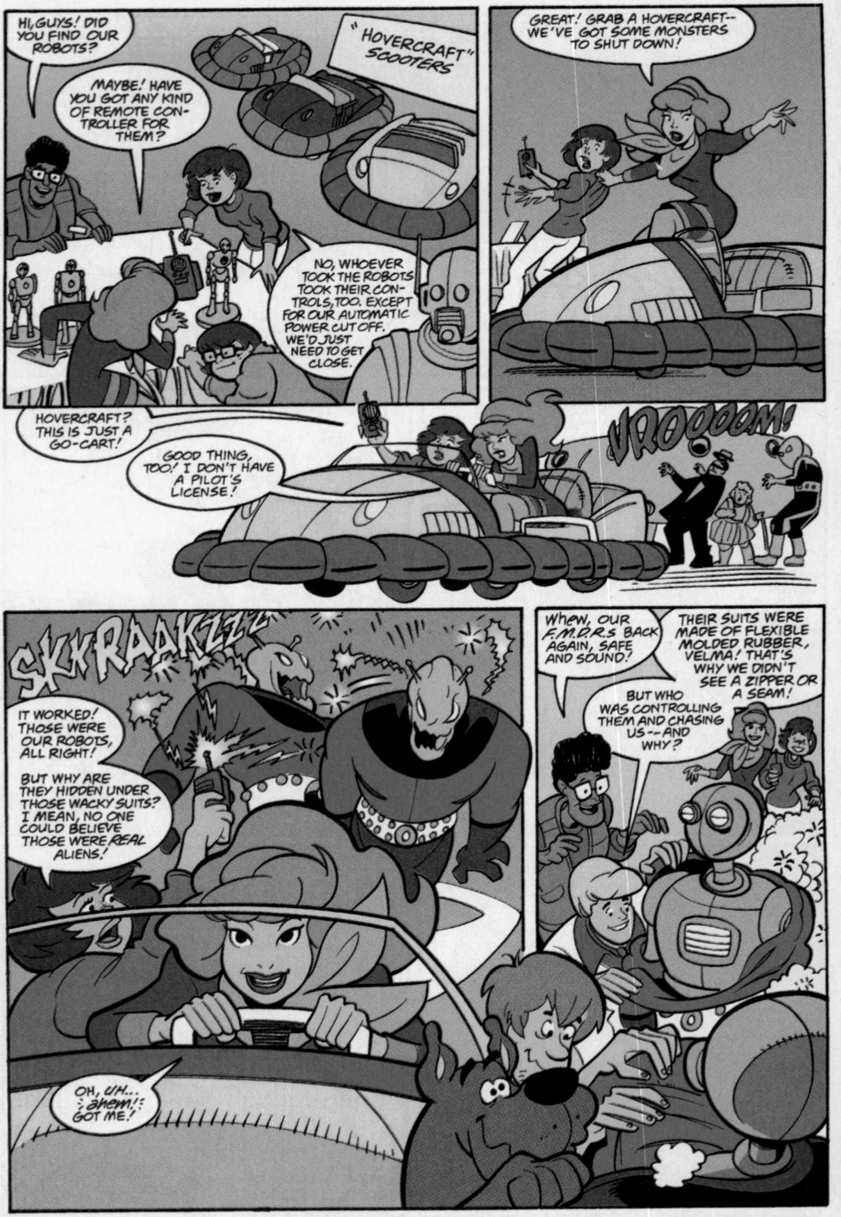
HI, GUYS! DID YOU FIND OUR ROBOTS?
MAYBE! HAVE YOU GOT ANY KIND OF REMOTE CONTROLLER FOR THEM?
"HOVERCRAFT" SCOOTERS
NO, WHOEVER TOOK THE ROBOTS TOOK THEIR CONTROLS, TOO. EXCEPT FOR OUR AUTOMATIC POWER CUT OFF. WE'D JUST NEED TO GET CLOSE.
GREAT! GRAB A HOVERCRAFT-- WE'VE GOT SOME MONSTERS TO SHUT DOWN!
HOVERCRAFT? THIS IS JUST A GO-CART!
GOOD THING, TOO! I DON'T HAVE A PILOT'S LICENSE!
VROOOOOM!
SKKRAAKZZZ
IT WORKED! THOSE WERE OUR ROBOTS, ALL RIGHT!
BUT WHY ARE THEY HIDDEN UNDER THOSE WACKY SUITS? I MEAN, NO ONE COULD BELIEVE THOSE WERE REAL ALIENS!
OH, UH... ahem! GOT ME!
Whew, OUR F.M.D.R.s BACK AGAIN, SAFE AND SOUND!
THEIR SUITS WERE MADE OF FLEXIBLE MOLDED RUBBER, VELMA! THAT'S WHY WE DIDN'T SEE A ZIPPER OR A SEAM!
BUT WHO WAS CONTROLLING THEM AND CHASING US--AND WHY?

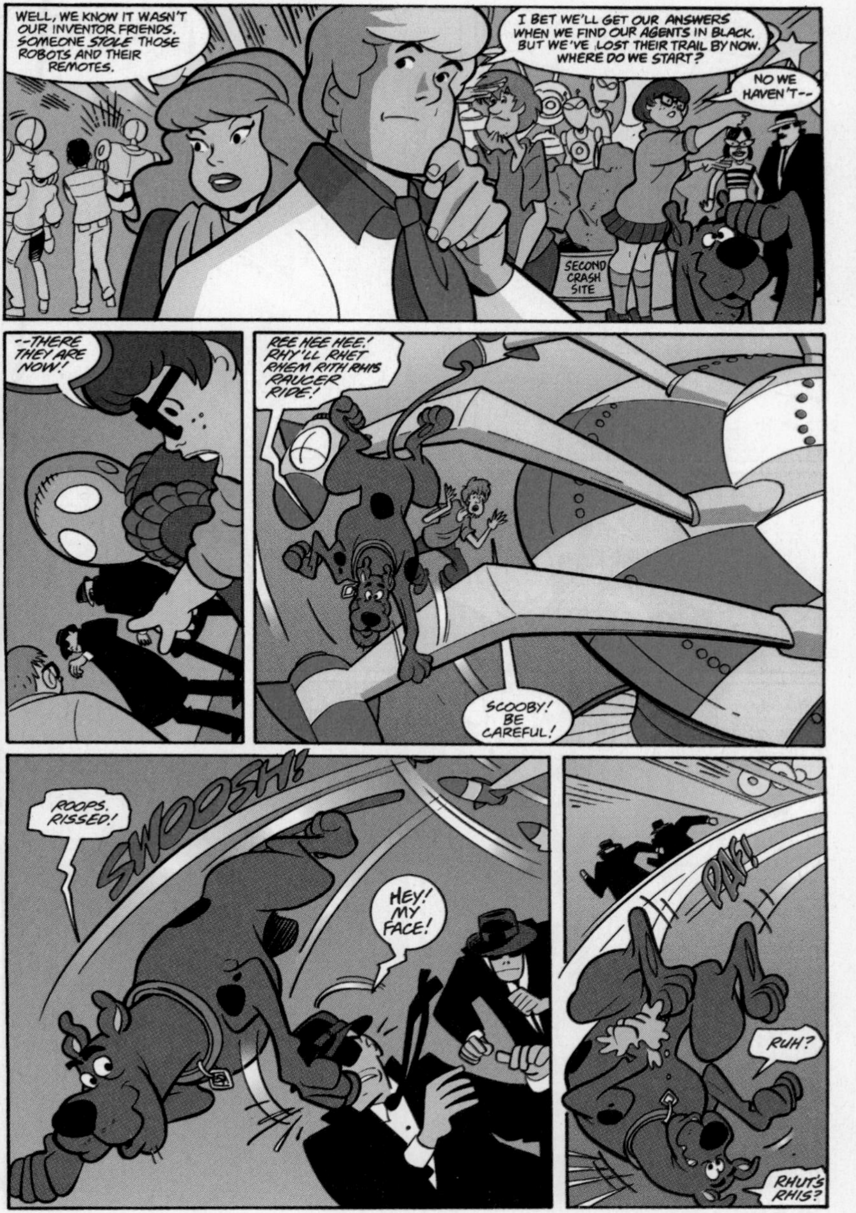
WELL, WE KNOW IT WASN'T OUR INVENTOR FRIENDS. SOMEONE STOLE THOSE ROBOTS AND THEIR REMOTES.
I BET WE'LL GET OUR ANSWERS WHEN WE FIND OUR AGENTS IN BLACK. BUT WE'VE LOST THEIR TRAIL BY NOW. WHERE DO WE START?
NO WE HAVEN'T--
SECOND CRASH SITE
--THERE THEY ARE NOW!
REE HEE HEE! RHY'LL RHET RHEM RITH RHIS RAUCER RIDE!
SCOOBY! BE CAREFUL!
ROOPS. RISSED!
SWOOSH!
HEY! MY FACE!
RUH?
RHUT'S RHIS?

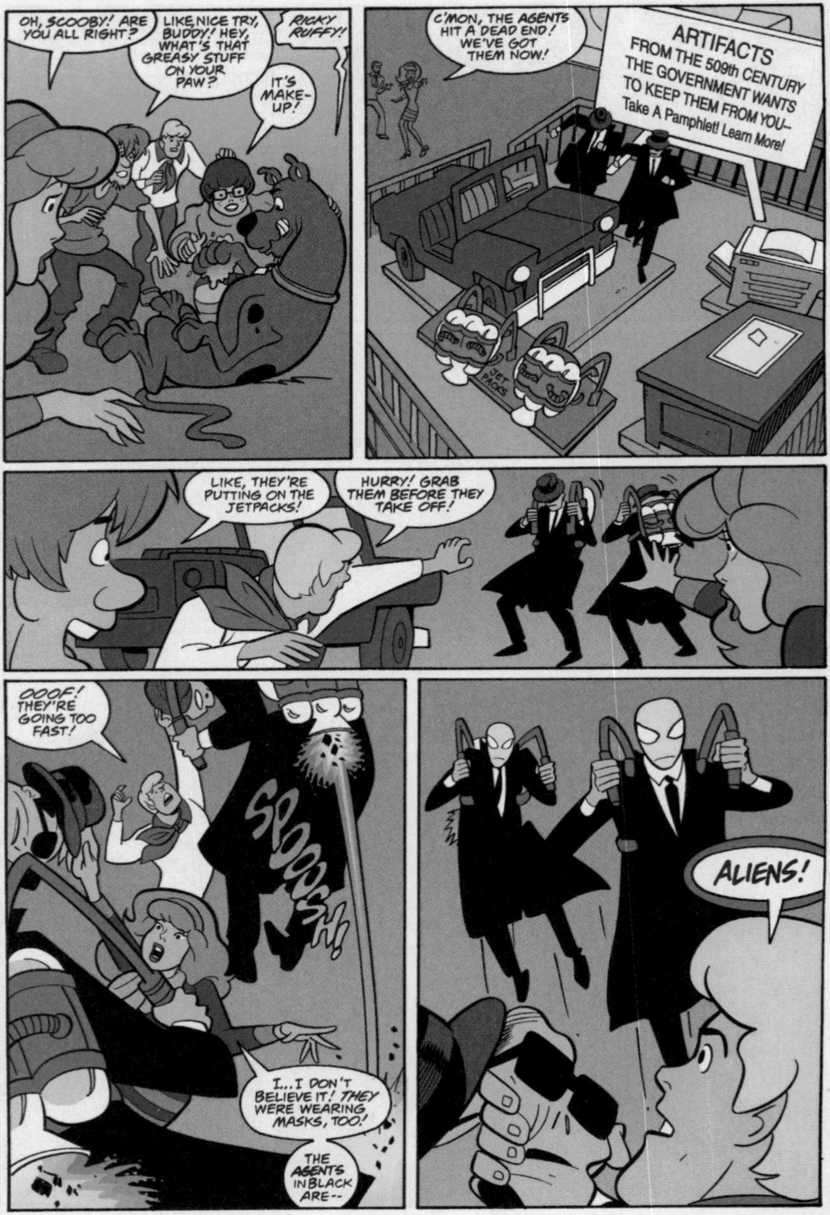
OH, SCOOBY! ARE YOU ALL RIGHT?
LIKE, NICE TRY, BUDDY! HEY, WHAT'S THAT GREASY STUFF ON YOUR PAW?
RICKY RUFFY!
IT'S MAKE-UP!
C'MON, THE AGENTS HIT A DEAD END! WE'VE GOT THEM NOW!
ARTIFACTS
FROM THE 509th CENTURY
THE GOVERNMENT WANTS
TO KEEP THEM FROM YOU--
Take A Pamphlet! Learn More!
JET PACKS
LIKE, THEY'RE PUTTING ON THE JETPACKS!
HURRY! GRAB THEM BEFORE THEY TAKE OFF!
OOOF! THEY'RE GOING TOO FAST!
SPOOOOSH!
I...I DON'T BELIEVE IT! THEY WERE WEARING MASKS, TOO!
THE AGENTS IN BLACK ARE--
ALIENS!

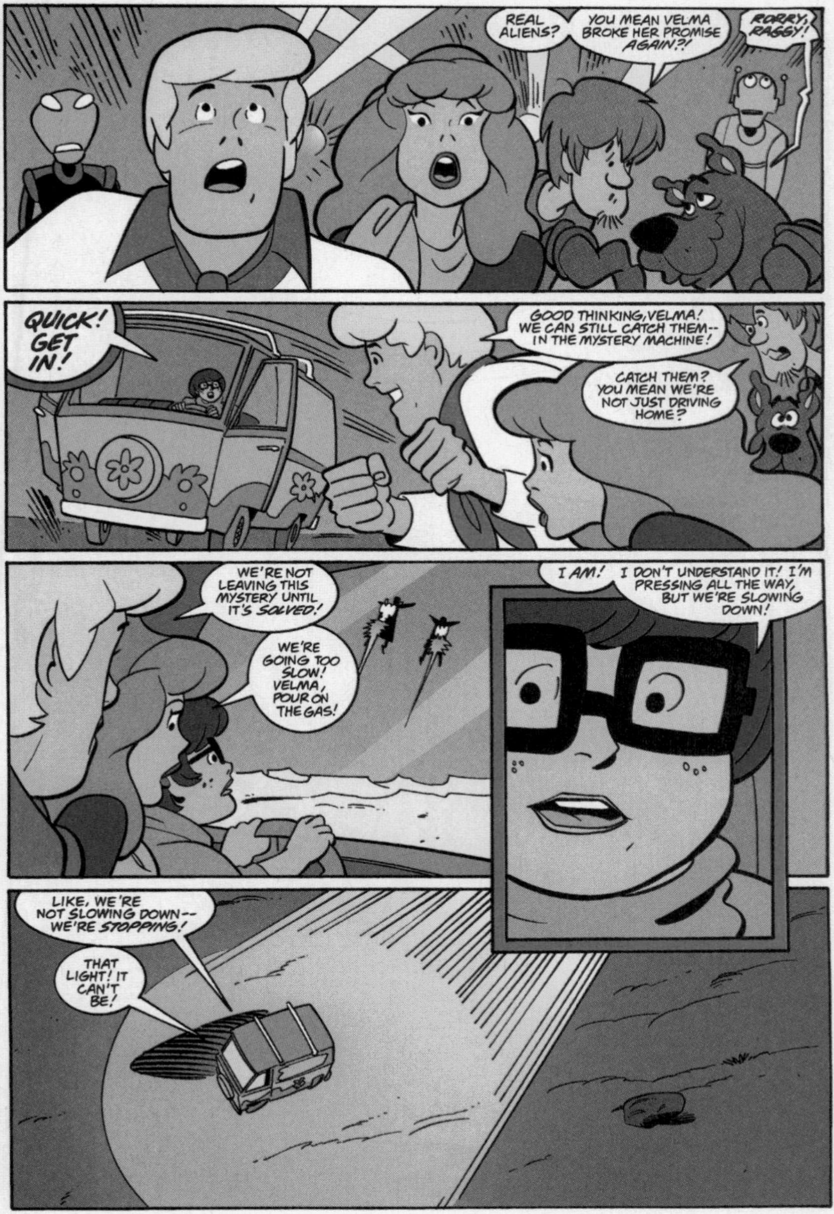
REAL ALIENS?
YOU MEAN VELMA BROKE HER PROMISE AGAIN?!
RORRY, RAGGY!
QUICK! GET IN!
GOOD THINKING, VELMA! WE CAN STILL CATCH THEM-- IN THE MYSTERY MACHINE!
CATCH THEM? YOU MEAN WE'RE NOT JUST DRIVING HOME?
WE'RE NOT LEAVING THIS MYSTERY UNTIL IT'S SOLVED!
WE'RE GOING TOO SLOW! VELMA, POUR ON THE GAS!
I AM!
I DON'T UNDERSTAND IT! I'M PRESSING ALL THE WAY, BUT WE'RE SLOWING DOWN!
LIKE, WE'RE NOT SLOWING DOWN-- WE'RE STOPPING!
THAT LIGHT! IT CAN'T BE!

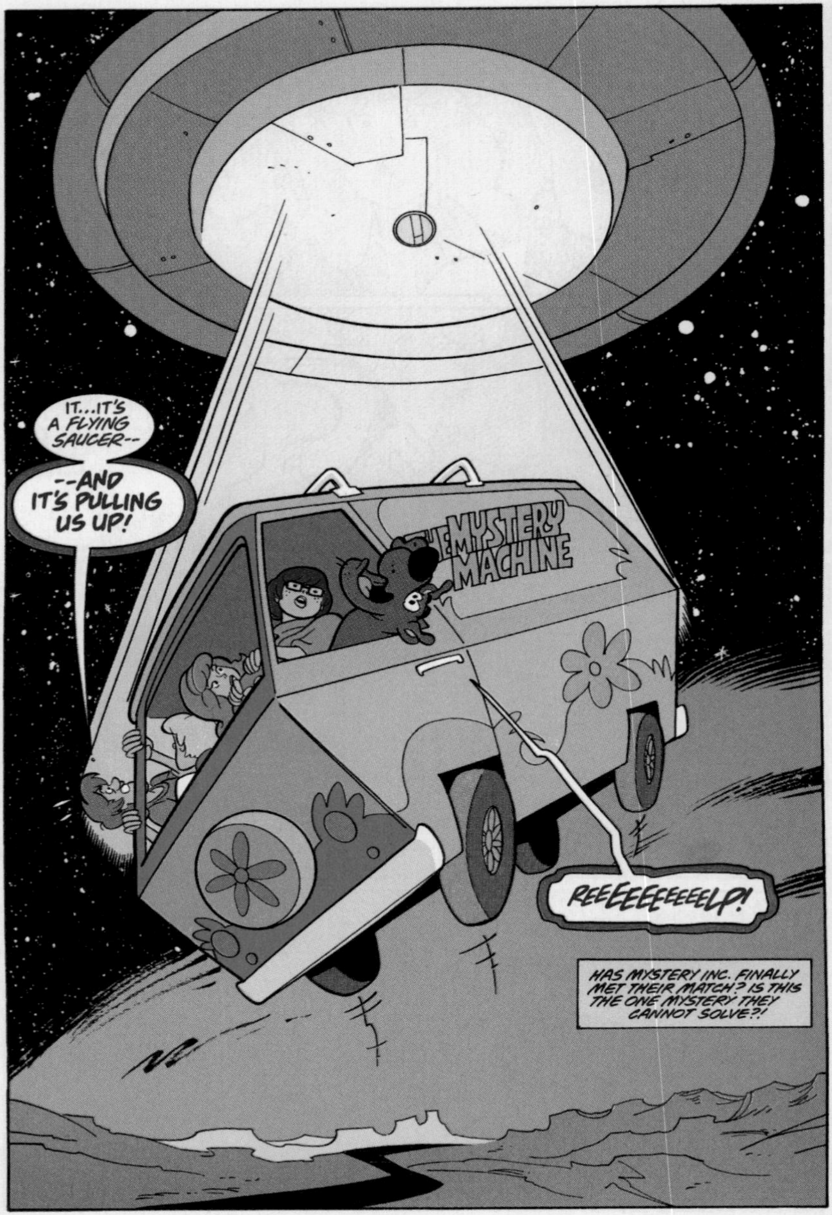

IT...IT'S A FLYING SAUCER--
--AND IT'S PULLING US UP!
THE MYSTERY MACHINE
REEEEEEEEEELP!
HAS MYSTERY INC. FINALLY MET THEIR MATCH? IS THIS THE ONE MYSTERY THEY CANNOT SOLVE?!

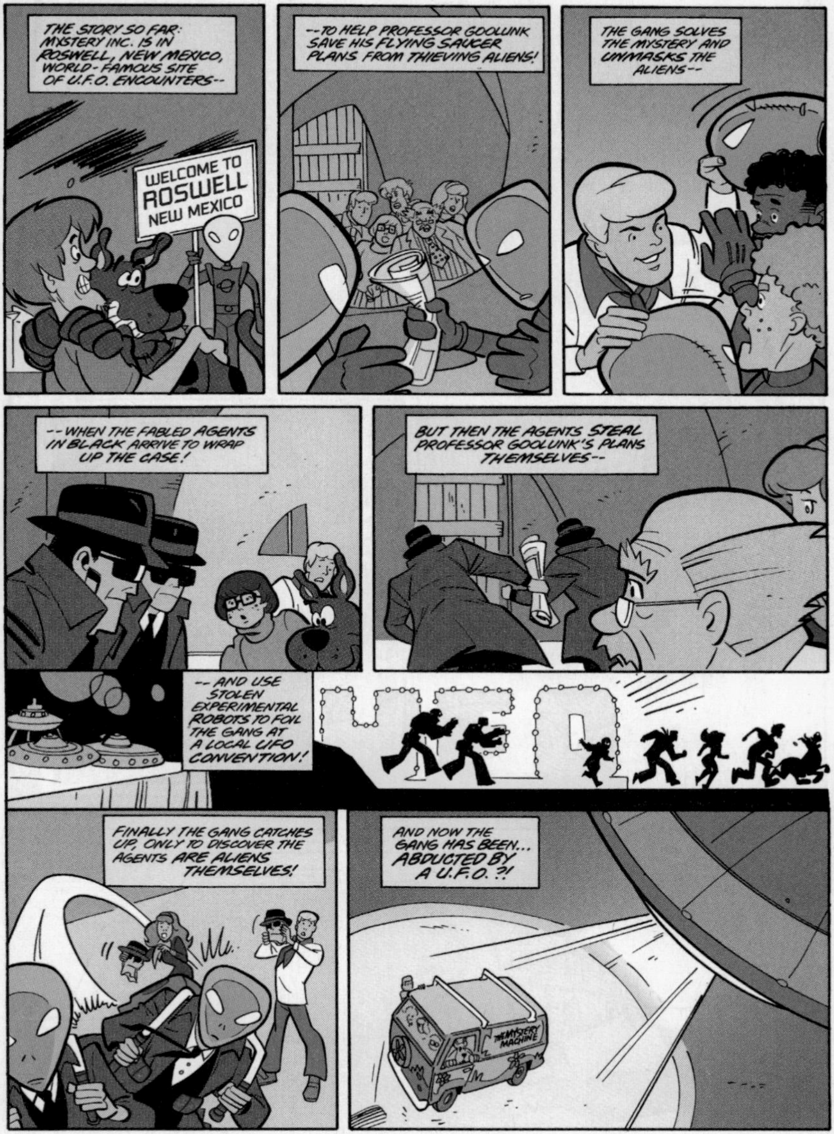

THE STORY SO FAR: MYSTERY INC. IS IN ROSWELL, NEW MEXICO, WORLD-FAMOUS SITE OF U.F.O. ENCOUNTERS--
WELCOME TO ROSWELL NEW MEXICO
--TO HELP PROFESSOR GOOLUNK SAVE HIS FLYING SAUCER PLANS FROM THIEVING ALIENS!
THE GANG SOLVES THE MYSTERY AND UNMASKS THE ALIENS--
--WHEN THE FABLED AGENTS IN BLACK ARRIVE TO WRAP UP THE CASE!
BUT THEN THE AGENTS STEAL PROFESSOR GOOLUNK'S PLANS THEMSELVES--
--AND USE STOLEN EXPERIMENTAL ROBOTS TO FOIL THE GANG AT A LOCAL UFO CONVENTION!
FINALLY THE GANG CATCHES UP, ONLY TO DISCOVER THE AGENTS ARE ALIENS THEMSELVES!
AND NOW THE GANG HAS BEEN... ABDUCTED BY A U.F.O.?!
THE MYSTERY MACHINE

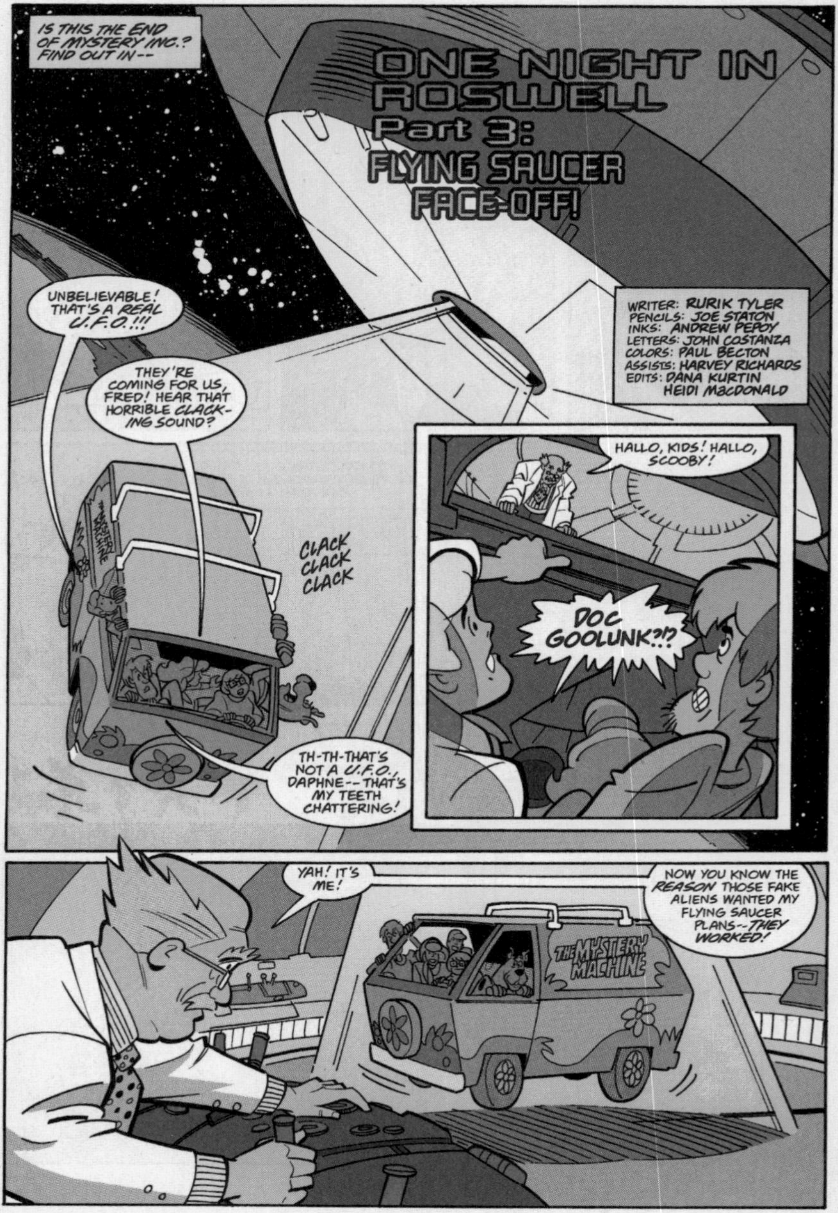

IS THIS THE END OF MYSTERY INC.? FIND OUT IN--
ONE NIGHT IN ROSWELL
Part 3:
FLYING SAUCER FACE-OFF!
WRITER: RURIK TYLER
PENCILS: JOE STATON
INKS: ANDREW PEPOY
LETTERS: JOHN COSTANZA
COLORS: PAUL BECTON
ASSISTS: HARVEY RICHARDS
EDITS: DANA KURTIN
HEIDI MacDONALD
UNBELIEVABLE! THAT'S A REAL U.F.O.!!!
THEY'RE COMING FOR US, FRED! HEAR THAT HORRIBLE CLACKING SOUND?
CLACK CLACK CLACK
TH-TH-THAT'S NOT A U.F.O., DAPHNE-- THAT'S MY TEETH CHATTERING!
HALLO, KIDS! HALLO, SCOOBY!
DOC GOOLUNK?!?
YAH! IT'S ME!
NOW YOU KNOW THE REASON THOSE FAKE ALIENS WANTED MY FLYING SAUCER PLANS--THEY WORKED!
THE MYSTERY MACHINE

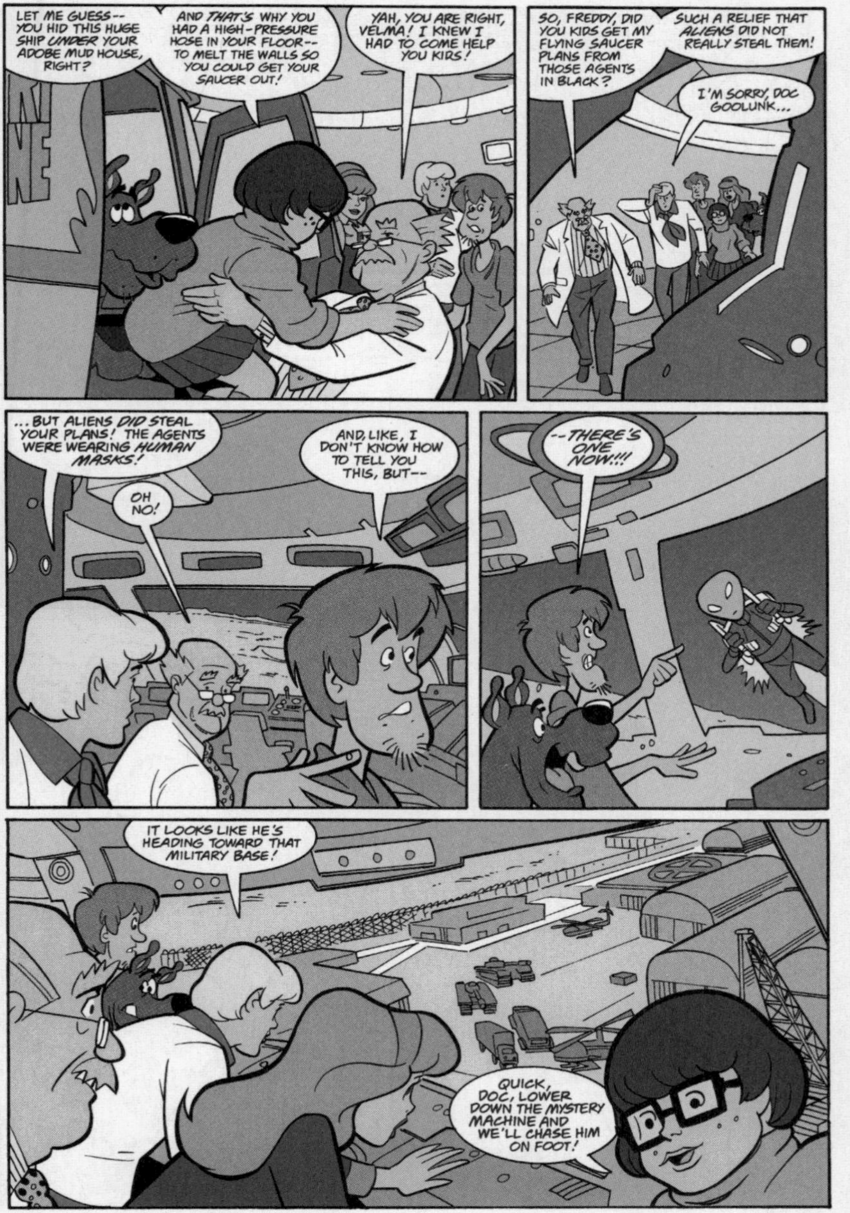
LET ME GUESS-- YOU HID THIS HUGE SHIP *UNDER* YOUR ADOBE MUD HOUSE, RIGHT?
AND *THAT'S* WHY YOU HAD A HIGH-PRESSURE HOSE IN YOUR FLOOR-- TO MELT THE WALLS SO YOU COULD GET YOUR SAUCER OUT!
YAH, YOU ARE RIGHT, VELMA! I KNEW I HAD TO COME HELP YOU KIDS!
SO, FREDDY, DID YOU KIDS GET MY FLYING SAUCER PLANS FROM THOSE AGENTS IN BLACK?
SUCH A RELIEF THAT *ALIENS* DID NOT REALLY STEAL THEM!
I'M SORRY, DOC GOOLUNK...
...BUT ALIENS *DID* STEAL YOUR PLANS! THE AGENTS WERE WEARING *HUMAN MASKS*!
OH NO!
AND, LIKE, I DON'T KNOW HOW TO TELL YOU THIS, BUT--
--*THERE'S ONE NOW!!!*
IT LOOKS LIKE HE'S HEADING TOWARD THAT MILITARY BASE!
QUICK, DOC, LOWER DOWN THE MYSTERY MACHINE AND WE'LL CHASE HIM ON FOOT!

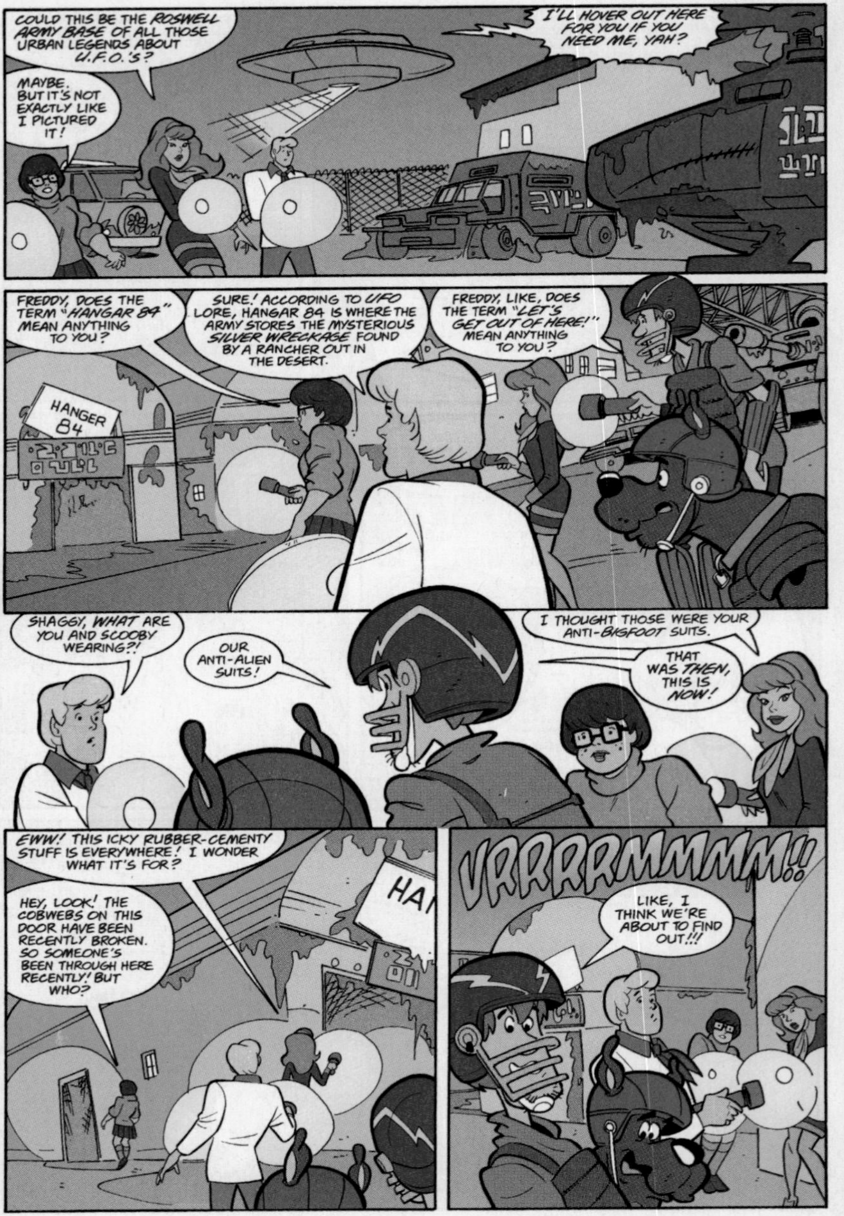
COULD THIS BE THE ROSWELL ARMY BASE OF ALL THOSE URBAN LEGENDS ABOUT U.F.O.'S?
I'LL HOVER OUT HERE FOR YOU IF YOU NEED ME, YAH?
MAYBE. BUT IT'S NOT EXACTLY LIKE I PICTURED IT!
FREDDY, DOES THE TERM "HANGAR 84" MEAN ANYTHING TO YOU?
SURE! ACCORDING TO UFO LORE, HANGAR 84 IS WHERE THE ARMY STORES THE MYSTERIOUS SILVER WRECKAGE FOUND BY A RANCHER OUT IN THE DESERT.
FREDDY, LIKE, DOES THE TERM "LET'S GET OUT OF HERE!" MEAN ANYTHING TO YOU?
HANGER 84
SHAGGY, WHAT ARE YOU AND SCOOBY WEARING?!
OUR ANTI-ALIEN SUITS!
I THOUGHT THOSE WERE YOUR ANTI-BIGFOOT SUITS.
THAT WAS THEN, THIS IS NOW!
EWW! THIS ICKY RUBBER-CEMENTY STUFF IS EVERYWHERE! I WONDER WHAT IT'S FOR?
HEY, LOOK! THE COBWEBS ON THIS DOOR HAVE BEEN RECENTLY BROKEN. SO SOMEONE'S BEEN THROUGH HERE RECENTLY! BUT WHO?
VRRRRMMMM!!
LIKE, I THINK WE'RE ABOUT TO FIND OUT!!!

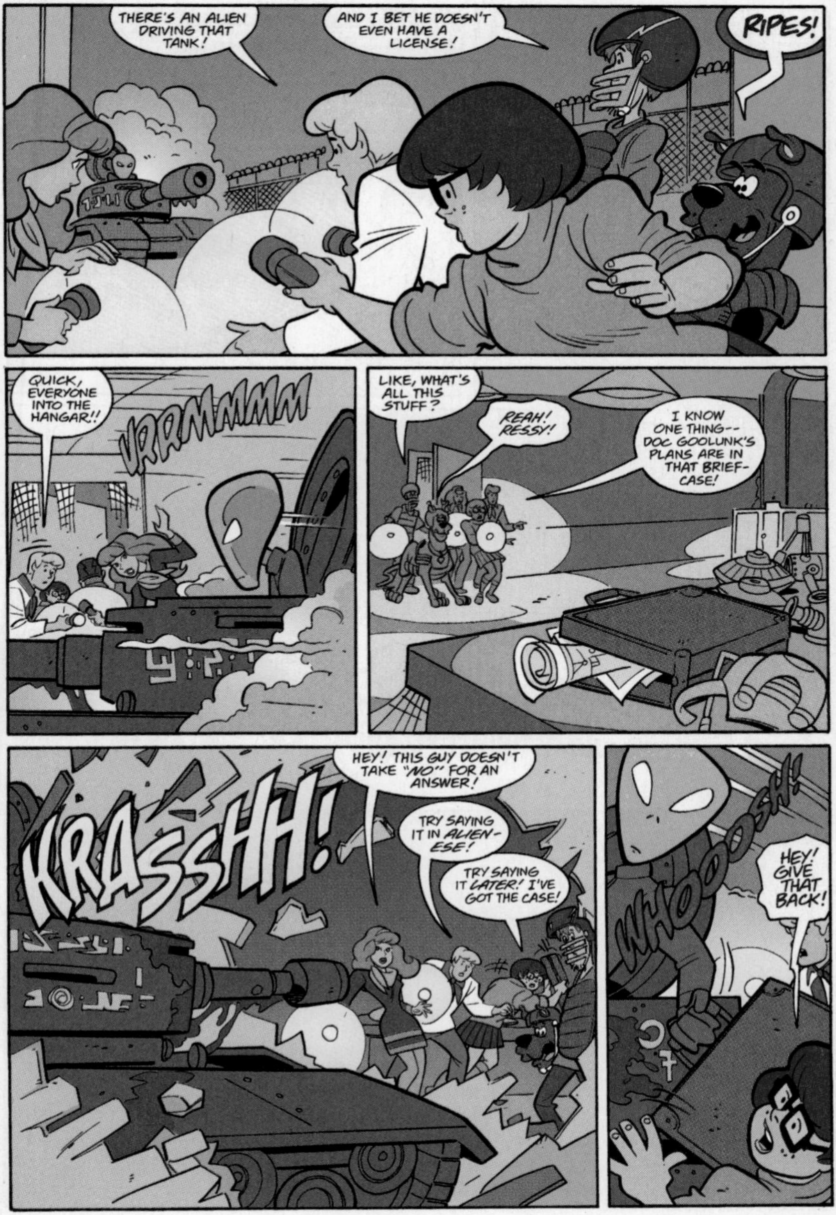
THERE'S AN ALIEN DRIVING THAT TANK!
AND I BET HE DOESN'T EVEN HAVE A LICENSE!
RIPES!
QUICK, EVERYONE INTO THE HANGAR!!
VRRMMMM
LIKE, WHAT'S ALL THIS STUFF?
REAH! RESSY!
I KNOW ONE THING-- DOC GOOLUNK'S PLANS ARE IN THAT BRIEF-CASE!
KRASSHH!
HEY! THIS GUY DOESN'T TAKE "NO" FOR AN ANSWER!
TRY SAYING IT IN ALIEN-ESE!
TRY SAYING IT LATER! I'VE GOT THE CASE!
WHOOOOSH!
HEY! GIVE THAT BACK!

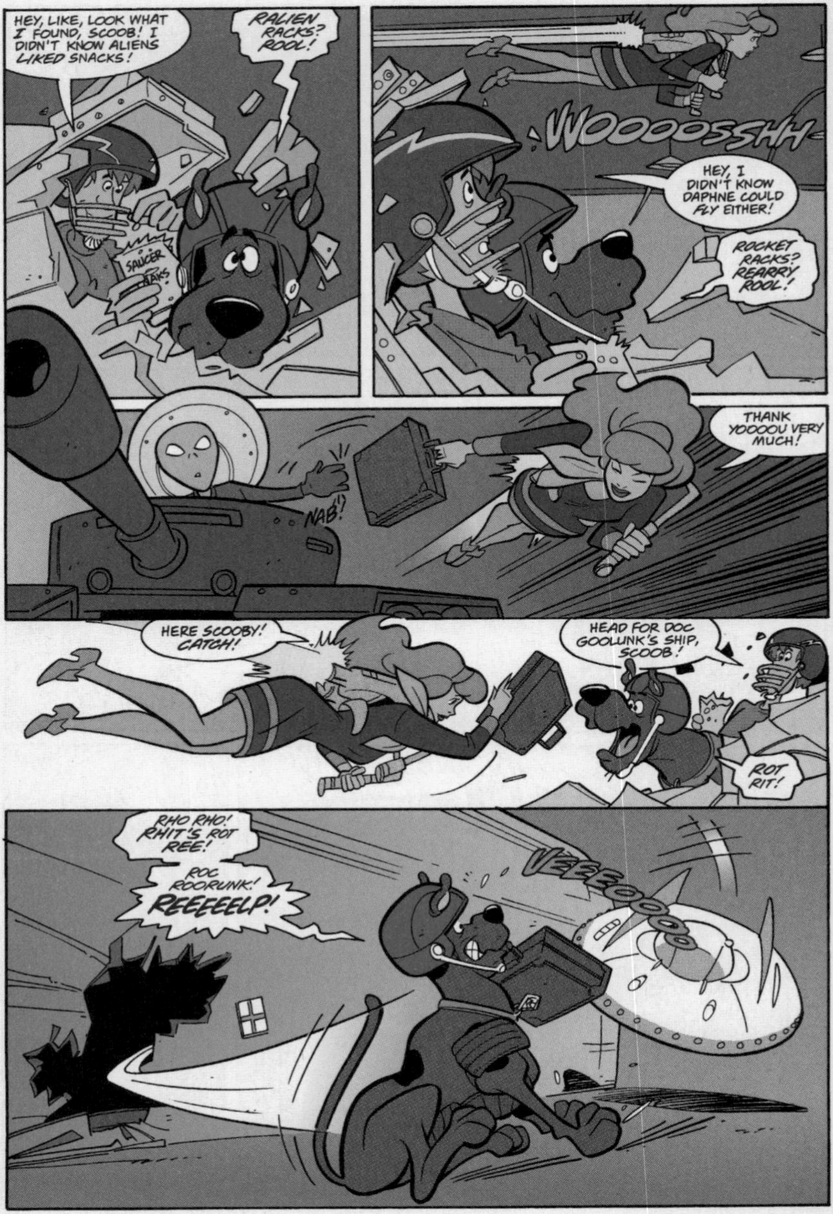
HEY, LIKE, LOOK WHAT I FOUND, SCOOB! I DIDN'T KNOW ALIENS LIKED SNACKS!
RALIEN RACKS? ROOL!
SAUCER SNAKS
WOOOOOSSHH
HEY, I DIDN'T KNOW DAPHNE COULD FLY EITHER!
ROCKET RACKS? REARRY ROOL!
NAB!
THANK YOOOOU VERY MUCH!
HERE SCOOBY! CATCH!
HEAD FOR DOC GOOLUNK'S SHIP, SCOOB!
ROT RIT!
RHO RHO! RHIT'S ROT REE!
ROC ROORUNK! REEEEELP!
VEEEOOOO

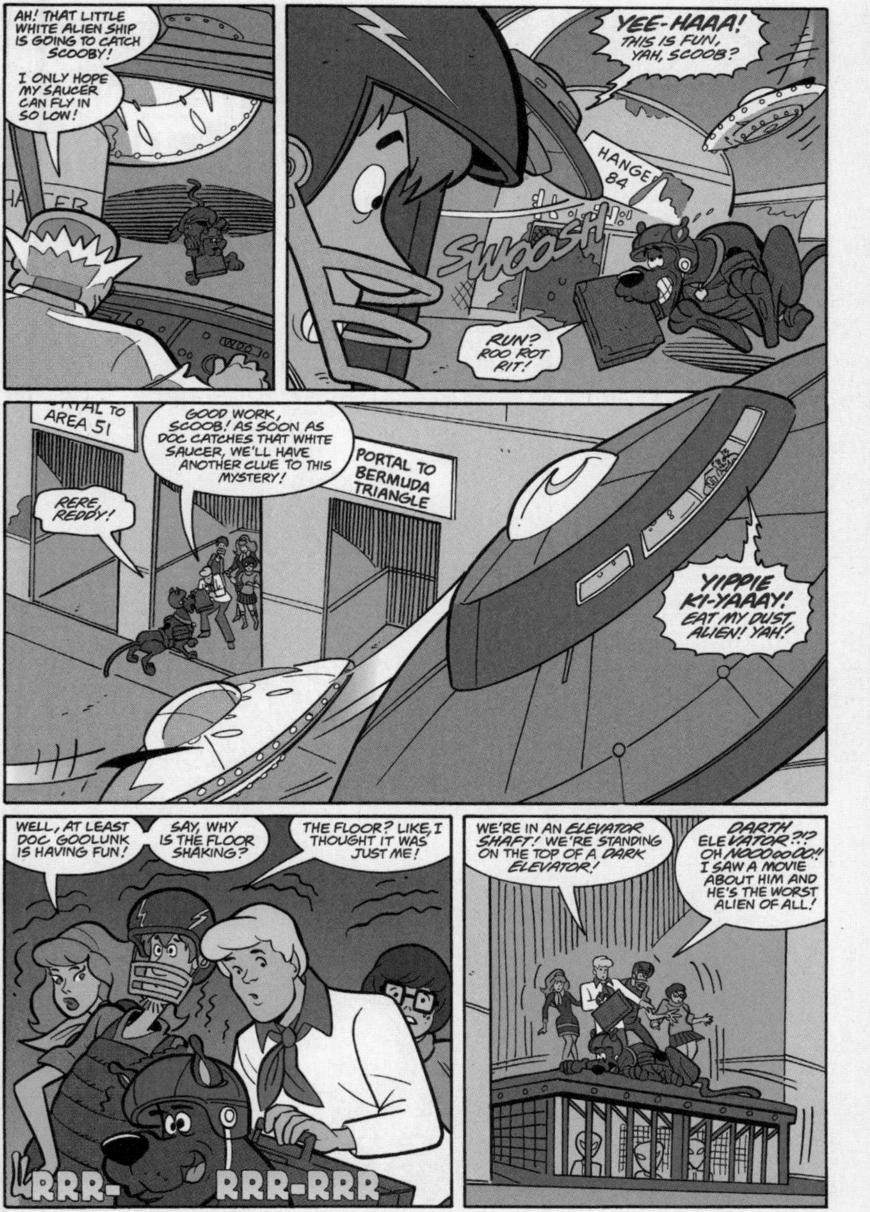
AH! THAT LITTLE WHITE ALIEN SHIP IS GOING TO CATCH SCOOBY!
I ONLY HOPE MY SAUCER CAN FLY IN SO LOW!
YEE-HAAA! THIS IS FUN, YAH, SCOOB?
HANGER 84
SWOOSH
RUN? ROO ROT RIT!
AREA 51
GOOD WORK, SCOOB! AS SOON AS DOC CATCHES THAT WHITE SAUCER, WE'LL HAVE ANOTHER CLUE TO THIS MYSTERY!
PORTAL TO BERMUDA TRIANGLE
RERE, REDDY!
YIPPIE KI-YAAAY! EAT MY DUST, ALIEN! YAH!
WELL, AT LEAST DOC GOOLUNK IS HAVING FUN!
SAY, WHY IS THE FLOOR SHAKING?
THE FLOOR? LIKE, I THOUGHT IT WAS JUST ME!
RRR- RRR-RRR
WE'RE IN AN ELEVATOR SHAFT! WE'RE STANDING ON THE TOP OF A DARK ELEVATOR!
DARTH ELEVATOR?!? OH NOOOooOO!! I SAW A MOVIE ABOUT HIM AND HE'S THE WORST ALIEN OF ALL!

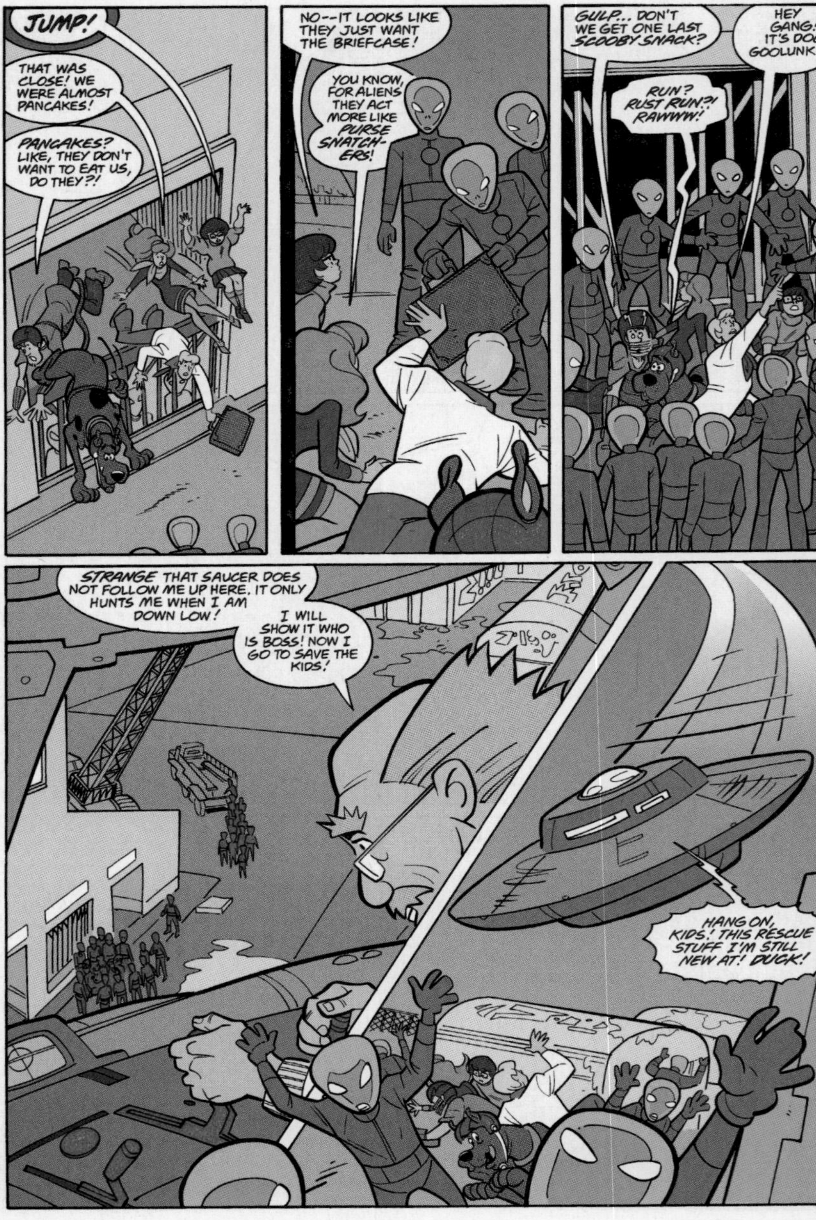
JUMP!
THAT WAS CLOSE! WE WERE ALMOST PANCAKES!
PANCAKES? LIKE, THEY DON'T WANT TO EAT US, DO THEY?!
NO--IT LOOKS LIKE THEY JUST WANT THE BRIEFCASE!
YOU KNOW, FOR ALIENS THEY ACT MORE LIKE PURSE SNATCHERS!
GULP... DON'T WE GET ONE LAST SCOOBY SNACK?
HEY GANG! IT'S DOC GOOLUNK!
RUN? RUST RUN?! RAWWW!
STRANGE THAT SAUCER DOES NOT FOLLOW ME UP HERE. IT ONLY HUNTS ME WHEN I AM DOWN LOW!
I WILL SHOW IT WHO IS BOSS! NOW I GO TO SAVE THE KIDS!
HANG ON, KIDS! THIS RESCUE STUFF I'M STILL NEW AT! DUCK!

GAK! AGAIN THE SAUCER COMES TO ME DOWN LOW!

WATCH THE CRAZY DRIVING, WHITE SHIP! YOU WILL MAKE US BOTH CRASH!

VOOOM

GO, DOC GOOLUNK!

THAT WHITE SHIP SURE DOES FLY WEIRD. IT'S LIKE IT'S ON A STRING!

RAGGY! RAGGY, ROOK!

ANOTHER SAUCER? WHAT IS THIS? A USED CAR LOT FOR SPACEMEN?

WSSSHHH

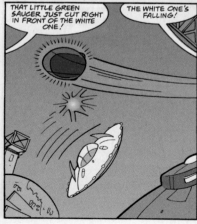

THAT LITTLE GREEN SAUCER JUST CUT RIGHT IN FRONT OF THE WHITE ONE!

THE WHITE ONE'S FALLING!

CRASSHHH!

LOOK OUT!

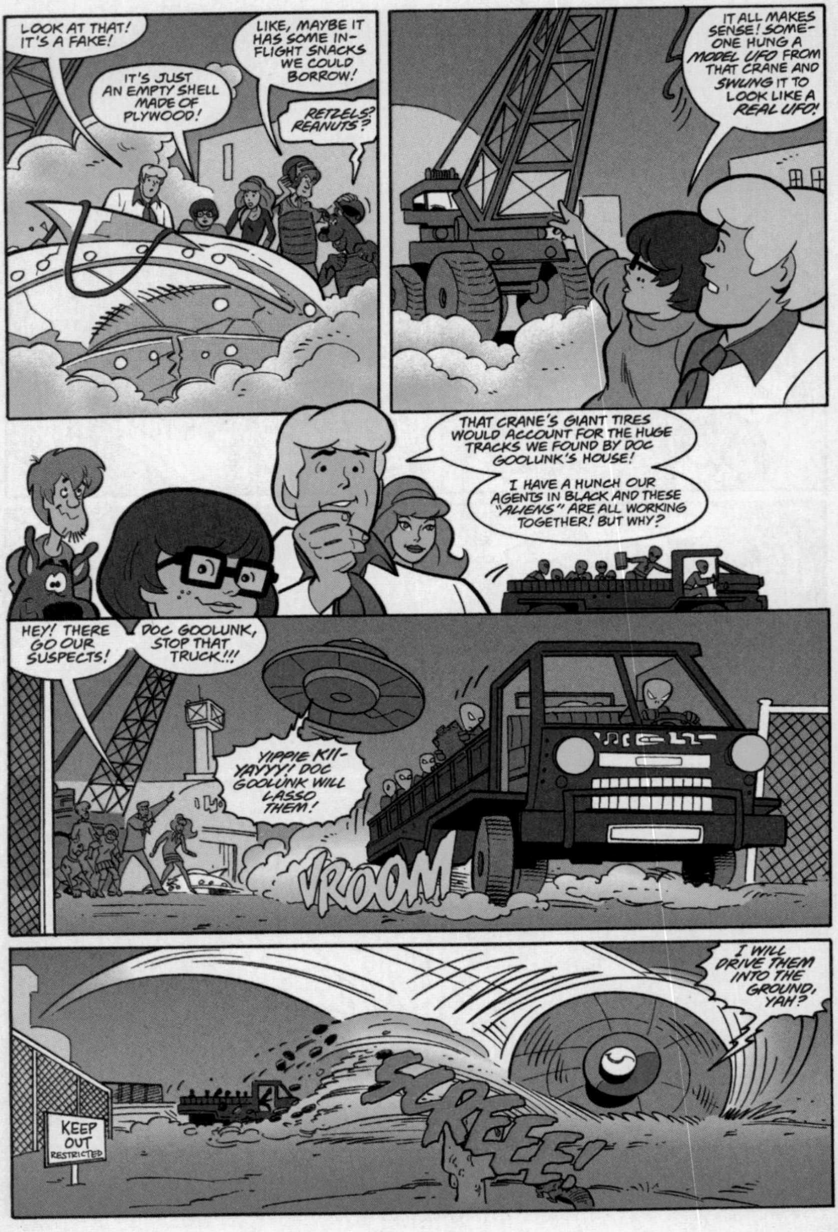

LOOK AT THAT! IT'S A FAKE!
IT'S JUST AN EMPTY SHELL MADE OF PLYWOOD!
LIKE, MAYBE IT HAS SOME IN-FLIGHT SNACKS WE COULD BORROW!
RETZELS? REANUTS?
IT ALL MAKES SENSE! SOMEONE HUNG A MODEL UFO FROM THAT CRANE AND SWUNG IT TO LOOK LIKE A REAL UFO!
THAT CRANE'S GIANT TIRES WOULD ACCOUNT FOR THE HUGE TRACKS WE FOUND BY DOC GOOLUNK'S HOUSE!
I HAVE A HUNCH OUR AGENTS IN BLACK AND THESE "ALIENS" ARE ALL WORKING TOGETHER! BUT WHY?
HEY! THERE GO OUR SUSPECTS!
DOC GOOLUNK, STOP THAT TRUCK!!!
YIPPIE KII-YAYYY! DOC GOOLUNK WILL LASSO THEM!
VROOM
I WILL DRIVE THEM INTO THE GROUND, YAH?
SCREEE!
KEEP OUT RESTRICTED

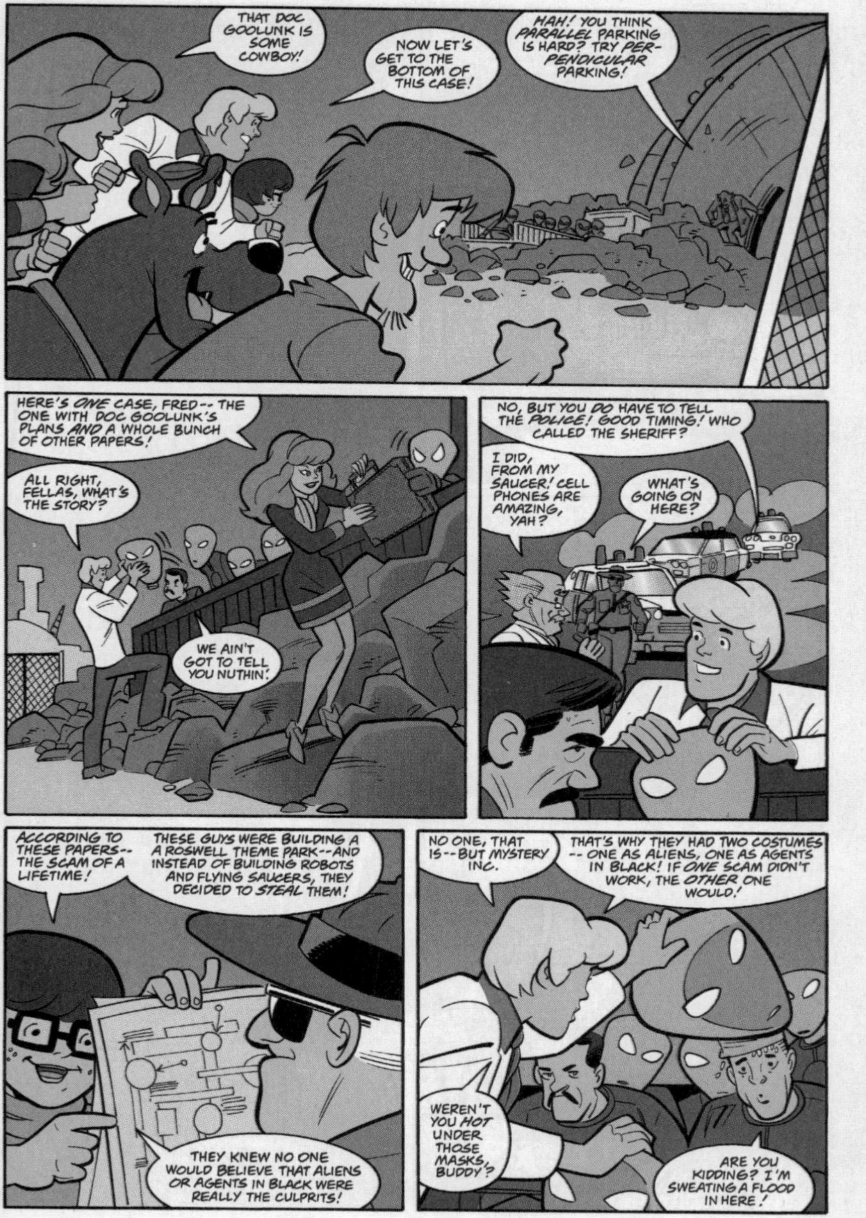
THAT DOC GOOLUNK IS SOME COWBOY!
NOW LET'S GET TO THE BOTTOM OF THIS CASE!
HAH! YOU THINK PARALLEL PARKING IS HARD? TRY PER-PENDICULAR PARKING!
HERE'S ONE CASE, FRED-- THE ONE WITH DOC GOOLUNK'S PLANS AND A WHOLE BUNCH OF OTHER PAPERS!
ALL RIGHT, FELLAS, WHAT'S THE STORY?
WE AIN'T GOT TO TELL YOU NUTHIN'.
NO, BUT YOU DO HAVE TO TELL THE POLICE! GOOD TIMING! WHO CALLED THE SHERIFF?
I DID, FROM MY SAUCER! CELL PHONES ARE AMAZING, YAH?
WHAT'S GOING ON HERE?
ACCORDING TO THESE PAPERS-- THE SCAM OF A LIFETIME!
THESE GUYS WERE BUILDING A A ROSWELL THEME PARK--AND INSTEAD OF BUILDING ROBOTS AND FLYING SAUCERS, THEY DECIDED TO STEAL THEM!
THEY KNEW NO ONE WOULD BELIEVE THAT ALIENS OR AGENTS IN BLACK WERE REALLY THE CULPRITS!
NO ONE, THAT IS--BUT MYSTERY INC.
THAT'S WHY THEY HAD TWO COSTUMES -- ONE AS ALIENS, ONE AS AGENTS IN BLACK! IF ONE SCAM DIDN'T WORK, THE OTHER ONE WOULD!
WEREN'T YOU HOT UNDER THOSE MASKS, BUDDY?
ARE YOU KIDDING? I'M SWEATING A FLOOD IN HERE!

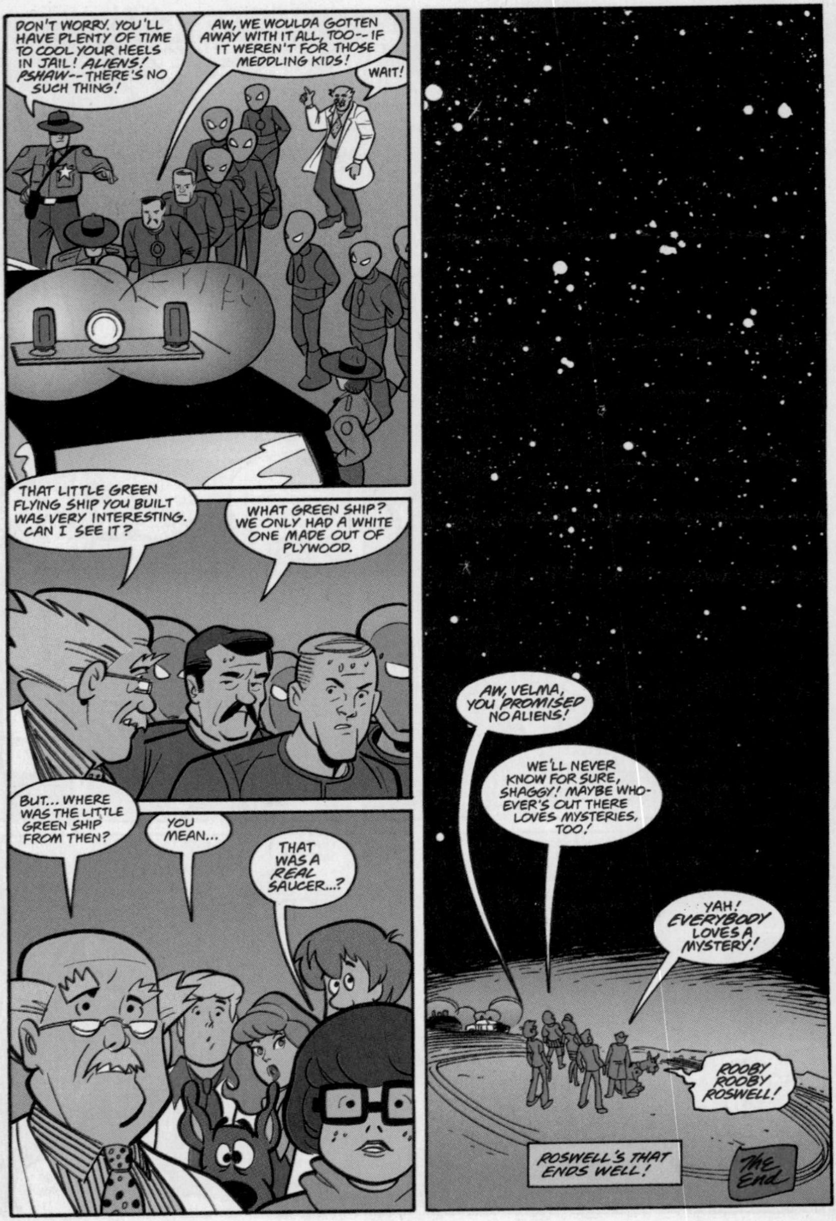
DON'T WORRY. YOU'LL HAVE PLENTY OF TIME TO COOL YOUR HEELS IN JAIL! ALIENS! PSHAW-- THERE'S NO SUCH THING!
AW, WE WOULDA GOTTEN AWAY WITH IT ALL, TOO-- IF IT WEREN'T FOR THOSE MEDDLING KIDS!
WAIT!
THAT LITTLE GREEN FLYING SHIP YOU BUILT WAS VERY INTERESTING. CAN I SEE IT?
WHAT GREEN SHIP? WE ONLY HAD A WHITE ONE MADE OUT OF PLYWOOD.
BUT... WHERE WAS THE LITTLE GREEN SHIP FROM THEN?
YOU MEAN...
THAT WAS A REAL SAUCER...?
AW, VELMA, YOU PROMISED NO ALIENS!
WE'LL NEVER KNOW FOR SURE, SHAGGY! MAYBE WHO-EVER'S OUT THERE LOVES MYSTERIES, TOO!
YAH! EVERYBODY LOVES A MYSTERY!
ROOBY ROOBY ROSWELL!
ROSWELL'S THAT ENDS WELL!
THE End

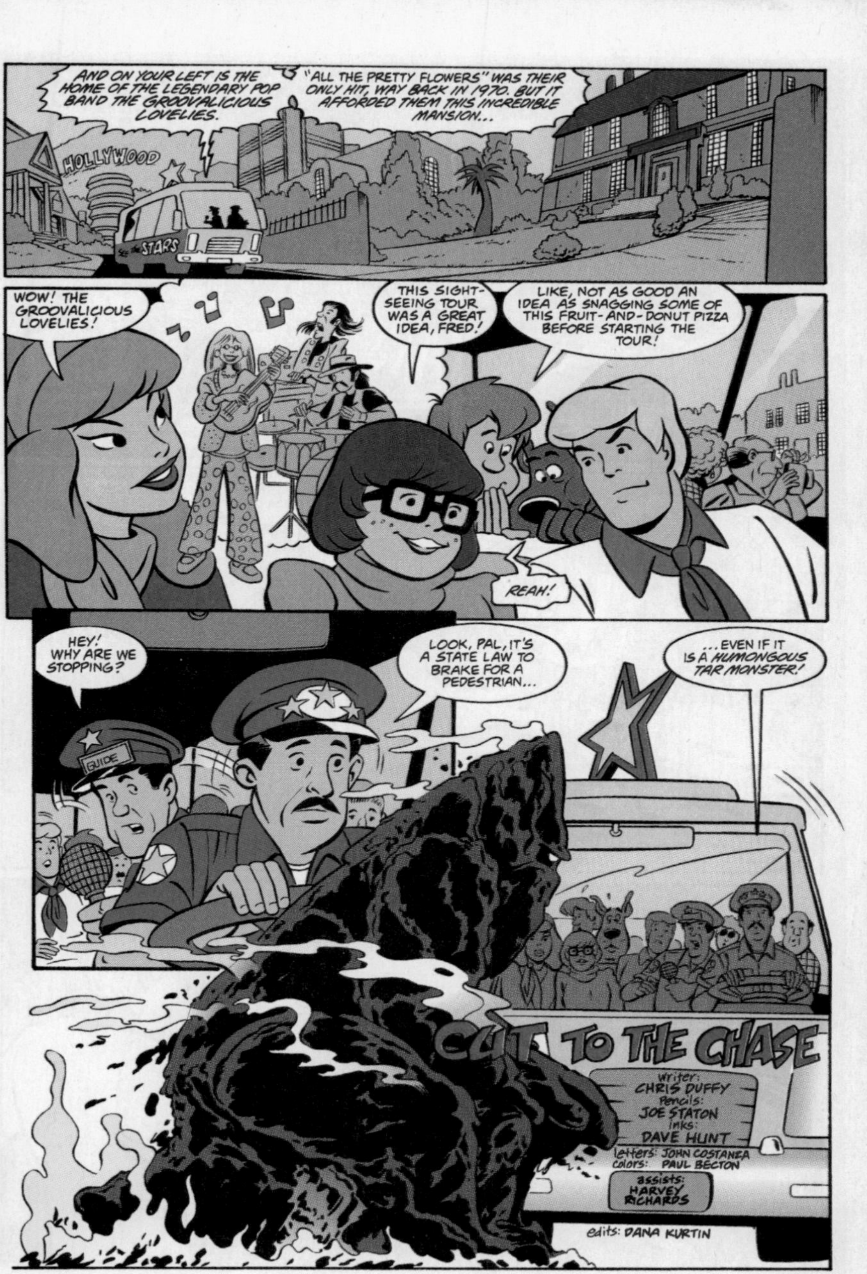
AND ON YOUR LEFT IS THE HOME OF THE LEGENDARY POP BAND THE GROOVALICIOUS LOVELIES.
"ALL THE PRETTY FLOWERS" WAS THEIR ONLY HIT, WAY BACK IN 1970. BUT IT AFFORDED THEM THIS INCREDIBLE MANSION...
HOLLYWOOD
SEE THE STARS
WOW! THE GROOVALICIOUS LOVELIES!
THIS SIGHT-SEEING TOUR WAS A GREAT IDEA, FRED!
LIKE, NOT AS GOOD AN IDEA AS SNAGGING SOME OF THIS FRUIT-AND-DONUT PIZZA BEFORE STARTING THE TOUR!
REAH!
HEY! WHY ARE WE STOPPING?
LOOK, PAL, IT'S A STATE LAW TO BRAKE FOR A PEDESTRIAN...
...EVEN IF IT IS A HUMONGOUS TAR MONSTER!
GUIDE
CUT TO THE CHASE
writer: CHRIS DUFFY
pencils: JOE STATON
inks: DAVE HUNT
letters: JOHN COSTANZA
colors: PAUL BECTON
assists: HARVEY RICHARDS
edits: DANA KURTIN

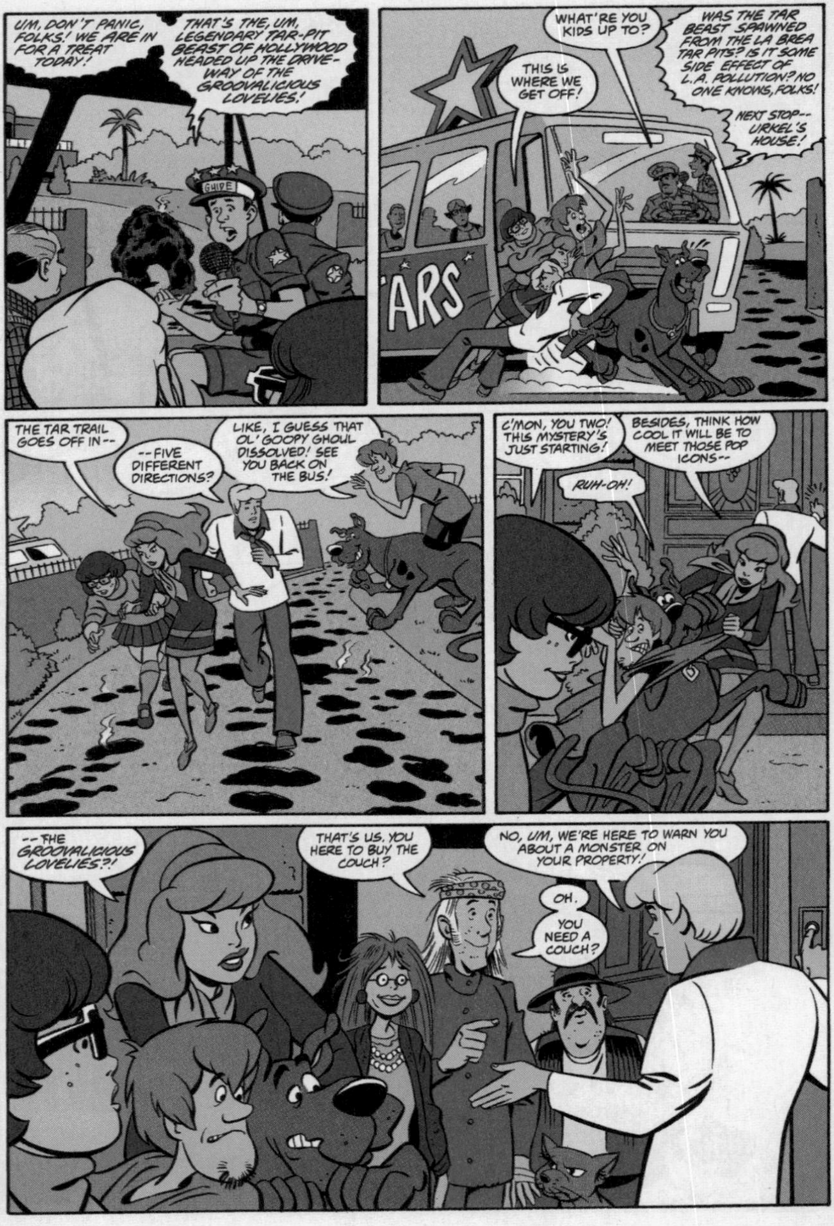
UM, DON'T PANIC, FOLKS! WE ARE IN FOR A TREAT TODAY!
THAT'S THE, UM, LEGENDARY TAR-PIT BEAST OF HOLLYWOOD HEADED UP THE DRIVE-WAY OF THE GROOVALICIOUS LOVELIES!
GUIDE
WHAT'RE YOU KIDS UP TO?
THIS IS WHERE WE GET OFF!
WAS THE TAR BEAST SPAWNED FROM THE LA BREA TAR PITS? IS IT SOME SIDE EFFECT OF L.A. POLLUTION? NO ONE KNOWS, FOLKS!
NEXT STOP-- URKEL'S HOUSE!
TARS
THE TAR TRAIL GOES OFF IN--
--FIVE DIFFERENT DIRECTIONS?
LIKE, I GUESS THAT OL' GOOPY GHOUL DISSOLVED! SEE YOU BACK ON THE BUS!
C'MON, YOU TWO! THIS MYSTERY'S JUST STARTING!
BESIDES, THINK HOW COOL IT WILL BE TO MEET THOSE POP ICONS--
RUH-OH!
--THE GROOVALICIOUS LOVELIES?!
THAT'S US. YOU HERE TO BUY THE COUCH?
NO, UM, WE'RE HERE TO WARN YOU ABOUT A MONSTER ON YOUR PROPERTY!
OH.
YOU NEED A COUCH?

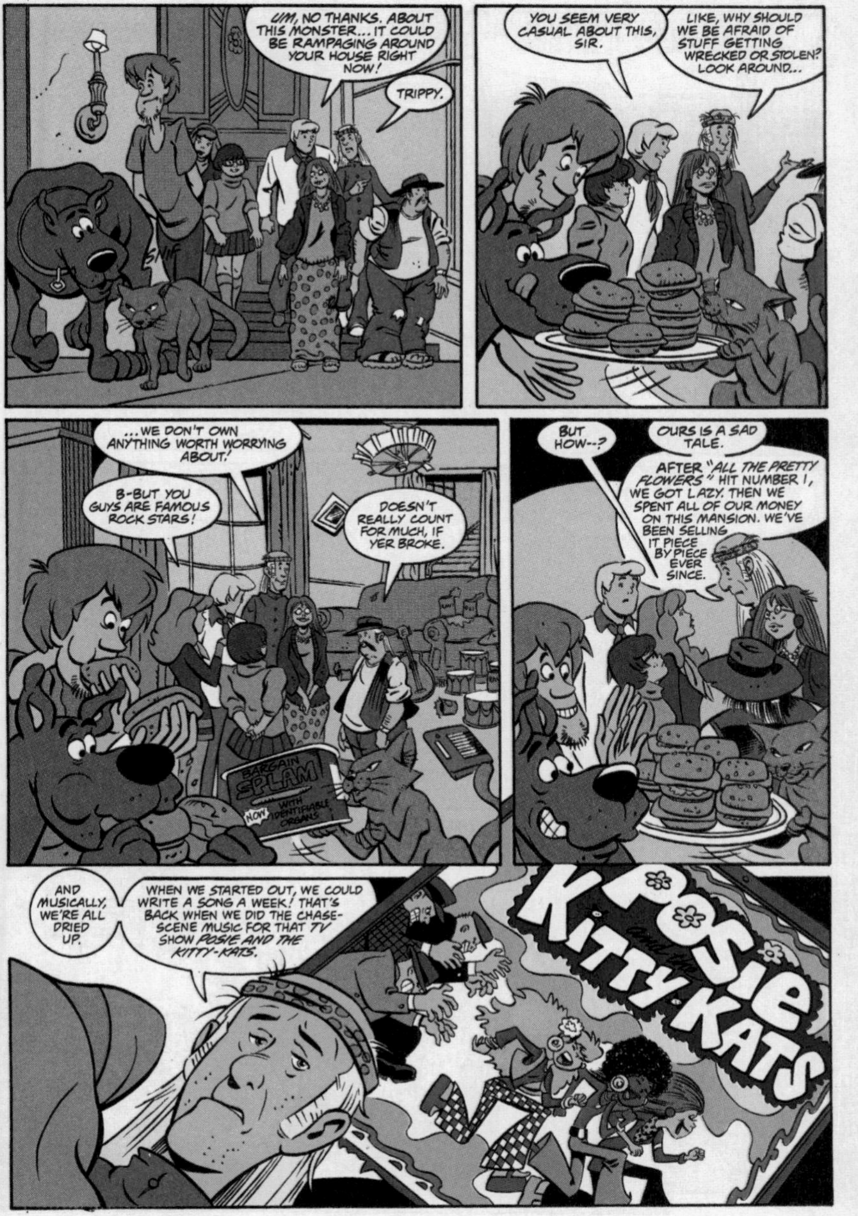
UM, NO THANKS. ABOUT THIS MONSTER... IT COULD BE RAMPAGING AROUND YOUR HOUSE RIGHT NOW!
TRIPPY.
SNIF
YOU SEEM VERY CASUAL ABOUT THIS, SIR.
LIKE, WHY SHOULD WE BE AFRAID OF STUFF GETTING WRECKED OR STOLEN? LOOK AROUND...
...WE DON'T OWN ANYTHING WORTH WORRYING ABOUT!
B-BUT YOU GUYS ARE FAMOUS ROCK STARS!
DOESN'T REALLY COUNT FOR MUCH, IF YER BROKE.
BARGAIN SPLAM
NOW WITH IDENTIFIABLE ORGANS
BUT HOW--?
OURS IS A SAD TALE.
AFTER "ALL THE PRETTY FLOWERS" HIT NUMBER 1, WE GOT LAZY. THEN WE SPENT ALL OF OUR MONEY ON THIS MANSION. WE'VE BEEN SELLING IT PIECE BY PIECE EVER SINCE.
AND MUSICALLY, WE'RE ALL DRIED UP.
WHEN WE STARTED OUT, WE COULD WRITE A SONG A WEEK! THAT'S BACK WHEN WE DID THE CHASE-SCENE MUSIC FOR THAT TV SHOW POSIE AND THE KITTY-KATS.
Posie and the Kitty-Kats

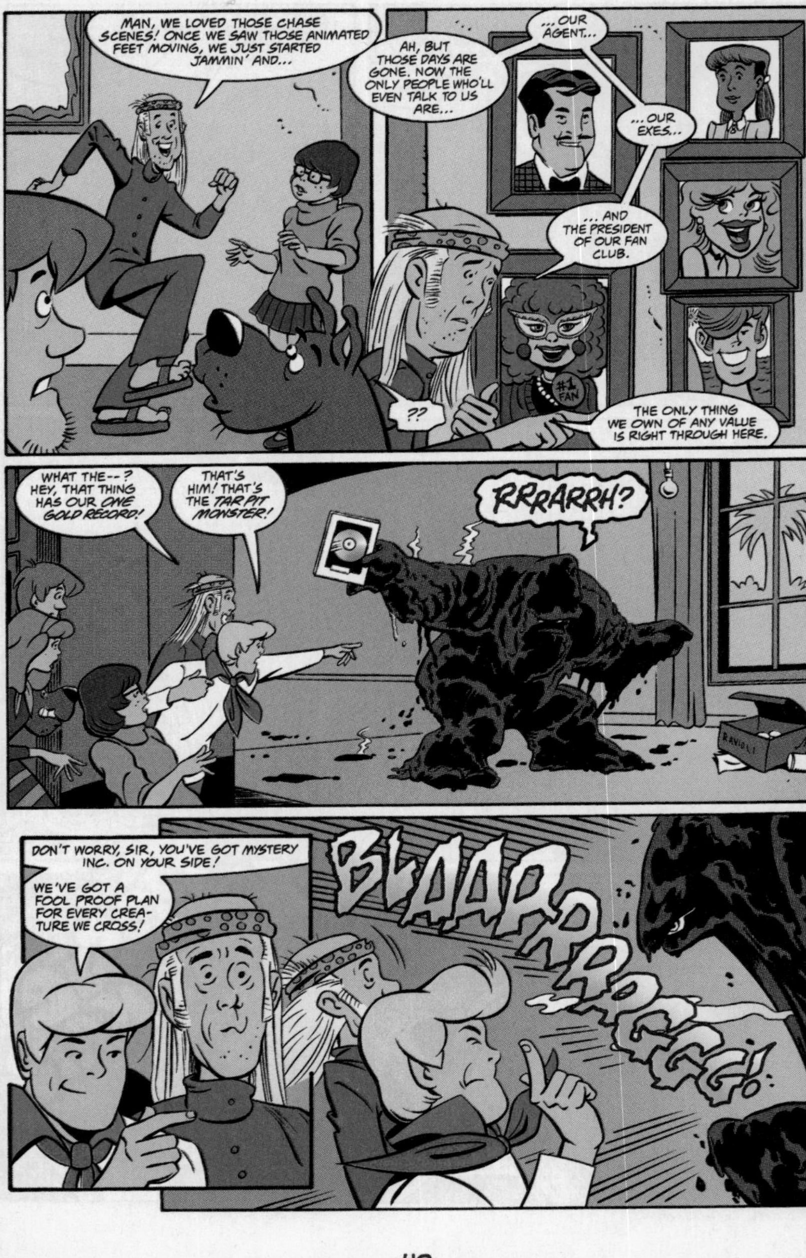

MAN, WE LOVED THOSE CHASE SCENES! ONCE WE SAW THOSE ANIMATED FEET MOVING, WE JUST STARTED JAMMIN' AND...
AH, BUT THOSE DAYS ARE GONE. NOW THE ONLY PEOPLE WHO'LL EVEN TALK TO US ARE...
...OUR AGENT...
...OUR EXES...
...AND THE PRESIDENT OF OUR FAN CLUB.
#1 FAN
??
THE ONLY THING WE OWN OF ANY VALUE IS RIGHT THROUGH HERE.
WHAT THE--? HEY, THAT THING HAS OUR ONE GOLD RECORD!
THAT'S HIM! THAT'S THE TAR PIT MONSTER!
RRRARRH?
RAVIOLI
DON'T WORRY, SIR, YOU'VE GOT MYSTERY INC. ON YOUR SIDE!
WE'VE GOT A FOOL PROOF PLAN FOR EVERY CREATURE WE CROSS!
BLAARRROGGG!

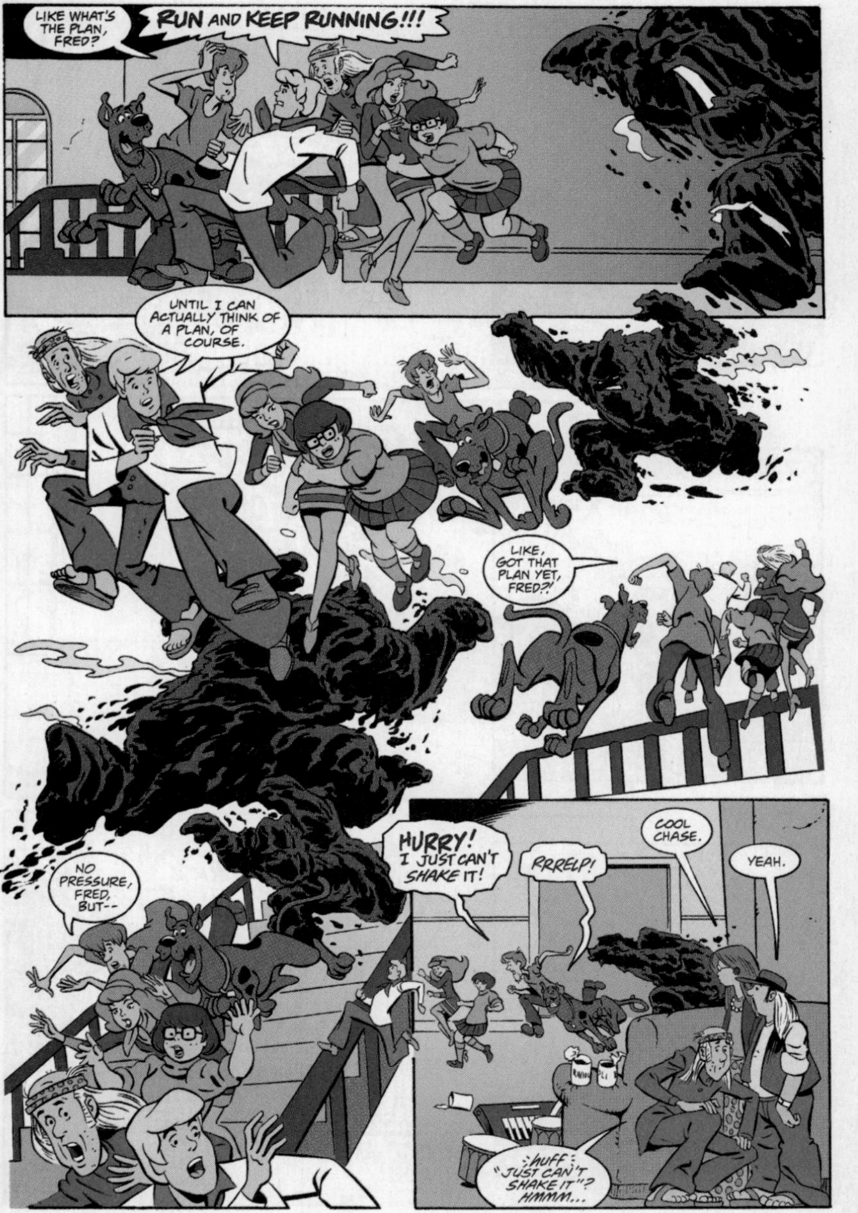
LIKE WHAT'S THE PLAN, FRED?
RUN AND KEEP RUNNING!!!
UNTIL I CAN ACTUALLY THINK OF A PLAN, OF COURSE.
LIKE, GOT THAT PLAN YET, FRED?!
NO PRESSURE, FRED, BUT--
HURRY! I JUST CAN'T SHAKE IT!
RRRELP!
COOL CHASE.
YEAH.
huff "JUST CAN'T SHAKE IT"? HMMM...

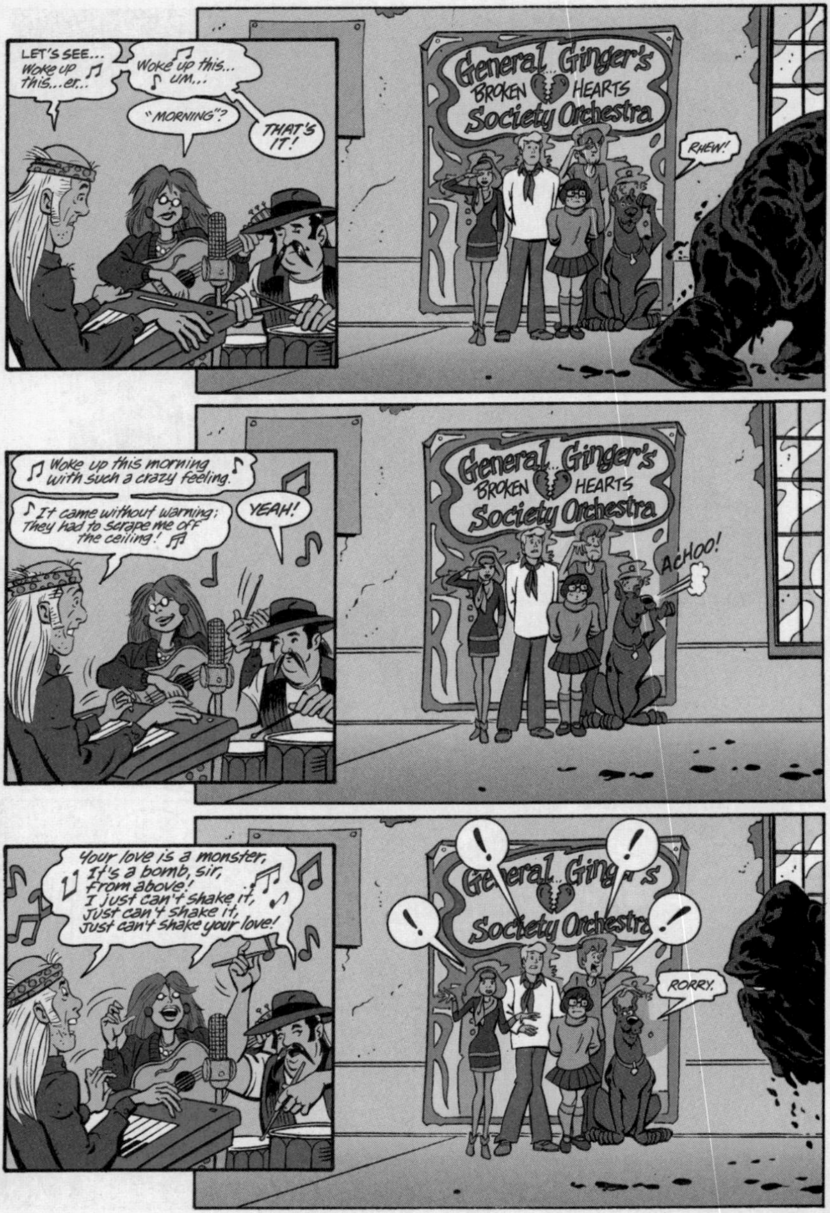
LET'S SEE... Woke up this...er...
Woke up this... um...
"MORNING"?
THAT'S IT!
General Ginger's BROKEN HEARTS Society Orchestra
RHEW!
Woke up this morning with such a crazy feeling.
It came without warning; They had to scrape me off the ceiling!
YEAH!
General Ginger's BROKEN HEARTS Society Orchestra
ACHOO!
Your love is a monster, It's a bomb, sir, from above! I just can't shake it, Just can't shake it, Just can't shake your love!
!
!
!
!
RORRY.

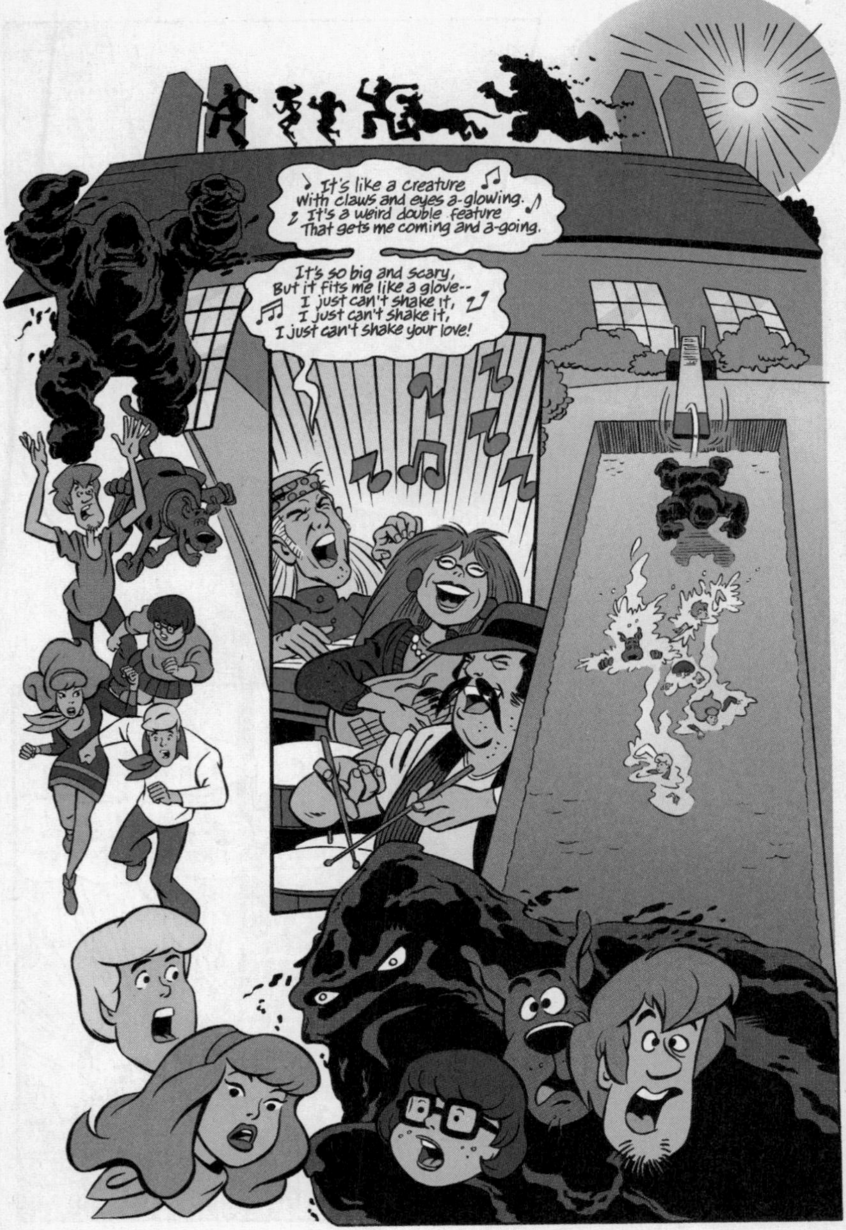
It's like a creature with claws and eyes a-glowing. It's a weird double feature That gets me coming and a-going.
It's so big and scary, But it fits me like a glove-- I just can't shake it, I just can't shake it, I just can't shake your love!

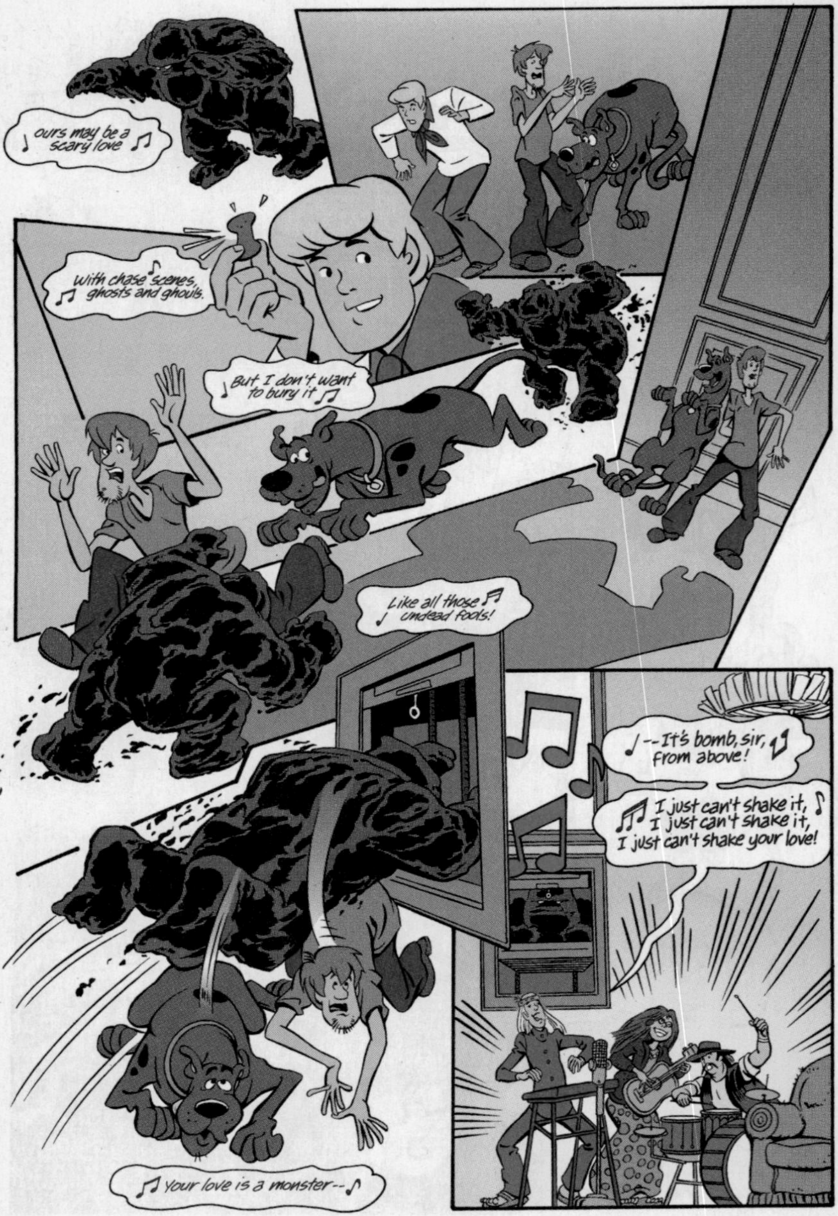
ours may be a scary love
With chase scenes, ghosts and ghouls.
But I don't want to bury it
Like all those undead fools!
--It's bomb, sir, from above!
I just can't shake it, I just can't shake it, I just can't shake your love!
Your love is a monster--

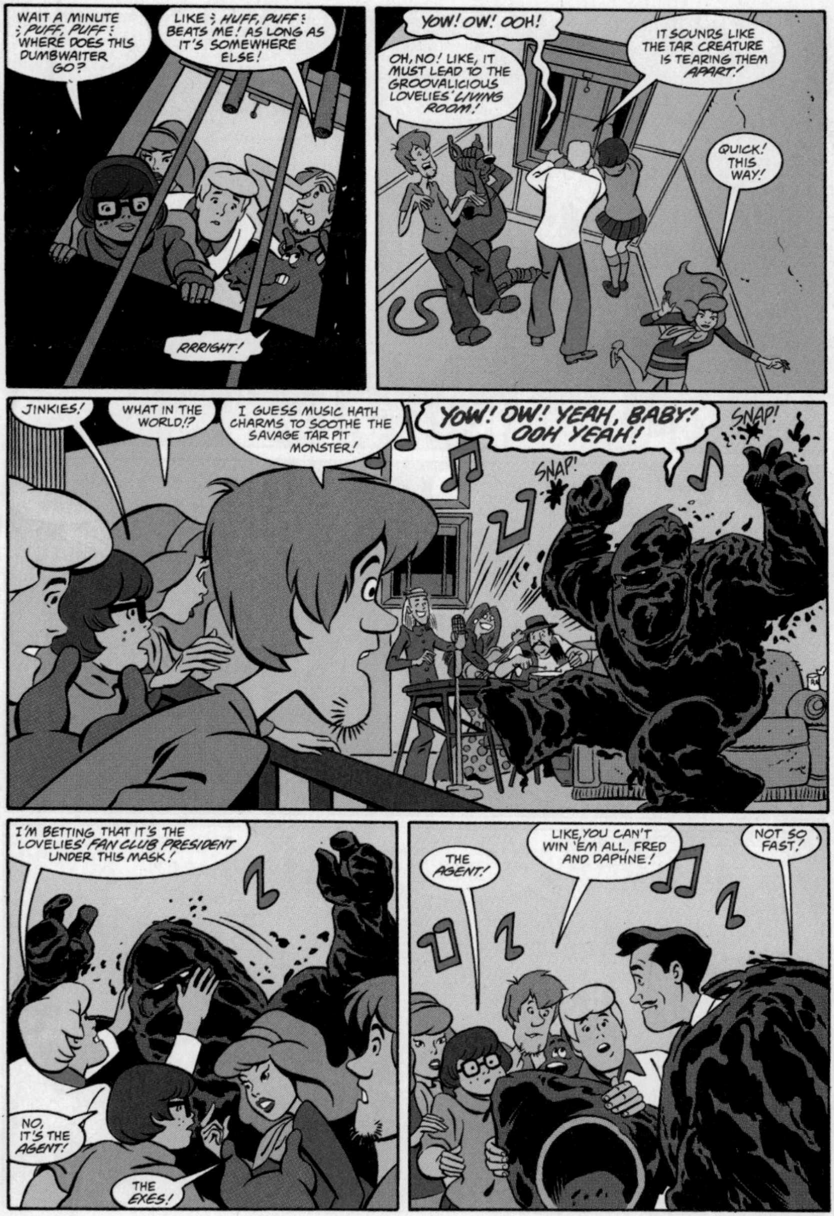
WAIT A MINUTE ⁝ PUFF, PUFF ⁝ WHERE DOES THIS DUMBWAITER GO?
LIKE ⁝ HUFF, PUFF ⁝ BEATS ME! AS LONG AS IT'S SOMEWHERE ELSE!
RRRIGHT!
YOW! OW! OOH!
OH, NO! LIKE, IT MUST LEAD TO THE GROOVALICIOUS LOVELIES' LIVING ROOM!
IT SOUNDS LIKE THE TAR CREATURE IS TEARING THEM APART!
QUICK! THIS WAY!
JINKIES!
WHAT IN THE WORLD!?
I GUESS MUSIC HATH CHARMS TO SOOTHE THE SAVAGE TAR PIT MONSTER!
YOW! OW! YEAH, BABY! OOH YEAH!
SNAP!
SNAP!
I'M BETTING THAT IT'S THE LOVELIES' FAN CLUB PRESIDENT UNDER THIS MASK!
NO, IT'S THE AGENT!
THE EXES!
THE AGENT!
LIKE, YOU CAN'T WIN 'EM ALL, FRED AND DAPHNE!
NOT SO FAST!

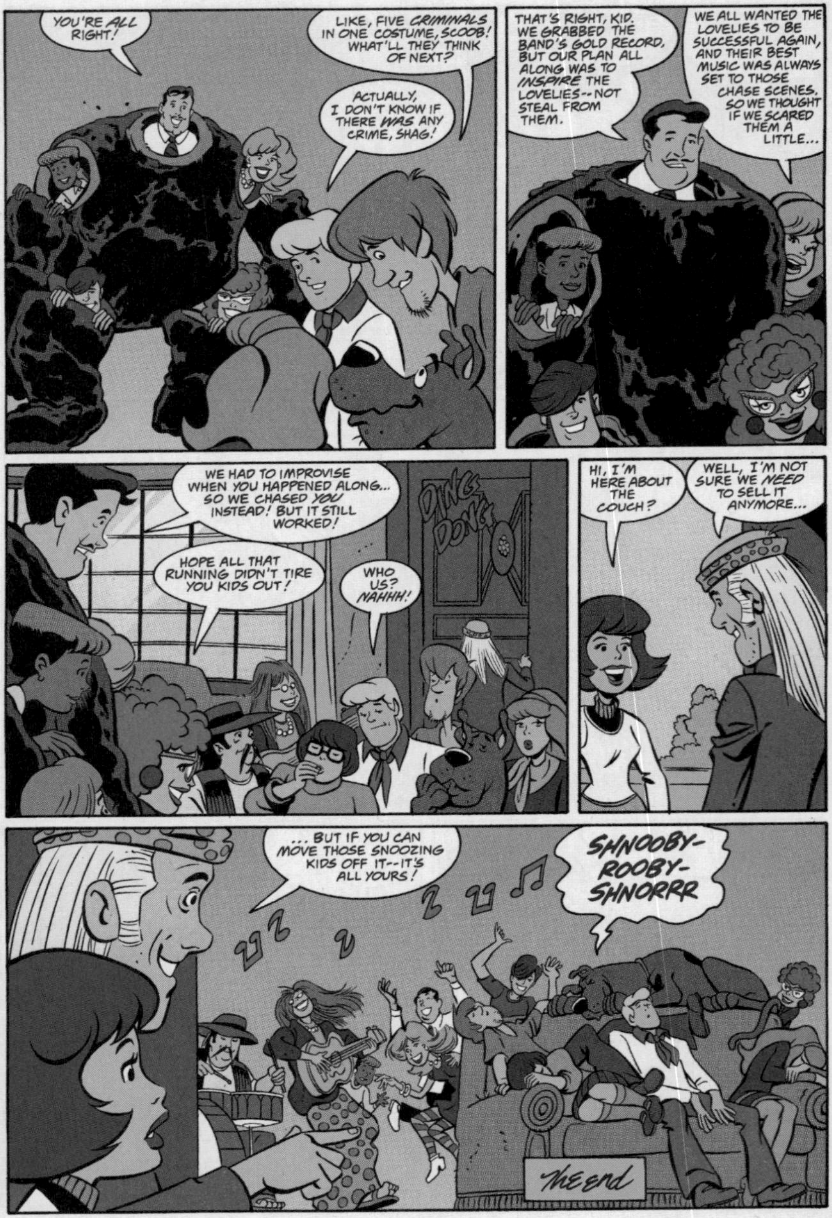
YOU'RE ALL RIGHT!
LIKE, FIVE CRIMINALS IN ONE COSTUME, SCOOB! WHAT'LL THEY THINK OF NEXT?
ACTUALLY, I DON'T KNOW IF THERE WAS ANY CRIME, SHAG!
THAT'S RIGHT, KID. WE GRABBED THE BAND'S GOLD RECORD, BUT OUR PLAN ALL ALONG WAS TO INSPIRE THE LOVELIES--NOT STEAL FROM THEM.
WE ALL WANTED THE LOVELIES TO BE SUCCESSFUL AGAIN, AND THEIR BEST MUSIC WAS ALWAYS SET TO THOSE CHASE SCENES. SO WE THOUGHT IF WE SCARED THEM A LITTLE...
WE HAD TO IMPROVISE WHEN YOU HAPPENED ALONG... SO WE CHASED YOU INSTEAD! BUT IT STILL WORKED!
DING DONG
HOPE ALL THAT RUNNING DIDN'T TIRE YOU KIDS OUT!
WHO US? NAHHH!
HI, I'M HERE ABOUT THE COUCH?
WELL, I'M NOT SURE WE NEED TO SELL IT ANYMORE...
...BUT IF YOU CAN MOVE THOSE SNOOZING KIDS OFF IT--IT'S ALL YOURS!
SHNOOBY-ROOBY-SHNORRR
The End

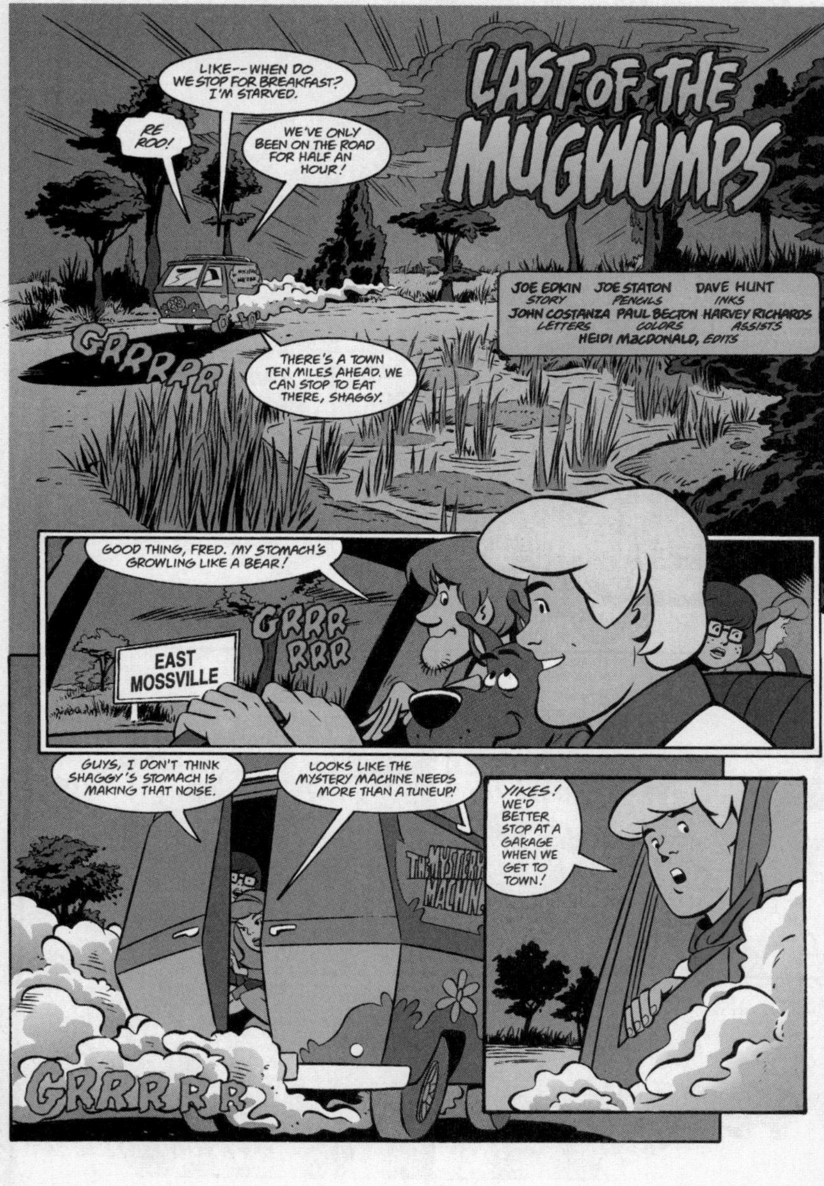
LAST OF THE MUGWUMPS
LIKE--WHEN DO WE STOP FOR BREAKFAST? I'M STARVED.
RE ROO!
WE'VE ONLY BEEN ON THE ROAD FOR HALF AN HOUR!
GRRRRR
JOE EDKIN STORY JOE STATON PENCILS DAVE HUNT INKS
JOHN COSTANZA LETTERS PAUL BECTON COLORS HARVEY RICHARDS ASSISTS
HEIDI MacDONALD, EDITS
THERE'S A TOWN TEN MILES AHEAD. WE CAN STOP TO EAT THERE, SHAGGY.
GOOD THING, FRED. MY STOMACH'S GROWLING LIKE A BEAR!
GRRRRRR
EAST MOSSVILLE
GUYS, I DON'T THINK SHAGGY'S STOMACH IS MAKING THAT NOISE.
LOOKS LIKE THE MYSTERY MACHINE NEEDS MORE THAN A TUNEUP!
THE MYSTERY MACHINE
YIKES! WE'D BETTER STOP AT A GARAGE WHEN WE GET TO TOWN!
GRRRRR

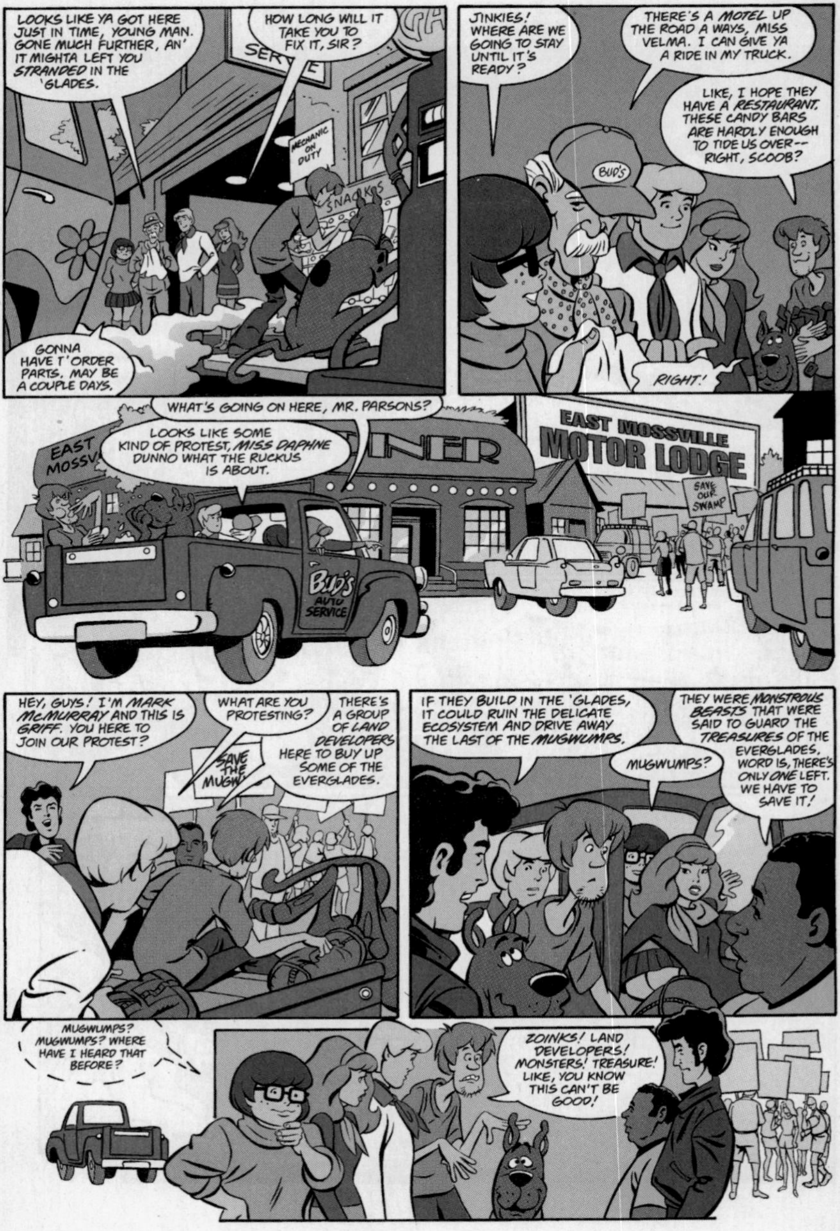
LOOKS LIKE YA GOT HERE JUST IN TIME, YOUNG MAN. GONE MUCH FURTHER, AN' IT MIGHTA LEFT YOU STRANDED IN THE 'GLADES.
HOW LONG WILL IT TAKE YOU TO FIX IT, SIR?
MECHANIC ON DUTY
GONNA HAVE T'ORDER PARTS. MAY BE A COUPLE DAYS.
JINKIES! WHERE ARE WE GOING TO STAY UNTIL IT'S READY?
THERE'S A MOTEL UP THE ROAD A WAYS, MISS VELMA. I CAN GIVE YA A RIDE IN MY TRUCK.
LIKE, I HOPE THEY HAVE A RESTAURANT. THESE CANDY BARS ARE HARDLY ENOUGH TO TIDE US OVER-- RIGHT, SCOOB?
BUD'S
RIGHT!
WHAT'S GOING ON HERE, MR. PARSONS?
LOOKS LIKE SOME KIND OF PROTEST, MISS DAPHNE. DUNNO WHAT THE RUCKUS IS ABOUT.
EAST MOSSVILLE MOTOR LODGE
SAVE OUR SWAMP
BUD'S AUTO SERVICE
HEY, GUYS! I'M MARK McMURRAY AND THIS IS GRIFF. YOU HERE TO JOIN OUR PROTEST?
WHAT ARE YOU PROTESTING?
THERE'S A GROUP OF LAND DEVELOPERS HERE TO BUY UP SOME OF THE EVERGLADES.
IF THEY BUILD IN THE 'GLADES, IT COULD RUIN THE DELICATE ECOSYSTEM AND DRIVE AWAY THE LAST OF THE MUGWUMPS.
MUGWUMPS?
THEY WERE MONSTROUS BEASTS THAT WERE SAID TO GUARD THE TREASURES OF THE EVERGLADES. WORD IS, THERE'S ONLY ONE LEFT. WE HAVE TO SAVE IT!
MUGWUMPS? MUGWUMPS? WHERE HAVE I HEARD THAT BEFORE?
ZOINKS! LAND DEVELOPERS! MONSTERS! TREASURE! LIKE, YOU KNOW THIS CAN'T BE GOOD!

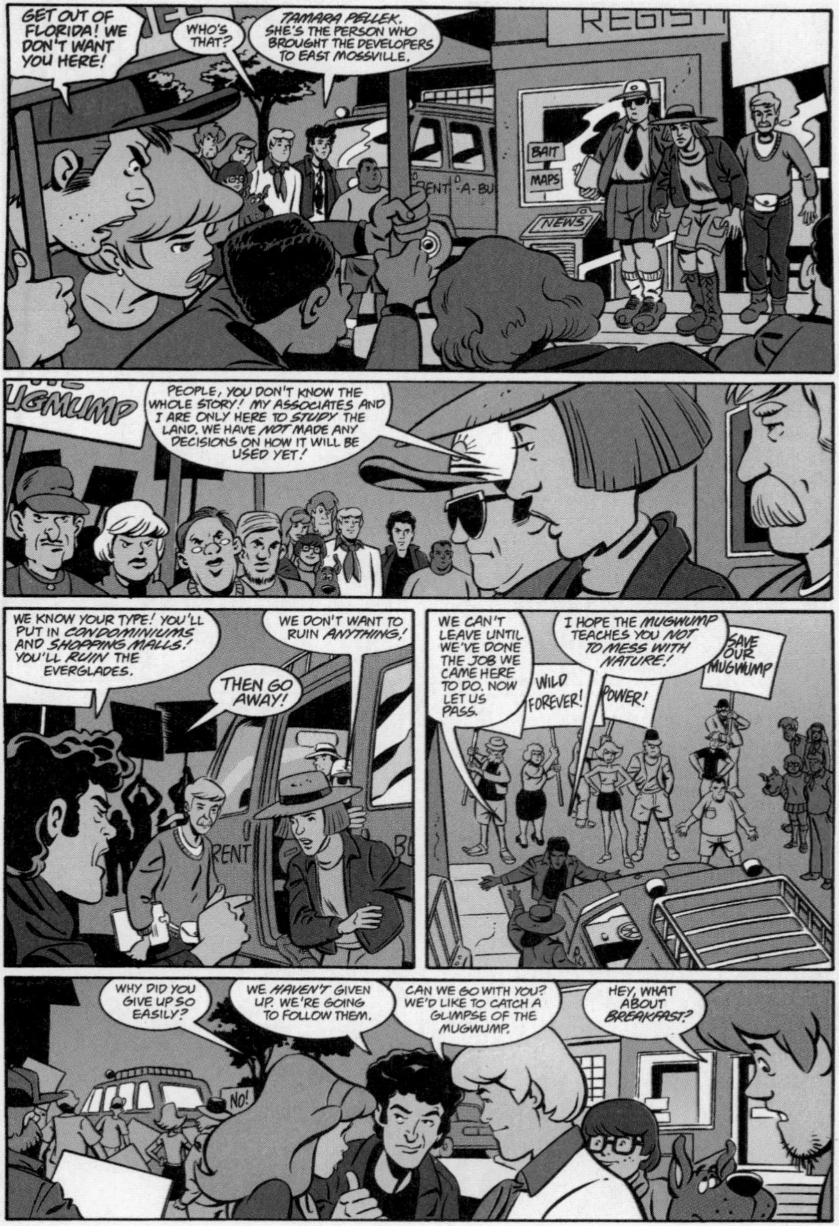
GET OUT OF FLORIDA! WE DON'T WANT YOU HERE!
WHO'S THAT?
TAMARA PELLEK. SHE'S THE PERSON WHO BROUGHT THE DEVELOPERS TO EAST MOSSVILLE.
REGIST
BAIT
MAPS
NEWS
RENT-A-BU
MUGWUMP
PEOPLE, YOU DON'T KNOW THE WHOLE STORY! MY ASSOCIATES AND I ARE ONLY HERE TO STUDY THE LAND. WE HAVE NOT MADE ANY DECISIONS ON HOW IT WILL BE USED YET!
WE KNOW YOUR TYPE! YOU'LL PUT IN CONDOMINIUMS AND SHOPPING MALLS! YOU'LL RUIN THE EVERGLADES.
WE DON'T WANT TO RUIN ANYTHING!
THEN GO AWAY!
RENT
WE CAN'T LEAVE UNTIL WE'VE DONE THE JOB WE CAME HERE TO DO. NOW LET US PASS.
I HOPE THE MUGWUMP TEACHES YOU NOT TO MESS WITH NATURE!
WILD FOREVER!
POWER!
SAVE OUR MUGWUMP
WHY DID YOU GIVE UP SO EASILY?
WE HAVEN'T GIVEN UP. WE'RE GOING TO FOLLOW THEM.
CAN WE GO WITH YOU? WE'D LIKE TO CATCH A GLIMPSE OF THE MUGWUMP.
HEY, WHAT ABOUT BREAKFAST?
NO!

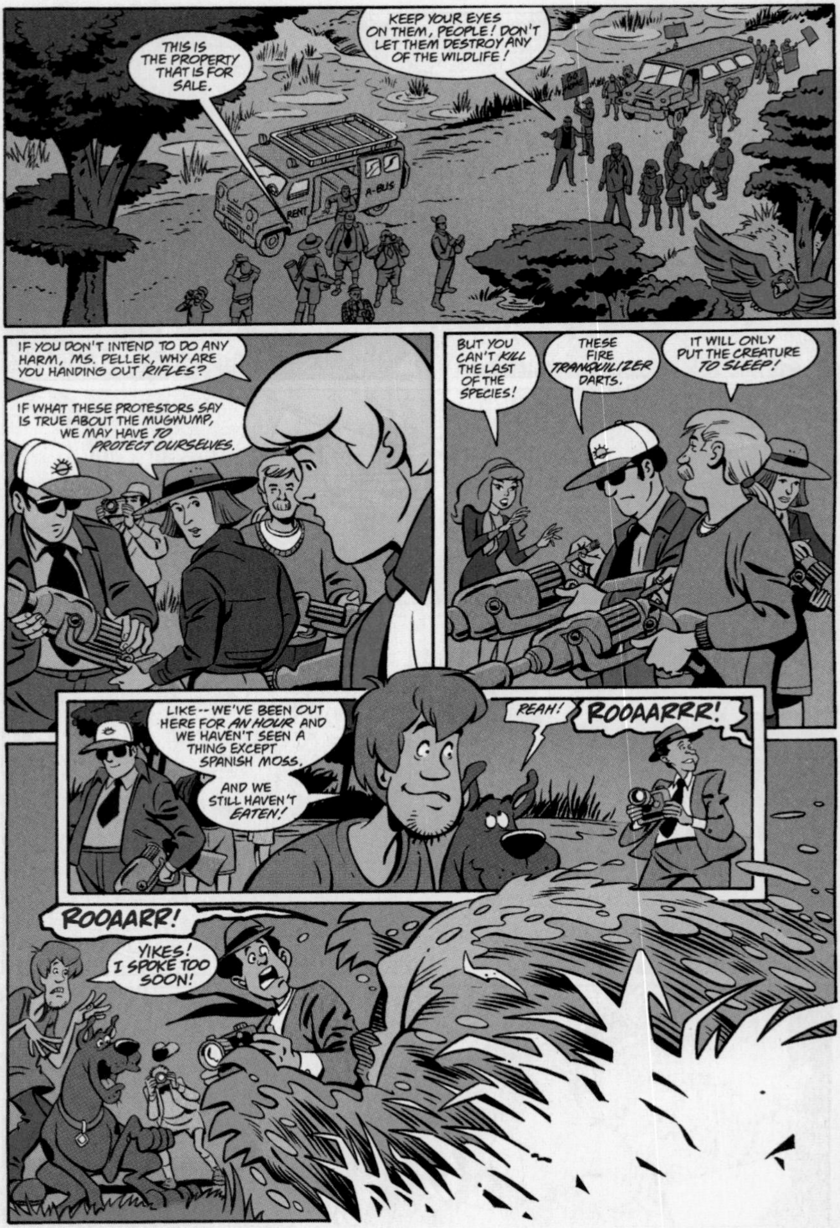
THIS IS THE PROPERTY THAT IS FOR SALE.
KEEP YOUR EYES ON THEM, PEOPLE! DON'T LET THEM DESTROY ANY OF THE WILDLIFE!
RENT A-BUS
IF YOU DON'T INTEND TO DO ANY HARM, MS. PELLEK, WHY ARE YOU HANDING OUT RIFLES?
IF WHAT THESE PROTESTORS SAY IS TRUE ABOUT THE MUGWUMP, WE MAY HAVE TO PROTECT OURSELVES.
BUT YOU CAN'T KILL THE LAST OF THE SPECIES!
THESE FIRE TRANQUILIZER DARTS.
IT WILL ONLY PUT THE CREATURE TO SLEEP!
LIKE--WE'VE BEEN OUT HERE FOR AN HOUR AND WE HAVEN'T SEEN A THING EXCEPT SPANISH MOSS.
AND WE STILL HAVEN'T EATEN!
REAH!
ROOAARRR!
ROOAARR!
YIKES! I SPOKE TOO SOON!

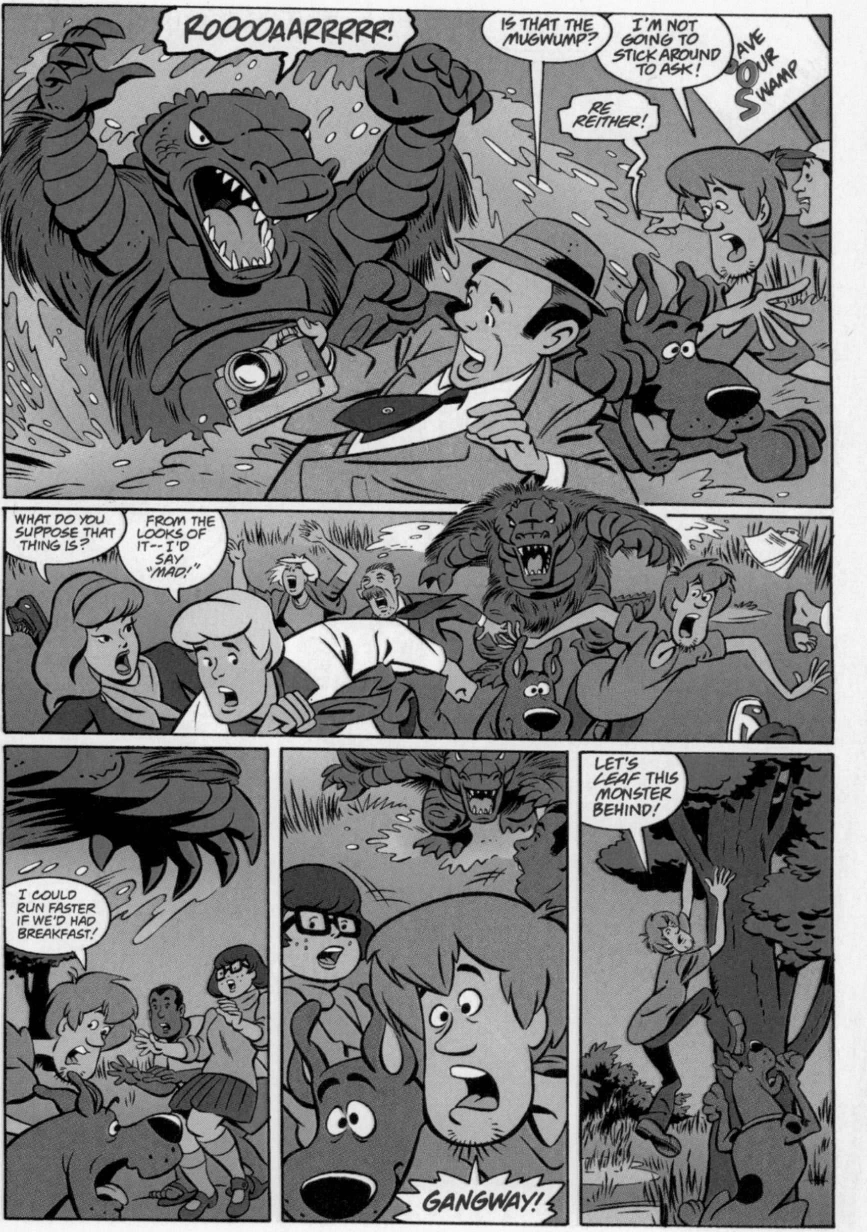
ROOOOAARRRRR!
IS THAT THE MUGWUMP?
I'M NOT GOING TO STICK AROUND TO ASK!
RE REITHER!
SAVE OUR SWAMP
WHAT DO YOU SUPPOSE THAT THING IS?
FROM THE LOOKS OF IT-- I'D SAY "MAD!"
I COULD RUN FASTER IF WE'D HAD BREAKFAST!
GANGWAY!
LET'S LEAF THIS MONSTER BEHIND!

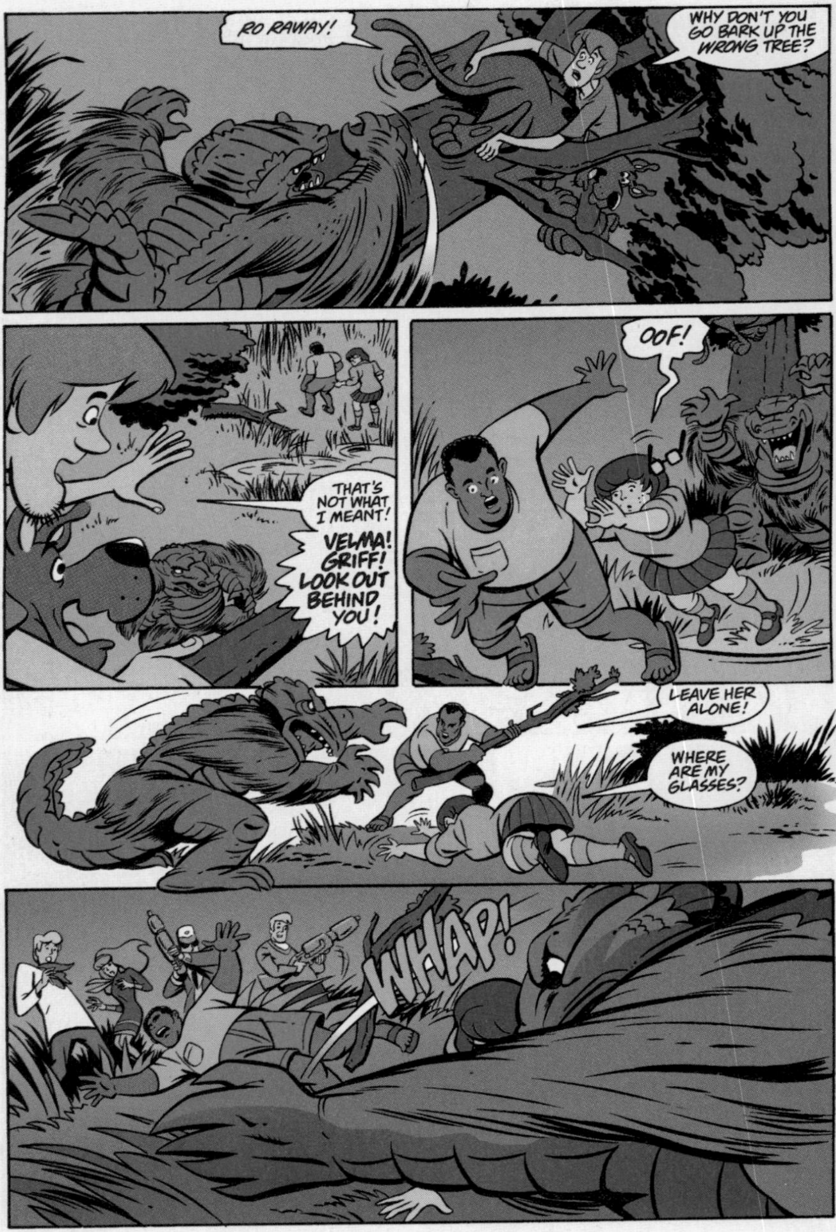
RO RAWAY!
WHY DON'T YOU GO BARK UP THE WRONG TREE?
THAT'S NOT WHAT I MEANT!
VELMA! GRIFF! LOOK OUT BEHIND YOU!
OOF!
LEAVE HER ALONE!
WHERE ARE MY GLASSES?
WHAP!

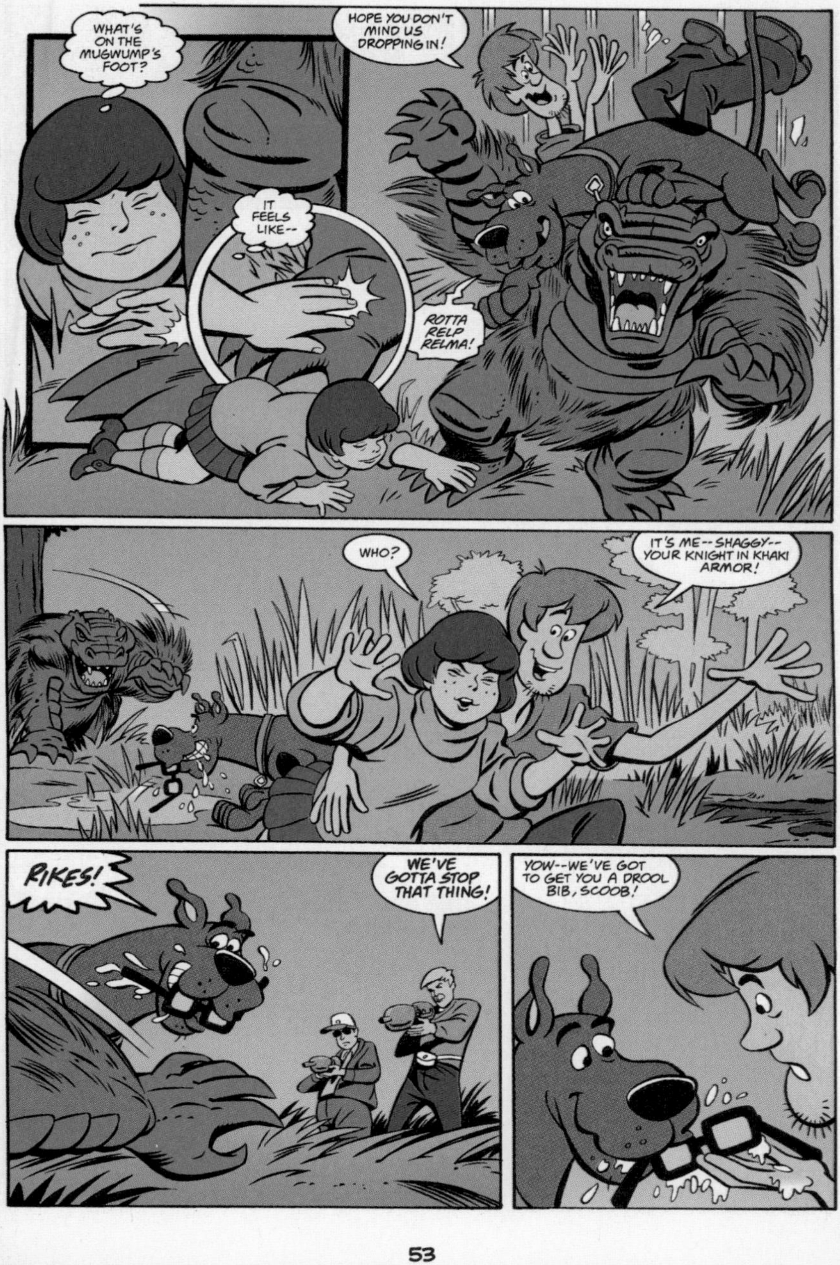
WHAT'S ON THE MUGWUMP'S FOOT?
IT FEELS LIKE--
HOPE YOU DON'T MIND US DROPPING IN!
ROTTA RELP RELMA!
WHO?
IT'S ME--SHAGGY--YOUR KNIGHT IN KHAKI ARMOR!
RIKES!
WE'VE GOTTA STOP THAT THING!
YOW--WE'VE GOT TO GET YOU A DROOL BIB, SCOOB!

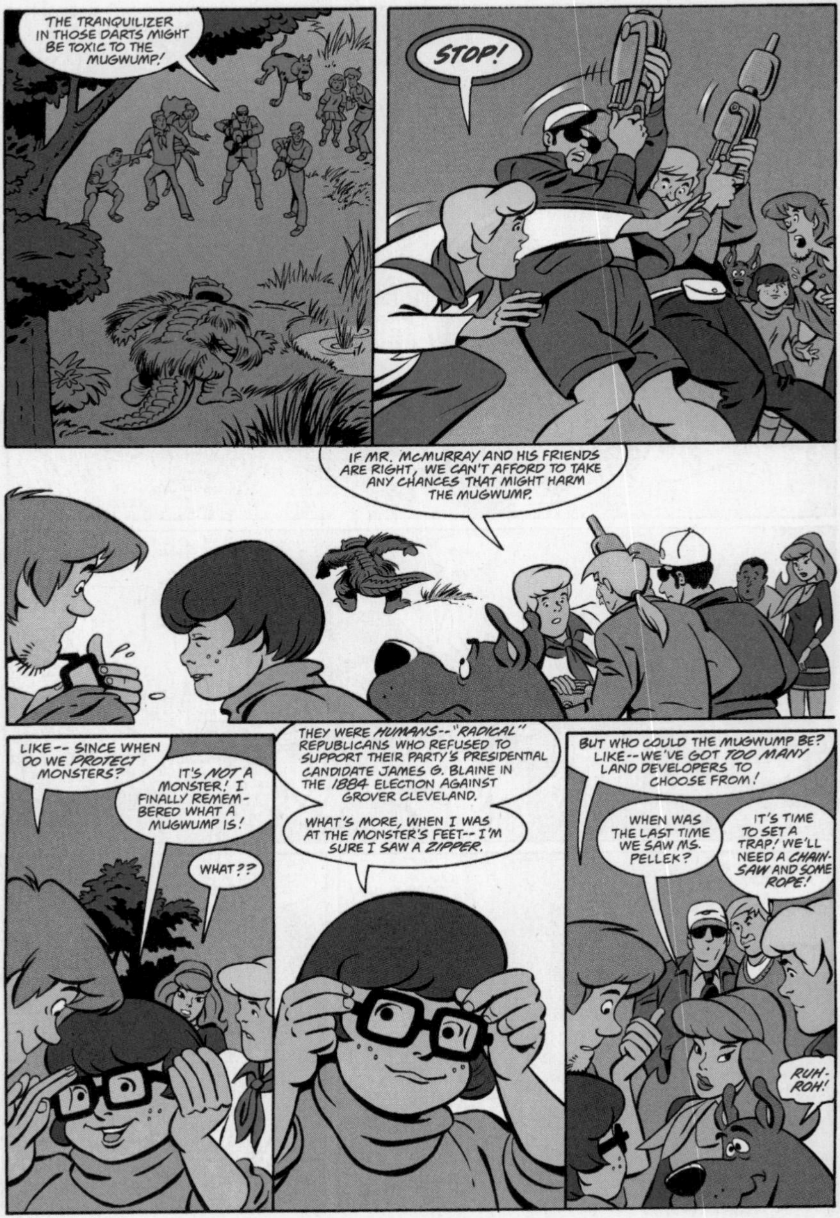
THE TRANQUILIZER IN THOSE DARTS MIGHT BE TOXIC TO THE MUGWUMP!
STOP!
IF MR. McMURRAY AND HIS FRIENDS ARE RIGHT, WE CAN'T AFFORD TO TAKE ANY CHANCES THAT MIGHT HARM THE MUGWUMP.
LIKE-- SINCE WHEN DO WE PROTECT MONSTERS?
IT'S NOT A MONSTER! I FINALLY REMEMBERED WHAT A MUGWUMP IS!
WHAT??
THEY WERE HUMANS--"RADICAL" REPUBLICANS WHO REFUSED TO SUPPORT THEIR PARTY'S PRESIDENTIAL CANDIDATE JAMES G. BLAINE IN THE 1884 ELECTION AGAINST GROVER CLEVELAND.
WHAT'S MORE, WHEN I WAS AT THE MONSTER'S FEET-- I'M SURE I SAW A ZIPPER.
BUT WHO COULD THE MUGWUMP BE? LIKE--WE'VE GOT TOO MANY LAND DEVELOPERS TO CHOOSE FROM!
WHEN WAS THE LAST TIME WE SAW MS. PELLEK?
IT'S TIME TO SET A TRAP! WE'LL NEED A CHAINSAW AND SOME ROPE!
RUH-ROH!

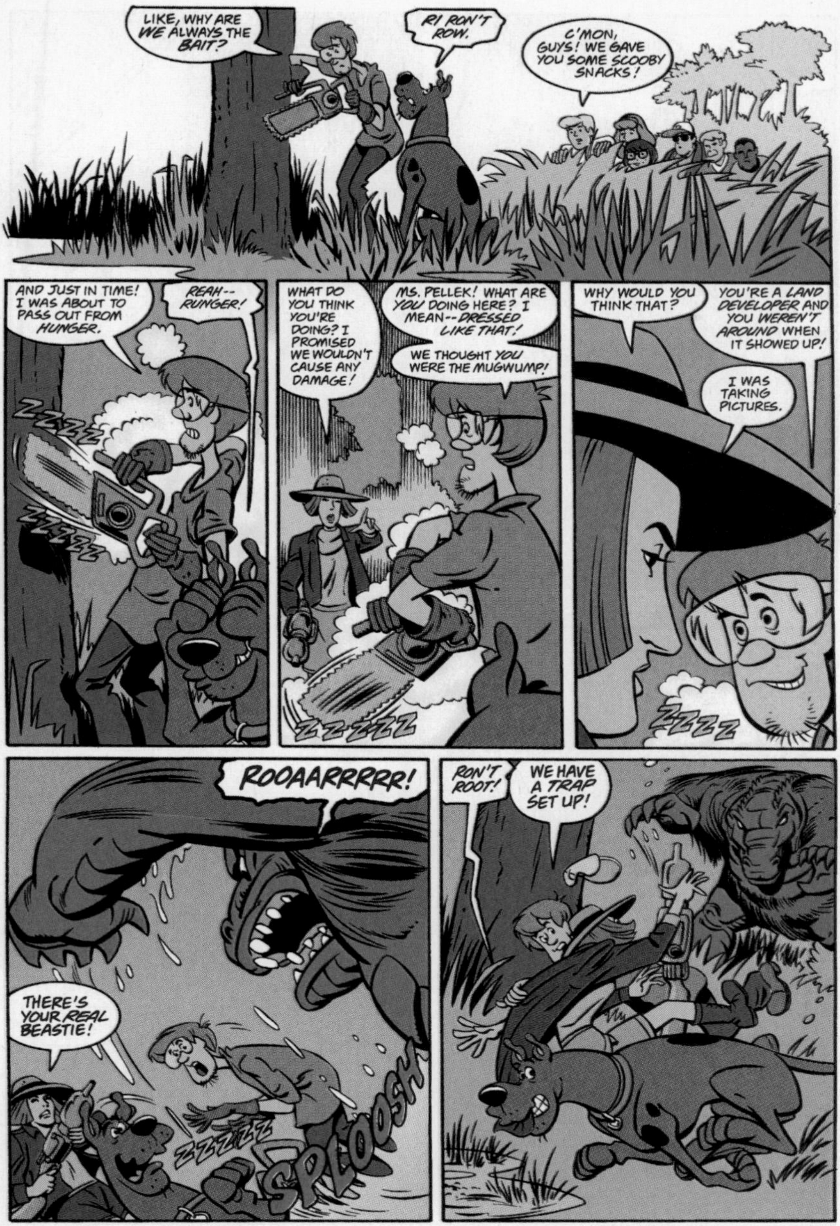

LIKE, WHY ARE WE ALWAYS THE BAIT?
RI RON'T ROW.
C'MON, GUYS! WE GAVE YOU SOME SCOOBY SNACKS!
AND JUST IN TIME! I WAS ABOUT TO PASS OUT FROM HUNGER.
REAH-- RUNGER!
ZZZZZ
ZZZZZ
WHAT DO YOU THINK YOU'RE DOING? I PROMISED WE WOULDN'T CAUSE ANY DAMAGE!
MS. PELLEK! WHAT ARE YOU DOING HERE? I MEAN--DRESSED LIKE THAT!
WE THOUGHT YOU WERE THE MUGWUMP!
ZZZZZZ
WHY WOULD YOU THINK THAT?
YOU'RE A LAND DEVELOPER AND YOU WEREN'T AROUND WHEN IT SHOWED UP!
I WAS TAKING PICTURES.
ZZZZ
ROOAARRRRR!
THERE'S YOUR REAL BEASTIE!
ZZZZZZ
SPLOOSH
RON'T ROOT!
WE HAVE A TRAP SET UP!

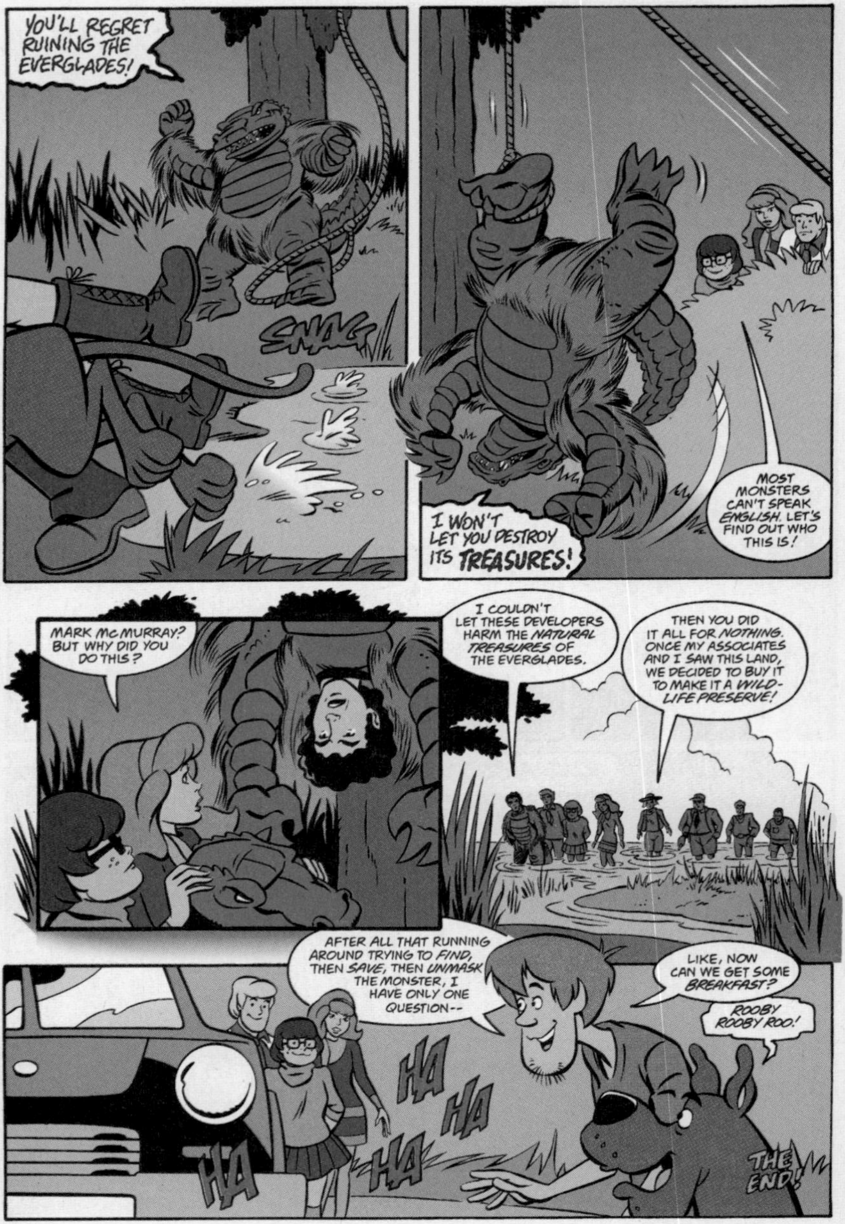
YOU'LL REGRET RUINING THE EVERGLADES!
SNAG
I WON'T LET YOU DESTROY ITS TREASURES!
MOST MONSTERS CAN'T SPEAK ENGLISH. LET'S FIND OUT WHO THIS IS!
MARK McMURRAY? BUT WHY DID YOU DO THIS?
I COULDN'T LET THESE DEVELOPERS HARM THE NATURAL TREASURES OF THE EVERGLADES.
THEN YOU DID IT ALL FOR NOTHING. ONCE MY ASSOCIATES AND I SAW THIS LAND, WE DECIDED TO BUY IT TO MAKE IT A WILD-LIFE PRESERVE!
AFTER ALL THAT RUNNING AROUND TRYING TO FIND, THEN SAVE, THEN UNMASK THE MONSTER, I HAVE ONLY ONE QUESTION--
LIKE, NOW CAN WE GET SOME BREAKFAST?
ROOBY ROOBY ROO!
HA
HA
HA
HA
THE END!

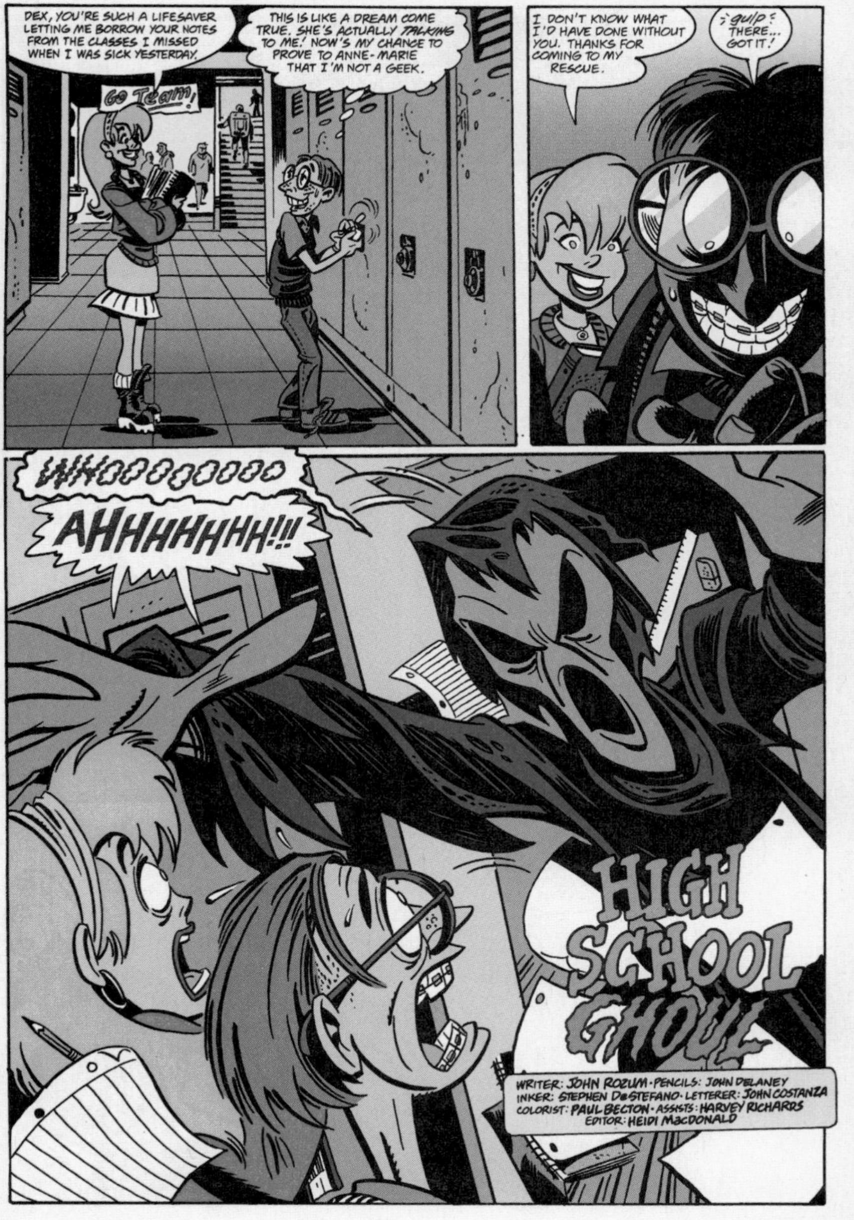

DEX, YOU'RE SUCH A LIFESAVER LETTING ME BORROW YOUR NOTES FROM THE CLASSES I MISSED WHEN I WAS SICK YESTERDAY.
THIS IS LIKE A DREAM COME TRUE. SHE'S ACTUALLY TALKING TO ME! NOW'S MY CHANCE TO PROVE TO ANNE-MARIE THAT I'M NOT A GEEK.
Go Team!
I DON'T KNOW WHAT I'D HAVE DONE WITHOUT YOU. THANKS FOR COMING TO MY RESCUE.
gulp THERE... GOT IT!
WHOOOOOOOO
AHHHHHHH!!!
HIGH SCHOOL GHOUL
WRITER: JOHN ROZUM · PENCILS: JOHN DELANEY
INKER: STEPHEN DeSTEFANO · LETTERER: JOHN COSTANZA
COLORIST: PAUL BECTON · ASSISTS: HARVEY RICHARDS
EDITOR: HEIDI MacDONALD

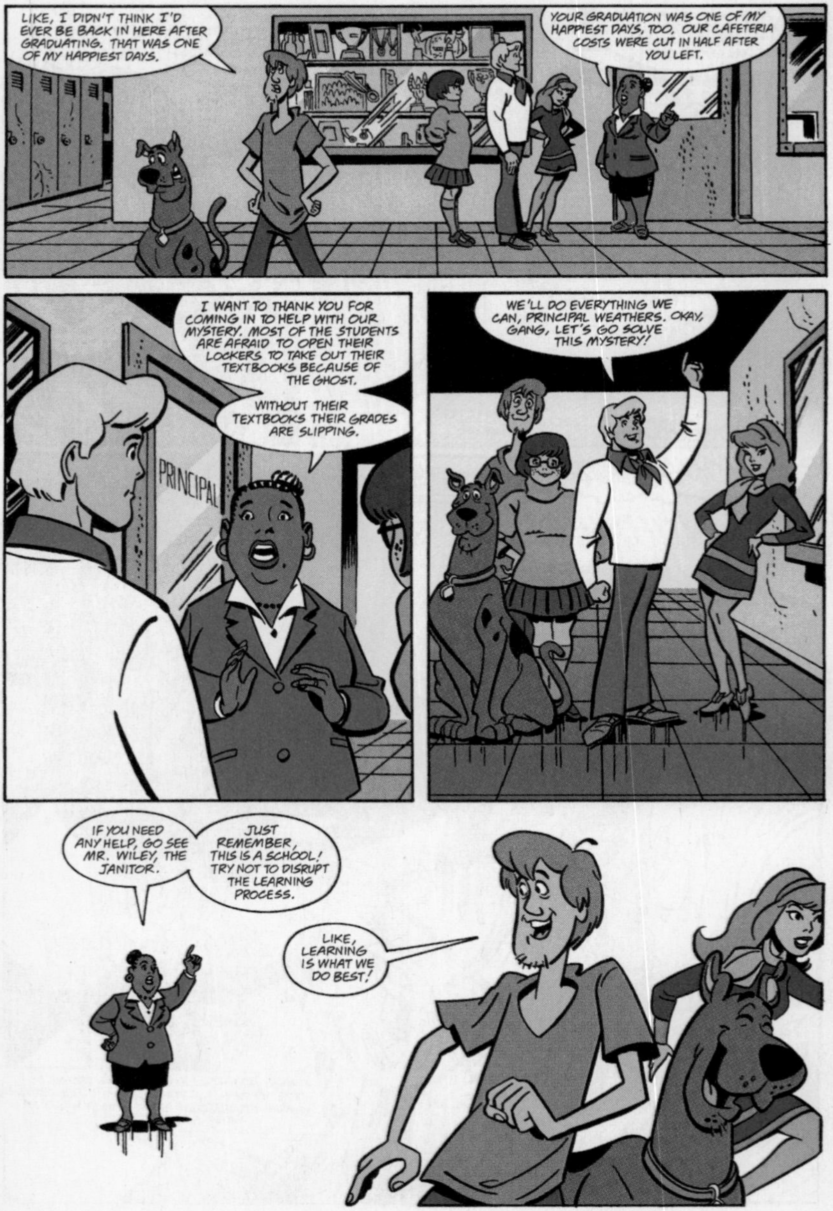
LIKE, I DIDN'T THINK I'D EVER BE BACK IN HERE AFTER GRADUATING. THAT WAS ONE OF MY HAPPIEST DAYS.
YOUR GRADUATION WAS ONE OF MY HAPPIEST DAYS, TOO. OUR CAFETERIA COSTS WERE CUT IN HALF AFTER YOU LEFT.
I WANT TO THANK YOU FOR COMING IN TO HELP WITH OUR MYSTERY. MOST OF THE STUDENTS ARE AFRAID TO OPEN THEIR LOCKERS TO TAKE OUT THEIR TEXTBOOKS BECAUSE OF THE GHOST.
WITHOUT THEIR TEXTBOOKS THEIR GRADES ARE SLIPPING.
PRINCIPAL
WE'LL DO EVERYTHING WE CAN, PRINCIPAL WEATHERS. OKAY, GANG, LET'S GO SOLVE THIS MYSTERY!
IF YOU NEED ANY HELP, GO SEE MR. WILEY, THE JANITOR.
JUST REMEMBER, THIS IS A SCHOOL! TRY NOT TO DISRUPT THE LEARNING PROCESS.
LIKE, LEARNING IS WHAT WE DO BEST!

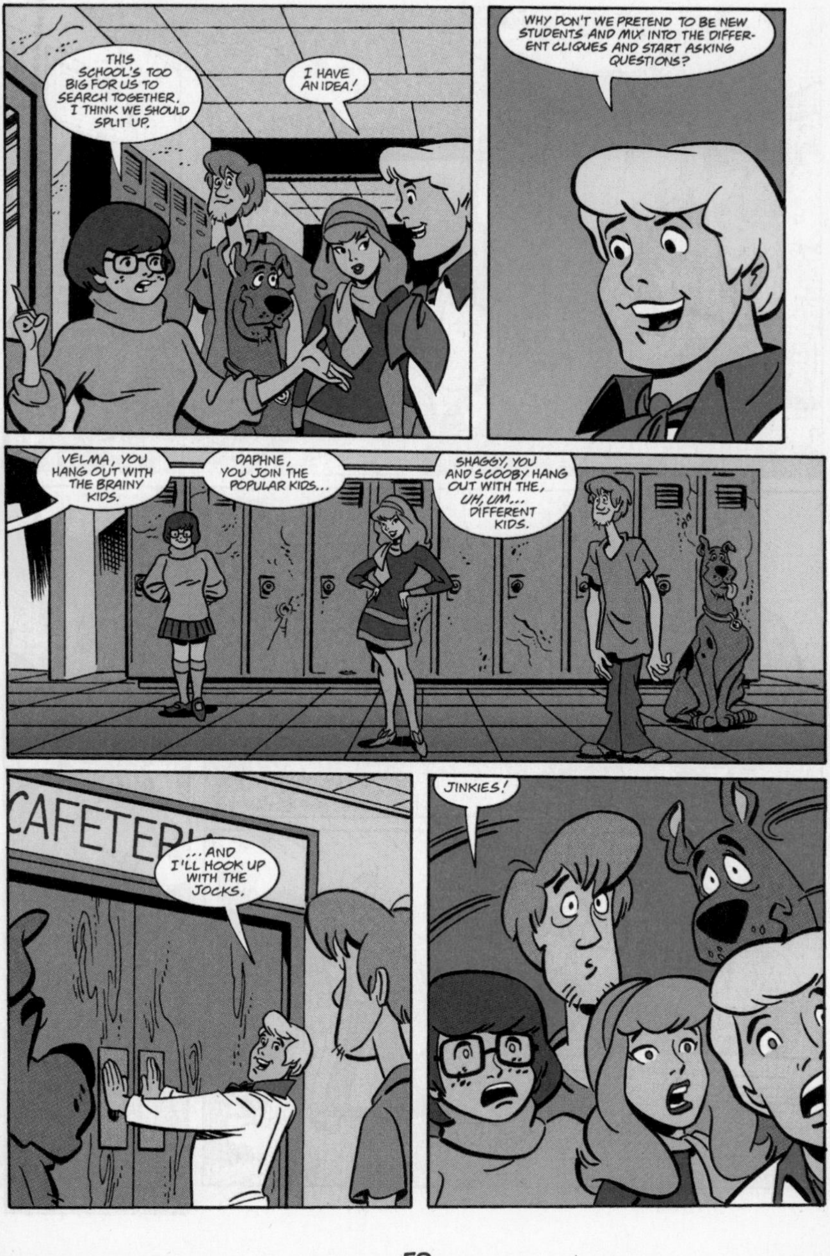
THIS SCHOOL'S TOO BIG FOR US TO SEARCH TOGETHER. I THINK WE SHOULD SPLIT UP.
I HAVE AN IDEA!
WHY DON'T WE PRETEND TO BE NEW STUDENTS AND MIX INTO THE DIFFERENT CLIQUES AND START ASKING QUESTIONS?
VELMA, YOU HANG OUT WITH THE BRAINY KIDS.
DAPHNE, YOU JOIN THE POPULAR KIDS...
SHAGGY, YOU AND SCOOBY HANG OUT WITH THE, UH, UM... DIFFERENT KIDS.
CAFETER
...AND I'LL HOOK UP WITH THE JOCKS.
JINKIES!

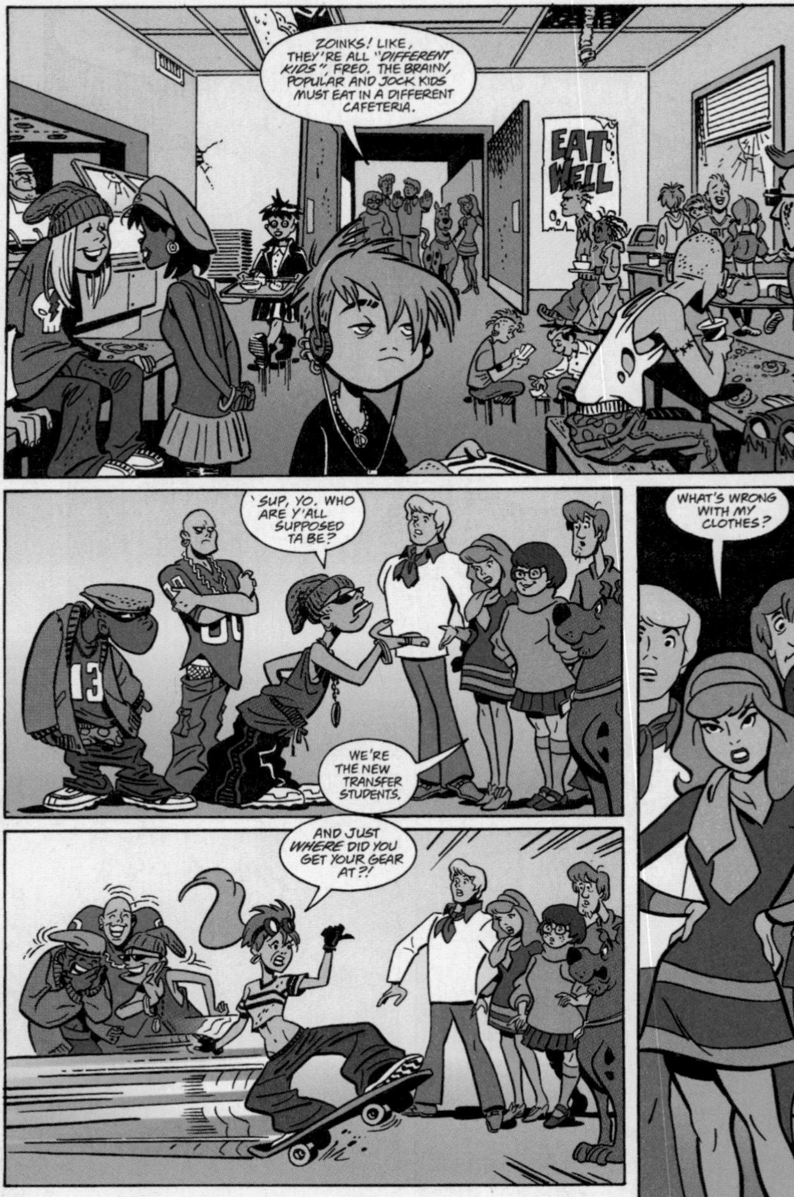
ZOINKS! LIKE, THEY'RE ALL "DIFFERENT KIDS", FRED. THE BRAINY, POPULAR AND JOCK KIDS MUST EAT IN A DIFFERENT CAFETERIA.
EAT WELL
'SUP, YO. WHO ARE Y'ALL SUPPOSED TA BE?
WE'RE THE NEW TRANSFER STUDENTS.
WHAT'S WRONG WITH MY CLOTHES?
AND JUST WHERE DID YOU GET YOUR GEAR AT?!

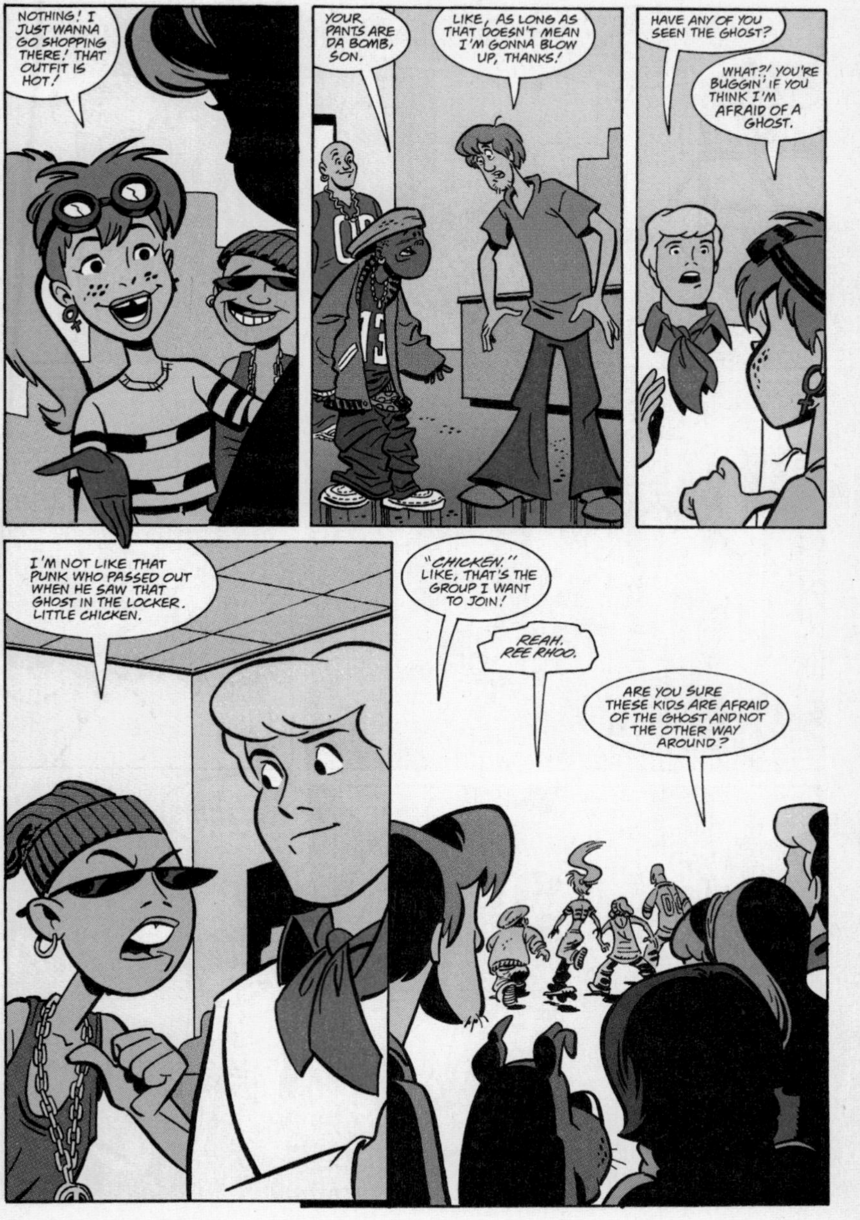
NOTHING! I JUST WANNA GO SHOPPING THERE! THAT OUTFIT IS HOT!
YOUR PANTS ARE DA BOMB, SON.
LIKE, AS LONG AS THAT DOESN'T MEAN I'M GONNA BLOW UP, THANKS!
HAVE ANY OF YOU SEEN THE GHOST?
WHAT?! YOU'RE BUGGIN' IF YOU THINK I'M AFRAID OF A GHOST.
I'M NOT LIKE THAT PUNK WHO PASSED OUT WHEN HE SAW THAT GHOST IN THE LOCKER. LITTLE CHICKEN.
"CHICKEN." LIKE, THAT'S THE GROUP I WANT TO JOIN!
REAH. REE RHOO.
ARE YOU SURE THESE KIDS ARE AFRAID OF THE GHOST AND NOT THE OTHER WAY AROUND?

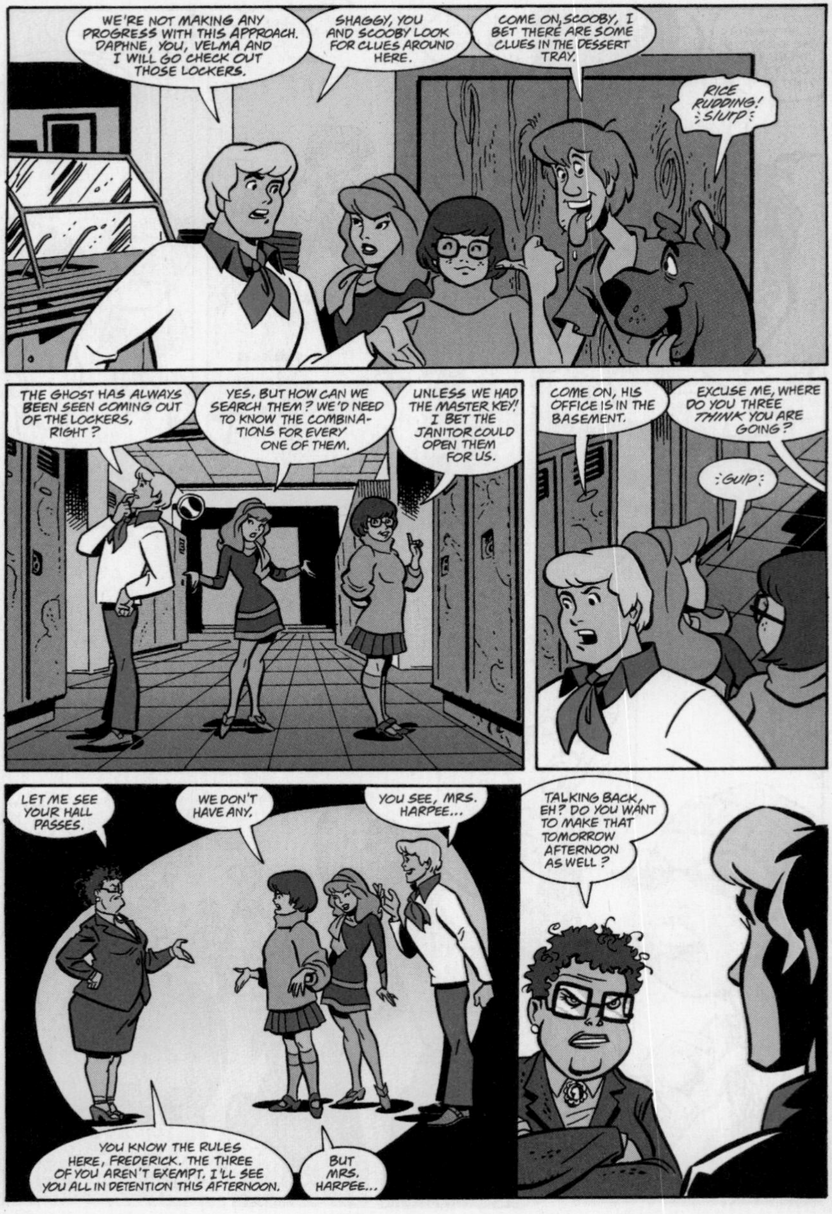
WE'RE NOT MAKING ANY PROGRESS WITH THIS APPROACH. DAPHNE, YOU, VELMA AND I WILL GO CHECK OUT THOSE LOCKERS.
SHAGGY, YOU AND SCOOBY LOOK FOR CLUES AROUND HERE.
COME ON, SCOOBY, I BET THERE ARE SOME CLUES IN THE DESSERT TRAY.
RICE RUDDING! Slurp
THE GHOST HAS ALWAYS BEEN SEEN COMING OUT OF THE LOCKERS, RIGHT?
YES, BUT HOW CAN WE SEARCH THEM? WE'D NEED TO KNOW THE COMBINATIONS FOR EVERY ONE OF THEM.
UNLESS WE HAD THE MASTER KEY! I BET THE JANITOR COULD OPEN THEM FOR US.
COME ON, HIS OFFICE IS IN THE BASEMENT.
EXCUSE ME, WHERE DO YOU THREE THINK YOU ARE GOING?
Gulp
LET ME SEE YOUR HALL PASSES.
WE DON'T HAVE ANY.
YOU SEE, MRS. HARPEE...
YOU KNOW THE RULES HERE, FREDERICK. THE THREE OF YOU AREN'T EXEMPT. I'LL SEE YOU ALL IN DETENTION THIS AFTERNOON.
BUT MRS. HARPEE...
TALKING BACK, EH? DO YOU WANT TO MAKE THAT TOMORROW AFTERNOON AS WELL?

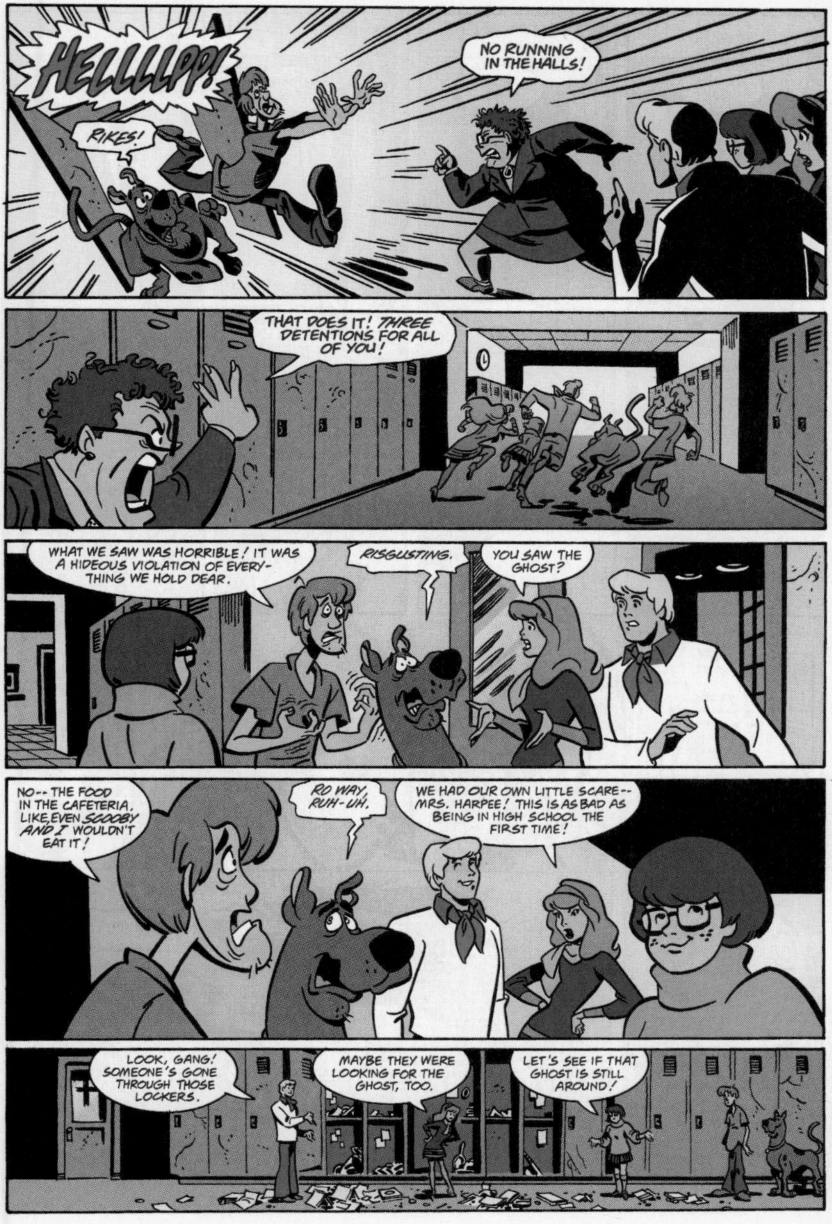
HELLLLLPP!
RIKES!
NO RUNNING IN THE HALLS!
THAT DOES IT! THREE DETENTIONS FOR ALL OF YOU!
WHAT WE SAW WAS HORRIBLE! IT WAS A HIDEOUS VIOLATION OF EVERYTHING WE HOLD DEAR.
RISGUSTING.
YOU SAW THE GHOST?
NO-- THE FOOD IN THE CAFETERIA. LIKE, EVEN SCOOBY AND I WOULDN'T EAT IT!
RO WAY, RUH-UH.
WE HAD OUR OWN LITTLE SCARE-- MRS. HARPEE! THIS IS AS BAD AS BEING IN HIGH SCHOOL THE FIRST TIME!
LOOK, GANG! SOMEONE'S GONE THROUGH THOSE LOCKERS.
MAYBE THEY WERE LOOKING FOR THE GHOST, TOO.
LET'S SEE IF THAT GHOST IS STILL AROUND!

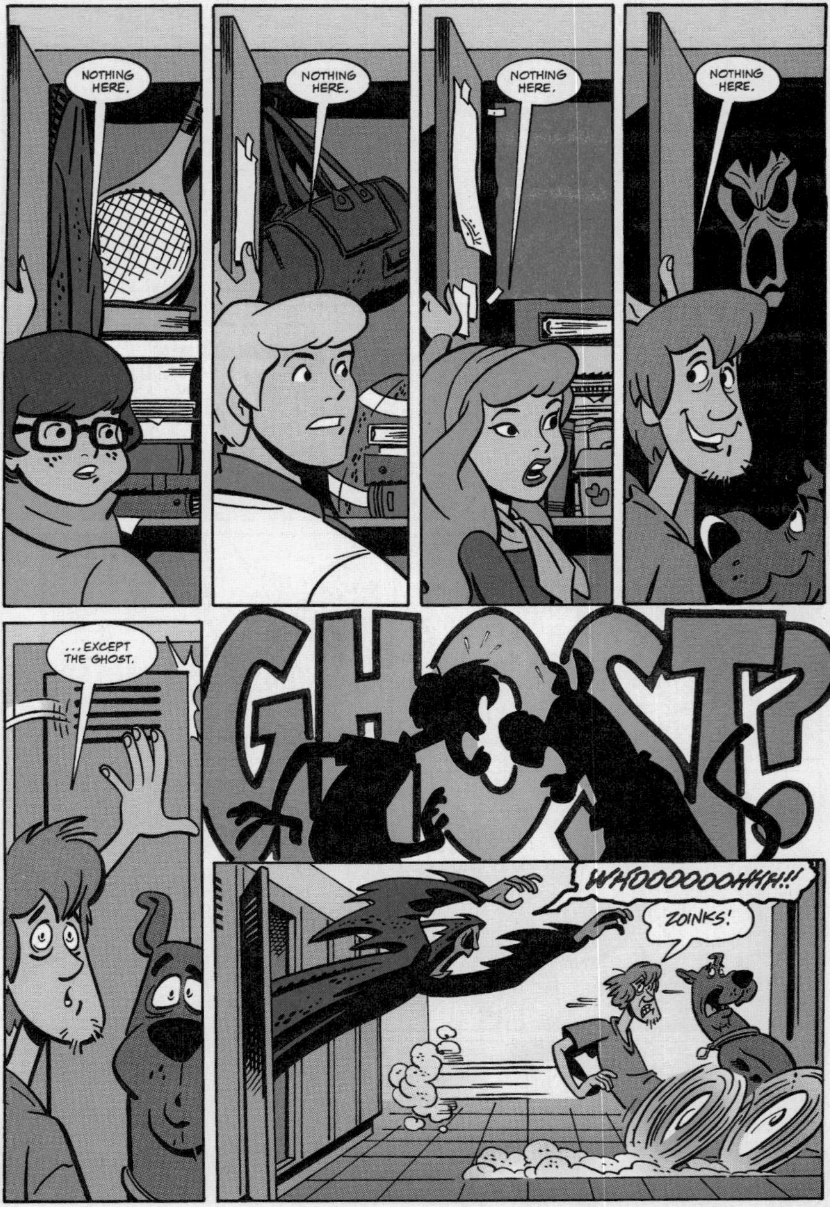

NOTHING HERE.
NOTHING HERE.
NOTHING HERE.
NOTHING HERE.
...EXCEPT THE GHOST.
GHOST?
WHOOOOOOOHHH!!
ZOINKS!

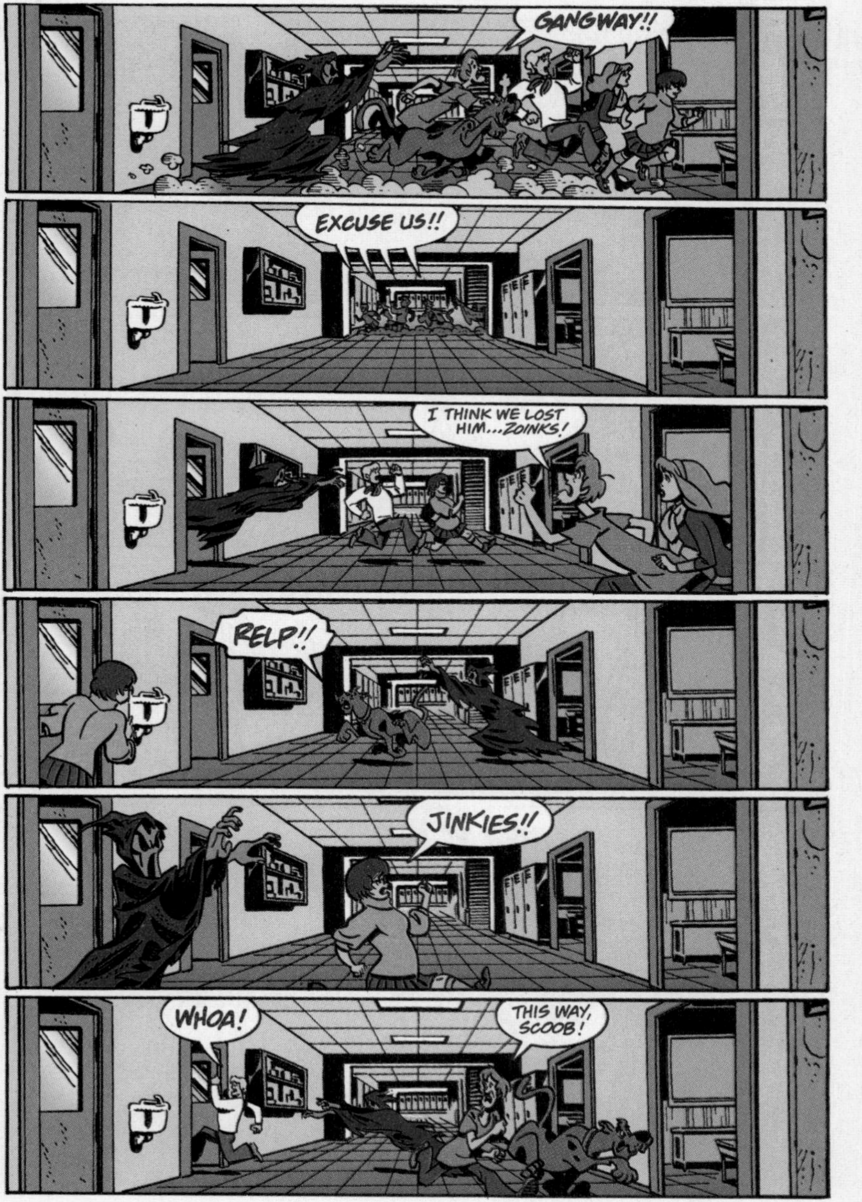
GANGWAY!!
EXCUSE US!!
I THINK WE LOST HIM...ZOINKS!
RELP!!
JINKIES!!
WHOA!
THIS WAY, SCOOB!

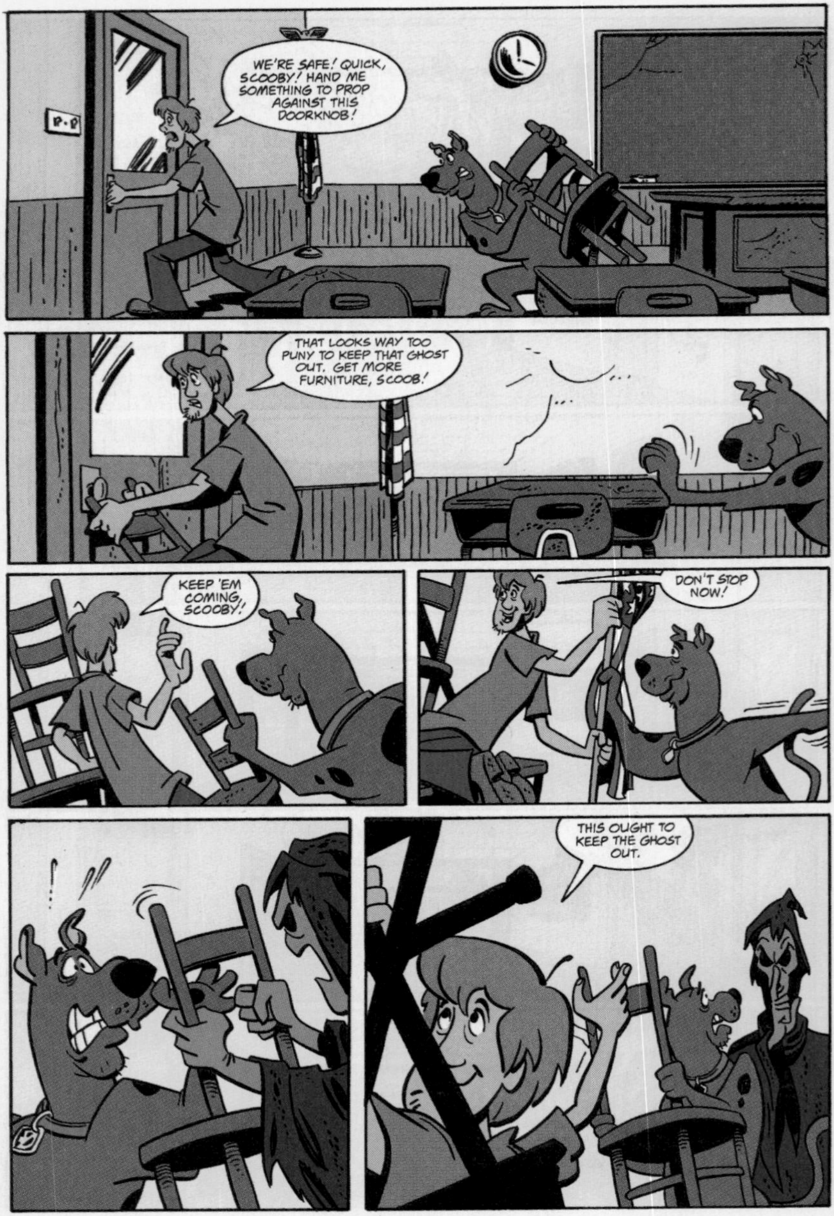
WE'RE SAFE! QUICK, SCOOBY! HAND ME SOMETHING TO PROP AGAINST THIS DOORKNOB!
THAT LOOKS WAY TOO PUNY TO KEEP THAT GHOST OUT. GET MORE FURNITURE, SCOOB!
KEEP 'EM COMING, SCOOBY!
DON'T STOP NOW!
THIS OUGHT TO KEEP THE GHOST OUT.

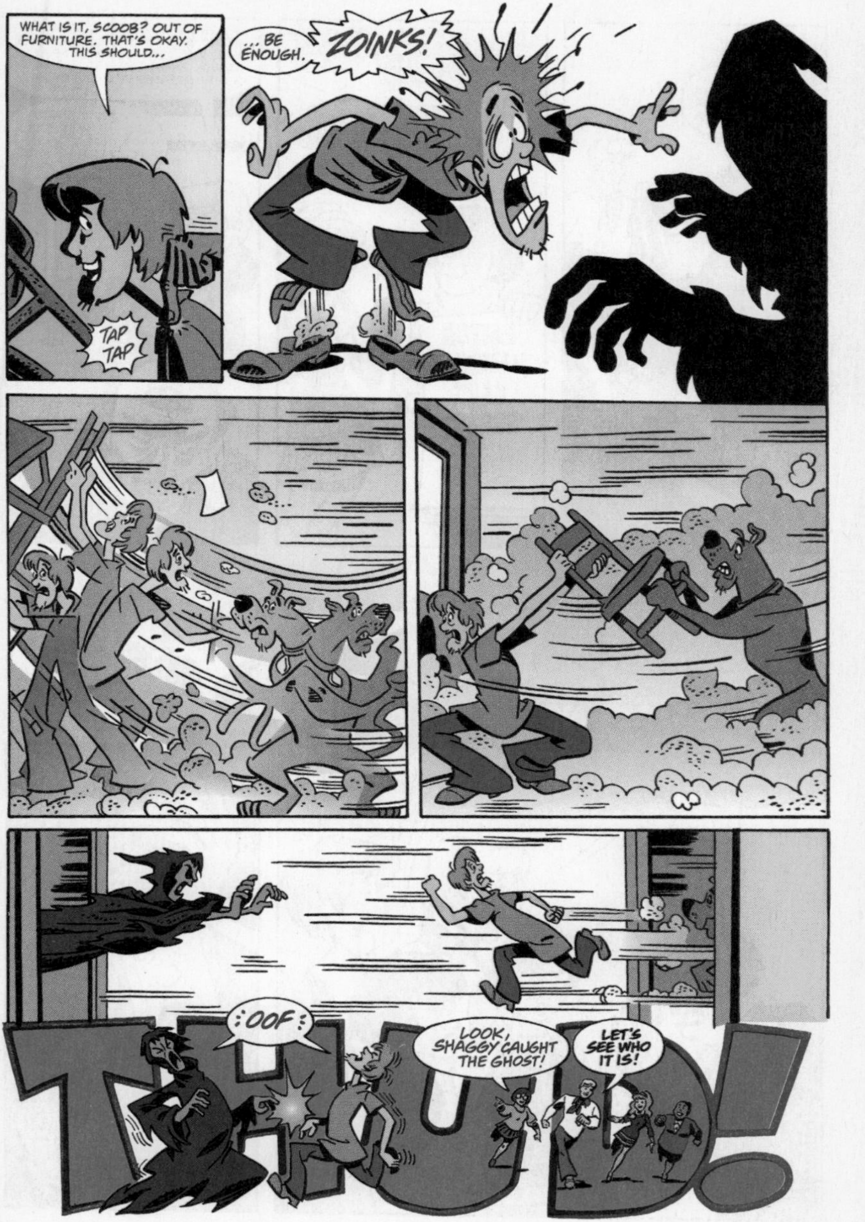
WHAT IS IT, SCOOB? OUT OF FURNITURE. THAT'S OKAY. THIS SHOULD...
TAP TAP
... BE ENOUGH.
ZOINKS!
OOF
THUD!
LOOK, SHAGGY CAUGHT THE GHOST!
LET'S SEE WHO IT IS!

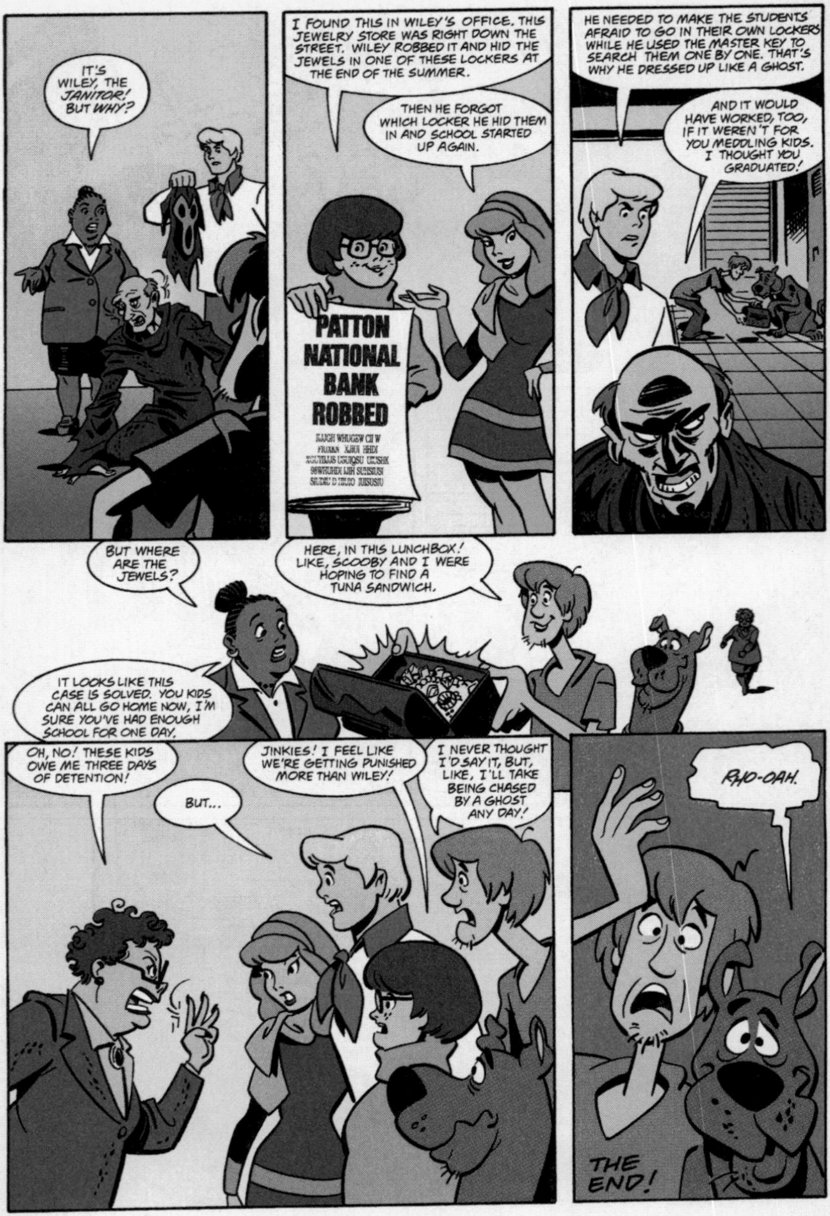
IT'S WILEY, THE JANITOR! BUT WHY?
I FOUND THIS IN WILEY'S OFFICE. THIS JEWELRY STORE WAS RIGHT DOWN THE STREET. WILEY ROBBED IT AND HID THE JEWELS IN ONE OF THESE LOCKERS AT THE END OF THE SUMMER.
THEN HE FORGOT WHICH LOCKER HE HID THEM IN AND SCHOOL STARTED UP AGAIN.
PATTON NATIONAL BANK ROBBED
HE NEEDED TO MAKE THE STUDENTS AFRAID TO GO IN THEIR OWN LOCKERS WHILE HE USED THE MASTER KEY TO SEARCH THEM ONE BY ONE. THAT'S WHY HE DRESSED UP LIKE A GHOST.
AND IT WOULD HAVE WORKED, TOO, IF IT WEREN'T FOR YOU MEDDLING KIDS. I THOUGHT YOU GRADUATED!
BUT WHERE ARE THE JEWELS?
HERE, IN THIS LUNCHBOX! LIKE, SCOOBY AND I WERE HOPING TO FIND A TUNA SANDWICH.
IT LOOKS LIKE THIS CASE IS SOLVED. YOU KIDS CAN ALL GO HOME NOW, I'M SURE YOU'VE HAD ENOUGH SCHOOL FOR ONE DAY.
OH, NO! THESE KIDS OWE ME THREE DAYS OF DETENTION!
BUT...
JINKIES! I FEEL LIKE WE'RE GETTING PUNISHED MORE THAN WILEY!
I NEVER THOUGHT I'D SAY IT, BUT, LIKE, I'LL TAKE BEING CHASED BY A GHOST ANY DAY!
RHO-OAH.
THE END!

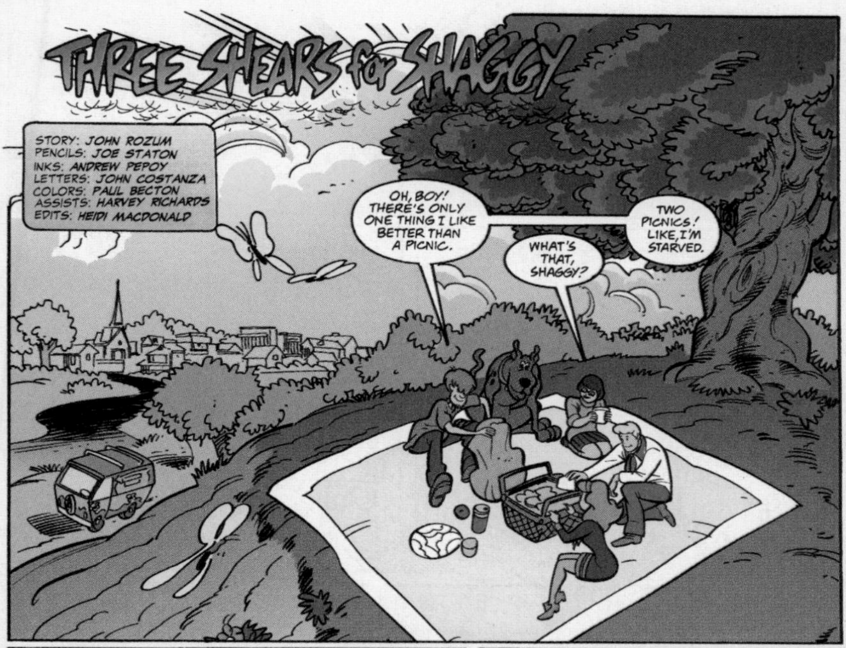
THREE SHEARS for SHAGGY
STORY: JOHN ROZUM
PENCILS: JOE STATON
INKS: ANDREW PEPOY
LETTERS: JOHN COSTANZA
COLORS: PAUL BECTON
ASSISTS: HARVEY RICHARDS
EDITS: HEIDI MACDONALD
OH, BOY! THERE'S ONLY ONE THING I LIKE BETTER THAN A PICNIC.
WHAT'S THAT, SHAGGY?
TWO PICNICS! LIKE, I'M STARVED.

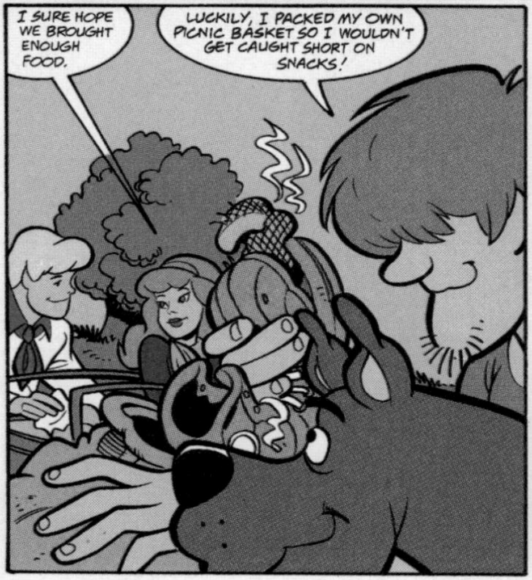
I SURE HOPE WE BROUGHT ENOUGH FOOD.
LUCKILY, I PACKED MY OWN PICNIC BASKET SO I WOULDN'T GET CAUGHT SHORT ON SNACKS!

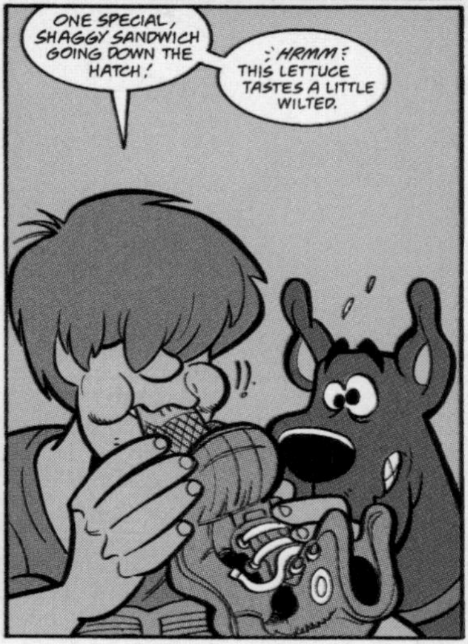
ONE SPECIAL, SHAGGY SANDWICH GOING DOWN THE HATCH!
HRMM
THIS LETTUCE TASTES A LITTLE WILTED.

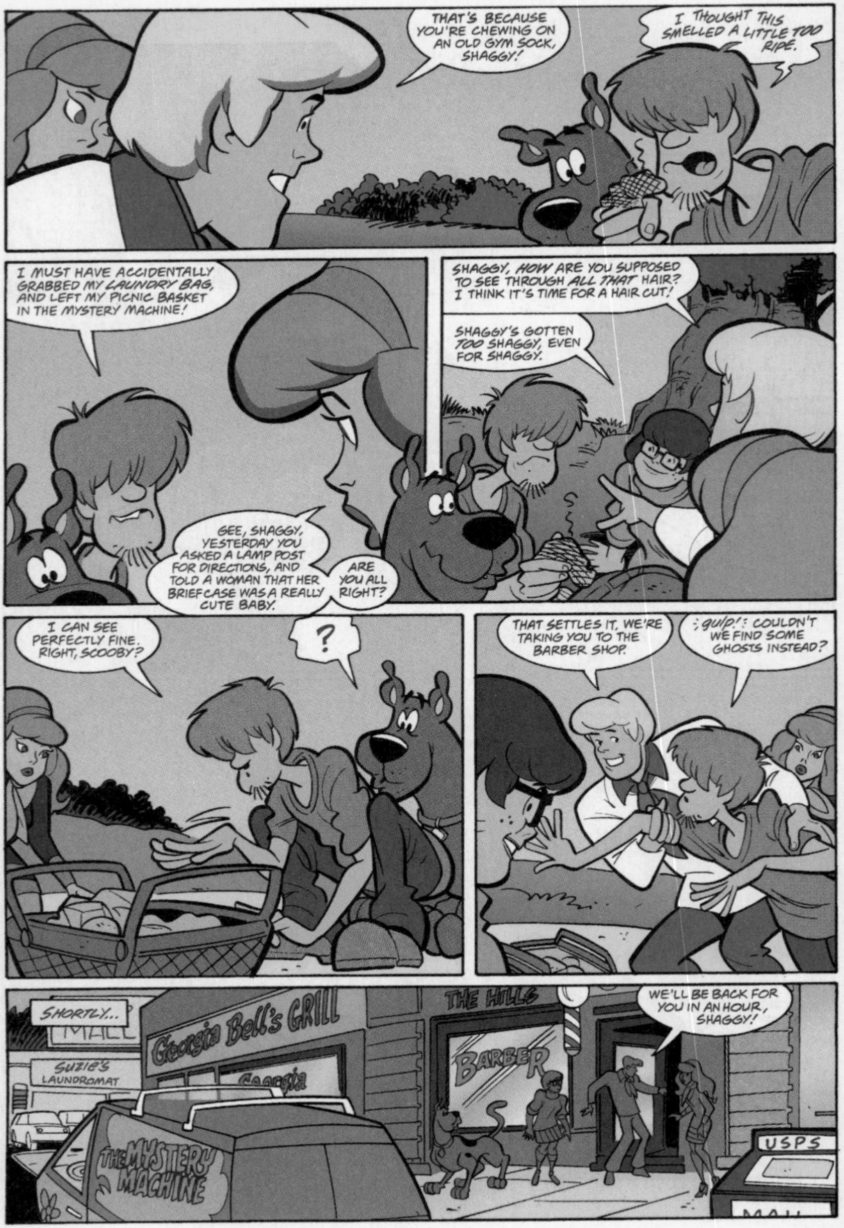
THAT'S BECAUSE YOU'RE CHEWING ON AN OLD GYM SOCK, SHAGGY!
I THOUGHT THIS SMELLED A LITTLE TOO RIPE.
I MUST HAVE ACCIDENTALLY GRABBED MY LAUNDRY BAG, AND LEFT MY PICNIC BASKET IN THE MYSTERY MACHINE!
GEE, SHAGGY, YESTERDAY YOU ASKED A LAMP POST FOR DIRECTIONS, AND TOLD A WOMAN THAT HER BRIEFCASE WAS A REALLY CUTE BABY.
ARE YOU ALL RIGHT?
SHAGGY, HOW ARE YOU SUPPOSED TO SEE THROUGH ALL THAT HAIR? I THINK IT'S TIME FOR A HAIR CUT!
SHAGGY'S GOTTEN TOO SHAGGY, EVEN FOR SHAGGY.
I CAN SEE PERFECTLY FINE. RIGHT, SCOOBY?
?
THAT SETTLES IT, WE'RE TAKING YOU TO THE BARBER SHOP.
;gulp!; COULDN'T WE FIND SOME GHOSTS INSTEAD?
SHORTLY...
MALL
Georgia Bell's GRILL
Georgia
SUZIE'S LAUNDROMAT
THE HILLS
BARBER
THE MYSTERY MACHINE
WE'LL BE BACK FOR YOU IN AN HOUR, SHAGGY!
USPS
MAIL

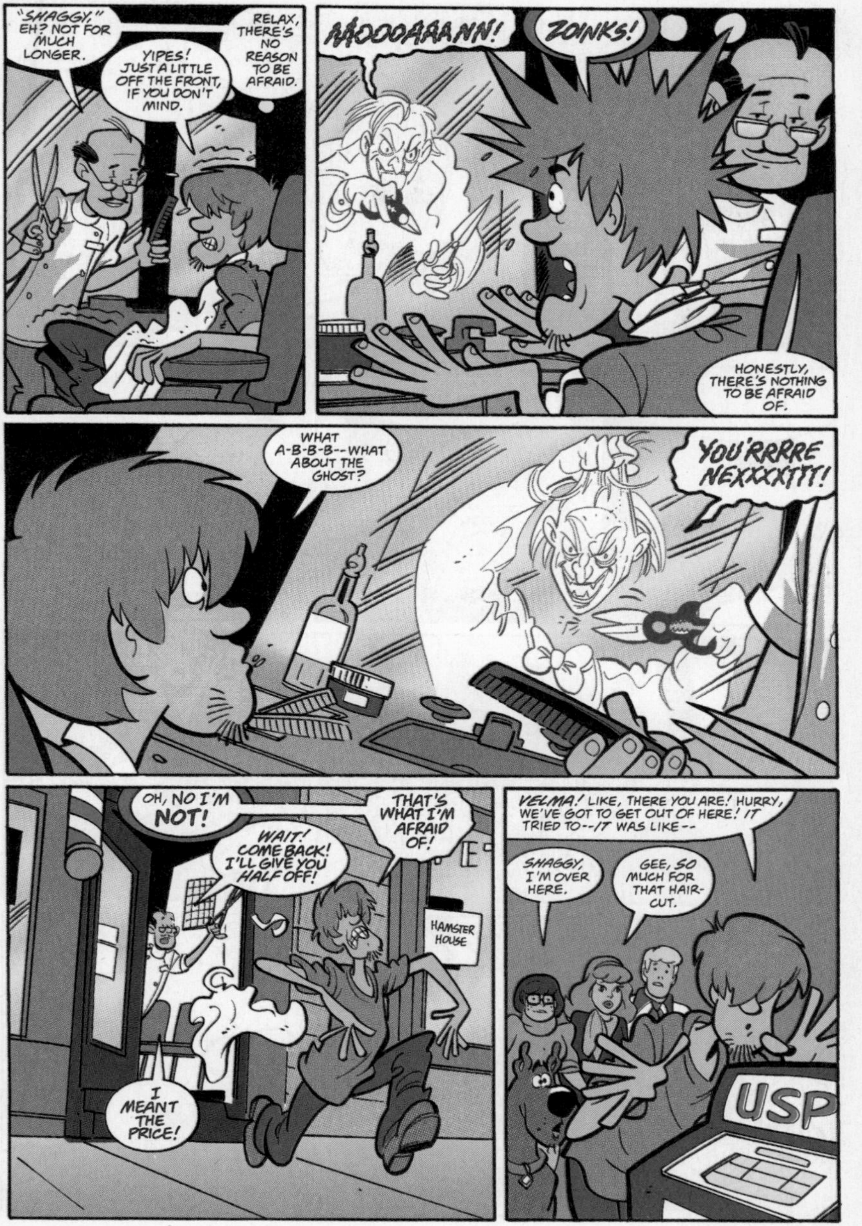
"SHAGGY," EH? NOT FOR MUCH LONGER.
YIPES! JUST A LITTLE OFF THE FRONT, IF YOU DON'T MIND.
RELAX, THERE'S NO REASON TO BE AFRAID.
MOOOAAAANN!
ZOINKS!
HONESTLY, THERE'S NOTHING TO BE AFRAID OF.
WHAT A-B-B-B--WHAT ABOUT THE GHOST?
YOU'RRRRE NEXXXXTTT!
OH, NO I'M NOT!
THAT'S WHAT I'M AFRAID OF!
WAIT! COME BACK! I'LL GIVE YOU HALF OFF!
HAMSTER HOUSE
I MEANT THE PRICE!
VELMA! LIKE, THERE YOU ARE! HURRY, WE'VE GOT TO GET OUT OF HERE! IT TRIED TO--IT WAS LIKE--
SHAGGY, I'M OVER HERE.
GEE, SO MUCH FOR THAT HAIR-CUT.
USP

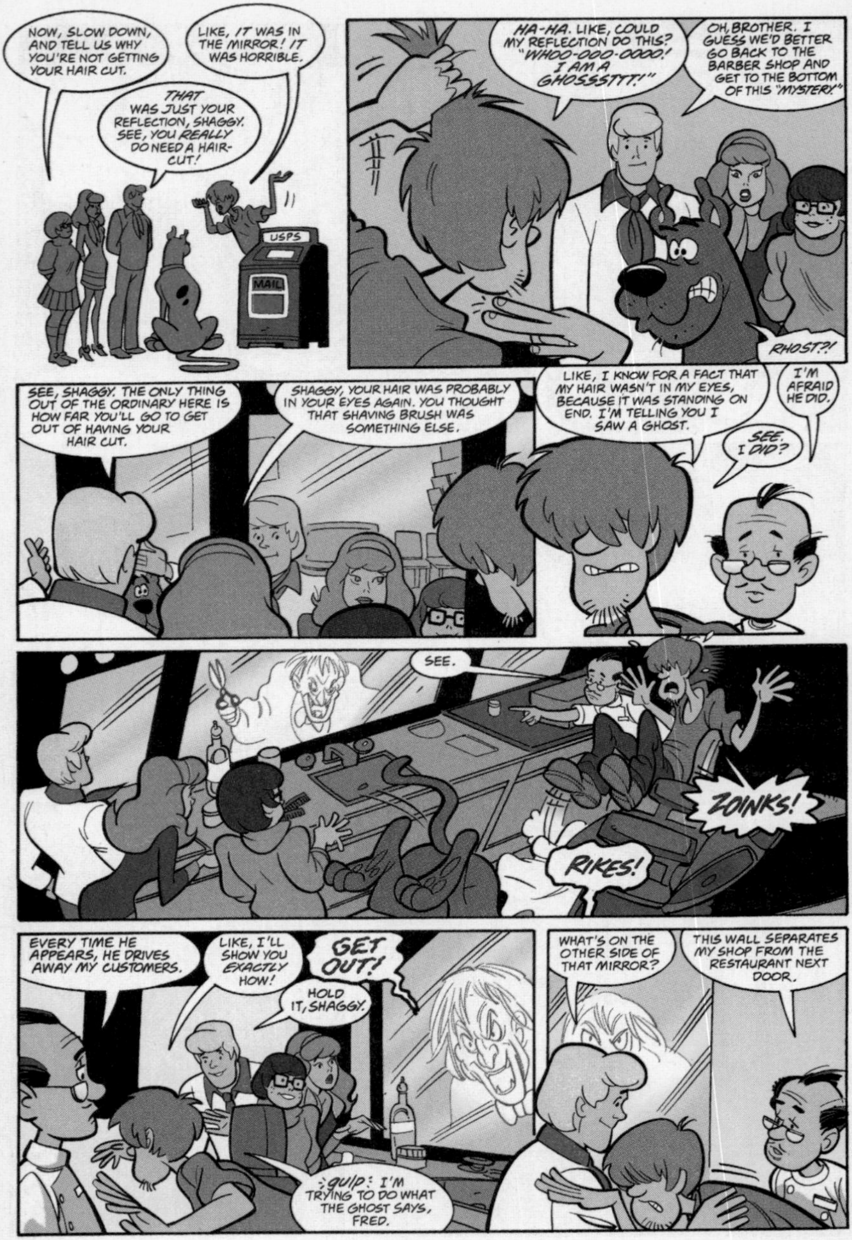
NOW, SLOW DOWN, AND TELL US WHY YOU'RE NOT GETTING YOUR HAIR CUT.
LIKE, IT WAS IN THE MIRROR! IT WAS HORRIBLE.
THAT WAS JUST YOUR REFLECTION, SHAGGY. SEE, YOU REALLY DO NEED A HAIR-CUT!
USPS
MAIL
HA-HA. LIKE, COULD MY REFLECTION DO THIS? "WHOO-OOO-OOOO! I AM A GHOSSSTTT!"
OH, BROTHER. I GUESS WE'D BETTER GO BACK TO THE BARBER SHOP AND GET TO THE BOTTOM OF THIS "MYSTERY."
RHOST?!
SEE, SHAGGY. THE ONLY THING OUT OF THE ORDINARY HERE IS HOW FAR YOU'LL GO TO GET OUT OF HAVING YOUR HAIR CUT.
SHAGGY, YOUR HAIR WAS PROBABLY IN YOUR EYES AGAIN. YOU THOUGHT THAT SHAVING BRUSH WAS SOMETHING ELSE.
LIKE, I KNOW FOR A FACT THAT MY HAIR WASN'T IN MY EYES, BECAUSE IT WAS STANDING ON END. I'M TELLING YOU I SAW A GHOST.
I'M AFRAID HE DID.
SEE. I DID?
SEE.
ZOINKS!
RIKES!
EVERY TIME HE APPEARS, HE DRIVES AWAY MY CUSTOMERS.
LIKE, I'LL SHOW YOU EXACTLY HOW!
GET OUT!
HOLD IT, SHAGGY.
:gulp: I'M TRYING TO DO WHAT THE GHOST SAYS, FRED.
WHAT'S ON THE OTHER SIDE OF THAT MIRROR?
THIS WALL SEPARATES MY SHOP FROM THE RESTAURANT NEXT DOOR.

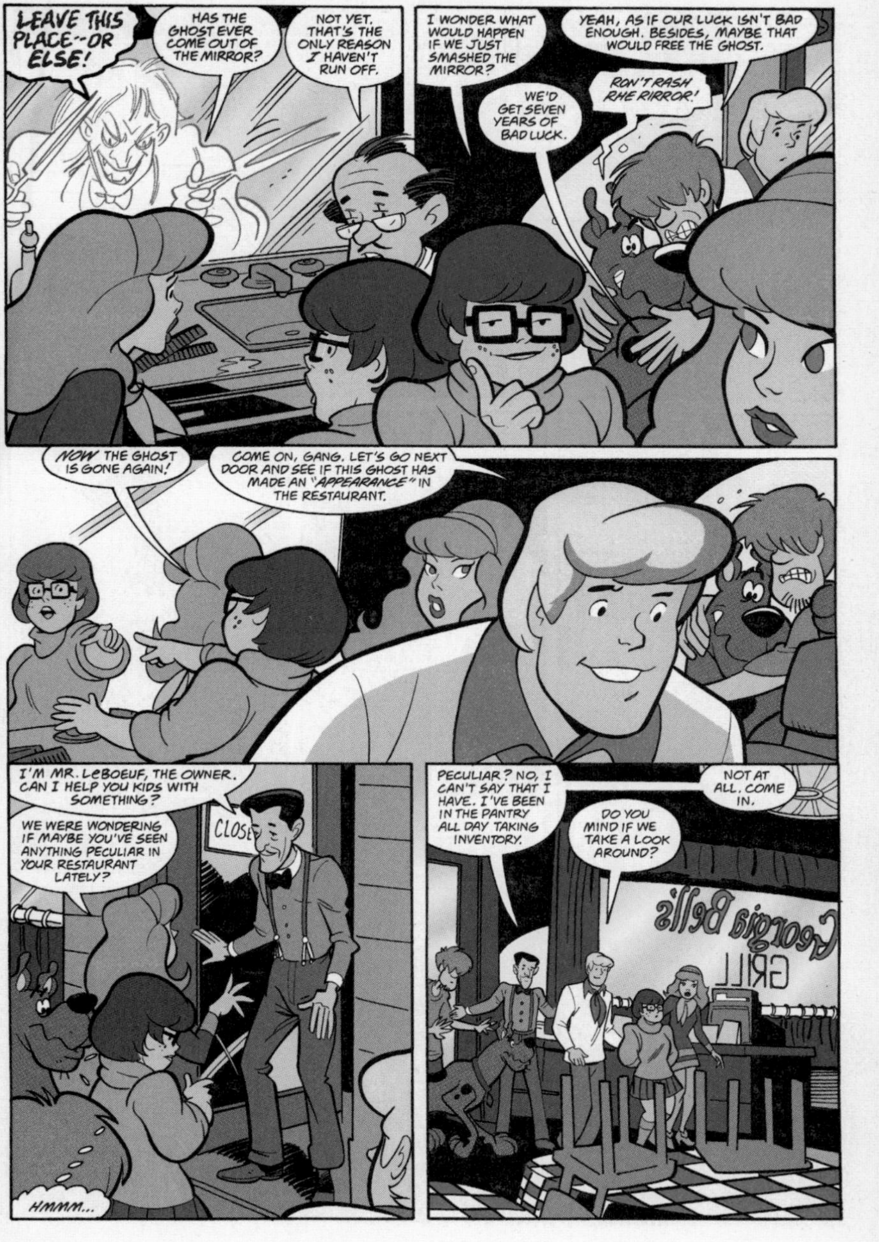

LEAVE THIS PLACE--OR ELSE!
HAS THE GHOST EVER COME OUT OF THE MIRROR?
NOT YET. THAT'S THE ONLY REASON I HAVEN'T RUN OFF.
I WONDER WHAT WOULD HAPPEN IF WE JUST SMASHED THE MIRROR?
WE'D GET SEVEN YEARS OF BAD LUCK.
YEAH, AS IF OUR LUCK ISN'T BAD ENOUGH. BESIDES, MAYBE THAT WOULD FREE THE GHOST.
RON'T RASH RHE RIRROR!
NOW THE GHOST IS GONE AGAIN!
COME ON, GANG. LET'S GO NEXT DOOR AND SEE IF THIS GHOST HAS MADE AN "APPEARANCE" IN THE RESTAURANT.
I'M MR. LeBOEUF, THE OWNER. CAN I HELP YOU KIDS WITH SOMETHING?
WE WERE WONDERING IF MAYBE YOU'VE SEEN ANYTHING PECULIAR IN YOUR RESTAURANT LATELY?
CLOSE
HMMM...
PECULIAR? NO, I CAN'T SAY THAT I HAVE. I'VE BEEN IN THE PANTRY ALL DAY TAKING INVENTORY.
DO YOU MIND IF WE TAKE A LOOK AROUND?
NOT AT ALL. COME IN.
Georgia Bell's
GRILL

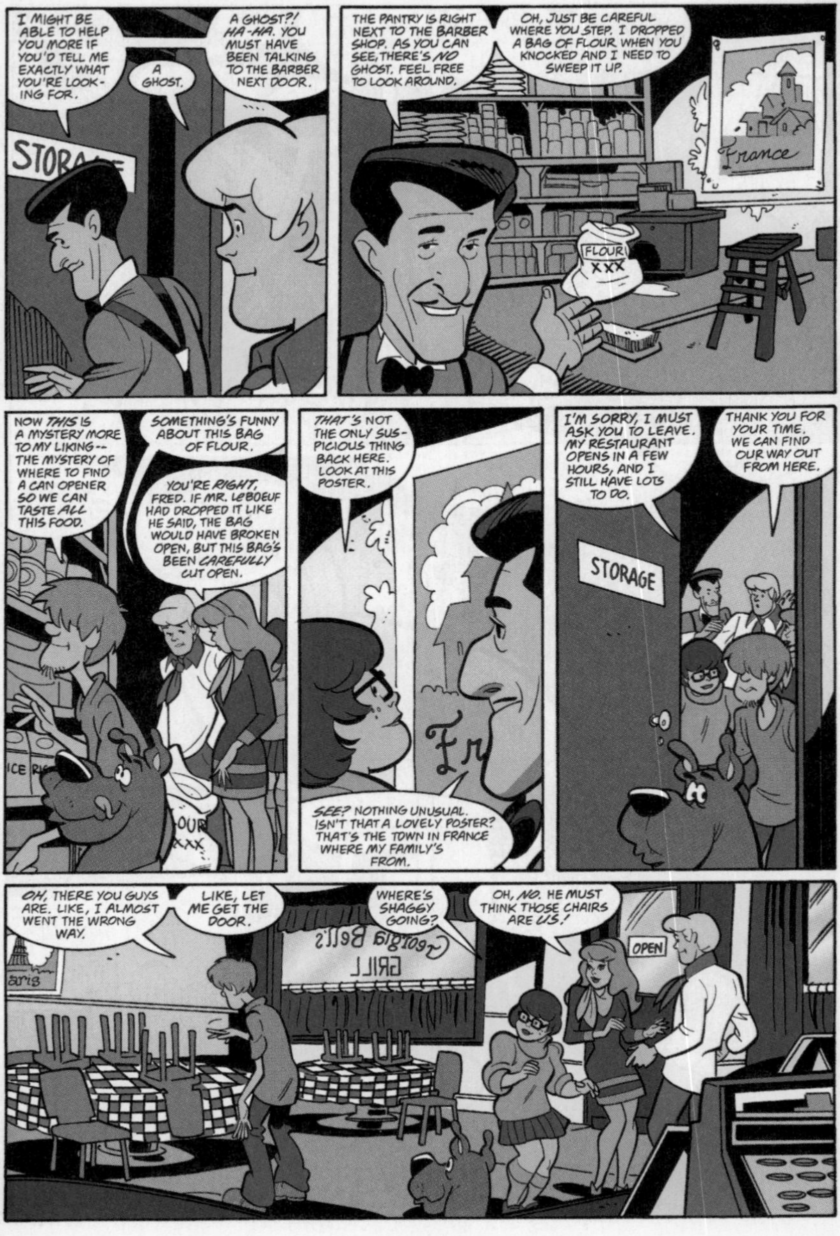

I MIGHT BE ABLE TO HELP YOU MORE IF YOU'D TELL ME EXACTLY WHAT YOU'RE LOOK-ING FOR.
A GHOST.
A GHOST?! HA-HA. YOU MUST HAVE BEEN TALKING TO THE BARBER NEXT DOOR.
STORA
THE PANTRY IS RIGHT NEXT TO THE BARBER SHOP. AS YOU CAN SEE, THERE'S NO GHOST. FEEL FREE TO LOOK AROUND.
OH, JUST BE CAREFUL WHERE YOU STEP. I DROPPED A BAG OF FLOUR WHEN YOU KNOCKED AND I NEED TO SWEEP IT UP.
France
FLOUR XXX
NOW THIS IS A MYSTERY MORE TO MY LIKING -- THE MYSTERY OF WHERE TO FIND A CAN OPENER SO WE CAN TASTE ALL THIS FOOD.
SOMETHING'S FUNNY ABOUT THIS BAG OF FLOUR.
YOU'RE RIGHT, FRED. IF MR. LeBOEUF HAD DROPPED IT LIKE HE SAID, THE BAG WOULD HAVE BROKEN OPEN, BUT THIS BAG'S BEEN CAREFULLY CUT OPEN.
THAT'S NOT THE ONLY SUS-PICIOUS THING BACK HERE. LOOK AT THIS POSTER.
SEE? NOTHING UNUSUAL. ISN'T THAT A LOVELY POSTER? THAT'S THE TOWN IN FRANCE WHERE MY FAMILY'S FROM.
I'M SORRY, I MUST ASK YOU TO LEAVE. MY RESTAURANT OPENS IN A FEW HOURS, AND I STILL HAVE LOTS TO DO.
THANK YOU FOR YOUR TIME. WE CAN FIND OUR WAY OUT FROM HERE.
STORAGE
OH, THERE YOU GUYS ARE. LIKE, I ALMOST WENT THE WRONG WAY.
LIKE, LET ME GET THE DOOR.
WHERE'S SHAGGY GOING?
OH, NO. HE MUST THINK THOSE CHAIRS ARE US!
OPEN
Georgia Bell's GRILL

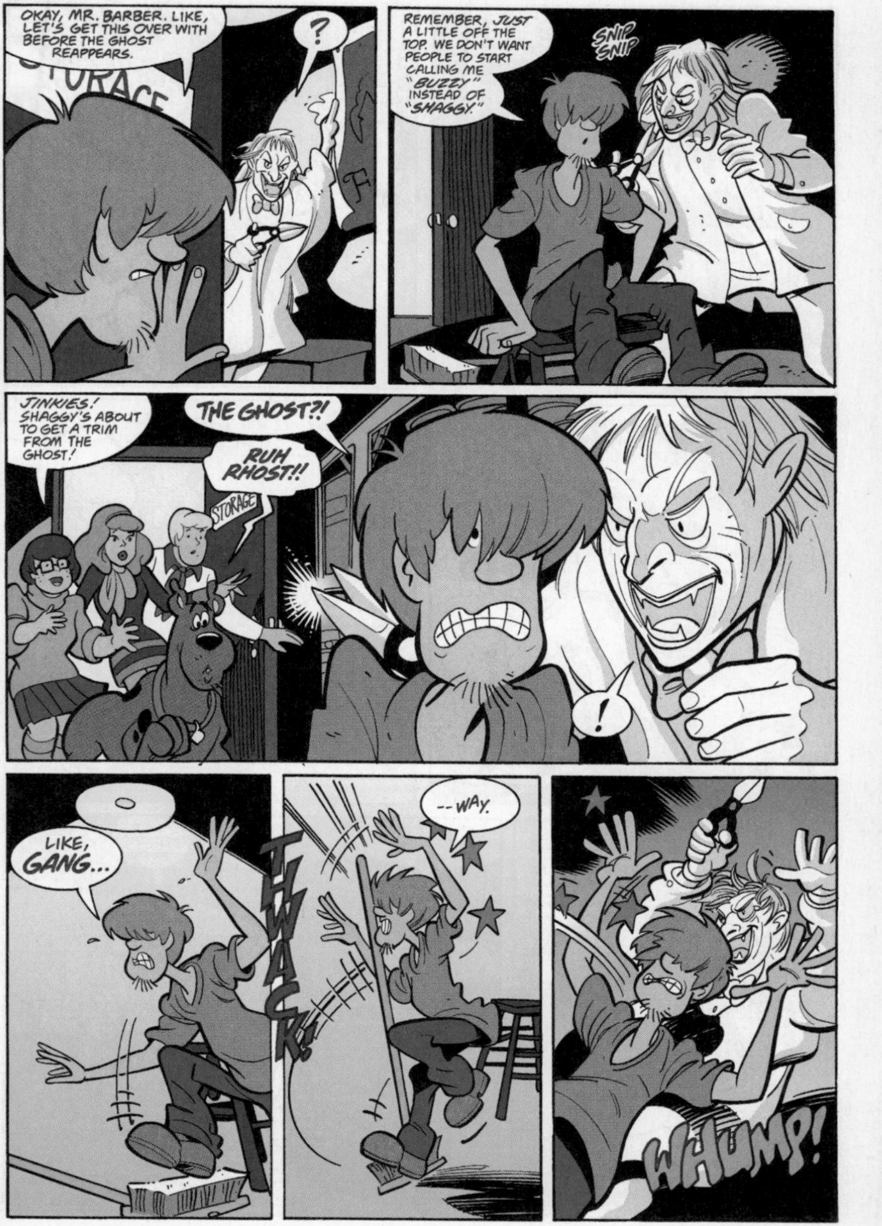

OKAY, MR. BARBER. LIKE, LET'S GET THIS OVER WITH BEFORE THE GHOST REAPPEARS.
?
REMEMBER, JUST A LITTLE OFF THE TOP. WE DON'T WANT PEOPLE TO START CALLING ME "BUZZY" INSTEAD OF "SHAGGY."
SNIP SNIP
JINKIES! SHAGGY'S ABOUT TO GET A TRIM FROM THE GHOST!
THE GHOST?!
RUH RHOST!!
STORAGE
!
LIKE, GANG...
THWACK!
-- WAY.
WHUMP!

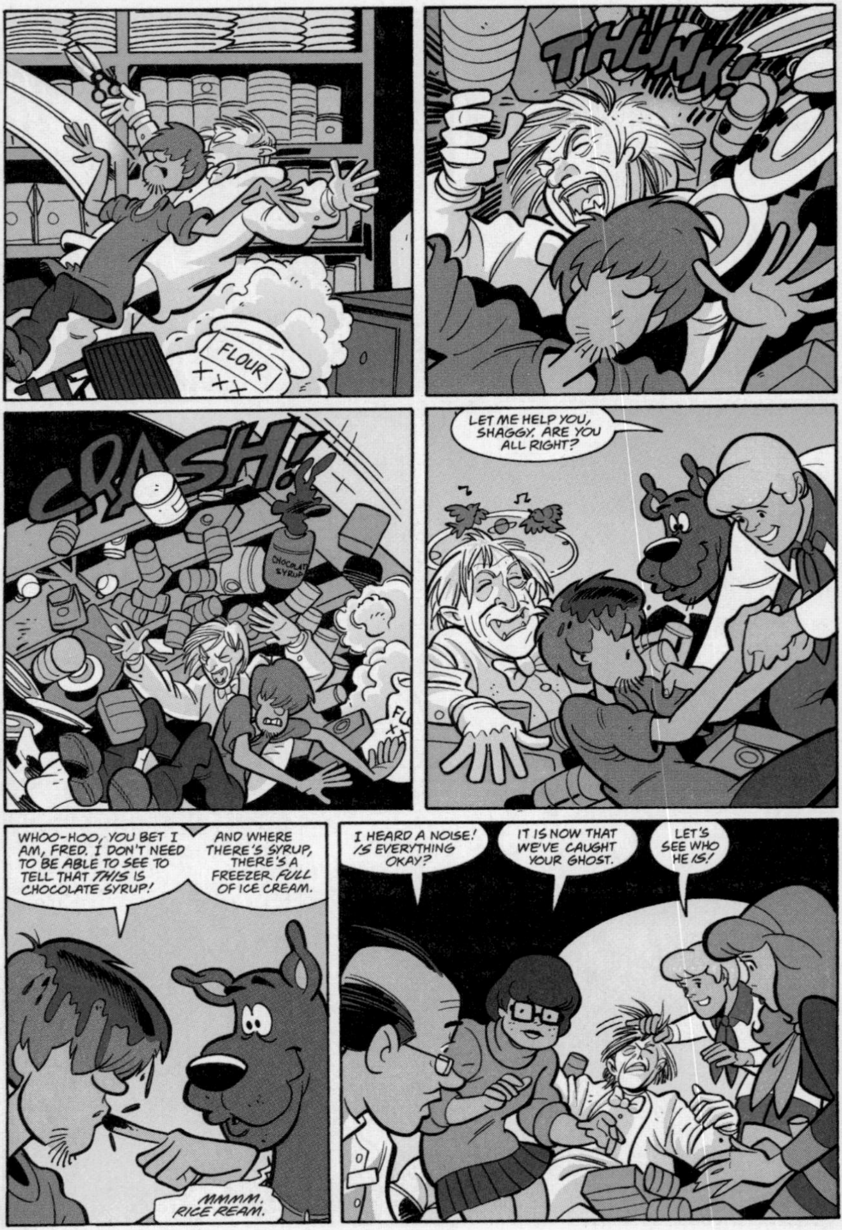

FLOUR
THUNK!
CRASH!
CHOCOLATE SYRUP
LET ME HELP YOU, SHAGGY. ARE YOU ALL RIGHT?
WHOO-HOO, YOU BET I AM, FRED. I DON'T NEED TO BE ABLE TO SEE TO TELL THAT *THIS* IS CHOCOLATE SYRUP!
AND WHERE THERE'S SYRUP, THERE'S A FREEZER *FULL* OF ICE CREAM.
MMMMM. RICE REAM.
I HEARD A NOISE! *IS* EVERYTHING OKAY?
IT IS NOW THAT WE'VE CAUGHT YOUR GHOST.
LET'S SEE WHO HE *IS*!

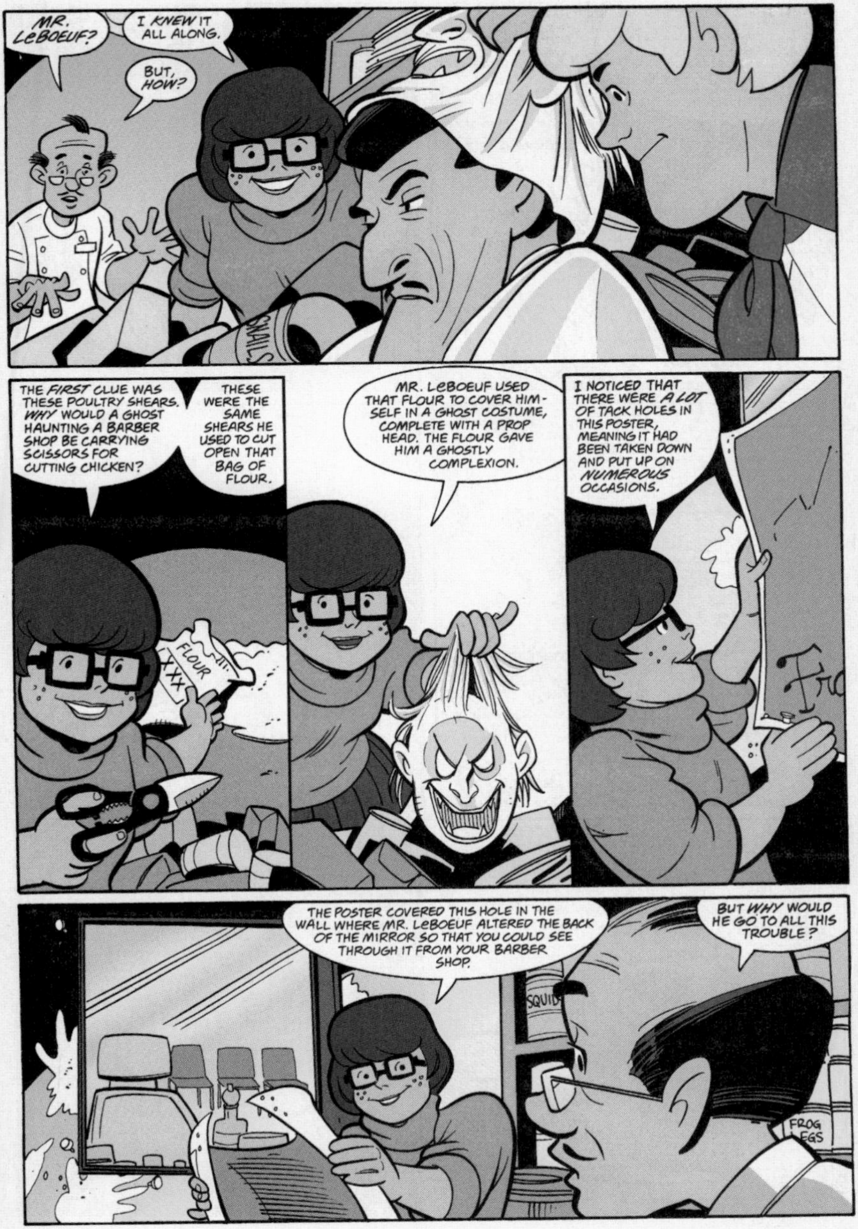
MR. LeBOEUF?
I KNEW IT ALL ALONG.
BUT, HOW?
SNAILS
THE FIRST CLUE WAS THESE POULTRY SHEARS. WHY WOULD A GHOST HAUNTING A BARBER SHOP BE CARRYING SCISSORS FOR CUTTING CHICKEN?
THESE WERE THE SAME SHEARS HE USED TO CUT OPEN THAT BAG OF FLOUR.
FLOUR
XXX
MR. LeBOEUF USED THAT FLOUR TO COVER HIMSELF IN A GHOST COSTUME, COMPLETE WITH A PROP HEAD. THE FLOUR GAVE HIM A GHOSTLY COMPLEXION.
I NOTICED THAT THERE WERE A LOT OF TACK HOLES IN THIS POSTER, MEANING IT HAD BEEN TAKEN DOWN AND PUT UP ON NUMEROUS OCCASIONS.
THE POSTER COVERED THIS HOLE IN THE WALL WHERE MR. LeBOEUF ALTERED THE BACK OF THE MIRROR SO THAT YOU COULD SEE THROUGH IT FROM YOUR BARBER SHOP.
BUT WHY WOULD HE GO TO ALL THIS TROUBLE?
SQUID
FROG LEGS

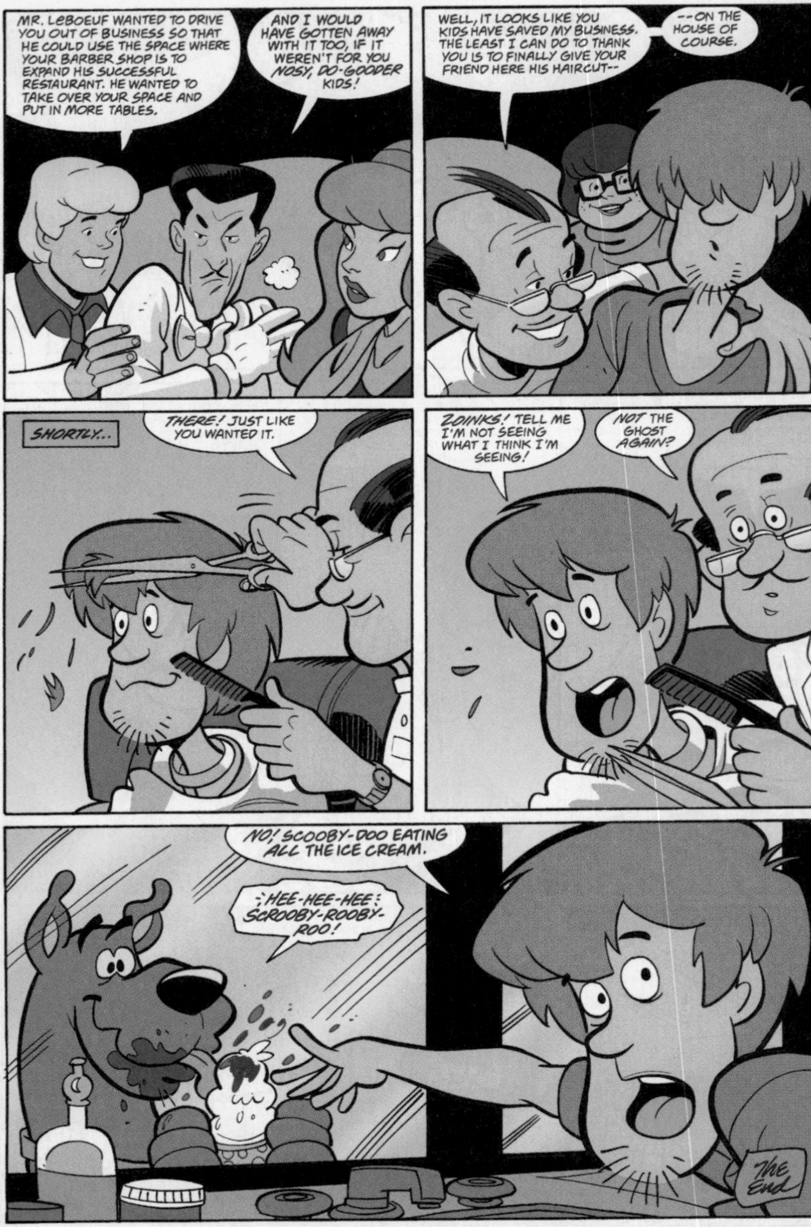

MR. LeBOEUF WANTED TO DRIVE YOU OUT OF BUSINESS SO THAT HE COULD USE THE SPACE WHERE YOUR BARBER SHOP IS TO EXPAND HIS SUCCESSFUL RESTAURANT. HE WANTED TO TAKE OVER YOUR SPACE AND PUT IN MORE TABLES.
AND I WOULD HAVE GOTTEN AWAY WITH IT TOO, IF IT WEREN'T FOR YOU NOSY, DO-GOODER KIDS!
WELL, IT LOOKS LIKE YOU KIDS HAVE SAVED MY BUSINESS. THE LEAST I CAN DO TO THANK YOU IS TO FINALLY GIVE YOUR FRIEND HERE HIS HAIRCUT--
--ON THE HOUSE OF COURSE.
SHORTLY...
THERE! JUST LIKE YOU WANTED IT.
ZOINKS! TELL ME I'M NOT SEEING WHAT I THINK I'M SEEING!
NOT THE GHOST AGAIN?
NO! SCOOBY-DOO EATING ALL THE ICE CREAM.
HEE-HEE-HEE SCROOBY-ROOBY-ROO!
The End

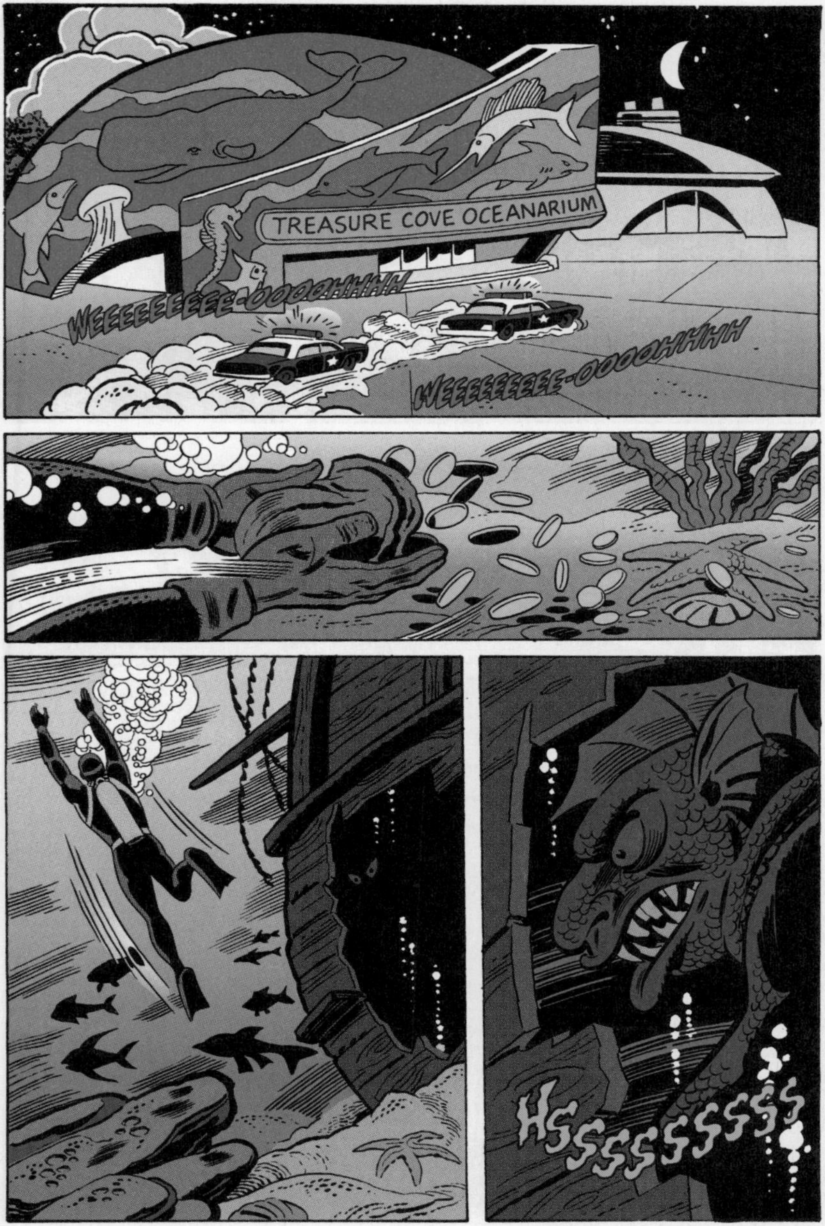
TREASURE COVE OCEANARIUM
WEEEEEEEEE-OOOOHHHHH
WEEEEEEEEE-OOOOHHHHH
HSSSSSSSSSS

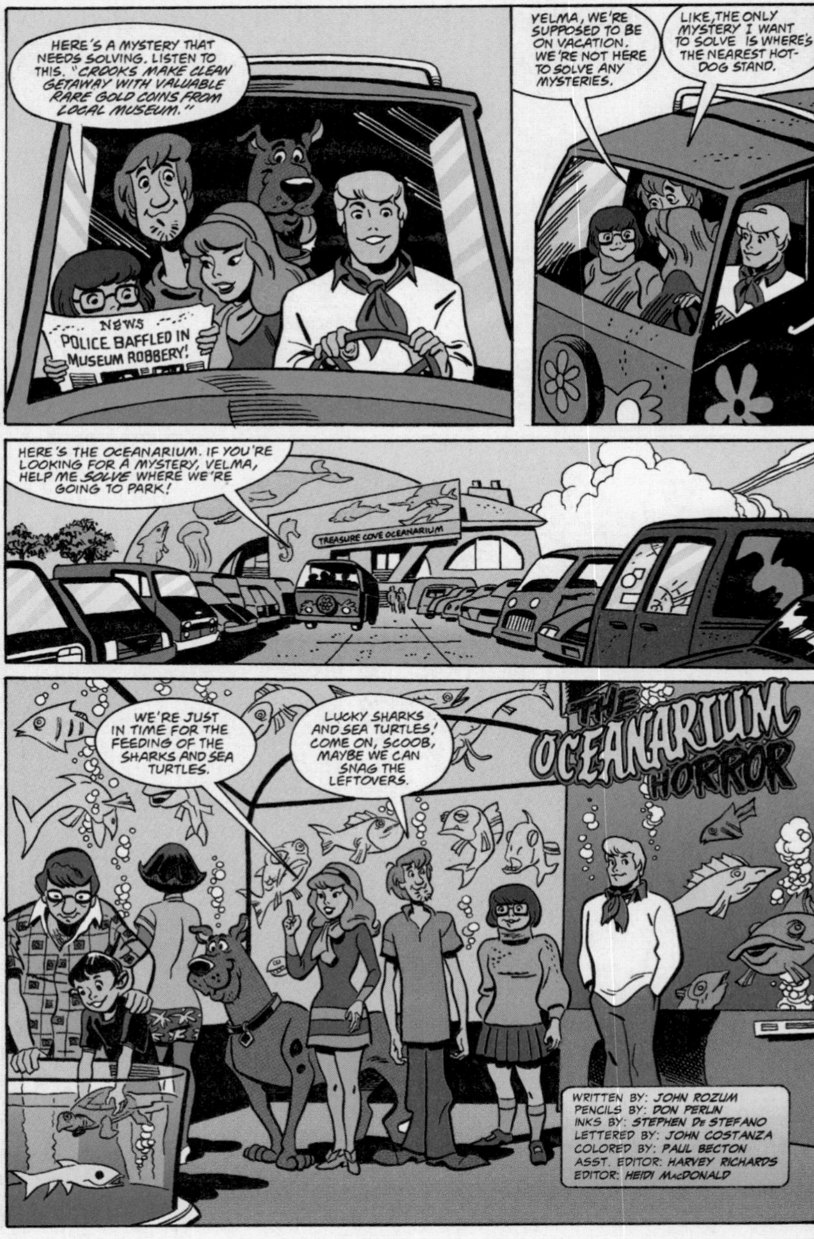
HERE'S A MYSTERY THAT NEEDS SOLVING. LISTEN TO THIS. "CROOKS MAKE CLEAN GETAWAY WITH VALUABLE RARE GOLD COINS FROM LOCAL MUSEUM."
NEWS
POLICE BAFFLED IN MUSEUM ROBBERY!
VELMA, WE'RE SUPPOSED TO BE ON VACATION. WE'RE NOT HERE TO SOLVE ANY MYSTERIES.
LIKE, THE ONLY MYSTERY I WANT TO SOLVE IS WHERE'S THE NEAREST HOT-DOG STAND.
HERE'S THE OCEANARIUM. IF YOU'RE LOOKING FOR A MYSTERY, VELMA, HELP ME SOLVE WHERE WE'RE GOING TO PARK!
TREASURE COVE OCEANARIUM
WE'RE JUST IN TIME FOR THE FEEDING OF THE SHARKS AND SEA TURTLES.
LUCKY SHARKS AND SEA TURTLES! COME ON, SCOOB, MAYBE WE CAN SNAG THE LEFTOVERS.
THE OCEANARIUM HORROR
WRITTEN BY: JOHN ROZUM
PENCILS BY: DON PERLIN
INKS BY: STEPHEN DE STEFANO
LETTERED BY: JOHN COSTANZA
COLORED BY: PAUL BECTON
ASST. EDITOR: HARVEY RICHARDS
EDITOR: HEIDI MACDONALD

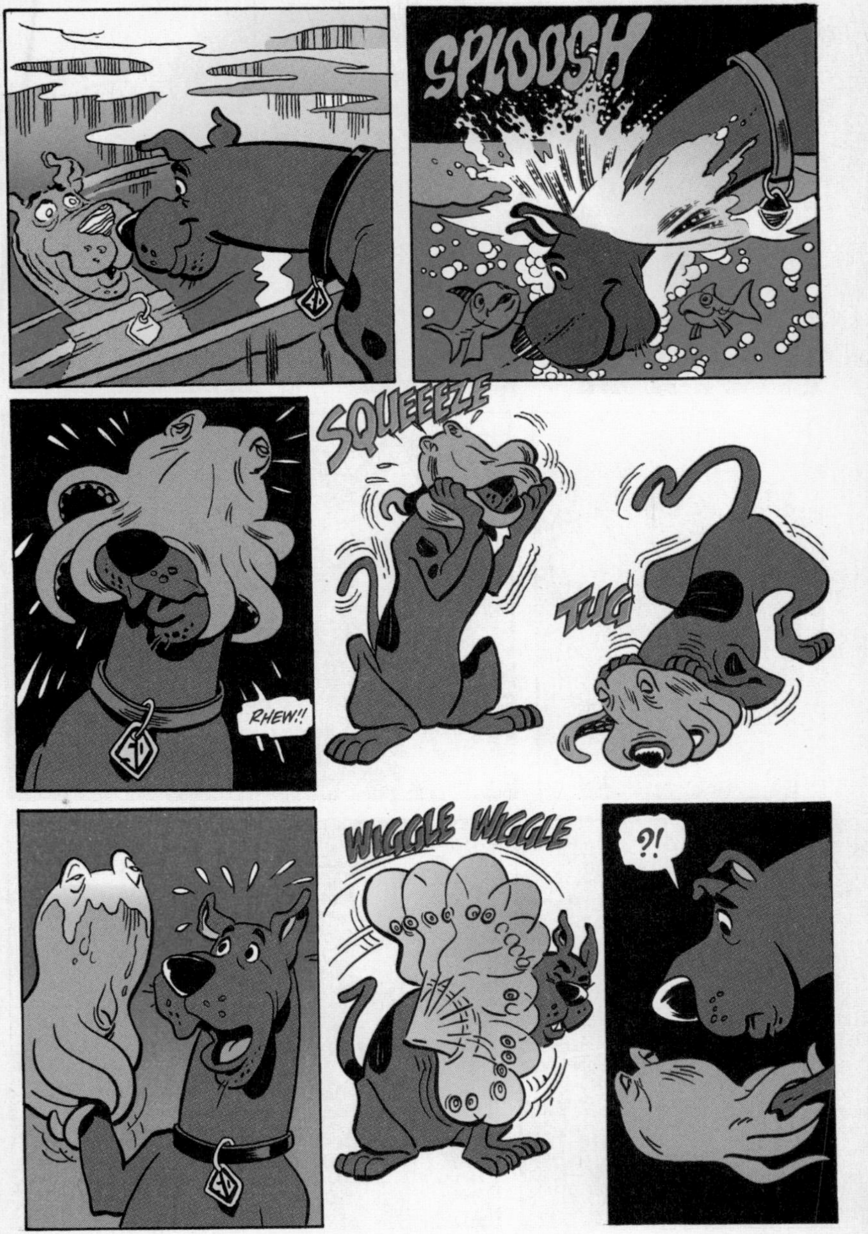
SPLOOSH
RHEW!!
SQUEEEZE
TUG
WIGGLE WIGGLE
?!

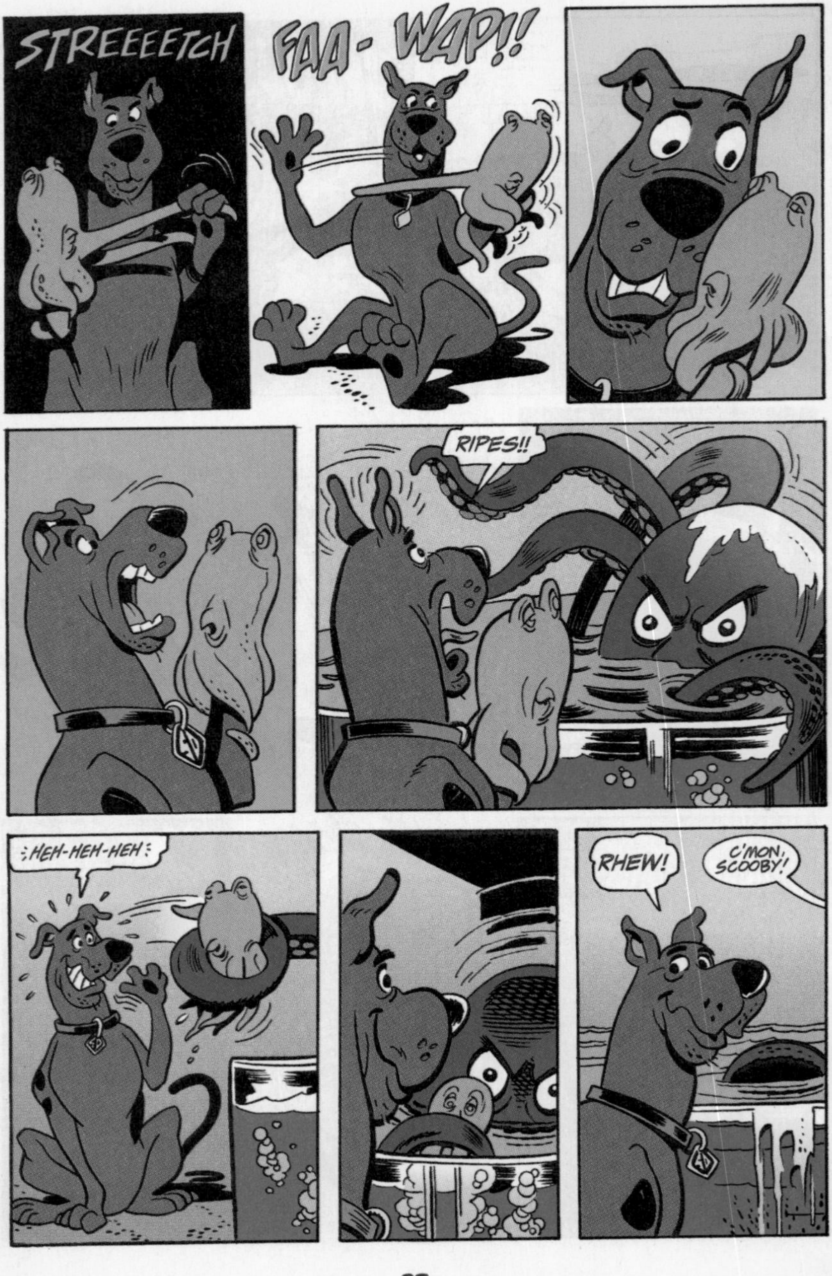
STREEEEETCH
FAA-WAP!!
RIPES!!
HEH-HEH-HEH
RHEW!
C'MON, SCOOBY!

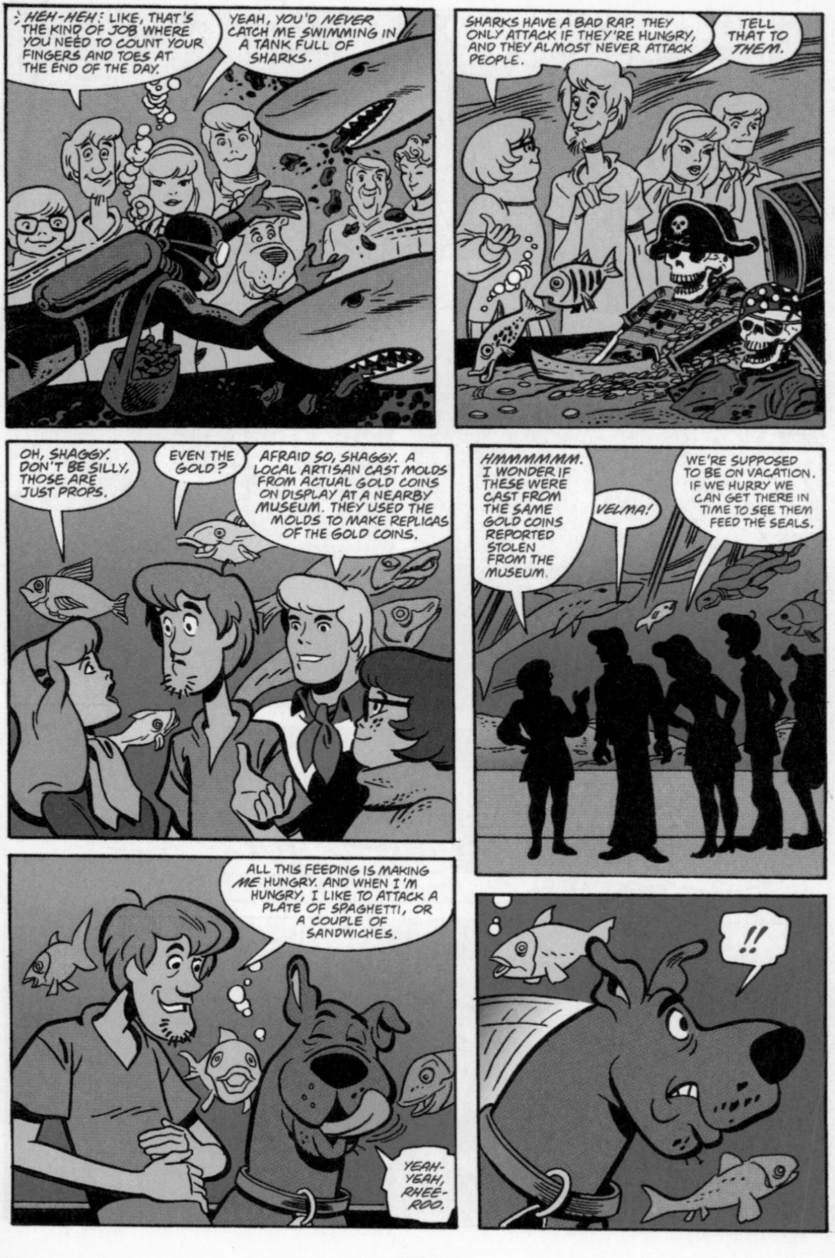
HEH-HEH: LIKE, THAT'S THE KIND OF JOB WHERE YOU NEED TO COUNT YOUR FINGERS AND TOES AT THE END OF THE DAY.
YEAH, YOU'D NEVER CATCH ME SWIMMING IN A TANK FULL OF SHARKS.
SHARKS HAVE A BAD RAP. THEY ONLY ATTACK IF THEY'RE HUNGRY, AND THEY ALMOST NEVER ATTACK PEOPLE.
TELL THAT TO THEM.
OH, SHAGGY. DON'T BE SILLY, THOSE ARE JUST PROPS.
EVEN THE GOLD?
AFRAID SO, SHAGGY. A LOCAL ARTISAN CAST MOLDS FROM ACTUAL GOLD COINS ON DISPLAY AT A NEARBY MUSEUM. THEY USED THE MOLDS TO MAKE REPLICAS OF THE GOLD COINS.
HMMMMMM. I WONDER IF THESE WERE CAST FROM THE SAME GOLD COINS REPORTED STOLEN FROM THE MUSEUM.
VELMA!
WE'RE SUPPOSED TO BE ON VACATION. IF WE HURRY WE CAN GET THERE IN TIME TO SEE THEM FEED THE SEALS.
ALL THIS FEEDING IS MAKING ME HUNGRY. AND WHEN I'M HUNGRY, I LIKE TO ATTACK A PLATE OF SPAGHETTI, OR A COUPLE OF SANDWICHES.
YEAH-YEAH, RHEE-ROO.
!!

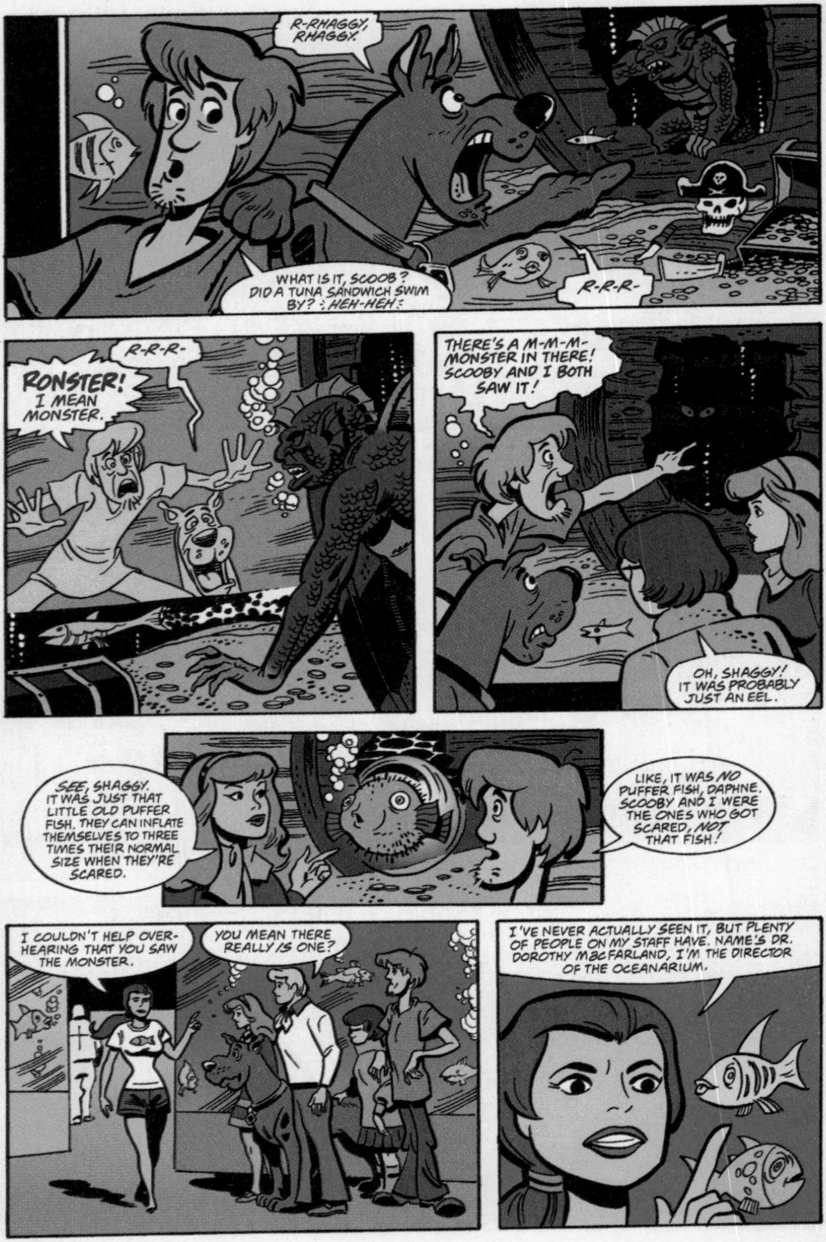

R-RHAGGY, RHAGGY.
WHAT IS IT, SCOOB? DID A TUNA SANDWICH SWIM BY? HEH-HEH
R-R-R-
R-R-R-
RONSTER! I MEAN MONSTER.
THERE'S A M-M-M-MONSTER IN THERE! SCOOBY AND I BOTH SAW IT!
OH, SHAGGY! IT WAS PROBABLY JUST AN EEL.
SEE, SHAGGY. IT WAS JUST THAT LITTLE OLD PUFFER FISH. THEY CAN INFLATE THEMSELVES TO THREE TIMES THEIR NORMAL SIZE WHEN THEY'RE SCARED.
LIKE, IT WAS NO PUFFER FISH, DAPHNE. SCOOBY AND I WERE THE ONES WHO GOT SCARED, NOT THAT FISH!
I COULDN'T HELP OVER-HEARING THAT YOU SAW THE MONSTER.
YOU MEAN THERE REALLY IS ONE?
I'VE NEVER ACTUALLY SEEN IT, BUT PLENTY OF PEOPLE ON MY STAFF HAVE. NAME'S DR. DOROTHY MacFARLAND, I'M THE DIRECTOR OF THE OCEANARIUM.

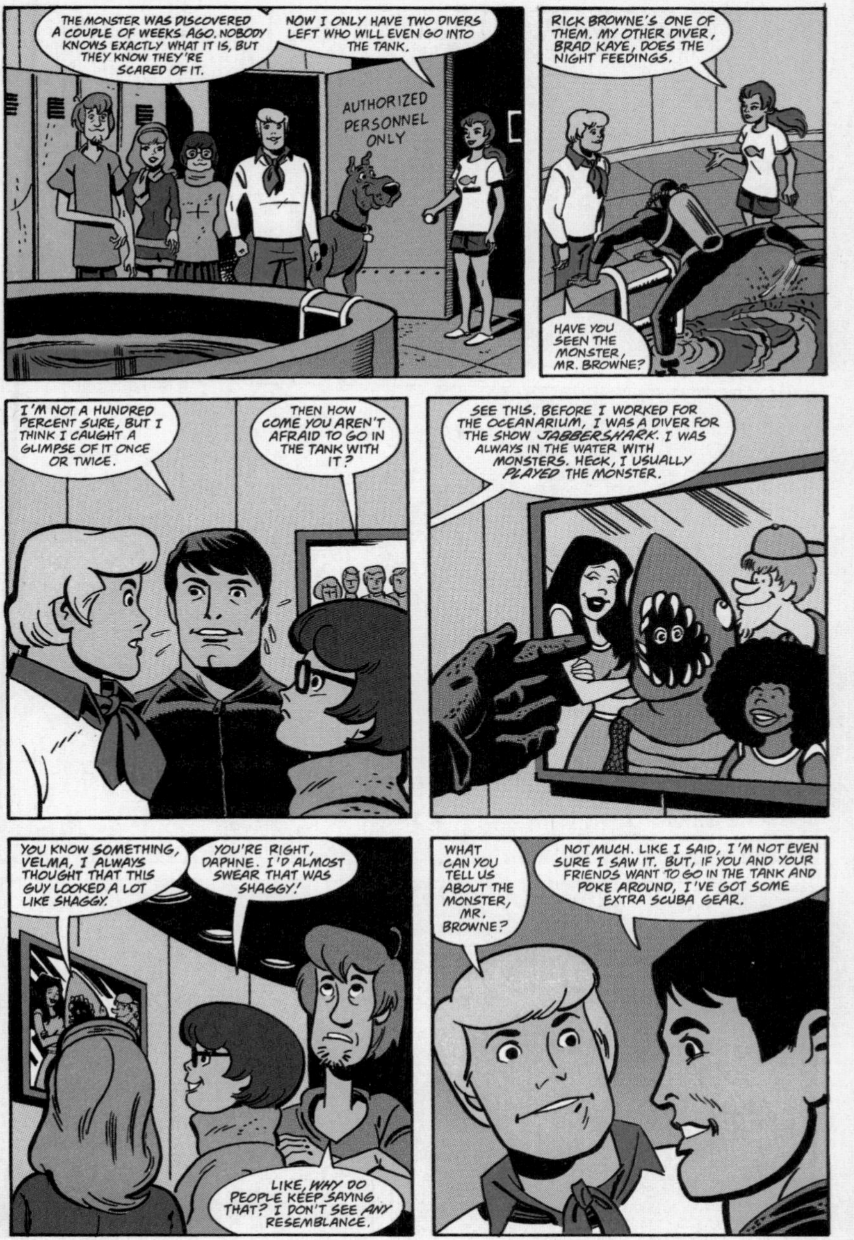
THE MONSTER WAS DISCOVERED A COUPLE OF WEEKS AGO. NOBODY KNOWS EXACTLY WHAT IT IS, BUT THEY KNOW THEY'RE SCARED OF IT.
NOW I ONLY HAVE TWO DIVERS LEFT WHO WILL EVEN GO INTO THE TANK.
AUTHORIZED PERSONNEL ONLY
RICK BROWNE'S ONE OF THEM. MY OTHER DIVER, BRAD KAYE, DOES THE NIGHT FEEDINGS.
HAVE YOU SEEN THE MONSTER, MR. BROWNE?
I'M NOT A HUNDRED PERCENT SURE, BUT I THINK I CAUGHT A GLIMPSE OF IT ONCE OR TWICE.
THEN HOW COME YOU AREN'T AFRAID TO GO IN THE TANK WITH IT?
SEE THIS. BEFORE I WORKED FOR THE OCEANARIUM, I WAS A DIVER FOR THE SHOW JABBERSHARK. I WAS ALWAYS IN THE WATER WITH MONSTERS. HECK, I USUALLY PLAYED THE MONSTER.
YOU KNOW SOMETHING, VELMA, I ALWAYS THOUGHT THAT THIS GUY LOOKED A LOT LIKE SHAGGY.
YOU'RE RIGHT, DAPHNE. I'D ALMOST SWEAR THAT WAS SHAGGY!
LIKE, WHY DO PEOPLE KEEP SAYING THAT? I DON'T SEE ANY RESEMBLANCE.
WHAT CAN YOU TELL US ABOUT THE MONSTER, MR. BROWNE?
NOT MUCH. LIKE I SAID, I'M NOT EVEN SURE I SAW IT. BUT, IF YOU AND YOUR FRIENDS WANT TO GO IN THE TANK AND POKE AROUND, I'VE GOT SOME EXTRA SCUBA GEAR.

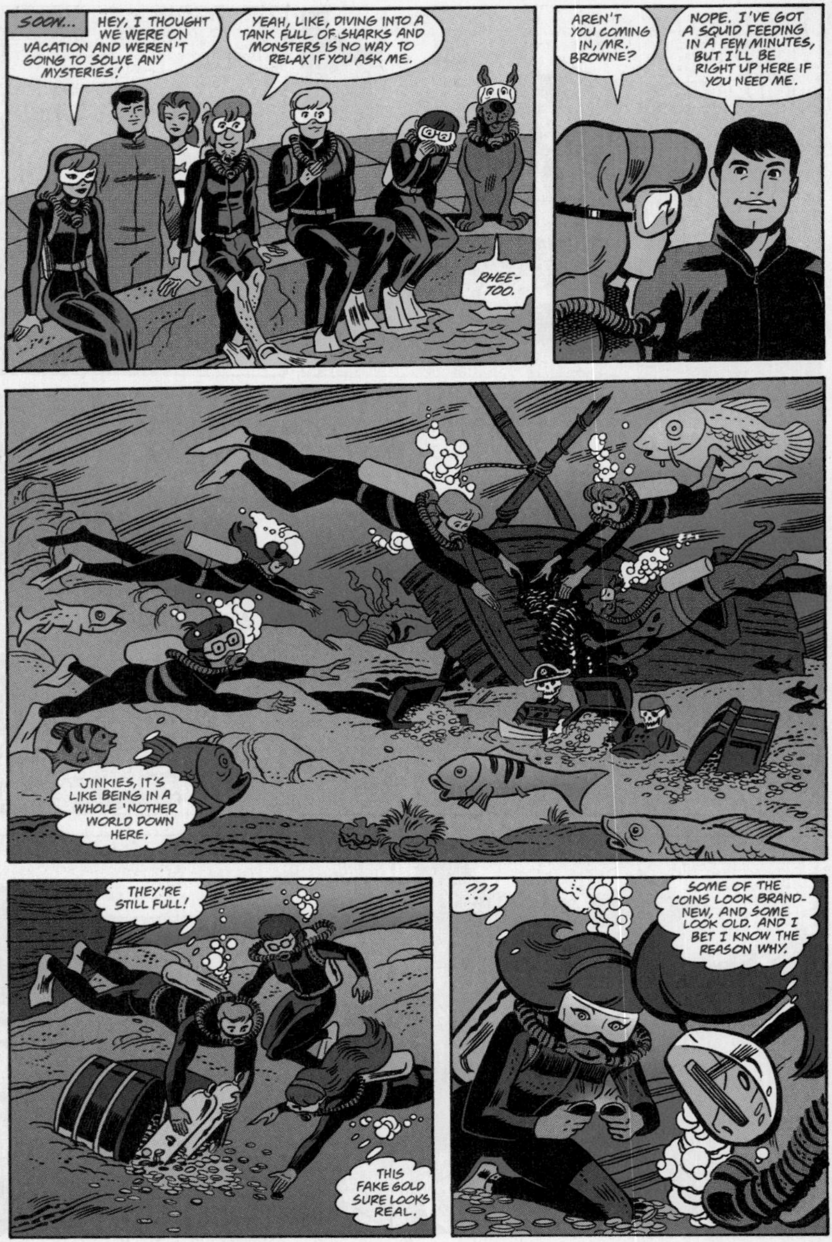
SOON...
HEY, I THOUGHT WE WERE ON VACATION AND WEREN'T GOING TO SOLVE ANY MYSTERIES!
YEAH, LIKE, DIVING INTO A TANK FULL OF SHARKS AND MONSTERS IS NO WAY TO RELAX IF YOU ASK ME.
RHEE-TOO.
AREN'T YOU COMING IN, MR. BROWNE?
NOPE. I'VE GOT A SQUID FEEDING IN A FEW MINUTES, BUT I'LL BE RIGHT UP HERE IF YOU NEED ME.
JINKIES, IT'S LIKE BEING IN A WHOLE 'NOTHER WORLD DOWN HERE.
THEY'RE STILL FULL!
THIS FAKE GOLD SURE LOOKS REAL.
???
SOME OF THE COINS LOOK BRAND-NEW, AND SOME LOOK OLD. AND I BET I KNOW THE REASON WHY.

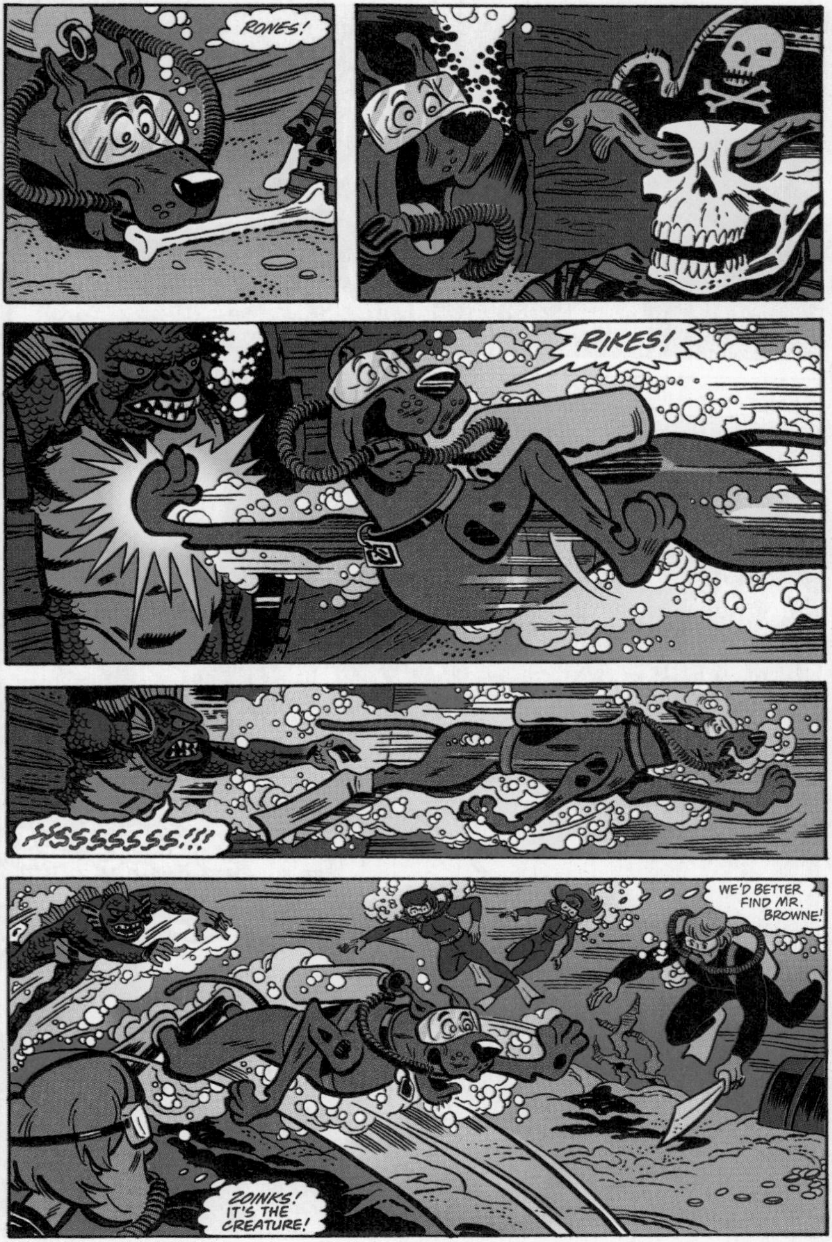
RONES!
RIKES!
HSSSSSSSS!!!
WE'D BETTER FIND MR. BROWNE!
ZOINKS! IT'S THE CREATURE!

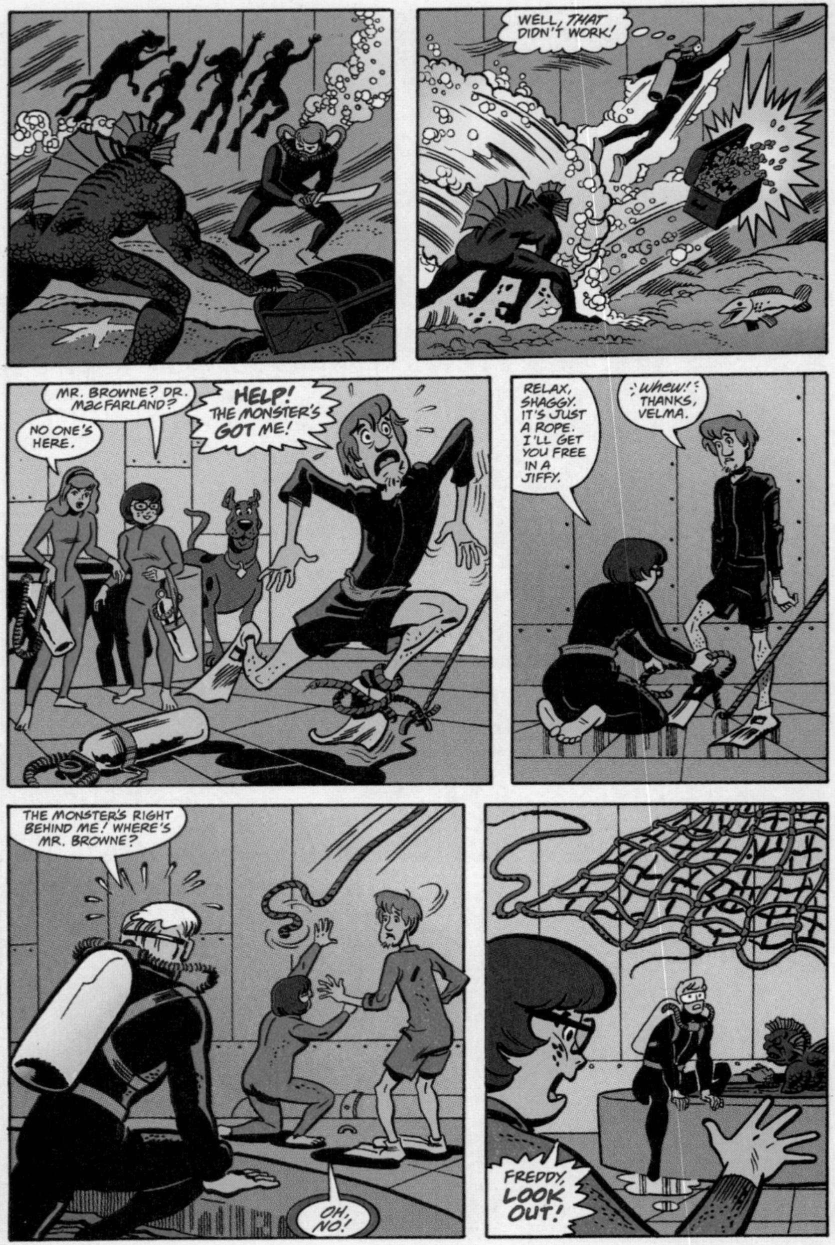

WELL, THAT DIDN'T WORK!
MR. BROWNE? DR. MACFARLAND?
NO ONE'S HERE.
HELP! THE MONSTER'S GOT ME!
RELAX, SHAGGY. IT'S JUST A ROPE. I'LL GET YOU FREE IN A JIFFY.
Whew! THANKS, VELMA.
THE MONSTER'S RIGHT BEHIND ME! WHERE'S MR. BROWNE?
OH, NO!
FREDDY, LOOK OUT!

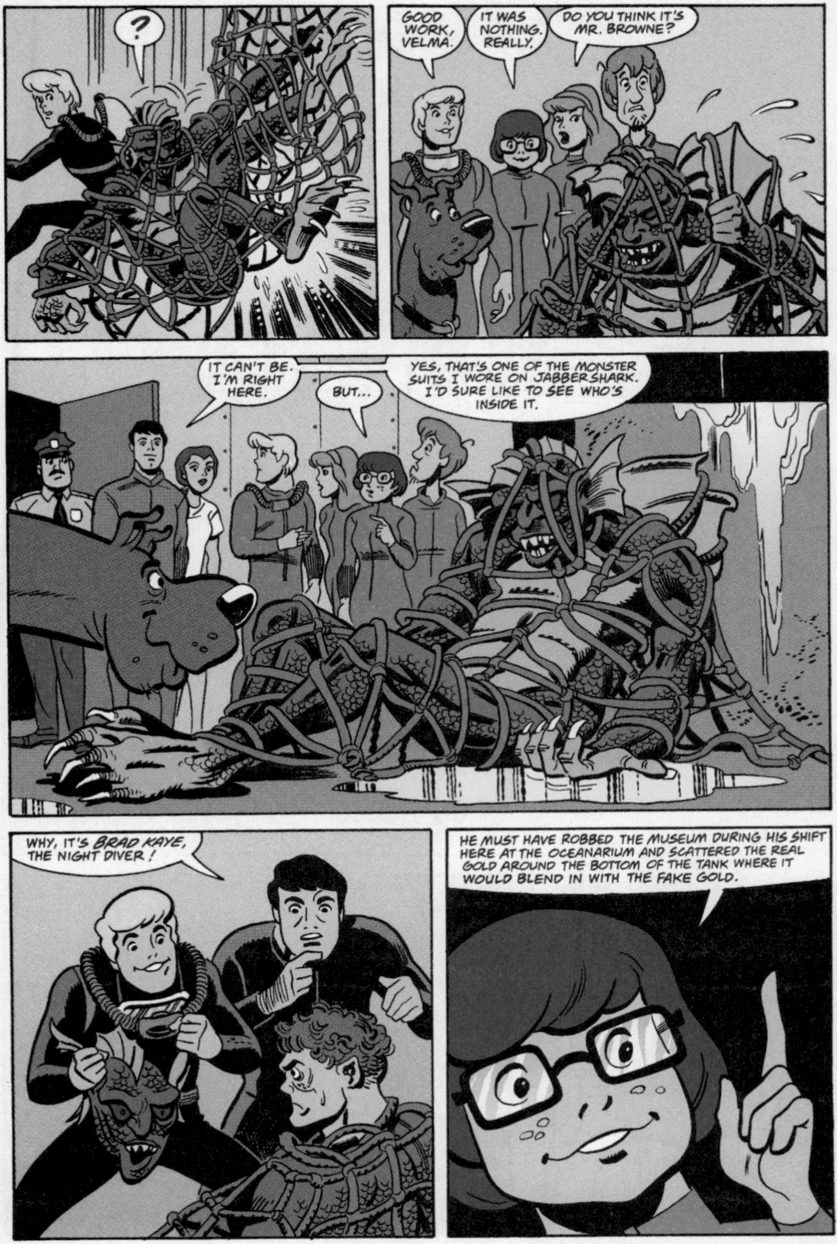
?
GOOD WORK, VELMA.
IT WAS NOTHING. REALLY.
DO YOU THINK IT'S MR. BROWNE?
IT CAN'T BE. I'M RIGHT HERE.
BUT...
YES, THAT'S ONE OF THE MONSTER SUITS I WORE ON JABBERSHARK. I'D SURE LIKE TO SEE WHO'S INSIDE IT.
WHY, IT'S BRAD KAYE, THE NIGHT DIVER!
HE MUST HAVE ROBBED THE MUSEUM DURING HIS SHIFT HERE AT THE OCEANARIUM AND SCATTERED THE REAL GOLD AROUND THE BOTTOM OF THE TANK WHERE IT WOULD BLEND IN WITH THE FAKE GOLD.

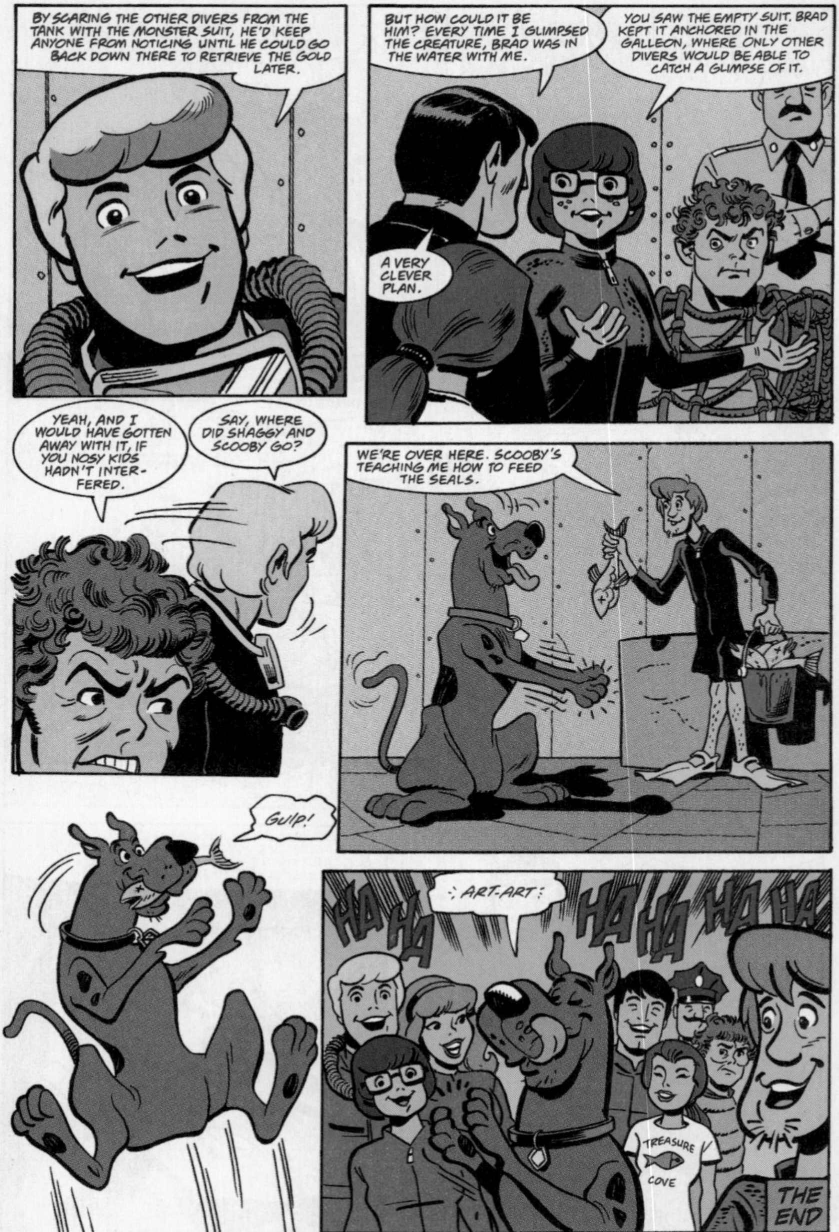

BY SCARING THE OTHER DIVERS FROM THE TANK WITH THE MONSTER SUIT, HE'D KEEP ANYONE FROM NOTICING UNTIL HE COULD GO BACK DOWN THERE TO RETRIEVE THE GOLD LATER.
BUT HOW COULD IT BE HIM? EVERY TIME I GLIMPSED THE CREATURE, BRAD WAS IN THE WATER WITH ME.
YOU SAW THE EMPTY SUIT. BRAD KEPT IT ANCHORED IN THE GALLEON, WHERE ONLY OTHER DIVERS WOULD BE ABLE TO CATCH A GLIMPSE OF IT.
A VERY CLEVER PLAN.
YEAH, AND I WOULD HAVE GOTTEN AWAY WITH IT, IF YOU NOSY KIDS HADN'T INTER-FERED.
SAY, WHERE DID SHAGGY AND SCOOBY GO?
WE'RE OVER HERE. SCOOBY'S TEACHING ME HOW TO FEED THE SEALS.
GULP!
ART-ART
HA HA HA HA HA HA HA
TREASURE COVE
THE END

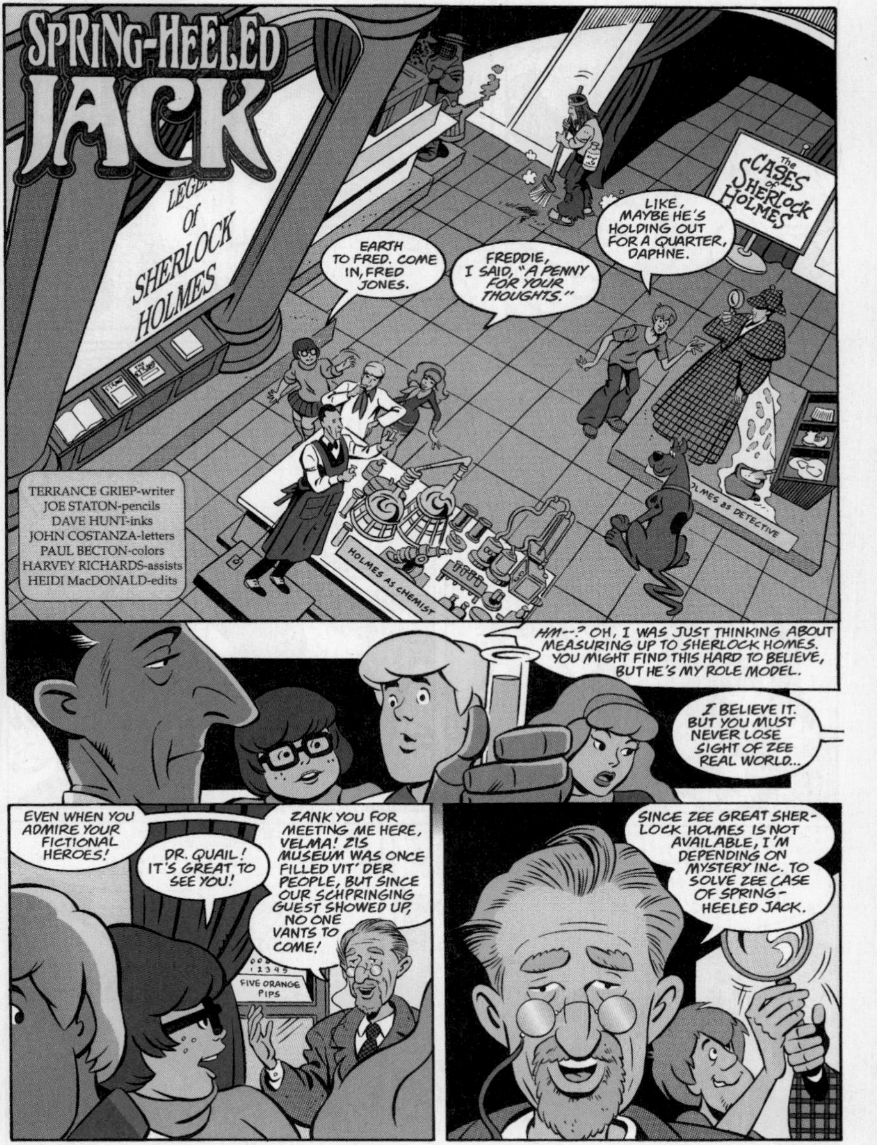
SPRING-HEELED JACK
LEGENDS of SHERLOCK HOLMES
The CASES of SHERLOCK HOLMES
EARTH TO FRED. COME IN, FRED JONES.
FREDDIE, I SAID, "A PENNY FOR YOUR THOUGHTS."
LIKE, MAYBE HE'S HOLDING OUT FOR A QUARTER, DAPHNE.
TERRANCE GRIEP-writer
JOE STATON-pencils
DAVE HUNT-inks
JOHN COSTANZA-letters
PAUL BECTON-colors
HARVEY RICHARDS-assists
HEIDI MacDONALD-edits
HOLMES AS CHEMIST
HOLMES AS DETECTIVE
HM--? OH, I WAS JUST THINKING ABOUT MEASURING UP TO SHERLOCK HOMES. YOU MIGHT FIND THIS HARD TO BELIEVE, BUT HE'S MY ROLE MODEL.
I BELIEVE IT. BUT YOU MUST NEVER LOSE SIGHT OF ZEE REAL WORLD...
EVEN WHEN YOU ADMIRE YOUR FICTIONAL HEROES!
DR. QUAIL! IT'S GREAT TO SEE YOU!
ZANK YOU FOR MEETING ME HERE, VELMA! ZIS MUSEUM WAS ONCE FILLED VIT' DER PEOPLE, BUT SINCE OUR SCHPRINGING GUEST SHOWED UP, NO ONE VANTS TO COME!
FIVE ORANGE PIPS
SINCE ZEE GREAT SHERLOCK HOLMES IS NOT AVAILABLE, I'M DEPENDING ON MYSTERY INC. TO SOLVE ZEE CASE OF SPRING-HEELED JACK.

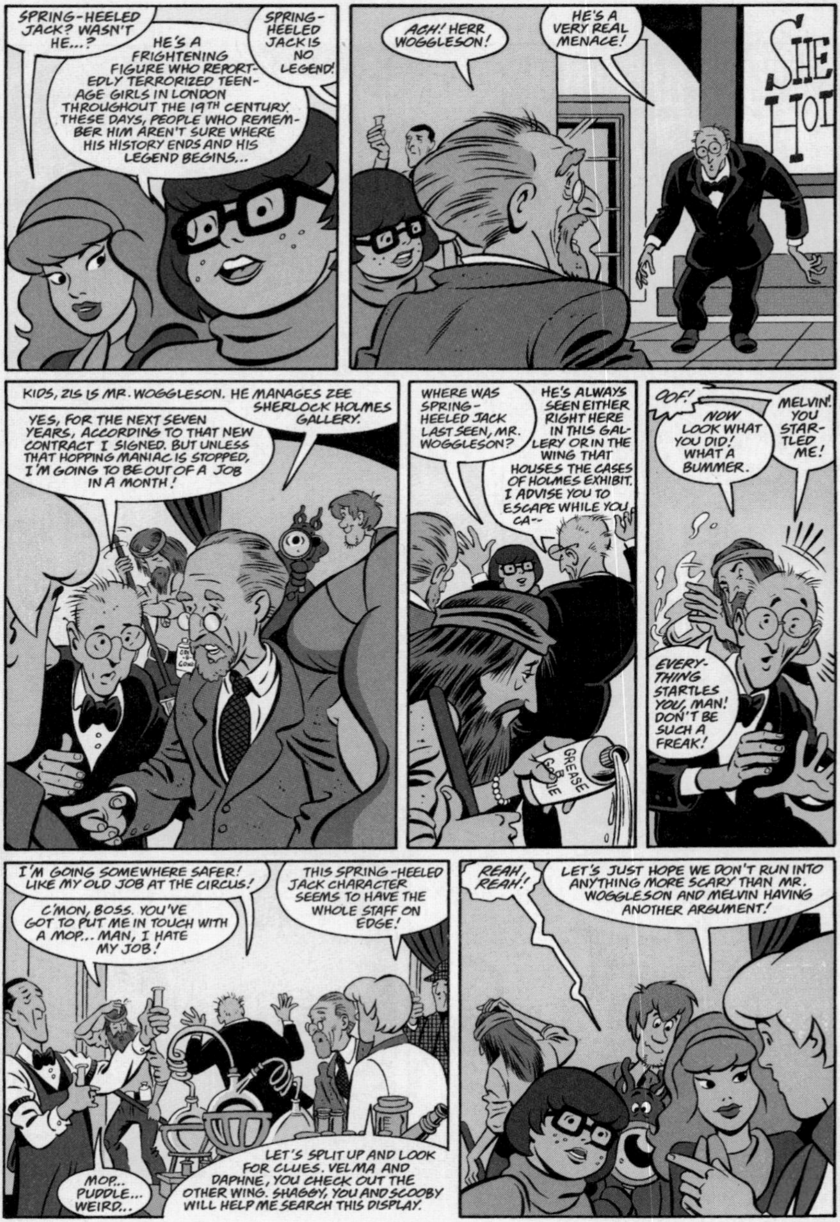

SPRING-HEELED JACK? WASN'T HE...?
HE'S A FRIGHTENING FIGURE WHO REPORTEDLY TERRORIZED TEENAGE GIRLS IN LONDON THROUGHOUT THE 19TH CENTURY. THESE DAYS, PEOPLE WHO REMEMBER HIM AREN'T SURE WHERE HIS HISTORY ENDS AND HIS LEGEND BEGINS...
SPRING-HEELED JACK IS NO LEGEND!
ACH! HERR WOGGLESON!
HE'S A VERY REAL MENACE!
KIDS, ZIS IS MR. WOGGLESON. HE MANAGES ZEE SHERLOCK HOLMES GALLERY.
YES, FOR THE NEXT SEVEN YEARS, ACCORDING TO THAT NEW CONTRACT I SIGNED. BUT UNLESS THAT HOPPING MANIAC IS STOPPED, I'M GOING TO BE OUT OF A JOB IN A MONTH!
WHERE WAS SPRING-HEELED JACK LAST SEEN, MR. WOGGLESON?
HE'S ALWAYS SEEN EITHER RIGHT HERE IN THIS GALLERY OR IN THE WING THAT HOUSES THE CASES OF HOLMES EXHIBIT. I ADVISE YOU TO ESCAPE WHILE YOU CA--
GREASE B GONE
OOF!
NOW LOOK WHAT YOU DID! WHAT A BUMMER.
MELVIN! YOU STARTLED ME!
EVERYTHING STARTLES YOU, MAN! DON'T BE SUCH A FREAK!
I'M GOING SOMEWHERE SAFER! LIKE MY OLD JOB AT THE CIRCUS!
C'MON, BOSS. YOU'VE GOT TO PUT ME IN TOUCH WITH A MOP... MAN, I HATE MY JOB!
THIS SPRING-HEELED JACK CHARACTER SEEMS TO HAVE THE WHOLE STAFF ON EDGE!
MOP... PUDDLE... WEIRD...
LET'S SPLIT UP AND LOOK FOR CLUES. VELMA AND DAPHNE, YOU CHECK OUT THE OTHER WING. SHAGGY, YOU AND SCOOBY WILL HELP ME SEARCH THIS DISPLAY.
REAH, REAH!
LET'S JUST HOPE WE DON'T RUN INTO ANYTHING MORE SCARY THAN MR. WOGGLESON AND MELVIN HAVING ANOTHER ARGUMENT!

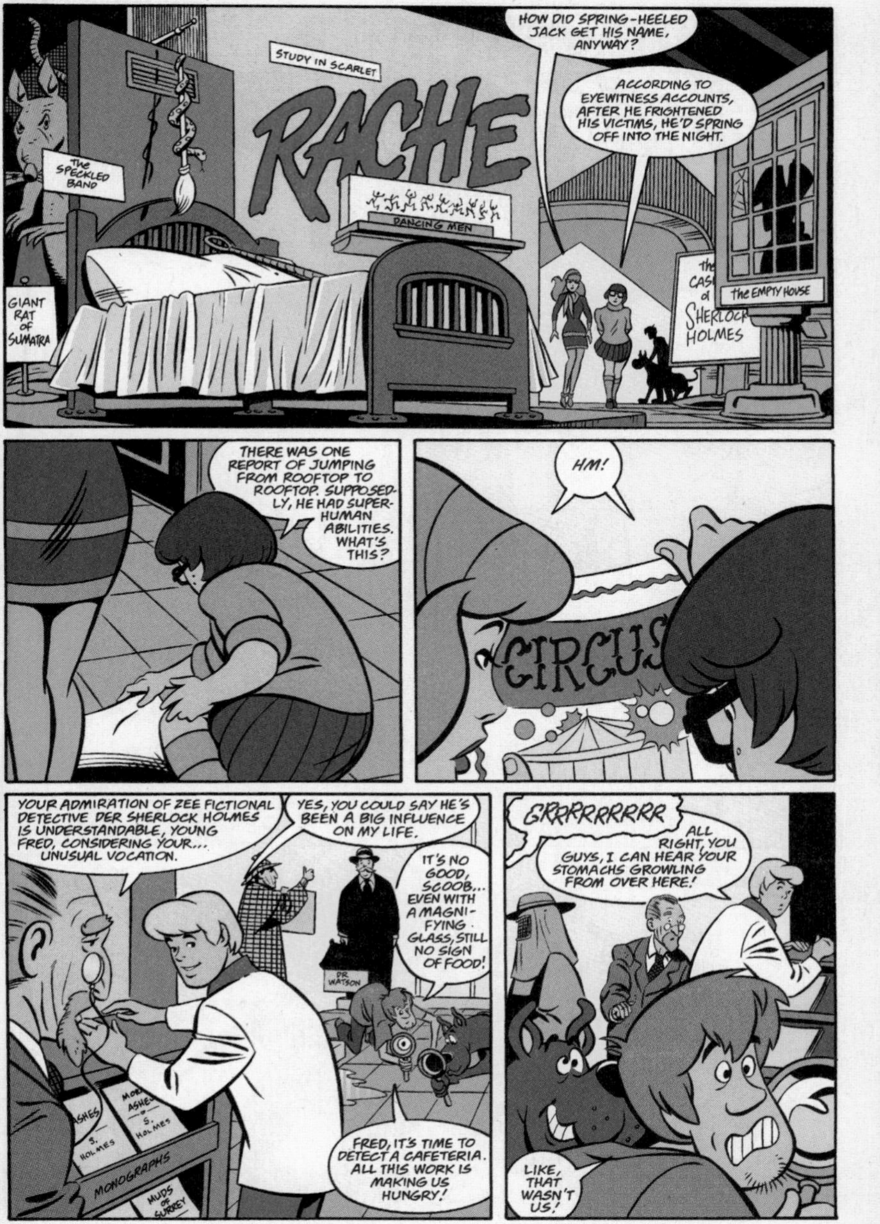

HOW DID SPRING-HEELED JACK GET HIS NAME, ANYWAY?
STUDY IN SCARLET
RACHE
The SPECKLED BAND
GIANT RAT OF SUMATRA
DANCING MEN
ACCORDING TO EYEWITNESS ACCOUNTS, AFTER HE FRIGHTENED HIS VICTIMS, HE'D SPRING OFF INTO THE NIGHT.
The CASE of SHERLOCK HOLMES
The EMPTY HOUSE
THERE WAS ONE REPORT OF JUMPING FROM ROOFTOP TO ROOFTOP. SUPPOSEDLY, HE HAD SUPER-HUMAN ABILITIES. WHAT'S THIS?
HM!
CIRCUS
YOUR ADMIRATION OF ZEE FICTIONAL DETECTIVE DER SHERLOCK HOLMES IS UNDERSTANDABLE, YOUNG FRED, CONSIDERING YOUR... UNUSUAL VOCATION.
YES, YOU COULD SAY HE'S BEEN A BIG INFLUENCE ON MY LIFE.
IT'S NO GOOD, SCOOB... EVEN WITH A MAGNIFYING GLASS, STILL NO SIGN OF FOOD!
DR. WATSON
ASHES S. HOLMES
MORE ASHES of S. HOLMES
MONOGRAPHS
MUDS OF SURREY
FRED, IT'S TIME TO DETECT A CAFETERIA. ALL THIS WORK IS MAKING US HUNGRY!
GRRRRRRRRR
ALL RIGHT, YOU GUYS, I CAN HEAR YOUR STOMACHS GROWLING FROM OVER HERE!
LIKE, THAT WASN'T US!

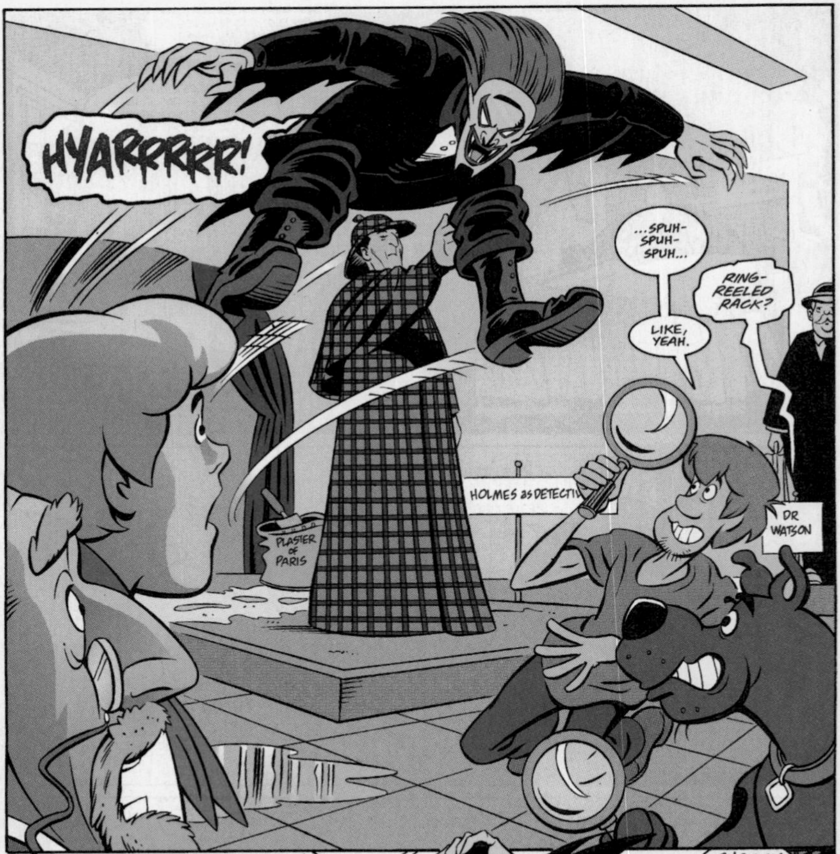
HYARRRRR!
...SPUH-SPUH-SPUH...
LIKE, YEAH.
RING-REELED RACK?
HOLMES as DETECTIVE
DR WATSON
PLASTER OF PARIS

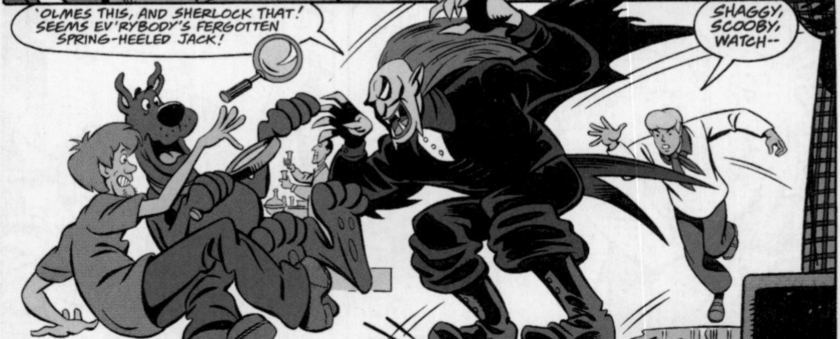
'OLMES THIS, AND SHERLOCK THAT! SEEMS EV'RYBODY'S FERGOTTEN SPRING-HEELED JACK!
SHAGGY, SCOOBY, WATCH--

OO-WAA-OOO-HH!

SSSLLL-YURPP!

MIST

KLONK!

OLMES as CHEMI

WHEN VICTORIA BEGAN 'ER RULE, MINE WAS A NAME SPOKEN IN FRIGHTENED WHISPERS.

WHERE WAS BALLY 'OLMES THEN, EH? WHERE WAS 'E?

The

HOLM

REDDIE!

ARE YOU OKAY?

The LEGEND Of ERLO

W-WATSON? IS THAT YOU, OLD FRIEND?

DR. WATSON...?

HOLMES

95

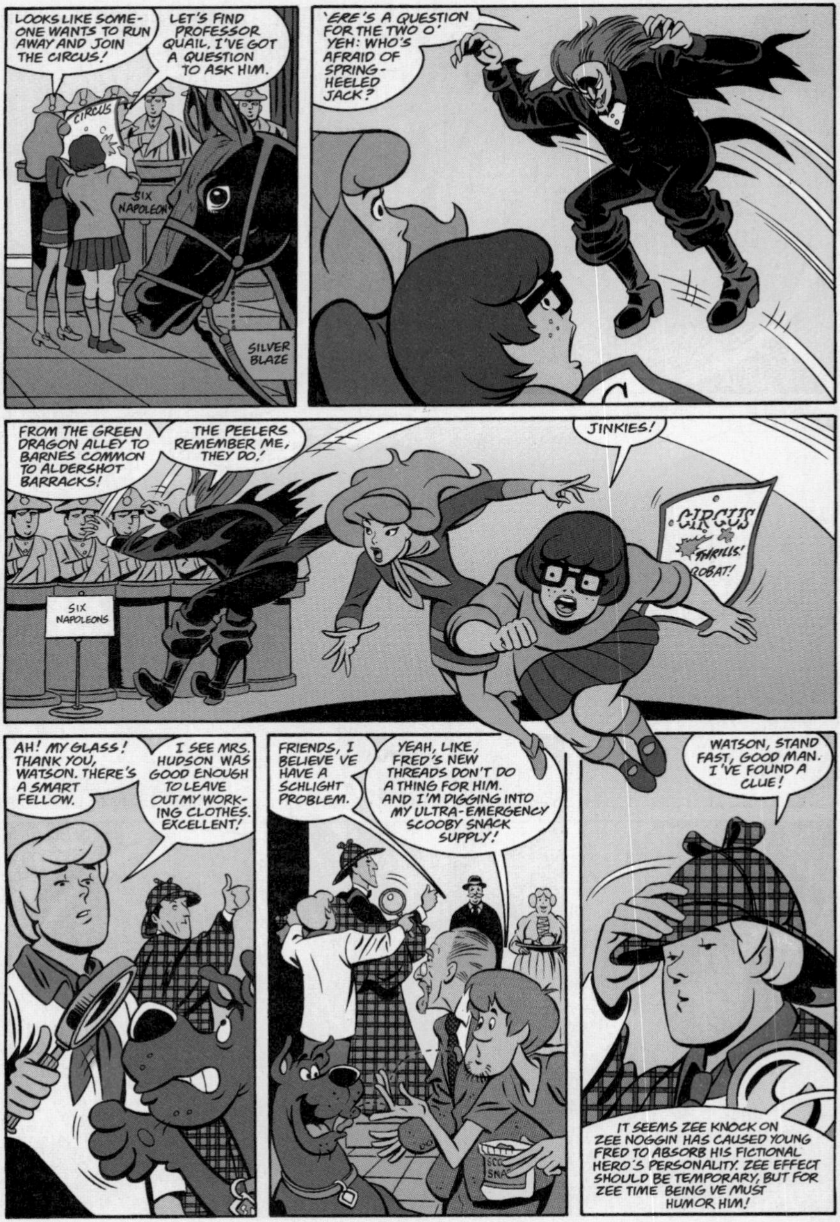

LOOKS LIKE SOME-ONE WANTS TO RUN AWAY AND JOIN THE CIRCUS!
LET'S FIND PROFESSOR QUAIL. I'VE GOT A QUESTION TO ASK HIM.
CIRCUS
SIX NAPOLEON
SILVER BLAZE
'ERE'S A QUESTION FOR THE TWO O' YEH: WHO'S AFRAID OF SPRING-HEELED JACK?
FROM THE GREEN DRAGON ALLEY TO BARNES COMMON TO ALDERSHOT BARRACKS!
THE PEELERS REMEMBER ME, THEY DO!
JINKIES!
SIX NAPOLEONS
CIRCUS
THRILLS!
ROBAT!
AH! MY GLASS! THANK YOU, WATSON. THERE'S A SMART FELLOW.
I SEE MRS. HUDSON WAS GOOD ENOUGH TO LEAVE OUT MY WORKING CLOTHES. EXCELLENT!
FRIENDS, I BELIEVE VE HAVE A SCHLIGHT PROBLEM.
YEAH, LIKE, FRED'S NEW THREADS DON'T DO A THING FOR HIM. AND I'M DIGGING INTO MY ULTRA-EMERGENCY SCOOBY SNACK SUPPLY!
WATSON, STAND FAST, GOOD MAN. I'VE FOUND A CLUE!
IT SEEMS ZEE KNOCK ON ZEE NOGGIN HAS CAUSED YOUNG FRED TO ABSORB HIS FICTIONAL HERO'S PERSONALITY. ZEE EFFECT SHOULD BE TEMPORARY, BUT FOR ZEE TIME BEING VE MUST HUMOR HIM!

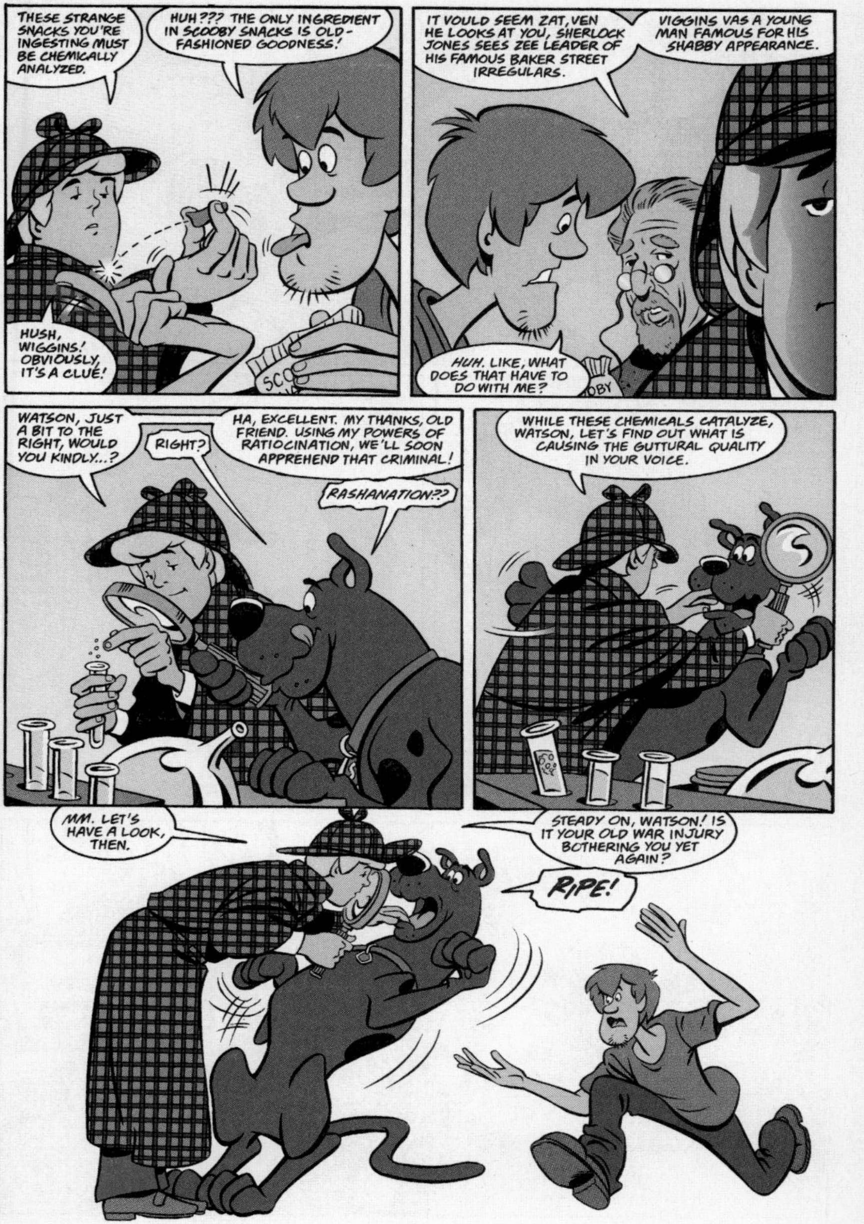

THESE STRANGE SNACKS YOU'RE INGESTING MUST BE CHEMICALLY ANALYZED.
HUH??? THE ONLY INGREDIENT IN SCOOBY SNACKS IS OLD-FASHIONED GOODNESS!
HUSH, WIGGINS! OBVIOUSLY, IT'S A CLUE!
SCO
IT VOULD SEEM ZAT, VEN HE LOOKS AT YOU, SHERLOCK JONES SEES ZEE LEADER OF HIS FAMOUS BAKER STREET IRREGULARS.
VIGGINS VAS A YOUNG MAN FAMOUS FOR HIS SHABBY APPEARANCE.
HUH. LIKE, WHAT DOES THAT HAVE TO DO WITH ME?
OBY
WATSON, JUST A BIT TO THE RIGHT, WOULD YOU KINDLY...?
RIGHT?
HA, EXCELLENT. MY THANKS, OLD FRIEND. USING MY POWERS OF RATIOCINATION, WE'LL SOON APPREHEND THAT CRIMINAL!
RASHANATION??
WHILE THESE CHEMICALS CATALYZE, WATSON, LET'S FIND OUT WHAT IS CAUSING THE GUTTURAL QUALITY IN YOUR VOICE.
MM. LET'S HAVE A LOOK, THEN.
STEADY ON, WATSON! IS IT YOUR OLD WAR INJURY BOTHERING YOU YET AGAIN?
RIPE!

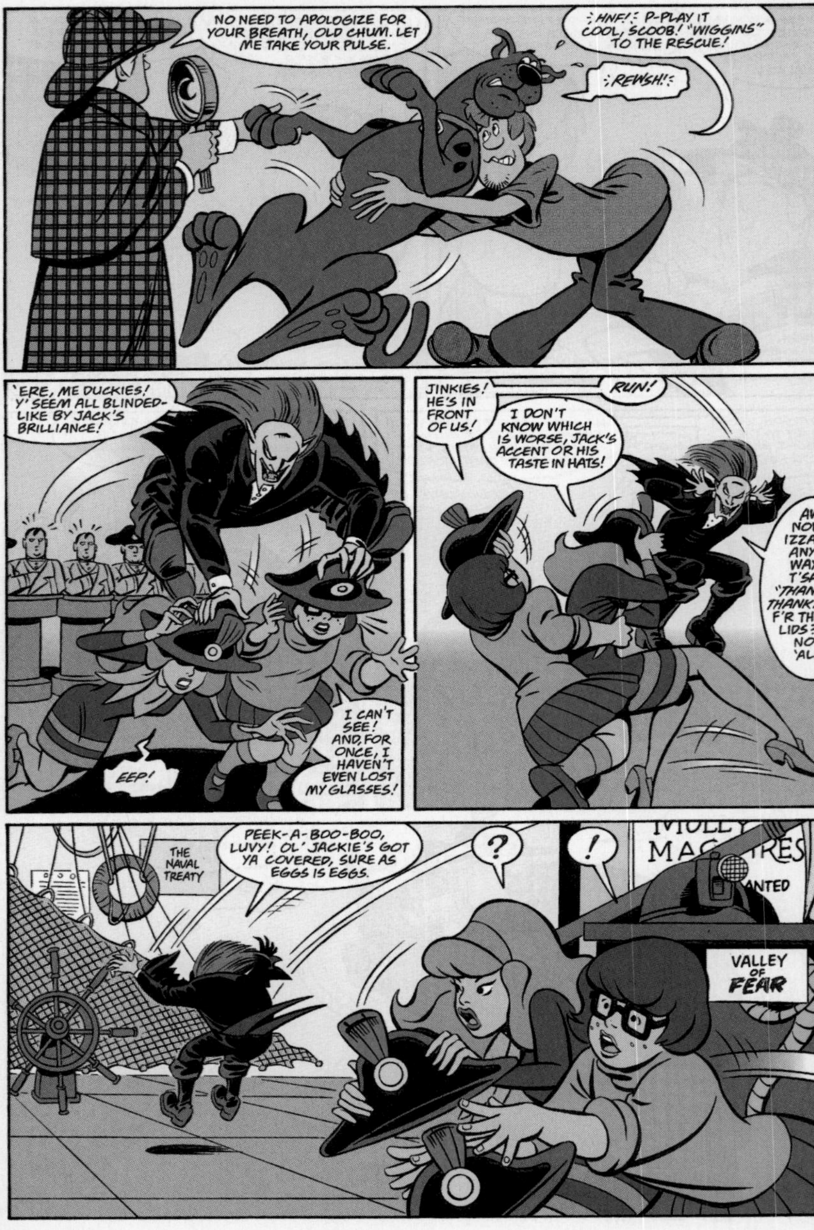
NO NEED TO APOLOGIZE FOR YOUR BREATH, OLD CHUM. LET ME TAKE YOUR PULSE.
HNF! P-PLAY IT COOL, SCOOB! "WIGGINS" TO THE RESCUE!
REWSH!
'ERE, ME DUCKIES! Y' SEEM ALL BLINDED-LIKE BY JACK'S BRILLIANCE!
I CAN'T SEE! AND, FOR ONCE, I HAVEN'T EVEN LOST MY GLASSES!
EEP!
JINKIES! HE'S IN FRONT OF US!
RUN!
I DON'T KNOW WHICH IS WORSE, JACK'S ACCENT OR HIS TASTE IN HATS!
AW, NOW IZZAT ANY WAY T'SAY, "THANKY THANKY" F'R THE LIDS? NOT 'ALF.
THE NAVAL TREATY
PEEK-A-BOO-BOO, LUVY! OL' JACKIE'S GOT YA COVERED, SURE AS EGGS IS EGGS.
?
!
MAG RES
ANTED
VALLEY OF FEAR

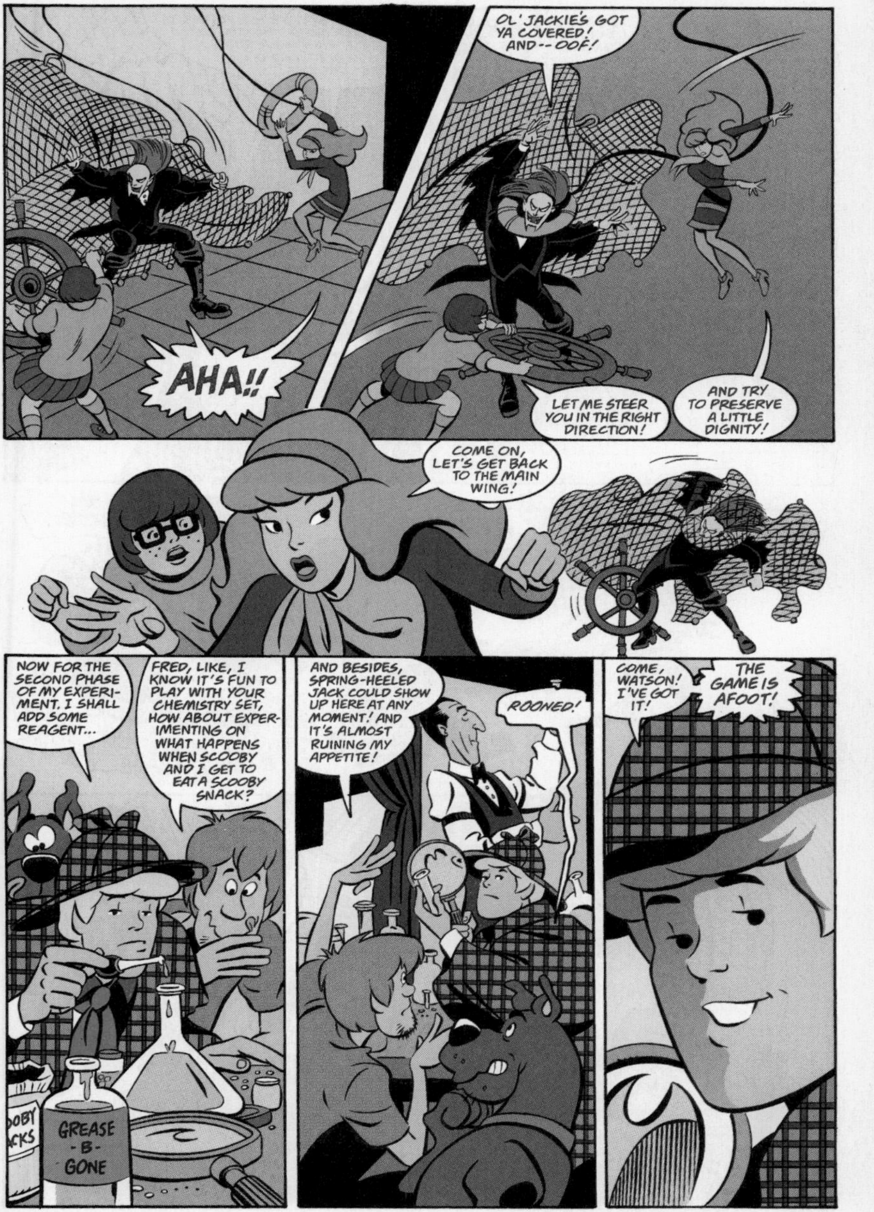

AHA!!
OL' JACKIE'S GOT YA COVERED! AND--OOF!
LET ME STEER YOU IN THE RIGHT DIRECTION!
AND TRY TO PRESERVE A LITTLE DIGNITY!
COME ON, LET'S GET BACK TO THE MAIN WING!
NOW FOR THE SECOND PHASE OF MY EXPERIMENT. I SHALL ADD SOME REAGENT...
FRED, LIKE, I KNOW IT'S FUN TO PLAY WITH YOUR CHEMISTRY SET, HOW ABOUT EXPERIMENTING ON WHAT HAPPENS WHEN SCOOBY AND I GET TO EAT A SCOOBY SNACK?
GREASE -B- GONE
AND BESIDES, SPRING-HEELED JACK COULD SHOW UP HERE AT ANY MOMENT! AND IT'S ALMOST RUINING MY APPETITE!
ROONED!
COME, WATSON! I'VE GOT IT!
THE GAME IS AFOOT!

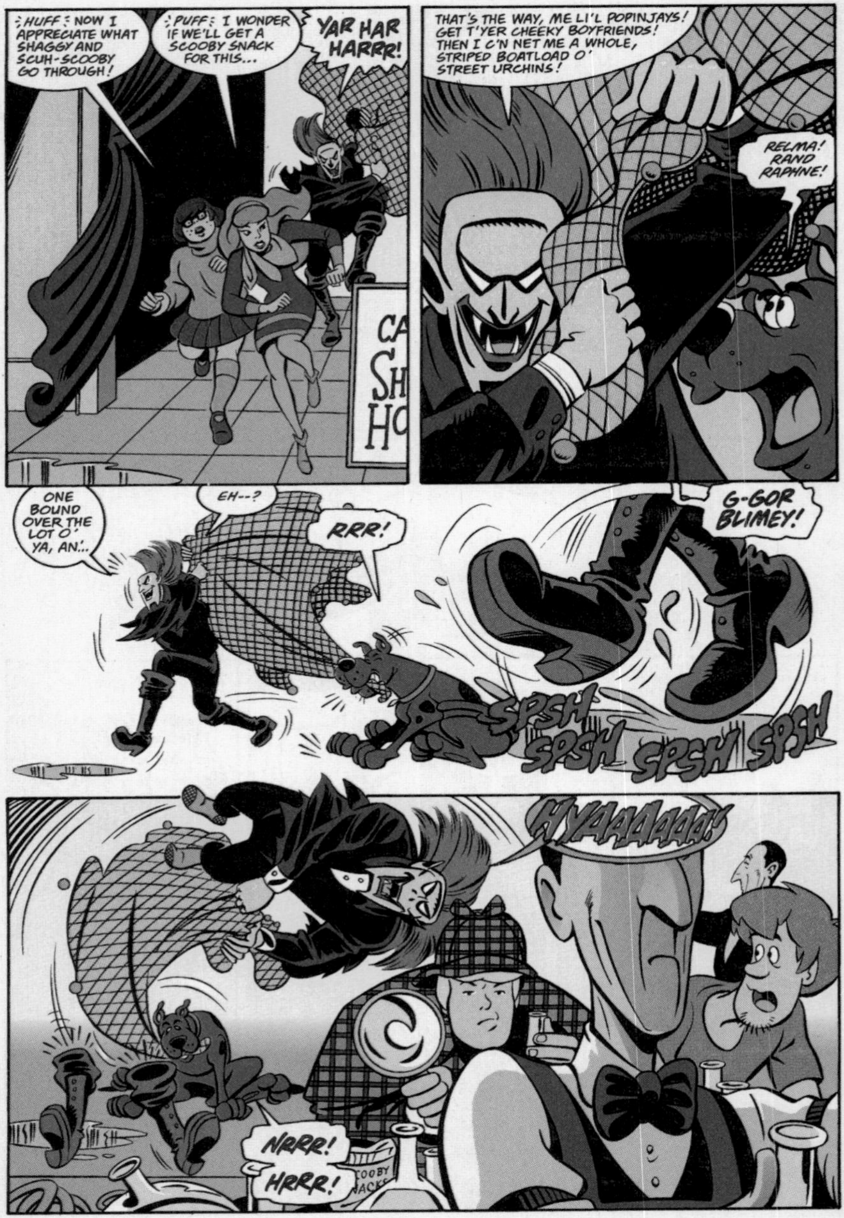

:HUFF: NOW I APPRECIATE WHAT SHAGGY AND SCUH-SCOOBY GO THROUGH!
:PUFF: I WONDER IF WE'LL GET A SCOOBY SNACK FOR THIS...
YAR HAR HARRR!
THAT'S THE WAY, ME LI'L POPINJAYS! GET T'YER CHEEKY BOYFRIENDS! THEN I C'N NET ME A WHOLE, STRIPED BOATLOAD O' STREET URCHINS!
RELMA! RAND RAPHNE!
ONE BOUND OVER THE LOT O' YA, AN'...
EH--?
RRR!
G-GOR BLIMEY!
SPSH
SPSH
SPSH
SPSH
HYAAAAAAA!
NRRR!
HRRR!

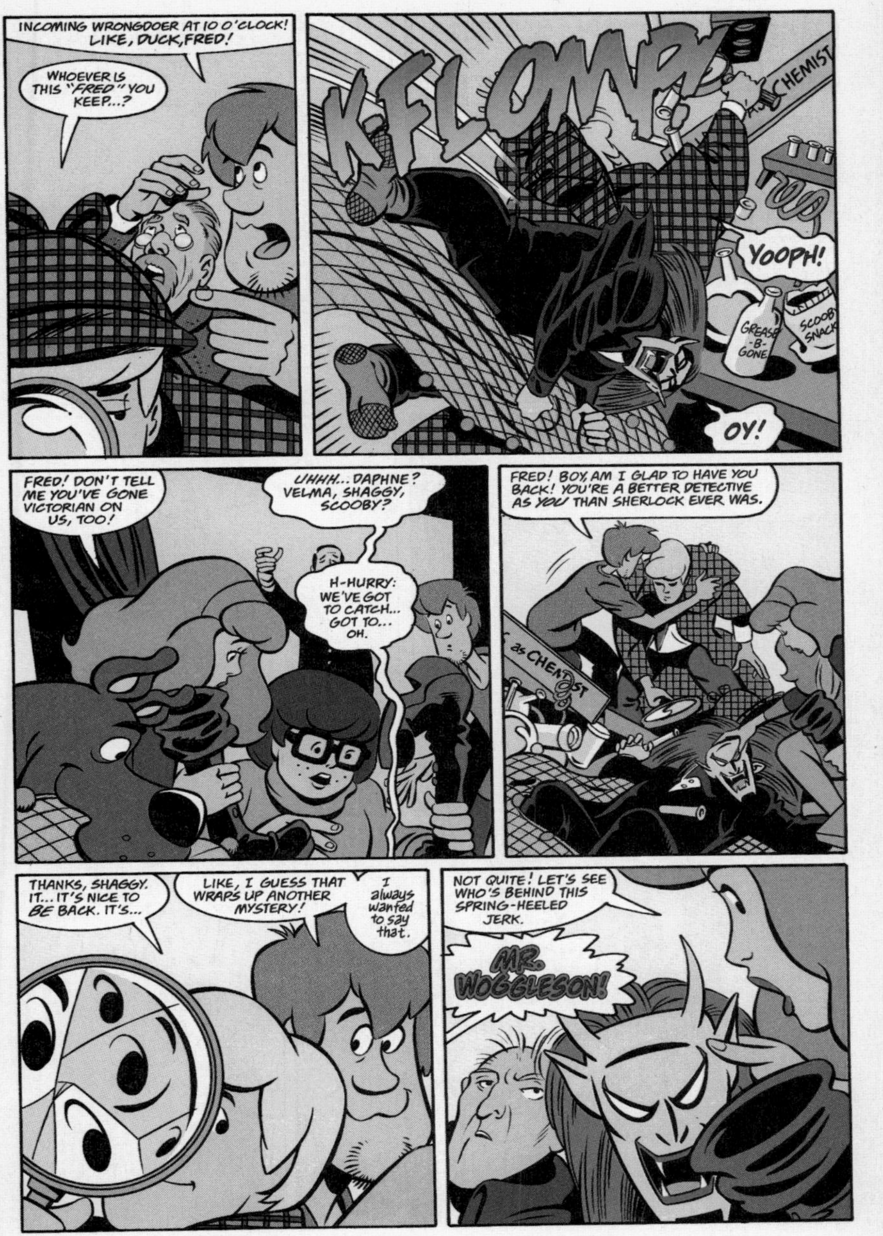

INCOMING WRONGDOER AT 10 O'CLOCK! LIKE, DUCK, FRED!
WHOEVER IS THIS "FRED" YOU KEEP...?
KFLOMP!
CHEMIST
YOOPH!
GREASE -B- GONE
SCOOBY SNACK
OY!
FRED! DON'T TELL ME YOU'VE GONE VICTORIAN ON US, TOO!
UHHH... DAPHNE? VELMA, SHAGGY, SCOOBY?
H-HURRY: WE'VE GOT TO CATCH... GOT TO... OH.
FRED! BOY, AM I GLAD TO HAVE YOU BACK! YOU'RE A BETTER DETECTIVE AS YOU THAN SHERLOCK EVER WAS.
as CHEMIST
THANKS, SHAGGY. IT... IT'S NICE TO BE BACK. IT'S...
LIKE, I GUESS THAT WRAPS UP ANOTHER MYSTERY!
I always wanted to say that.
NOT QUITE! LET'S SEE WHO'S BEHIND THIS SPRING-HEELED JERK.
MR. WOGGLESON!

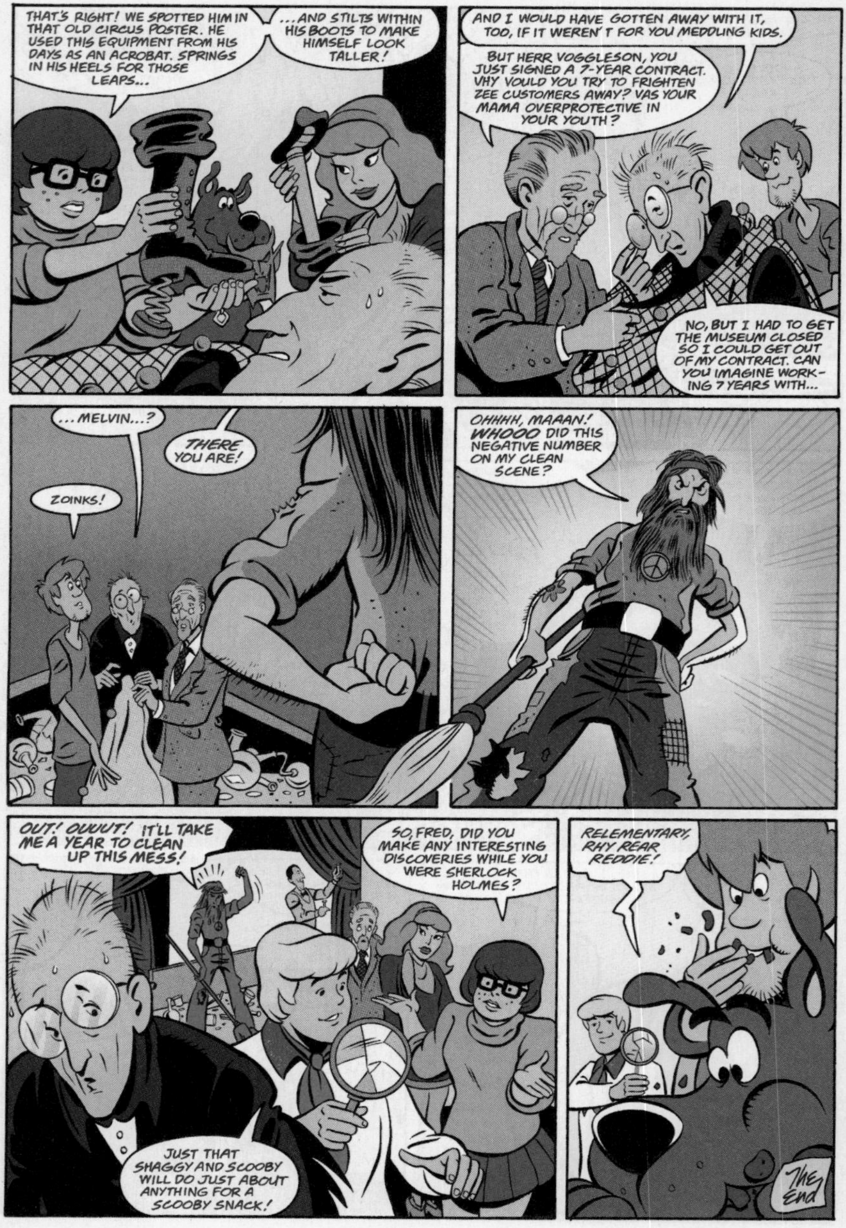
THAT'S RIGHT! WE SPOTTED HIM IN THAT OLD CIRCUS POSTER. HE USED THIS EQUIPMENT FROM HIS DAYS AS AN ACROBAT. SPRINGS IN HIS HEELS FOR THOSE LEAPS...
...AND STILTS WITHIN HIS BOOTS TO MAKE HIMSELF LOOK TALLER!
AND I WOULD HAVE GOTTEN AWAY WITH IT, TOO, IF IT WEREN'T FOR YOU MEDDLING KIDS.
BUT HERR VOGGLESON, YOU JUST SIGNED A 7-YEAR CONTRACT. VHY VOULD YOU TRY TO FRIGHTEN ZEE CUSTOMERS AWAY? VAS YOUR MAMA OVERPROTECTIVE IN YOUR YOUTH?
NO, BUT I HAD TO GET THE MUSEUM CLOSED SO I COULD GET OUT OF MY CONTRACT. CAN YOU IMAGINE WORKING 7 YEARS WITH...
...MELVIN...?
THERE YOU ARE!
ZOINKS!
OHHHH, MAAAN! WHOOO DID THIS NEGATIVE NUMBER ON MY CLEAN SCENE?
OUT! OUUUT! IT'LL TAKE ME A YEAR TO CLEAN UP THIS MESS!
SO, FRED, DID YOU MAKE ANY INTERESTING DISCOVERIES WHILE YOU WERE SHERLOCK HOLMES?
JUST THAT SHAGGY AND SCOOBY WILL DO JUST ABOUT ANYTHING FOR A SCOOBY SNACK!
RELEMENTARY, RHY REAR REDDIE!
THE END

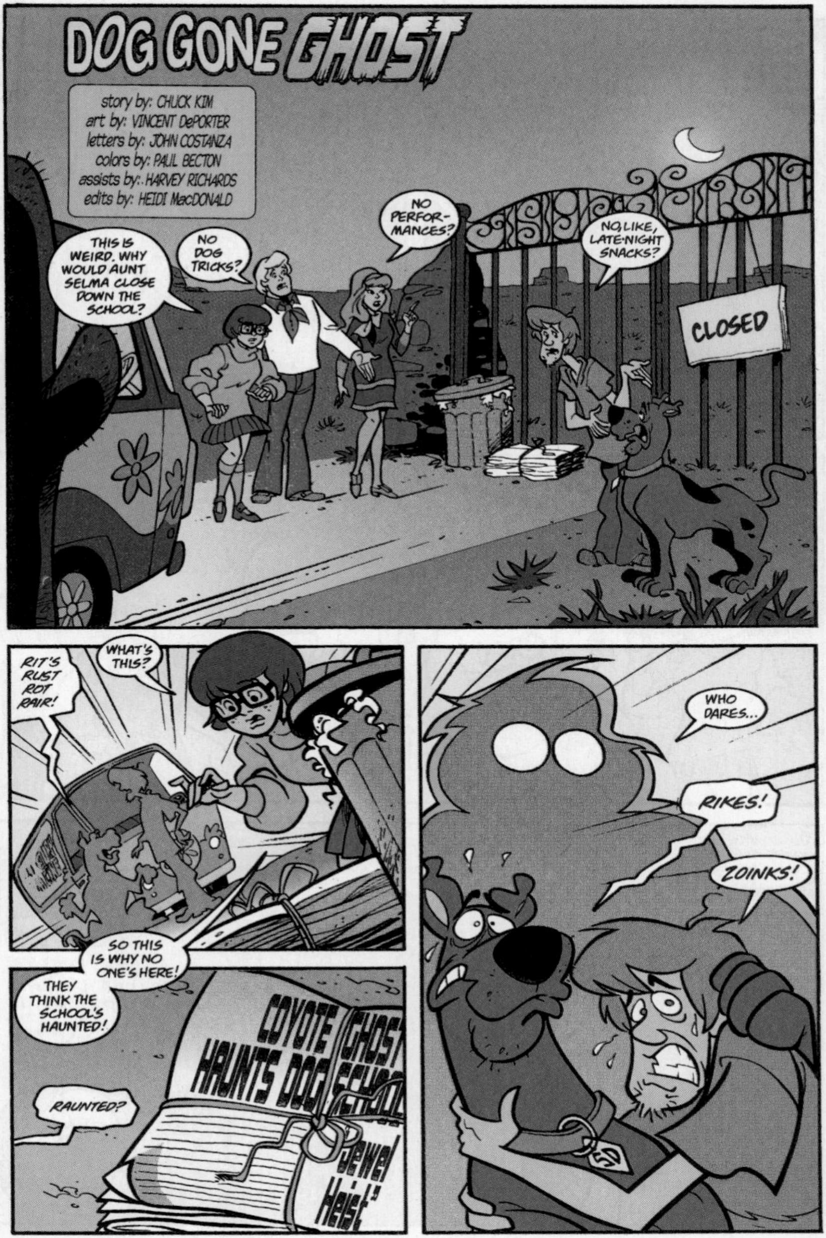
DOG GONE GHOST
story by: CHUCK KIM
art by: VINCENT DePORTER
letters by: JOHN COSTANZA
colors by: PAUL BECTON
assists by: HARVEY RICHARDS
edits by: HEIDI MacDONALD
THIS IS WEIRD. WHY WOULD AUNT SELMA CLOSE DOWN THE SCHOOL?
NO DOG TRICKS?
NO PERFORMANCES?
NO, LIKE, LATE-NIGHT SNACKS?
CLOSED
RIT'S RUST ROT RAIR!
WHAT'S THIS?
SO THIS IS WHY NO ONE'S HERE!
THEY THINK THE SCHOOL'S HAUNTED!
COYOTE GHOST HAUNTS DOG SCHOOL
Jewel Heist
RAUNTED?
WHO DARES...
RIKES!
ZOINKS!

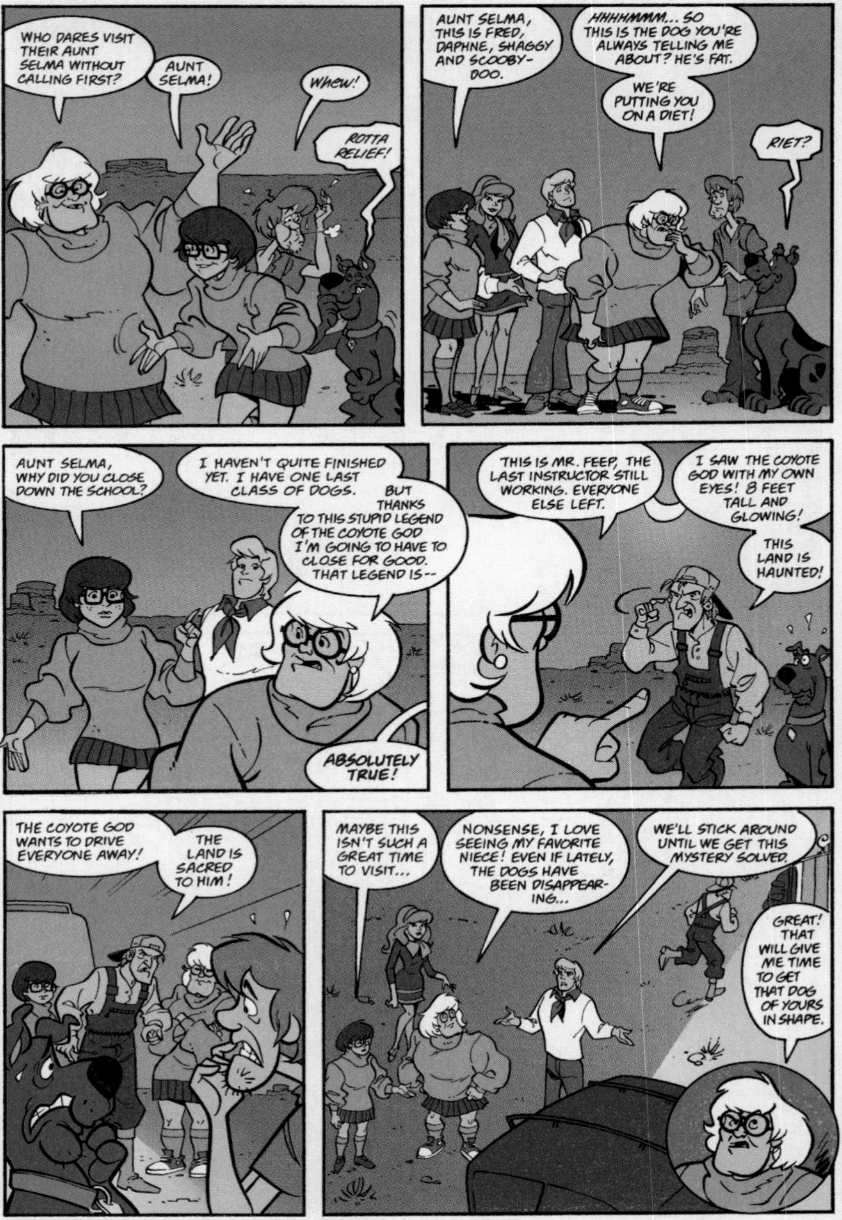
WHO DARES VISIT THEIR AUNT SELMA WITHOUT CALLING FIRST?
AUNT SELMA!
Whew!
ROTTA RELIEF!
AUNT SELMA, THIS IS FRED, DAPHNE, SHAGGY AND SCOOBY-DOO.
HHHHMMM... SO THIS IS THE DOG YOU'RE ALWAYS TELLING ME ABOUT? HE'S FAT.
WE'RE PUTTING YOU ON A DIET!
RIET?
AUNT SELMA, WHY DID YOU CLOSE DOWN THE SCHOOL?
I HAVEN'T QUITE FINISHED YET. I HAVE ONE LAST CLASS OF DOGS.
BUT THANKS TO THIS STUPID LEGEND OF THE COYOTE GOD I'M GOING TO HAVE TO CLOSE FOR GOOD. THAT LEGEND IS--
ABSOLUTELY TRUE!
THIS IS MR. FEEP, THE LAST INSTRUCTOR STILL WORKING. EVERYONE ELSE LEFT.
I SAW THE COYOTE GOD WITH MY OWN EYES! 8 FEET TALL AND GLOWING!
THIS LAND IS HAUNTED!
THE COYOTE GOD WANTS TO DRIVE EVERYONE AWAY!
THE LAND IS SACRED TO HIM!
MAYBE THIS ISN'T SUCH A GREAT TIME TO VISIT...
NONSENSE, I LOVE SEEING MY FAVORITE NIECE! EVEN IF LATELY, THE DOGS HAVE BEEN DISAPPEARING...
WE'LL STICK AROUND UNTIL WE GET THIS MYSTERY SOLVED.
GREAT! THAT WILL GIVE ME TIME TO GET THAT DOG OF YOURS IN SHAPE.

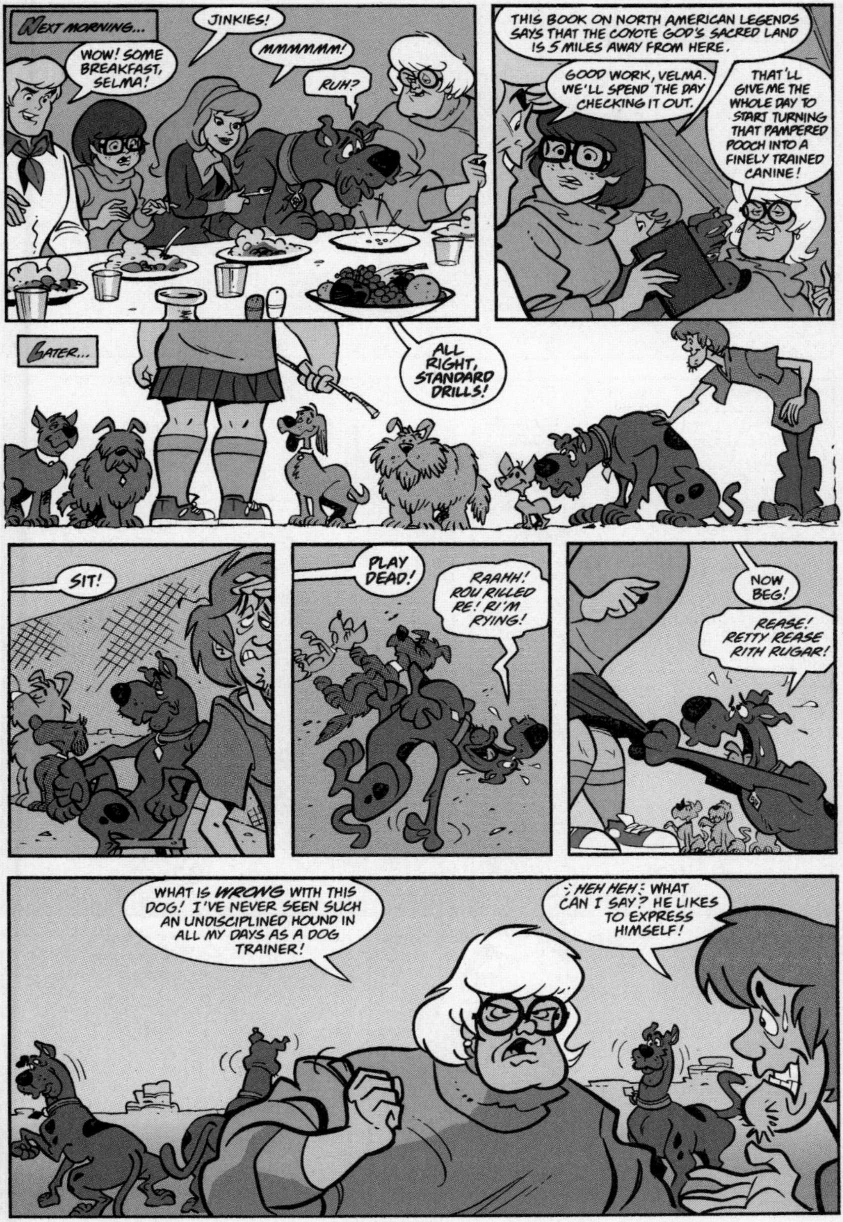
NEXT MORNING...
WOW! SOME BREAKFAST, SELMA!
JINKIES!
MMMMMMM!
RUH?
THIS BOOK ON NORTH AMERICAN LEGENDS SAYS THAT THE COYOTE GOD'S SACRED LAND IS 5 MILES AWAY FROM HERE.
GOOD WORK, VELMA. WE'LL SPEND THE DAY CHECKING IT OUT.
THAT'LL GIVE ME THE WHOLE DAY TO START TURNING THAT PAMPERED POOCH INTO A FINELY TRAINED CANINE!
LATER...
ALL RIGHT, STANDARD DRILLS!
SIT!
PLAY DEAD!
RAAHH! ROU RILLED RE! RI'M RYING!
NOW BEG!
REASE! RETTY REASE RITH RUGAR!
WHAT IS WRONG WITH THIS DOG! I'VE NEVER SEEN SUCH AN UNDISCIPLINED HOUND IN ALL MY DAYS AS A DOG TRAINER!
HEH HEH WHAT CAN I SAY? HE LIKES TO EXPRESS HIMSELF!

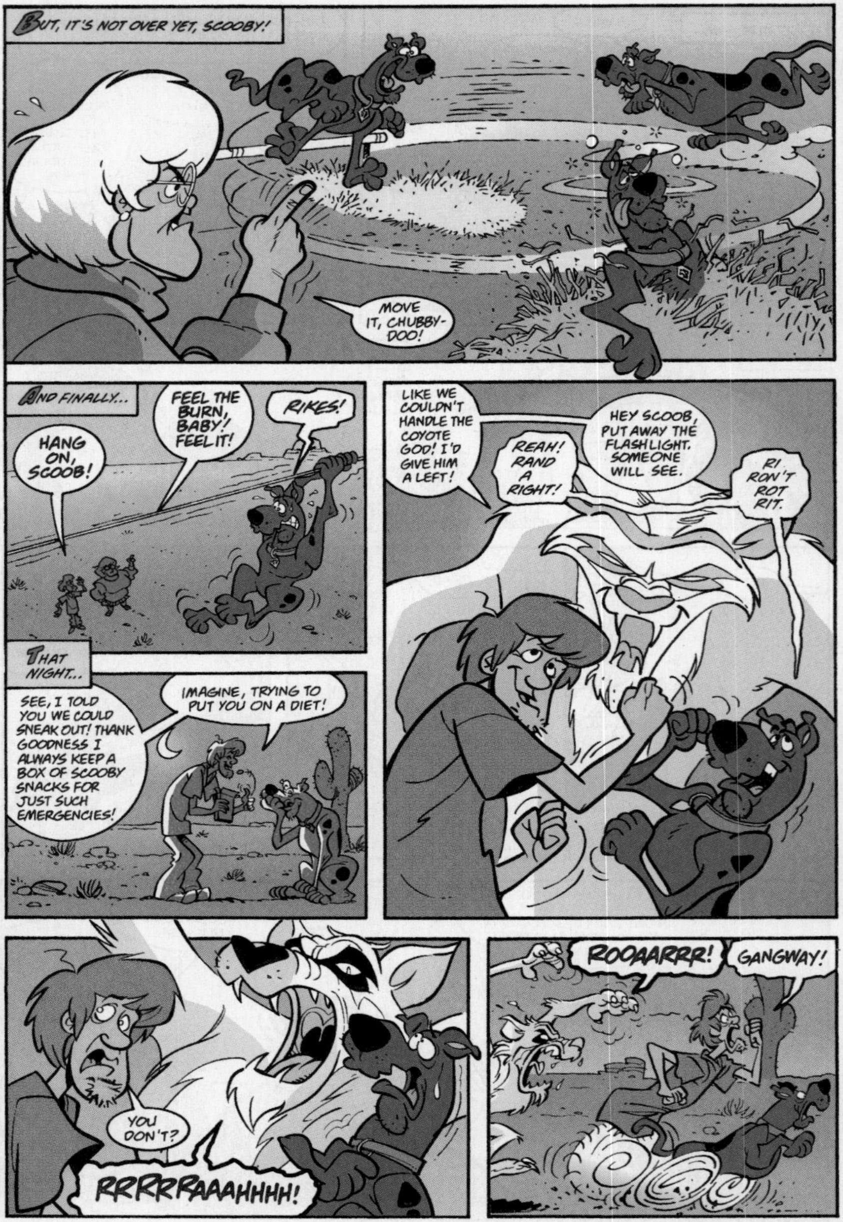
BUT, IT'S NOT OVER YET, SCOOBY!
MOVE IT, CHUBBY-DOO!
AND FINALLY...
HANG ON, SCOOB!
FEEL THE BURN, BABY! FEEL IT!
RIKES!
THAT NIGHT...
SEE, I TOLD YOU WE COULD SNEAK OUT! THANK GOODNESS I ALWAYS KEEP A BOX OF SCOOBY SNACKS FOR JUST SUCH EMERGENCIES!
IMAGINE, TRYING TO PUT YOU ON A DIET!
LIKE WE COULDN'T HANDLE THE COYOTE GOD! I'D GIVE HIM A LEFT!
REAH! RAND A RIGHT!
HEY SCOOB, PUT AWAY THE FLASHLIGHT. SOMEONE WILL SEE.
RI RON'T ROT RIT.
YOU DON'T?
RRRRRAAAHHHH!
ROOAARRR!
GANGWAY!

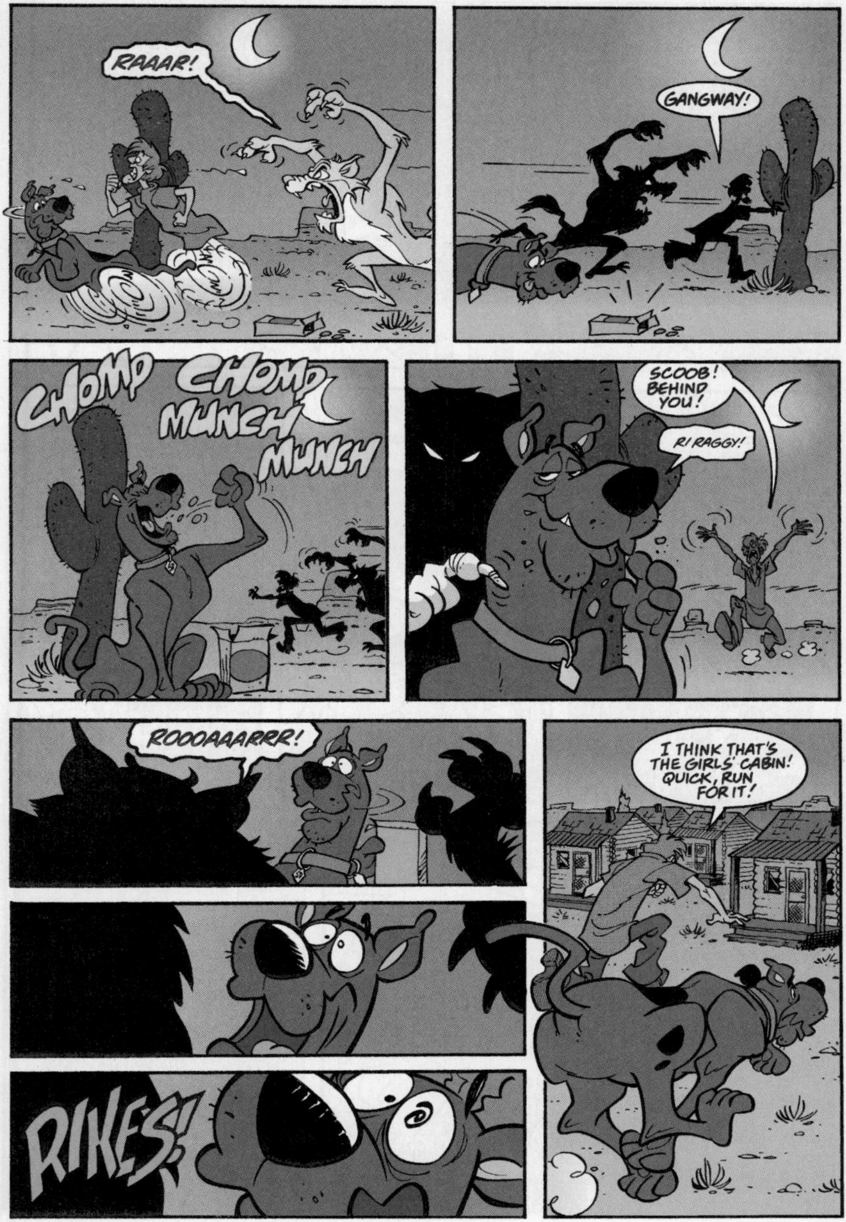
RAAAR!
GANGWAY!
CHOMP CHOMP MUNCH MUNCH
SCOOB! BEHIND YOU!
R! RAGGY!
ROOOAAARRR!
I THINK THAT'S THE GIRLS' CABIN! QUICK, RUN FOR IT!
RIKES!

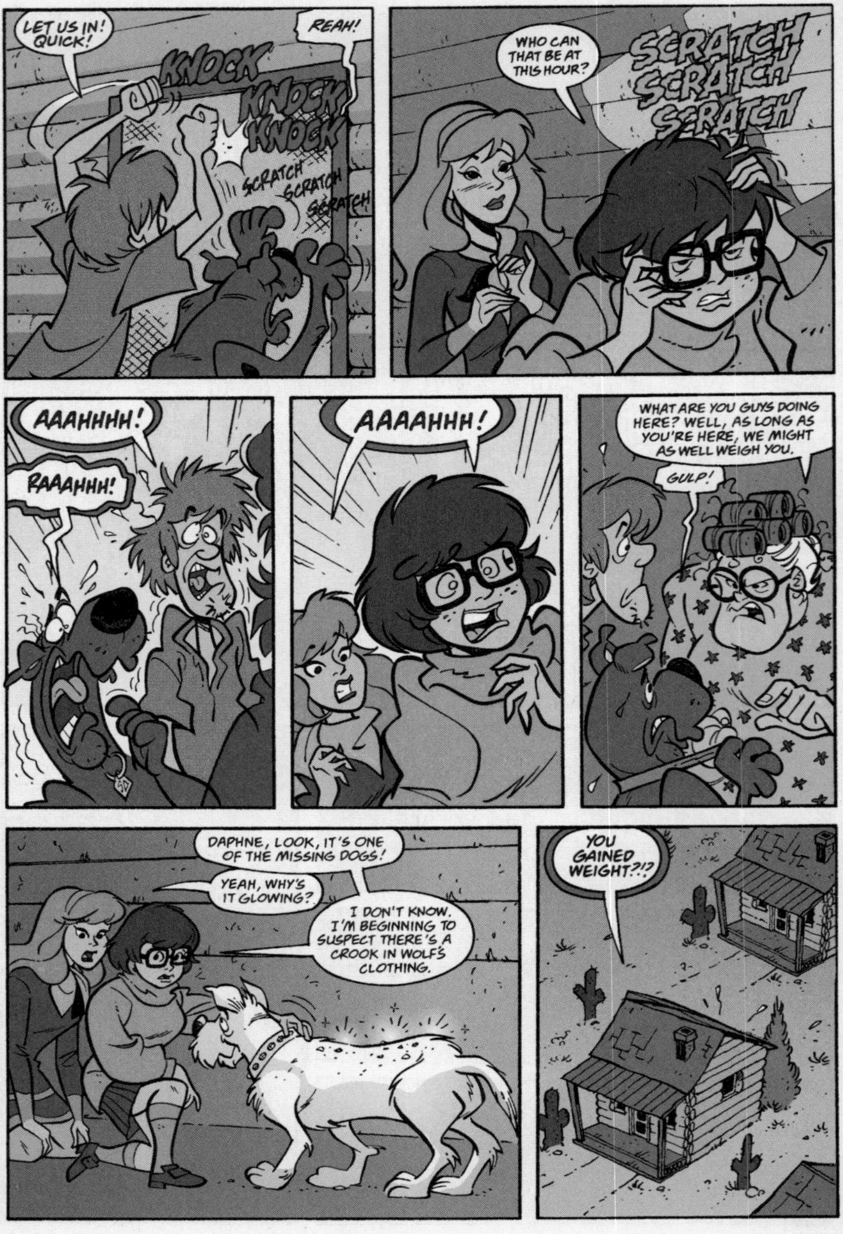
LET US IN! QUICK!
REAH!
KNOCK
KNOCK
KNOCK
SCRATCH
SCRATCH
SCRATCH
WHO CAN THAT BE AT THIS HOUR?
SCRATCH
SCRATCH
SCRATCH
AAAHHHH!
RAAAHHH!
AAAAHHH!
WHAT ARE YOU GUYS DOING HERE? WELL, AS LONG AS YOU'RE HERE, WE MIGHT AS WELL WEIGH YOU.
GULP!
DAPHNE, LOOK, IT'S ONE OF THE MISSING DOGS!
YEAH, WHY'S IT GLOWING?
I DON'T KNOW. I'M BEGINNING TO SUSPECT THERE'S A CROOK IN WOLF'S CLOTHING.
YOU GAINED WEIGHT?!?

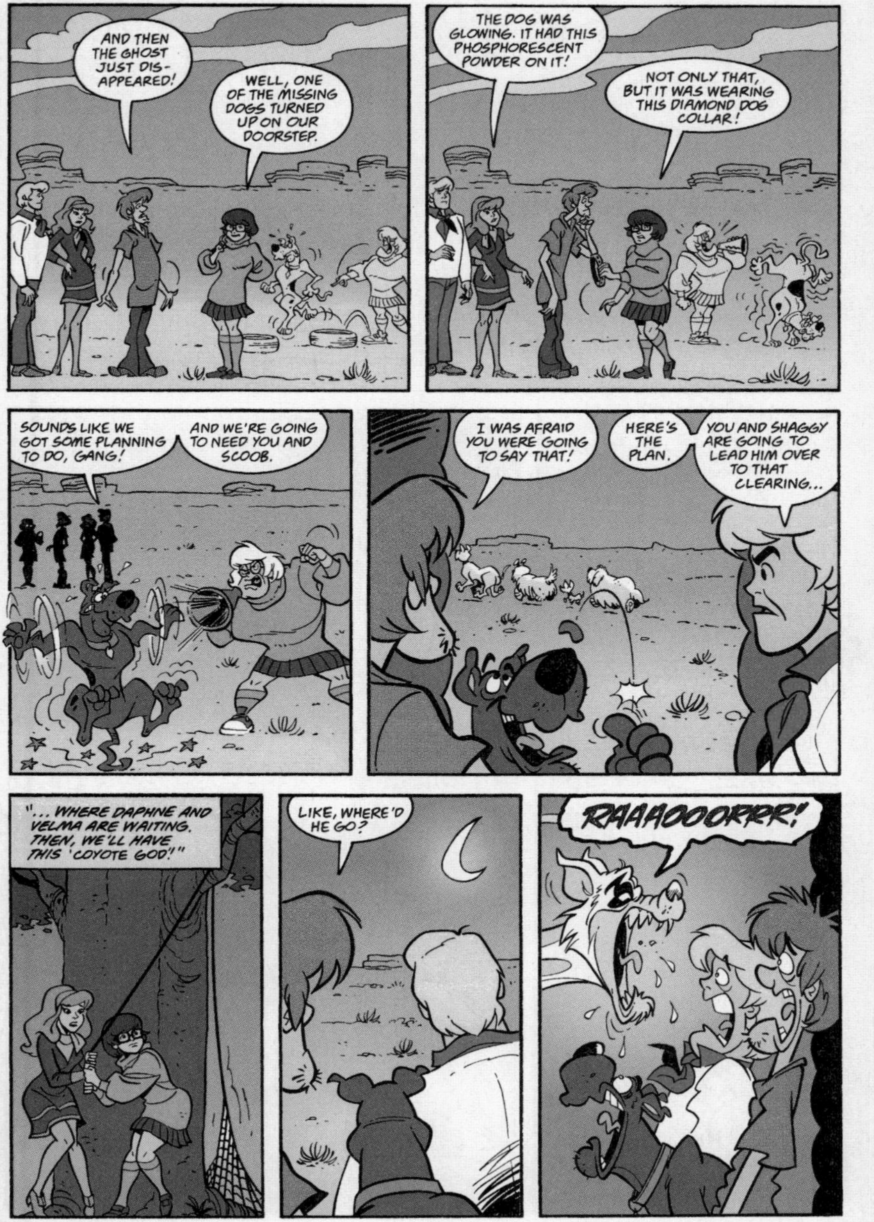
AND THEN THE GHOST JUST DIS-APPEARED!
WELL, ONE OF THE MISSING DOGS TURNED UP ON OUR DOORSTEP.
THE DOG WAS GLOWING. IT HAD THIS PHOSPHORESCENT POWDER ON IT!
NOT ONLY THAT, BUT IT WAS WEARING THIS DIAMOND DOG COLLAR!
SOUNDS LIKE WE GOT SOME PLANNING TO DO, GANG!
AND WE'RE GOING TO NEED YOU AND SCOOB.
I WAS AFRAID YOU WERE GOING TO SAY THAT!
HERE'S THE PLAN.
YOU AND SHAGGY ARE GOING TO LEAD HIM OVER TO THAT CLEARING...
"... WHERE DAPHNE AND VELMA ARE WAITING. THEN, WE'LL HAVE THIS 'COYOTE GOD'!"
LIKE, WHERE'D HE GO?
RAAAOOORRR!

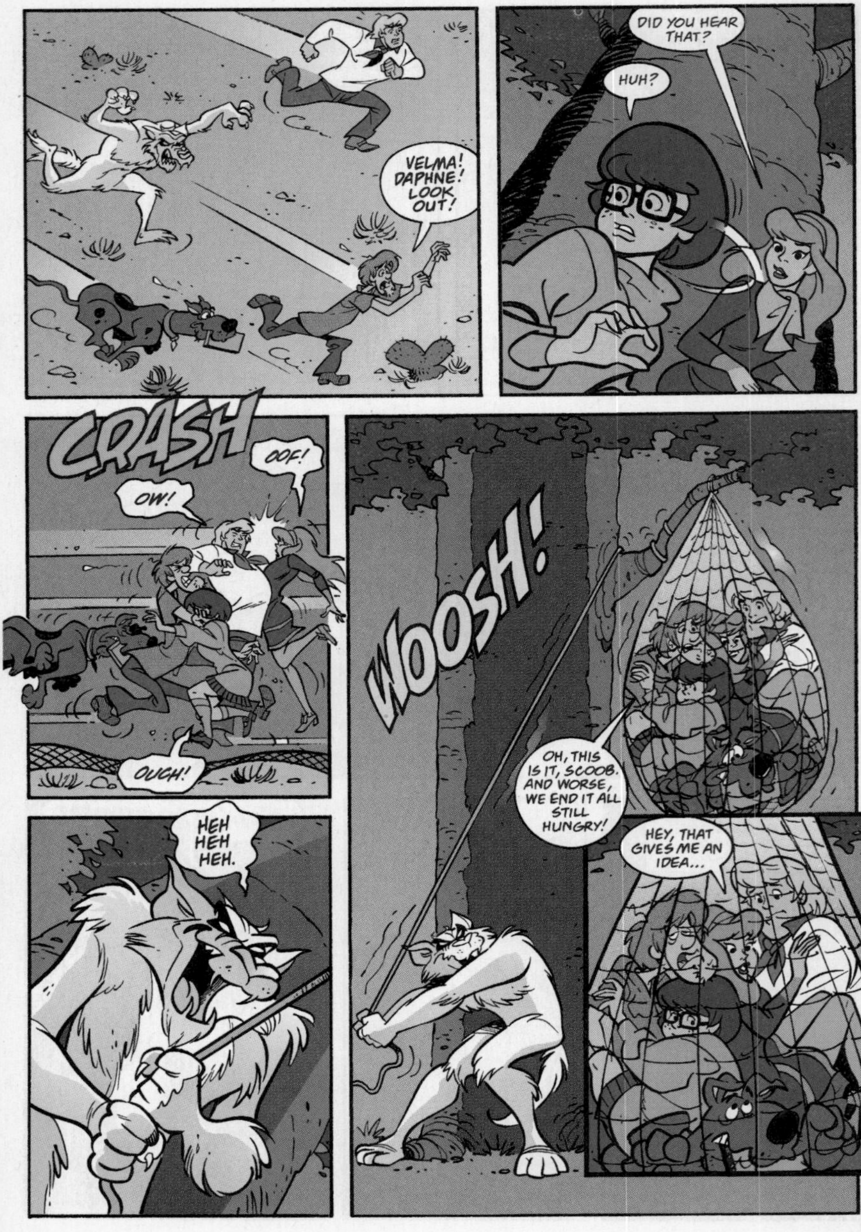
VELMA! DAPHNE! LOOK OUT!
DID YOU HEAR THAT?
HUH?
CRASH
OOF!
OW!
OUGH!
WOOSH!
OH, THIS IS IT, SCOOB. AND WORSE, WE END IT ALL STILL HUNGRY!
HEY, THAT GIVES ME AN IDEA...
HEH HEH HEH.

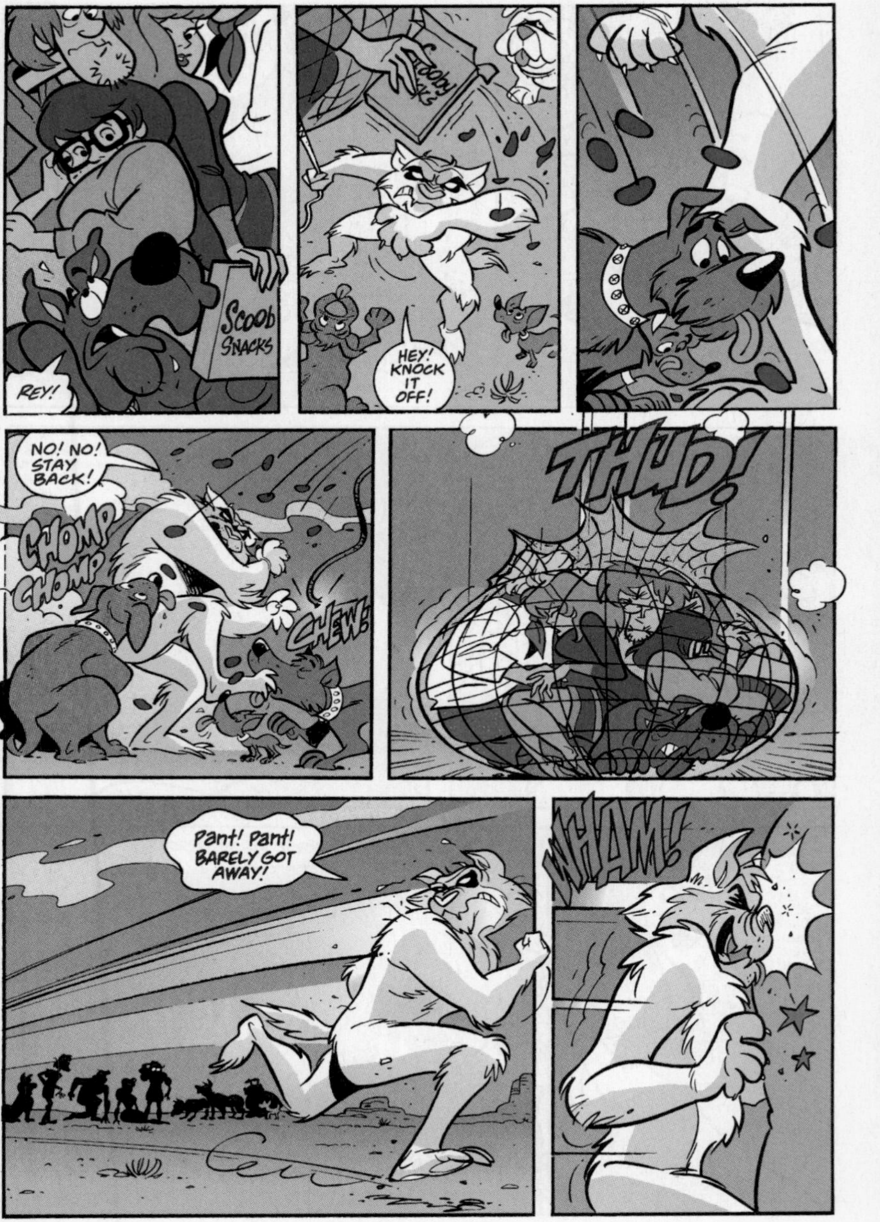

Scoob Snacks
REY!
Scooby Snacks
HEY! KNOCK IT OFF!
NO! NO! STAY BACK!
CHOMP CHOMP
CHEW!
THUD!
Pant! Pant! BARELY GOT AWAY!
WHAM!

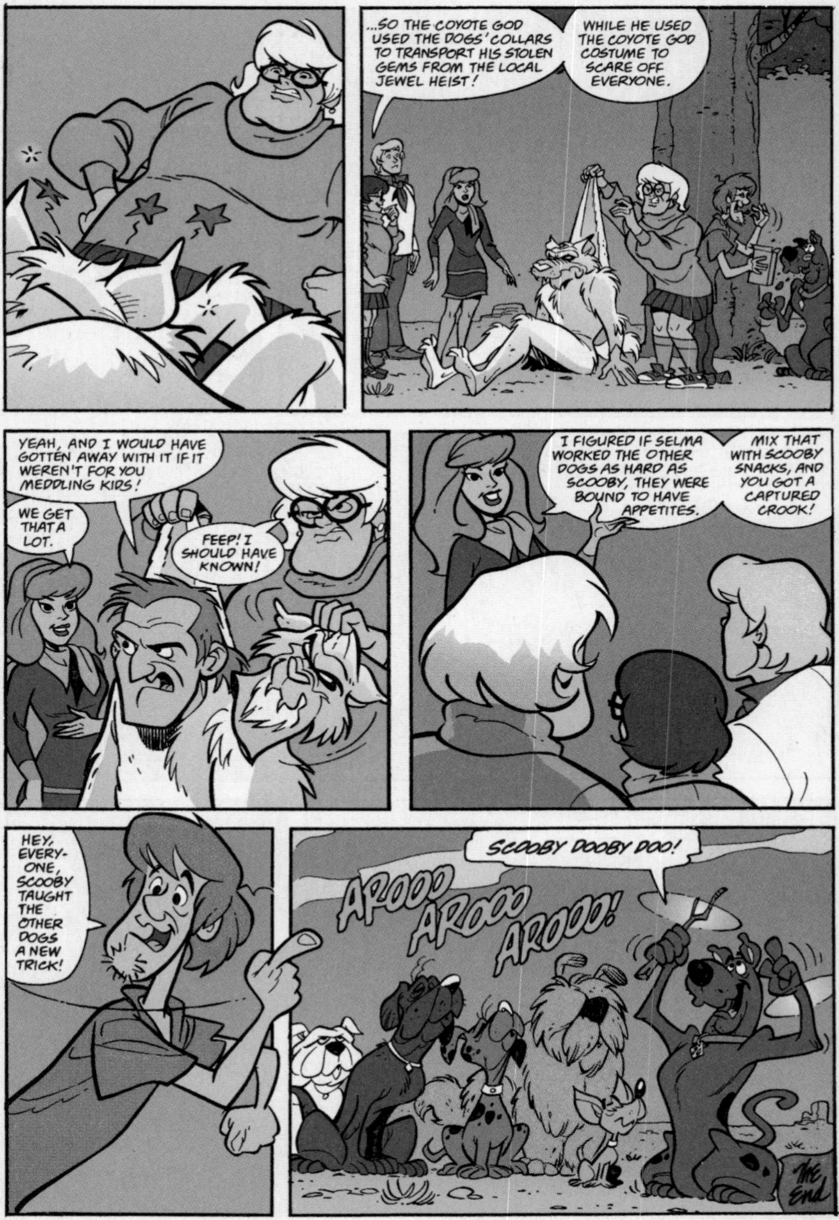
...SO THE COYOTE GOD USED THE DOGS' COLLARS TO TRANSPORT HIS STOLEN GEMS FROM THE LOCAL JEWEL HEIST!
WHILE HE USED THE COYOTE GOD COSTUME TO SCARE OFF EVERYONE.
YEAH, AND I WOULD HAVE GOTTEN AWAY WITH IT IF IT WEREN'T FOR YOU MEDDLING KIDS!
WE GET THAT A LOT.
FEEP! I SHOULD HAVE KNOWN!
I FIGURED IF SELMA WORKED THE OTHER DOGS AS HARD AS SCOOBY, THEY WERE BOUND TO HAVE APPETITES.
MIX THAT WITH SCOOBY SNACKS, AND YOU GOT A CAPTURED CROOK!
HEY, EVERY-ONE, SCOOBY TAUGHT THE OTHER DOGS A NEW TRICK!
SCOOBY DOOBY DOO!
AROOO AROOO AROOO!
THE End